"A wager then, my lady."

"A wager?"

"I will kiss you. If you enjoy my kiss, you owe me a dance."

"And if I do not?"

"I owe *you* a dance."

"That is no sporting wager, sir. You win the prize either way."

"Then you admit you are a prize worthy of the game."

She had to tilt her head to look up at him as he turned her in his arms. She could not ignore the feel of him as he brushed against her.

No one had ever called her a prize before.

Her lashes drifted downward in expectation even before his lips touched hers.

The kiss did not scream passion as much as it whispered pleasure. Feather-light like the softest touch of moonlight brushing her lips. She made a whimpering sound, then lifted on her toes to better drink in the sensation.

She hadn't realized the games had yet to begin . . .

By Melody Thomas

MELODY THOMAS

This Perfect Kiss

AVON
An Imprint of HarperCollinsPublishers

AVON BOOKS
An Imprint of HarperCollins*Publishers*
10 East 53rd Street
New York, New York 10022–5299

Copyright © 2011 by Laura Renken
ISBN 978–0–06–189876–1
www.avonromance.com

First Avon Books mass market printing: July 2011

Avon Trademark Reg. U.S. Pat. Off. and in Other Countries, Marca Registrada, Hecho en U.S.A.
HarperCollins® is a registered trademark of HarperCollins Publishers.

Printed in the U.S.A.

10 9 8 7 6 5 4 3 2 1

For Thomas, Brent, Ross, and Shari.
You are my heart. I love you.

Prologue

1775 Blackthorn Castle, Scotland
Golden Masquerade Ball

From the gilt-edged balcony overlooking the grand ballroom, she watched him move among the bustles of silks and satins that shifted like sunlight through polished glass.

Camden St. Giles, heir to the Carrick dynasty, was easily recognizable in the crowd of revelers. No wig covered his head. His dark hair, his height, enhanced by his royal blue wool uniform, set him apart from the other dignitaries and aristocrats surrounding him. He slowed as a young white-wigged woman stopped him. His head inclined toward her in a manner of ease as he listened to something that made him smile. But like the others who had tried before her, she failed to hold his attention for long, and soon he moved past her toward the glass doors.

His entrance into the ballroom earlier that evening had been as dramatic as that of two months ago, the day he had sailed his ship, the Royal Navy's *Endurance*—the flagship to the British vice admiral himself—dressed in full seagoing rig into full view of the shoreline.

She braced her hands on the polished balustrade and glided down the stairs.

A feather-adorned mask covered half her face and wrapped around her jaw like the golden talons of a hawk. Her cropped blond curls were tucked neatly beneath a tall pompadour wig. This one evening, she was part of her grandmother's aristocratic world, every bit a princess, as yard upon yard of frothy golden taffeta whispered with each step down the stairs and out onto the garden terrace.

For some, gold was the color of warmth and summer. For others, 'twas the color of great wealth. But for Christel Douglas, gold was the color of enchantment, a pair of shiny slippers and a magical spell cast by the strains of music drifting like light over the night.

All around her, the parkland twinkled with party lanterns set up along walkways and in the gardens. People milled around the lights and in the shadows, and footmen circulated among the revelers, offering trays of sweet wine and cakes. She snatched a glass of bubbly wine from a passing footman's tray and savored the large plump strawberry on the edge of the glass, all the while trying to keep a casual eye on her handsome quarry as he made his way down to the lower terrace away from the crowd.

Her heart raced. Would her intentions and desires be too obvious if he turned and saw her now? Would he recognize her? Christel knew only that if she left Scotland without telling Lord Camden everything in her heart, she would never have another chance. In another few weeks, he would choose his bride and be gone from her life forever.

She had just swallowed a bite of strawberry when a whisper touched her neck. "I know who you are," the owner of those warm lips said, bringing her around with a gasp.

"Leighton!"

Lord Leighton was Lord Camden's scapegrace younger brother, two years older than Christel. He wore a black mask with slits to reveal his eyes.

"I thought that was you up on the stairway," he said.

His discovery of her identity suddenly left her uncertain. Grams was already terribly disappointed in her, and the last thing she wanted was for her antics to publicly embarrass her grandmother again.

But realizing she was losing Lord Camden into the night, she edged around Leighton, only to be stopped as he wrapped his hand around her arm. "Why are you here? Surely you are not one of those addlebrained females running about hoping my brother will choose you for his bride!"

"Go away, Leighton," she whispered. "If you want to be concerned about someone, go visit Saundra. She is in bed with a sprained ankle and could not come tonight."

He dropped his grip on her arm. "Does she know you are here?"

Christel stepped away from him. "Why should she not? This is her mask." Her eyes narrowed. "Or did you think I was she when you placed your lips on my neck?"

"You should not be here, Christel," Leighton said softly. "Your grandmother has already summoned your uncle to fetch you away. Do you want to be banished forever from Scotland?"

"Since when do you care about my banishment? Or anything but your own interests?"

The emotion seemed to drain from him. Perhaps she had been too harsh. Didn't everyone look after their own interests first?

A group of men stood at the edge of the yard. One held a jug and waved him over. "'Tis your pride," he said dismissively, at the same time acknowledging the men's invitation with a lift of his chin. "As for me, I am off to enjoy other pleasures this night and shall leave you to yours."

"You are going to the cove? Are you—?"

"If I tell you, I will have to invite you. Give Saundra my love."

Watching him go, Christel did not understand why he just did not ask Saundra to marry him and have done with it.

With Leighton finally gone, Christel whirled and took the path leading to the lower terrace. Yet as she walked farther and farther away from the music, it soon became evident that she had lost Lord Camden to the night. In frustration, she stopped at the stone wall to look out at the cove, wishing the evening had not ended for her so soon. But she dared not return to the ballroom lest someone recognize her. What did it matter that she had not waltzed even once?

It mattered because tonight she was as beautiful as the twinkling lights. Her cousin and closest friend, Saundra, had oft said Christel could be quite "the rage" if she wanted. And until now, Christel had been content with not wanting to be anything like her beautiful cousin or half-sister, for it gave her a certain amount of independence to go unnoticed in the public's eye. She dressed the way she pleased and ventured where she pleased, even if it did displease Grams.

Then three weeks ago, she had accidentally met Lord Camden while she had been on the beach exploring the cove. He'd thought nothing of passing a young lad on the beach, so she'd been hidden in plain sight. He went to the cove every day on his wild stallion to swim. And she went every day and watched him. He was the most beautiful thing she had ever glimpsed rising from the spumelike mist, like some sea god carved from coral and flesh.

Tonight, she wore not the rags of an urchin, and she was not hiding behind lichen-encrusted rocks; she was dressed as a woman and was as beautiful as her cousin.

Out of sight of the gardens, the stars were alive in a velvet sky, a bit of silver in a golden world. She extended her arms and twirled, making her dress bell out like one of the plump roses that climbed the stone wall behind her. She had made this dress herself. One day, she would make something *of* herself, too, and be something more than a disappointment to Grams.

The scent of larkspur and juniper touched her nostrils. She smelled roses . . . and something else more elusive, mixing with the scent of earth and sea.

Tobacco.

Alerted to the presence of another, she instinctively ducked back into the protective shadows of a tall potted evergreen. Her heart beat so hard that she could scarcely breathe against the tightly laced corset, which lifted her small bosoms dramatically and made her waist nearly hand-span small. Catching her breath, she looked behind her into the shadows of ivy-covered stucco.

She could see little in the misty darkness, and she might not have seen the man at all amid the plant life except that she glimpsed his movement and knew he was leaning against the rock wall watching her. *Lord Camden!*

"Do not stop. I am rather enjoying the show."

Amusement laced his deeply masculine voice. His words were perfectly spoken, with just a hint of Scottish intonation for sensual flavor. He was a man who had been well educated, was someone comfortable with authority.

She did not move as he stepped out of the darkness into the circle of torchlight flickering in the breeze. The torchlight gave him a disreputable air that was in accord with his attire. He had removed the blue button-up outer jacket of his uniform and was dressed in a high-collar white shirt and button-up white waistcoat and white breeches.

He looked over his shoulder into the darkness, as if expecting that she was awaiting a rendezvous.

"I was on my way to the beach," she lied.

"Lord Carrick's gamekeeper is particular about trespassers on his beach," he said. "Especially if they go near the cove."

"He has a most vile reputation. The gamekeeper," she hastily confirmed. "Once he threatened to shoot a person just for chasing a rabbit onto his beach." She neglected to say that the alleged poacher had been herself and she had been ten at the time.

"Did he?"

"Aye, he is most particular. I think 'tis fortunate he did not wander down to the beach yesterday or he might have been shocked by the, uh . . . quite naked man emerging from the surf."

The tip of a cheroot glowed orange, brightened, then faded. Then she saw it drop onto the damp stones before the heel of his boot crushed it out. His gaze held a lazy aura of amusement, even as a hint of white flashed in the shadows of his face. "And you are?"

She lifted her chin. "I am Madam Pompadour, sir."

"You were on the beach yesterday?" He looked over the ledge of the wall to the pit of blackness below. "What were you doing down there . . . Madam Pompadour? The only people familiar with that cove are urchins and smugglers."

"On occasion, I do wander down there after a storm with the hope that I will find a great treasure." *But the only thing the sea has coughed up on its shore is small intriguing bits of shells and glass and an occasional naked man swimming in the surf.* "Once someone found a silver sorcerer's cup," she said, then blushed. "They say Merlin hails from Scotland. Have you ever heard of King Arthur? 'Tis my favorite childhood tale."

"You are a fan of tragedy?"

" 'Twas only a tragedy because Guinevere fell in love with a man she could not wed."

"Some would consider her adultery the only tragedy."

She kicked at a pebble. "Perhaps you have never been in love."

"How old are you?"

"Eighteen." It wasn't a total lie. She would be eighteen in two months.

"Ah, that explains it then." Folding his arms, he perched against the wall and seemed to study her with more than curiosity. "You are acquainted with Lord Carrick's family?"

She was finding it harder and harder to concentrate on maintaining an air of sophisticated detachment. "Who does *not* know the earl? A masquerade is held every year in honor of his birthday. This year it is also a celebration to honor his eldest son. He is a great hero."

The corners of his mouth crimped. "*Humph.* I am told the chap thinks rather highly of himself."

"The father or the son?" she asked.

"The son."

She covered her mouth with a gloved palm and laughed, for she had heard the same thing on occasion from Leighton. "He is only twenty-two, not so old, I think. And any man who has received a medal for valor in his service to the Crown cannot be too vain. He is the youngest captain of a ship of the line in the Royal Navy. All the Carrick earls have done their duty by the people and the Crown, most having served as captains and admirals for generations. 'Tis a very noble family."

"Indeed," he said, straight-faced.

He didn't know that she knew everything about him or that she had first met him through his portrait hanging prominently in the foyer, or that for years she had listened to his grandmother talk about him on the days the dowager would visit Grams at Rosecliffe.

He didn't know that the urchin he'd passed on the beach these past few weeks was she.

His gloved hand suddenly lifted her chin. "Madam Pompadour, you have been following me all evening. Why?"

No one had ever touched her quite like he did now, tenderness and possession at once, as if such a hand had been capable of holding the world.

"When I saw you yesterday looking out at the sea," she said, "you looked . . . alone. Nay, you looked solitary."

"I *was* alone," he teased in a low voice.

"There is a difference between being alone and being solitary."

She understood solitary.

Tipping her chin up, he gazed deeply into her eyes, and she saw that there was so much more that was a part of him he kept tucked away from the world. "Then your presence here at my side has nothing to do with wanting my body."

She raised her fingers to his jaw. "You looked very nice swimming, *Lord Camden*. Captain."

He gave a bark of laughter. "You spoil me with so much flattery."

Their gazes held, and he smiled at her. The first true smile she had seen from him. "You have me at a disadvantage, Madam Pompadour. You know who I am, but I do not know you."

"Perhaps if you were wearing a mask like everyone else, I would not have the advantage."

"Dance with me," he said suddenly.

An invisible gauntlet thrown, a subtle challenge. Something

swelled inside her chest, making breathing difficult. He had not danced all night, and to do so with her would draw the attention of a thousand guests. Rumors would circulate. People would want to know who she was. Suddenly her desire to reveal herself to him was no longer so simple when it included the rest of the world knowing.

Turning away from her, he dragged up his coat and shoved his arms into the sleeves. Full-dress blue cloth coat with one row of epaulettes on the left shoulder, gold lace around the lapels. "A wager then, my lady Pompadour."

She pulled her gaze from the gold buttons on his jacket. "A wager?"

"I will kiss you. If you enjoy my kiss, you owe me a dance for the pleasure."

"And if I do not . . . think your kiss pleasurable?"

"I owe *you* a dance."

She had to tilt her head to look up at him as he drew her into his arms. "That is no sporting wager, sir," she barely breathed the words. "You win the prize either way."

Conscious of the heat of his hand through the layers of her ribbed bodice, she could not ignore the feel of him as he held her provocatively against him. "Then you admit you are a prize worthy of the game," he replied.

No one had ever called her a prize before.

"Do we have a wager, my lady Pompadour?"

"I need no wager to let you kiss me, my lord."

Cupping her cheeks with his palms, he looked into her face. Her lashes drifted downward in expectation. His soft chuckle opened her eyes. "I usually know the name of a woman before I kiss her," he said.

A scar stretched the length of his hairline to his temple, but it was noticeable only with his hair swept off his forehead. Like now. "Do you? Always?"

"Always." His gaze dropped to her mouth. "What else do you know about me?"

She could barely think. He was not known as "the Barracuda" for no reason. For years, his exploits had been a bane to pirates and French privateers alike. He was a topic of much gossip and speculation, and though his charm was still evident in an occasional smile, he seemed to have bored long ago of the *ton*. He rarely came home. He was home for the summer now only to take the requisite bride.

But she said none of this. Instead, she smiled and said something purposefully provocative. "I like the way you look without a shirt."

She was cognizant of the heavy thudding of his heart. Or was that hers sending the blood rushing through her veins?

Then, as if in slow motion, he lowered his head and his mouth covered hers.

The kiss did not scream passion as much as it whispered pleasure. Feather light at first, like the softest touch of moonlight brushing her lips. She made a sound in the back of her throat, then lifted on her toes to better drink in the strange and wondrous sensations, only to feel him pull away as if he was slowly, deliberately testing her response.

His warm breath brushed over her lower cheek. "You taste like strawberries."

Where his formidable authority had lent him only certitude moments ago, she now heard something else in his voice.

The pads of his thumbs pressed into the curves just beneath her jaw. Her lashes fluttered open and she stared into eyes that were dark and dangerous. "You have never kissed a man before," he murmured.

That much about her was true. Men that she actually cared to meet were in short supply.

"I apologize if I have offended you with my wagers and games," he said against her mask.

He wasn't sorry. She could tell by the satisfied look in his eyes that he was pleased with her response. Her lips felt thick and hot. Unfamiliar. "You have not offended me," she said, and there was a rusty catch in her voice.

A subtle shift and he brought his mouth down on hers with a tender savagery that tightened his hand around her nape.

Then he was deepening the contact, dragging her head-first into a sensual tide so primal that any sense of will to protest was swept away by the roaring in her veins. His tongue slid past her parted lips, filling her with the taste of his heat and whiskey, the piercing intimacy of it igniting a hunger from deep inside her. Her half groan of surrender teetered on the brink of gasp, and lost beneath the sensuous assault, she arched instinctively against him. He seemed to want to inhale her. When he came up to breathe, she pulled air into her lungs, too.

She wrapped her clumsy arms around his neck, sinking deeper into the sea of wondrous sensations. She could feel the corded muscles of his arms and shoulders delineated against his coat. His thumbs splayed the sensitive undersides of her breast. An intense tremor shook her. The shock of his touch sent shivers knifing through the length of her body, and she turned her head away.

"Who are you?" he asked. "I know nothing about you."

I am no one, she realized.

But the wet sea air caressed her moist lips like a drug, loosening the words from her heart. "I like the sunset over the sea after a storm and the way the air smells in spring," she said, wanting him to know a minute piece of her self that had nothing to do with the magic of a golden night. "I love cold milk with warm bread. Roses and summertime. The smell of watercolors on canvas. I do not own a horse, but if I did, I would name him after a constellation."

I love you, her young heart said.

Her eyes had not moved from his, her uncertain gaze lowering without will to his lips. She could feel a strange heat run through her veins and into the pit of her stomach, before his gaze lowered to her mouth. She leaned into him to fill her senses with him and sensed caution, as if he recognized he was wading into dangerous waters.

"Which constellation?" The words vibrated against her cheek.

"Orion."

"Ahh, poor Orion," he chuckled against her lips, "he had the misfortune of falling in love with the virgin huntress

Diana, the archer goddess who discharged the fatal arrow that killed him."

" 'Twas in her grief that she placed him among the stars and made him the brightest constellation in the sky. The one that guides all seafarers home."

She returned her mouth to his. His palms slid to the curvature of her corseted waist, and he pulled her fully against him. "What do you want, Madam Pompadour?"

"I wish above all things to be seduced by you."

There was no mistaking the feel of him against her waist. Her heart raced and she pushed aside her nerves. She might have been an innocent when it came to sexual encounters, but she was not naïve about what men and women did with each other, how male and female fit together.

But no amount of inducement was pushing him beyond the initial kiss. "Remove your mask."

"Nay, my lord."

His hand covered her breast, tentative at first as he registered her start at the intimate touch, then boldly as he cupped her in his palm. He turned to the side, maneuvering her body against the ivy until he had neatly confined her between his arms and the stone wall.

His lips touched hers with heat. "I could take it off you."

"But then the seduction would lose its magic."

He cupped her chin, raising her face another fraction. Moonlight glanced off his hair. He kissed her, pressing his lips to hers without regard to tenderness, sending her blood racing through her veins like a potent aphrodisiac. He plunged his tongue in her mouth and she heard herself moaning with strange torment. The echo in his chest became a growl as his mouth trailed down her neck and lingered on her collarbone. Nothing could have prepared her for the hunger that seemed to grow inside her. She leaned into his body. His hair was soft and silky. He smelled exotic, with a hint of cool citrus.

"Is there a brother or father or uncle waiting in the shrubberies to launch at me? Call me out?" His breath was warm. "Expert swordsmen ready for an excuse to fillet me?"

"I have no brothers or father."

His breathing was harsh against her shoulder as he braced his hand against the wall and leaned with his head down. It was not precisely confusion she sensed but something akin to it. "Then why?"

Her lips trembled beneath his. "I . . . wish to know what it feels like."

She thought she heard him swear, but she didn't recognize the word he'd said, except by its tone.

"Surely, 'tis no sin to be a virgin," she ventured. As an invitation, she could not be clearer.

"You wish to escape a marriage by ruining yourself. You have picked me because you saw me naked on the beach and thought I would be . . . amenable to the idea?"

"I picked you because . . . because you are the most beautiful man I have ever seen. I mean you no harm. I will tell no one."

He laughed almost as if her words made him blush. He seemed gratified that his reaction was finally one she could interpret. "Are you trying to protect *my* reputation?" he asked.

"No one need know, my lord."

The cadence of his breathing changed. "*I* would know."

"It cannot be good for you to *think* so much."

He laughed, this time not with discomfort evident in his tone but with an acknowledgement that her words couldn't have been more true.

Footsteps and voices on the upper walkway caused them both to pause. Someone was walking down the pathway. Neither of them breathed. She shut her eyes. They stood in the shadows like coconspirators, the bastard daughter of an adulterer and England's hero and heir to an earldom. What would he have said if he'd known her mother had been known as Ayrshire's "Colonial whore"? That she was no lady at all.

The footsteps stopped. "My lord?" a voice called from the walkway to her left.

She heard the hiss of an oath against the soft shell of her ear. Shifting his weight, he shielded her from view. "What is it, Smolich?"

"I am sorry to disturb you, my lord, but your father is asking for you. The last set has begun and 'tis a half hour before midnight. Your grandmother is about to send out the cavalry to find you." Clearing his throat, he added, "I saw you come down here earlier and thought to warn you."

"Thank you, Smolich." Lord Camden seemed to consider his next words. He looked down at her. "You may reassure my grandmother that I am on my way inside. I would not have her disappointed."

"Aye, my lord."

Lord Camden hesitated for the briefest moment. She couldn't read him, but she sensed that his unaffected expression, like his appearance, was an illusion. The great hero of the Atlantic and West Indies, the Barracuda himself, was vulnerable to normal human emotion.

"I have never hidden in the flower vines before." He regarded her, trying to make out her thoughts. "But I have a feeling you have spent a great deal of time hiding and observing the world around you."

Placing his hands on her waist, he pulled her nearer, peering into her upturned face, trying to see behind the mask. It was to his credit, she realized, that he did not take it from her when she knew he could have. Remnants of music floated to her. "I will play your game, madam, but we will begin in the ballroom with a dance. Do you waltz?"

The waltz was a new dance that had become all the rage. "I do."

He looked up the path. "There will be others in the yard," he said. "I will leave first. You can follow when you are ready."

"You do not wish to be seen with me."

"Nay, my love. *You* do not wish to be seen coming from the shadows of the yard with me. It takes very little to ruin a reputation and even less to find yourself ostracized."

Her throat was suddenly tight and sore. She nodded, but as she watched him vanish in the thickening mist forming around her, she no longer felt so brave. A stone was in one of her shoes. She walked to the wall and leaned against the barrier to drag in breath. Removing her shoes, she lingered in the shadows as if the darkness had been a mask to cover the one she now wore. Her feet hurt. Everything hurt. It hurt to be a lady.

"He will turn away from you when he learns who you are?"

For a moment, Christel thought the words had been plucked from her own thoughts. She whirled toward the path. *Tia*.

A swish of silk and her half sister stood in front of her. The dress she wore was similar to Christel's, but Tia was taller, her eyes darker. The white wig she wore covered chestnut hair. That they shared the same father only made Christel her enemy.

"He is betrothed, you know."

Christel had heard the rumors. He had come home to wed.

"The papers will be signed next week. I heard Grams and the dowager talking tonight."

"You are lying."

Tia picked up Christel's golden slippers from the wall. "And you are a thief." She flicked gloved fingers over the gold painted pearls Christel had sewn into the molded fabric. "Did you get these pearls from *my* castoffs or Saundra's? Or did you steal them from Grams?"

Tears burned behind Christel's eyes. "Give them back." *Please.*

Tia held one slipper over the stone wall. Christel gasped but stopped herself from leaping after it. "Lady Etherton will be furious that you and Saundra traded places tonight. These belong to Saundra."

"Tell her then."

Christel knew Tia wouldn't; Tia fancied herself Saundra's best friend. Telling Saundra's mother that Christel and Saundra had traded places tonight would only bring Lady Etherton's wrath down upon her daughter.

"Saundra will wed his lordship at summer's end," Tia said.

Christel's heart stopped with a thud. "I— You said the papers were not signed. You are only telling me this lie because you hate me."

Tia swallowed hard. "If I hated you, I would throw this slipper over the cliff so you could never go inside to dance." Tears shimmered in Tia's eyes behind the mask. She drew back her arm and threw the slipper over the wall.

Christel cried out. Catching herself on the wall, she glimpsed a flash of gold in the moonlight as the shoe tumbled over the rocks to the beach far below.

"His lordship would never have picked someone like you, Christel Douglas."

Chapter 1

~~~~~~ ∞ ~~~~~~

Nine years later
London

"**I**f we do not leave on the tide, we will not get out of London, my lord." Captain Bentwell struggled to keep pace with Camden's limping stride. "The child's cabin has been heated as instructed."

With his daughter cradled in his arms, Camden St. Giles, the seventh earl of Carrick, turned east to look at the sliver of dawn breaking through the heavy clouds. He frowned. The trip to the docks had taken longer in the inclement weather, but even at this early hour, London's maritime district swarmed with activity on and off the water as everyone attempted to beat the snowstorm bearing down on the Thames.

"Then see that we get out, Bentwell," Lord Carrick said as the captain opened the door into the companionway.

"Aye, my lord."

Camden stepped over the coaming, following his daughter's stout nurse into the narrow corridor. Clearing his throat, Bentwell reluctantly added, "A woman came aboard late last night. She said she sailed from Boston—"

Camden came to a stop abruptly in front of his daughter's cabin. "This ship does not take passengers."

"I know, my lord." Bentwell hastily lowered his voice. "But she claims to be a cousin to your dead wife. On the chance that she spoke the truth, I put her in your quarters. I did not know what else to do."

Despite himself, Camden felt himself turn toward his quarters and hesitate. But not out of caution or anger. His wife had had two cousins, but only one had been living in the colonies.

Camden carefully handed his sleeping daughter to the nurse and told her to take Anna to her quarters. Mrs. Gables was like a stout brown workhorse, and he was sure that carrying a willowy eight-year-old to bed would prove to be no effort.

Bentwell was working to prepare the ship to sail on the tide ahead of the storm. Indeed, the man had performed a miracle just having this ship and its crew prepared in the short time Camden had given him. Only yesterday, a missive had come from Camden's solicitor reporting that Camden's grandmother was ill.

"See that my daughter is warmed sufficiently," Camden instructed the nurse. "I'll check on you both shortly."

Removing his hat and gloves and stomping the snow from his boots, Camden slipped an enameled watch from his waistcoat and checked the time. "The wind has come round, and if it backs up too far easterly we will have a bloody time trying to get out of here," he told Bentwell. "Have the customs officers finished their inspection?"

"Not yet, sir."

"I will see to my guest. You see to the ship."

Captain Bentwell slapped his hat back on his grizzled head. "Aye, sir," he hastily answered.

For a moment after Captain Bentwell left, Camden was alone in the narrow, dark corridor. The idea of confronting the woman who had once been a familiar centerpiece in his mind brought silence to his thoughts.

Nine years ago, he had first encountered his wife's unconventional barefoot and half-dressed cousin collecting shells on the beach below the cliffs of Blackthorn Castle. Christel Douglas had been a seventeen-year-old sprite, the by-blow daughter of Lady Harriet's oldest son, though he had not known this at the time. It had been the month of the Golden Masquerade Ball, the summer he had come home on leave from his duties with the Royal Navy to do his obligation to his family and marry.

He had not willingly allowed himself to think about her in years.

Yet his heart raced oddly as he opened the door to his quarters. Without removing his heavy woolen cloak, he ducked under the deck beams before walking into the adjoining chamber. In the drowsy predawn, he had to be satisfied with a ship's brass lanthorn to supply illumination. No one had come into the cabin to light the stove, and the room was cold even to him, and he was as cold-blooded as a man came in these climes.

He dropped his gloves and hat on a chair. Like the rest of the room's furnishings, it was bolted down.

A rustle sounded near the gallery window, followed by a low growl from a dog. The unwelcome canine interloper stood next to the cabin's other inhabitant behind his desk, as if his entrance had only just roused her from the window bench.

She raised a pistol and pointed it directly at him. 'Twas his own pistol from his desk. "Do not come any closer, sir. Not until I first have your word that you will not have me removed from this ship." She spoke in a familiar voice, commanding and cultured, with a slight hint of Scots in the drawl.

Whatever he had been expecting to see at that moment, it had not been some mangy hound and Christel Douglas threatening him.

He could not see her face in the shadows. She wore a thin cloak over a pair of woolen breeches tightened at the waist with rope, a loose shirt and ragged, turned-out boots. Her hair beneath a floppy felt hat curled around her chin and shoulders. He knew from memory that her hair was the color of freshly churned butter.

They had been on the opposite sides of a war. That she might have actually come to England to shoot him flitted through his brain. Walking forward, he said, "Do you always threaten to kill people you do not like? Or do you intend to hold a gun on me all the way to Scotland?"

She gasped. "Lord Carrick . . ."

He strode past her and, raising his arms like Moses parting the Red Sea, he yanked open the gallery curtains, letting light into the room.

He turned, and he was suddenly looking into eyes that were still the deep blue of the warm Aegean Sea. For a moment, neither spoke. He reached around her for the pistol. He did not have to trust Christel Douglas to respect her. "I do not take threats lightly, Christel. Especially from you."

Her chin lifted. "'Tis only that I was not sure 'twould be you or that you would remember me. I would not have fatally shot you."

"Then your aim has improved since the last time you attempted to shoot me?" He emptied the powder from the gun.

"That was a long time ago. I was target practicing. Besides"—she straightened—"if you had been a better rider, you would not have been tossed from your horse and knocked silly."

"Aye." He lobbed the empty pistol on a chair. "Then where would our lives be today? Hmm?"

"Exactly as we are, my lord. You would still have married my cousin and I would still have gone to Virginia."

She suddenly gave her attention to her tattered sleeve. He had never known her to be compliant or meek. Perhaps she was remembering that he had briefly awakened from her onerous target practice flat on his back with his head in her lap, looking up into those same blue-colored eyes. She had been wearing very little when he had come upon her after she had been swimming in the sea. It was the first time he had realized that the little urchin who had been following him around all that August had been no skinny child, and that she had been the one he had kissed at the ball.

"You vanished without ever explaining a bloody thing

to me, Christel. Then you left Scotland and sailed across the world."

"What was to explain? You were already betrothed to Saundra."

"I was always curious how you found that out," he said quietly, "since the news had yet to be announced to anyone, including her."

His hand moved to lift her chin into the light. The dog growled. She abruptly bent and gently soothed it with a touch. The display of unconditional affection reminded him of the ragamuffin girl he'd briefly known, who'd rescued birds and kittens and rabbits and anything else that had needed saving. Of a time when tenderness had not been such a rare commodity in his life.

Aye, he remembered Christel Douglas well enough. He had looked upon similar features for eight years of his life.

Turning away, he reached for a tin pannikin in the bookcase and filled it from a flask before raking her slender figure with a glance. "As I remember, you seem to lack a knack for proper attire and introductions. Why am I not surprised to see you dressed like a stable hand?"

"A woman traveling alone has many reasons not to trust a man," she said without looking up.

His eyes slid from her floppy hat to the tips of her mud-caked boots. "I hate to be the one to inform you, but no one would mistake you for a man even if you do smell like a side of smoked bacon." He held out the pannikin.

She snatched the cup and drank, then coughed delicately into her sleeve, causing him some amusement as she attempted not to choke on the fiery drink. "Rest assured, *my lord*," she rasped, "with your dislike of pork and my distrust of powerful men we should all get along famously."

With this blustery declaration, she lifted her watery gaze and the light fell full on her face beneath her hat's brim. Something inside him cracked. No longer holding his anger close to his chest, he wondered what fool notion had brought her across a hostile ocean a world away from her own. "What are you doing here, Christel?"

"I was on my way to Glasgow. Two weeks ago a storm diverted the ship from Boston to Lisbon for repairs. What was not confiscated from me in Spain was stolen yesterday when I arrived in London. It was only by chance that I learned you were here and that this was your ship."

"Let me rephrase. What are you doing on this side of the *Atlantic*?"

She cautiously set down the tin cup. "I . . . I received a letter in Williamsburg six months ago." While she spoke, she struggled to pull a crumpled, water-stained letter from beneath her shirt. "'Twas written by Saundra. She asked me to return to Scotland to be a governess for Anna."

"A *governess*?" His gaze hesitating on the tattered gloves covering her fingers, he took the letter from her hand and brought it nearer to the window for light. "Saundra has been dead almost two years."

"Do you think I do not know that? But that is Saundra's handwriting. It bears your wax seal. It came from Blackthorn Castle."

In the uneasy silence that followed, he flipped over the letter and studied the wax seal. He shoved his hand into his waistcoat pocket and withdrew the missive he had received last evening from his solicitor concerning the onset of his grandmother's illness. The signet wax seal matched the ring on his finger, down to the laurel leaves that framed the crossed swords. This ring had not left his finger in years. He had another that he kept locked in a desk in his library. Only Saundra and his grandmother had ever had access to the ring kept at Blackthorn Castle.

Saundra could not have written the letter unless someone had mailed it long after she had died. He found it impossible to believe his grandmother would have done such a thing without his consent. But still . . . His grandmother and Christel's had always been close friends. Or else the letter had merely got lost for almost two years.

"I was not aware you and Saundra communicated," he said so casually that the question seemed to startle her.

He looked up from the letter into her liquid blue eyes. "Why?" she asked. "Because I am the family scandal?"

"That is not what I meant," he said quietly.

"We wrote to each other often." She tucked her arms in her cloak. "Now that the war is over, you must know that there were many Scots sympathetic to the colonists' plight. Trade and communication between us did not cease because of an embargo."

"Us? I am English, Christel. The Carrick title is an English patent given to one of my ancestors two hundred years ago for successfully quelling a Scottish rebellion and hanging all its leaders. Had I known she was in league with Leighton and you, I would have put a stop to it."

The color seemed to drain from her face. "I—"

"You think I did not know my own brother worked with your uncle against me in the war?" He folded the letter, little caring that his voice was sharp. "Saundra may have kept in contact with you, I do not know. But if the individual who sent this letter knew anything about me, she would have known that hell would freeze over before I would ever ask a colonial urchin to be governess to my daughter."

"I beg your pardon."

"Please do. Someone should. You have a habit of popping in and out of my life like a hand full of mist. You present me with a letter mailed from a woman who has been dead sixteen months. And I should not consider this a joke?"

Her temper flashed hotly. "Acquit me, my lord. Whatever I have done to make you angry, I apologize. But if I have earned your animosity, then let it be for a sin I have actually committed."

The ship lurched. Bentwell had cast off the mooring lines. Knowing what was about to come, Camden braced his hand against the timber stretching across the ceiling as the ship climbed and dropped. Despite his lame leg, he rode the ship's movement as years of experience and practice supplanted the effects of the injury on the psyche. Miss Douglas attempted to catch her balance on the desk and missed. He hooked his arm around her waist and kept her from tumbling to the floor. He heard her breath catch as he brought her hard against him.

Beneath the layers of homespun, her skin was warm, her curves soft. Despite the pungent scent of her clothes, he held her tightly braced against him. There was nothing about her that should have intrigued him, yet he found his interest piqued despite himself.

"What *sins* have you committed since our last meeting, Miss Douglas?"

Shoving away from him, she captured his gaze. "I have not *murdered* you. Yet," she said, riding the pitch of the ship with more ease. "And for your information, I never considered for an instant that I was *not* qualified to be a governess." A calm seemed to settle over her, banishing all timidity. "My grandmother saw to that part of my education before . . . before I left Scotland."

Camden set his teeth and silently cursed himself. What was wrong with him? For a moment, all he could grasp was that she had made a dangerous trip halfway across the world alone. She could have been killed and no one would ever have known her fate.

He also knew that she had already endured hell coming from the war-torn Tidewater region in Virginia. He was no novice when it came to understanding what war did to people.

Despite her bravado, she was very much a person now in exile.

Much as he was.

Forcing his attention back to the letter, he refolded it as his gaze fell on the dog. He had forgotten the mutt was present.

"He is mine," she said defensively, kneeling beside the natty red and brown spotted dog as if she would protect it from being thrown into the Thames.

He had never had pets, and when he was a boy, he couldn't understand his own grandmother's doting over a hairy, yapping lap dog that had never missed an occasion to bite him.

"I am not going to toss either of you overboard, Christel." Pocketing the letter, he looked past her out the stern gallery window into a dim, snowy morn. "When was the last time you ate something?"

"Yesterday morning."

He turned and strode across the room to the adjoining chamber. The cold made his leg ache, and absently he rubbed his palm against his thigh as he opened the door and found his steward in the corridor, warming blankets in hand. He took one, then directed the rest to his daughter's chamber. "After you deliver those to Anna's room, bring hot water and soap to these quarters," he said. "Then bring our guest something to eat. Coffee?" he asked her.

"And something for my dog?"

"Will a plate of kippers suffice?"

At her nod, he allayed the information to his steward. "Have we any women's clothing on board?"

"Maybe sir," his steward said. "Captain Bentwell's wife keeps a trunk in his quarters."

Shutting the door, Camden turned back into the room.

As Miss Douglas and her mongrel stared back at him, he contemplated what he had got himself into.

"You will remove those clothes so I can have them burned." He jutted his chin toward the trunk in the far corner. "You can find something in there to wear. My robe should provide you adequate protection until we find you something more suitable. I trust the dog will not chew up anything."

"But these are your quarters. Where will you stay?"

He gathered up his hat and gloves to quit the room. "Accept my hospitality, Miss Douglas. I am not normally so accommodating."

She waited until he had opened the door before saying, "Thank you, my lord. You have saved our lives this day whether you like it or nay."

His hand froze on the latch and his gaze returned to hers. Any normal person would have been grateful for his aid. Yet with typical colonial impertinence, she seemed to reproach *him*, as if his character had been on trial in a room filled with his peers.

"I will repay you for any expenses you incur on my behalf," she said.

Camden's scowl gave way to a momentary lapse of amused silence. She could not afford one of his shirts. But her posture told him more eloquently than words that she intended to repay him every shilling if she had to dig turnips from the ground the rest of her life to do it.

He was not a man tolerant of emotions, especially his own, yet he found himself possessed of the need to lift her face back into light and ask her what the hell she could possibly do to support herself.

"Christel . . . Miss Douglas," he managed with patience, "if 'tis your conscience you need to appease, you may do what you think best."

"I have never thought you less than kind, my lord."

Her voice again arrested his hand on the door latch. Only this time it was the words spoken that made him turn. For they had not been facetious, nor had she meant to be hurtful.

He wanted to laugh. Saundra had not died thinking him kind.

But he could not force cynicism into his thoughts. There was none.

"And me with no reputation for civility. You, Miss Douglas, are still too trusting by far, or you would not be stranded and in need of my help." He cocked a brow, surprised that of everything he had been able to say, it had been the truth that had cowed her into silence. "*Now* do I have your leave to retire?"

Camden's steward was waiting for him in the corridor. "I put yer trunk in my cabin, my lord." Carrying a tray, he hurried forward and swung open the door to his quarters. "I am heating water for the girl's bath. She is young. I had heard she got out of Lisbon before they closed the port for cholera. She is fortunate to have made it this far alone. Why would a woman cross the Atlantic alone?"

"I do not know, Harry."

"Must have been desperate to come home."

Camden limped past the little Irishman into a cabin that was smaller than his privy closet. He dumped his cloak, hat and gloves on the bottom berth. The room had a washbasin and a narrow space next to the wall barely wide enough for Harry's sea bag and Camden's leather trunk.

His leg was so stiff that he could barely bend it to sit on the berth. His knees bumped the stove, but he welcomed the heat.

"I can see from here that leg's all swelled up," Red Harry said. "Let me take a look."

"Have mercy on me and bring me hot coffee."

The old steward shut the door. He had already made a pot of coffee and forced Camden to stand to accommodate his presence as he squeezed next to the washbasin, where he set the tray.

"That girl has come a long way," Red Harry said. "You ought be more patient with her. She is no' as strong as she seems."

"That girl survived Yorktown."

"So did you, my lord."

Camden yanked at his stock. "Duly chastised, Harry. As the oldest of the crew and more trustworthy than my own grandfather, you are tasked with her care. Make sure she eats a hearty meal. The galley will most probably be out of service once we enter the channel." He removed his jacket and ducked to look out the porthole. "Someone will also need to take that hound of hers to the hold. There is straw in the livestock stalls for his needs."

He scrubbed frost off the window. Outside, a forest of

masts sporting flags from several nations bobbed above a crowded watery surface and stood against a London skyline of tall brick buildings and chimneys billowing clouds of black smoke. The scene held little interest beyond a cursory glance to reassure him that his ship was leaving the quay. The voyage around the southern tip of England past Falmouth, then north into the Firth of Clyde, would last four, maybe five, days. By land with winter encroaching, the journey to Ayrshire would have lasted six weeks.

He could survive four or five days in close quarters with Christel.

Absently rubbing his thigh, he turned away from the porthole. Harry squeezed past him to the cupboard, forcing Camden to stand. Finding himself trapped against the bunk, the top of his head touching the ceiling and his shoulders pressing against the upper berth, he eyed his steward narrowly.

"Ye can toss me overboard if ye wish later," Red Harry said. "But right now ye will be lettin' me tend to that leg."

Red Harry removed a tin and, slapping a towel around his neck like a drover snapping a whip, turned. "Down with yer breeches and on your side, my lord."

"Dammit, Harry."

But the old hunched-over wolf stared Camden down as if he'd been a contrary pup. After a moment, Camden's hands fell to his waist and the next thing he knew, he was peeling down his breeches in the most humbling, humiliating way possible. He sat on the berth, accepting a flask of whiskey from his gaoler.

"You do understand you are the only man I would ever allow to torture me in this way."

The man's gnarled fingers kneaded foul-smelling balm into the swollen area around the ugly red scar just below Camden's hip. The scar stretched to his knee. "I have known wee babes who take better care of themselves," Red Harry muttered unpleasantly.

"Is that a tone of hostility I am hearing?"

"When ye be old and crippled like me you'll be wishin' you'd listened to me more, my lord. Ye should have stayed at Blackthorn Castle to begin with, where ye belong, my lord."

Tipping the flask, Camden let the warm liquid slide down his throat. "I *should* have listened when you thought moving to Naples would be a good idea."

"I never thought 'twould be a good idea. I only said any place would be warmer than England. I do no' fancy ye goin' anywhere but back to Blackthorn Castle." Red Harry wiped the oil from his hands on a towel and slapped it around his neck. "No one ever believed ye would walk away and leave the place to your blackguard brother."

"I do not intend to remain longer at Blackthorn Castle than I must to discharge my duty to Grandmother."

"You'll be returning to London to be with Miss Jordan then?"

Camden adjusted his clothes. "Are you tiring of London's gay life, or is it the company I keep?"

Red Harry knew better than to question Camden's relationship with Marie Jordan. The fact that he did surprised Camden.

Indeed, he was more than aware of the beautiful Miss Jordan's character. He just didn't care. He'd ceased finding relevance in society or its over-bloated opinion of itself long ago.

A knock sounded on the door. Camden answered it as he pulled a heavy sweater over his head. "We will reach Gravesend in an hour, my lord," Bentwell said. "The snow has turned to ice. We may need to take the ship farther east toward Calais to escape the brunt of the storm."

Camden had no intention of entering French waters with his daughter aboard. "Or we can skirt Dover and use the wind to our advantage in the straits."

Bentwell nodded. "Aye, the storm is coming in from the north. That could work. Could shave off half a day of travel if we time it right. The crew will like that. 'Tis bloody damn cold up there."

Camden shut the door and turned to Red Harry. "See that someone brings enough coal for the stoves in both Miss Douglas's room and my daughter's. I will be topside as soon as I finish down here."

After Red Harry scurried out, Camden stepped across the companionway and entered his daughter's cabin. He found her dressed warmly and lying on her bed asleep. Smoothing her hair from her face, he kissed her brow. The girl being eight years old, her beauty still possessed the angelic innocence of childhood, untarnished by the lessons of life. Asleep, she looked as fragile as the finest porcelain. Awake, she could be a mythical woodland sprite rumored to live in the woods surrounding Blackthorn Castle.

Anna was the one thing with which God had seen fit to bless him. Camden loved her more than he had ever loved anything, even more than his own life. Despite everything that Saundra had done, she had never alienated his daughter's affections from him. Anna was the reason he'd survived these hellish last years after Yorktown. She was the reason he'd learned to walk again. The reason that he lived. They had rarely been home since Saundra had died there almost two years ago.

"She had a restless night, my lord," the nurse said. "I think she will be glad to be returning home."

Camden wrapped her in fur. Warming bricks heated the interior sufficiently to render the chill less biting.

His daughter stirred and turned onto her back. "Are we going home now, Papa?"

He looked into her face and smoothed the hair back from her cheek. "Aye, lass."

"And I will be able to see Uncle Leighton and Grandmamma?"

Camden held back the frown that wanted to form just at the corners of his mouth. Somehow, his brother had managed to steal his daughter's heart, and Camden did not have it inside to hurt her more than she had already been hurt with her mother's passing. "Aye, Anna. They will be there."

She settled comfortably in the blankets as he wrapped the fur more tightly around her. "I am glad, Papa."

"The weather will be rough. I want you to stay in your cabin. You and I will share a cup of tea tonight."

"My doll, too?"

He chuckled. "Aye, your doll, too."

She smiled and turned back into her pillow. He looked over at Mrs. Gables and told her not to stand. Letting himself out of the cabin, he caught himself against the ship's sway as he shut the door. Two lanthorns on the wall knocked against the bulkhead. He looked over at his cabin, hesitated, then raised his hand and knocked.

The door swung open. Christel stood before him wearing his brown silk robe and carrying a stave bucket filled with soap and a towel. Her gaze shot up to his. "Oh."

The disappointment in her voice was so evident that he almost laughed. "Oh?"

Her other hand clutched the edges of the robe. A whisper of gold flashed just above the mounds of her breasts. "I thought you were Mr. Harold . . . ah, Red Harry. He took my dog to the hold. It has started to sleet." She held fast to the door. "Does the captain know what he is doing? Should we have left London in this weather?"

Camden raised a brow. "This is November," he said. "If I waited for the perfect day to leave London, I would be waiting until June."

"*You* are this ship's captain? I thought Captain Bentwell was."

"Mr. Bentwell runs the ship back and forth in trade between Glasgow and London and sometimes to Holland. But I am the captain of this ship." He looked past her toward the cupboard. "And as captain, I need my oilskin and a few of my belongings."

She stepped aside. He walked to the cupboard and

withdrew a few of his items. He could feel her eyes on him. His skin felt warm and discomforting, like he was catching a fever. As he sat on his berth to put on his boots, he made an effort not to look at her even as he knew she was standing in a shaft of daylight coming through the gallery windows.

He stomped the sealskin boots onto his feet, retrieved his fur hat and slicker, and stopped. She stood in front of him holding out his heavy woolen gloves. The ship labored against a swell. She tightened her hold on the bucket. His mouth softened.

"Do not leave this cabin."

"I would not dream of it."

His gaze dropped to her sassy mouth, and it occurred to him as he left the room that there was still much that was unsettled between them. And it had nothing to do with his marriage to Saundra or the fact that Christel left Scotland without ever telling him good-bye.

He had not known that she'd been in Yorktown that fateful year when tens of thousands of colonists had battled for the fate of a future nation. His ship, *Endurance*, had been one of the frigates in the British fleet that had gone to aid Cornwallis with a four-hundred-man crew. What had happened had been public record when the British had failed to break the French blockade.

What had not been public record was that most of the British fleet had become separated during a storm, leaving two ships behind and outnumbered nine to one come the dawn. There had been no chance for surrender. Rather than try to run, he had made the fateful decision to fight.

He'd lost two hundred souls under his command in the battle and would have lost his life, too, if not for the colonial ship that had fished the survivors out of the water. Captain Douglas's frigate had been a part of the battle that day, and first on the scene to pull many of the surviving British from the bay.

Camden had awakened in pain to Christel's voice in the field hospital outside Yorktown shortly before Cornwallis's surrender. He had spent weeks in and out of consciousness with her at his side, weeks more in interrogation before her uncle was able to get him put on a prisoner transport back to England. It had taken months to learn to walk again, and when he had, he'd faced an admiralty board and dishonor after the British defeat at Yorktown.

But even as life had a way of reminding him that everything came with a price, fate had worked itself out in the end. If Christel had not gone to Virginia, he would have probably died in Yorktown. And maybe Saundra would still be alive.

Chapter 2

~∞~

Christel came awake that evening to the loud groaning noise from the ship's seams as it plowed through choppy seas. She had crawled into bed after bathing herself and the dog merely to get warm.

Raking back damp tendrils of uncombed hair from her eyes, she sat up to find that the dog had leapt onto the bunk and wrapped itself in Lord Carrick's thick feather tick. Everything smelled like wet dog and feathers. She gasped upon seeing feathers on the ground.

"Oh, bad dog."

The hound licked her face. "Lord Carrick will kill us both. Off with you before someone finds you up here and banishes us both to the hold."

The dog leapt off the bed, and Christel crawled out to check the damage to the blankets. Wearing nothing more than one of Lord Carrick's white cambric shirts, she was painfully aware of the cold as she cleaned up the mess and found her way to the washbasin behind a screen.

Pausing to confront the woman in the silvered glass above the washbasin, she touched her hair. Her wheaten curls, once her pride and glory, wilted unevenly at her shoulders. Cutting her hair before she had left Boston had not been the hardest part of this journey. Seeing Camden St. Giles again was like stepping barefoot into a room filled with broken glass.

Absently rubbing her thumb across the face of her necklace, she walked around the cabin, studying the books locked behind glass, touching everything else as if by doing so she could develop a bond with her new temporary world. It was something she had always done from the days when she was a child, a habit that had begun after she had gone to live at Rosecliffe when she was twelve. It was her way to feel a part of her new world, which did not welcome her or treat her kindly.

His chambers were more practical than luxurious, with their display of polished brass and leather-covered chairs bolted to the floor, and a Persian rug that gave character to the tastes of the cabin's male owner.

She saw nothing that might have once belonged to Saundra. No ornaments or color that bespoke a woman's gentle touch. Everything was shiny and new and in its proper place, ruthlessly void of softness, like the polished brilliance of a diamond devoid of warmth.

Like Lord Carrick.

Even his appearance had bespoken a calculated elegance refined by his dark tailored clothes. The man Christel had met early this morning was not that restless young naval officer she had fallen in love with those many years ago in a world so far separated from the one where he now lived. If she could have found another way home, she would have.

But the Barracuda was not all ice and teeth and did have

a soft spot inside him. That morning she had heard him talking gently to a little girl in the adjoining cabin.

And just that fast it was as if the shadow had lifted from Christel's heart. Lord Carrick had not said Lady Anna was aboard the ship. That she might be so near raised Christel's spirits.

A knock sounded at the door, and Christel jumped back into the bunk as Lord Carrick's steward entered carrying a tray laden with food. He had introduced himself earlier as Red Harry. She had no idea why he possessed such a name, for there seemed to be nothing red about him except his nose.

He spied her awake. "I hoped ye be awake." He set down the tray at the end of the bunk. "I brought ye some nice fried pancakes, eggs and kippers to fill yer belly."

Christel pulled the tick to her neck as she attempted to maneuver nearer to the tray. It wasn't that she was shy. She'd bathed in streams with a regiment of soldiers a stone's throw over the trees. But she suddenly felt awkward and exposed wearing only Lord Carrick's shirt, sleeping in his cabin and his bed.

Red Harry chuckled as he turned to pick up the water tins littering the floor. "Ye need no' fear none over yer modesty," he said kindly. "I been wed three times, mum. None of 'em was legal, mind ye, but the point bein', I seen my fair share of ankles and other female"—he cleared his throat—"whatnots." He offered her a serviette. "The cap'n tasked me with yer care, so I am under me oath to be a gentleman."

A corner of her mouth lifted. The tick fell to her waist as she moved the tray onto her lap and began to eat. Nay, devour. The pancakes were more like flatbread, the eggs were runny and the sweet coffee had thick grounds on the bottom of the cup, but nothing had ever tasted better. "Thank you." She dabbed the corner of her mouth with her finger and smiled. "You would not by chance have a cow on board. I would love a glass of cold milk."

He chuckled, resettling the water tins in his arms. "No cows, lass. And you'll most likely be dinin' off pickled herring and hardtack the rest of the trip. The cap'n has closed the galley."

Approaching darkness prevented her from seeing outside the window. "Where are we?" she murmured over a mouthful while sharing a kipper with the dog. He had somehow snuck back up on the berth to better observe her tray without her noticing.

"Jest near Dover, mum. And this mutt be?" Red Harry asked.

Scratching between his ears, Christel nuzzled her nose against his neck. "I have no idea. I only just met him on the docks in London." With a mottled red-and-white spotted coat, he seemed to be a mishmash of breeds with perky ears and amber eyes and an equal need to belong. "He just found me."

The weathered face of the old man turned fatherly. "Did he now?" he said approvingly. "A dog knows a lot about a person's character, ye ken."

She patted the hound's head and fed him the last kipper from her tray. "Or perhaps he merely likes me because I feed him. Is that not right, boy? People oughtn't be so cruel," she said as if to herself, still miffed by Lord Carrick's curtness with her this morning.

Red Harry sniffed. "If it makes ye feel better, his lordship be harder on hisself than he is on others, lass."

It didn't make her feel better, but she finished her meal rather than state her sentiment aloud. "You have served Lord Carrick long?"

Red Harry closed the cupboard and walked past her with an armful of linens that had been behind the screen. "Been with his lordship from the day he took his first command ten years ago. Course he is no longer a captain in His Majesty's navy. . . . A lot has changed from those days."

She hoped he would reveal more. He didn't.

"It has been a long time since I have been back to Ayr. Is it the same, then?"

He withdrew the tinderbox from the cupboard and began lighting the lamps. "Gossip never changes as far as I can tell. But there still be gels standin' in line to be the next Countess Carrick, and his grandmother still be wantin' him to wed and settle down at Blackthorn like a proper lord should. And him in London instead with that Spanish mistress hangin' on his arm and causin' one scandal or another, and him carin' about nothin' at all, 'cept maybe his little girl."

The little steward snapped shut the glass casing on the copper lamp next to the door. "Me bein' only his lordship's loyal servant for nigh on ten years and savin' his life more than once, I am no' sayin' it be my business how he lives his life. People spend too much time sticking their noses in other people's affairs as is, and no one can accuse *me* of puttin' my nose where it does no' belong."

"I am sure his lordship can handle himself, Mr. Harry."

"My name be Red Harry. *Mister* makes me sound too old and formal. I be old enough without ye makin' me older than I am, and I ain't been a gentleman ever."

She smiled. "Then we are kindred spirits, Red Harry, for no one can accuse me of being much of a lady."

"Do no' fool yourself, lass," he said, his brown eyes softening. "Ye be beautiful like his lady wife. Ye could be her, ye ken."

Looking away, Christel tried not to resent the physical comparison. But she loved Saundra, and at once, she felt guilty for the thought.

"Mr. . . . er . . . Red Harry? Did you know my cousin, his wife?"

"Aye, I did, lass." He hesitated, as if he would measure his words, then said no more.

Red Harry took the tray and returned to present her with a gown, an assortment of underclothing, including boned stays, a stiffened petticoat, and sturdy shoes. Then he surprised her with a sewing box that had once been hers but that she had given to Saundra on her eighteenth birthday.

She threw off the bunk covers. "Where did you get this?"

"It belonged to her ladyship, lass. She kept her embroidery needles and threads inside. Do no' rightly know why 'tis still on board . . ." His voice trailed, and he busied himself with the latch. "I thought ye could use something inside. The dress might need a bit of altering."

She held the gown against her. A glance at herself made her laugh. "'Tis quite festive."

At her age, she would never have chosen to wear such a piece of muslin frippery, with its enthusiastic flower motif, but she decided that she would welcome the bright colors on such a dower day even if it meant gophering the frilled sleeves and hem with an iron.

"His lordship said fer me to tell ye the dress be yours."

She continued to gaze down at the gown. She had learned long ago never to accept charity from men without expecting to give something back. Yet, in this case, she didn't concern herself that Lord Carrick had designs on her person. He felt a responsibility toward her. And he *had* taken her clothes, after all. But that she found herself reminded of his benevolence bothered her as much as the fact that she was forced to accept it.

She smiled. "I am appreciative. I was not looking forward to arriving in Scotland barefoot and wearing only his robe." She peered out the ice-encrusted window and asked, "Has he been on deck all this time?"

"Aye, lass." Red Harry scratched his whiskers. "I do no' 'spect he will have the time even to eat. No' in this weather."

Christel spent this period of involuntary confinement sewing. By early afternoon the next day, before the seas had become so rough that she could no longer work, she had already removed the bottom flounce of lace to shorten the gown three inches, adding it to the sleeves and bodice so that it would cover more of her bosoms.

She held the dress to her body and, looking this way and that in the glass Red Harry had found for her, concluded she was still an excellent modiste. She could not deny the dress endowed her with springtime cheer, even if she was feeling less than cheerful herself.

After a supper of dried biscuits and herring, and feeling distinctly queasy, she changed into Lord Carrick's robe and readied herself for bed. Rolling up the sleeves to her elbows, she struggled to clean the scraps of cloth off the floor and brought the sewing box to the window bench. She stowed it beneath and sat, the dog at her feet. The animal, having found a secure place on the floor to endure the storm, was far wiser than she.

Lacing her fingers tightly in her lap, she looked outward toward a turbulent horizon and could not tell where the churning sky ended and the waves began. The sea was a powerful, living current and had killed her father and her uncle. She couldn't understand how any man could remain on deck in this cold.

She spied a two-masted ship. At first, she didn't pay attention, but then she saw the ship again, right to windward under full sail, a tactic oft used when one ship was following another. She straightened.

She did not hear the cabin door click open, only saw the dog's head suddenly come up. Startled, Christel turned and caught a flash of movement near the bulkhead. The door swung on its hinges with the ship's movements. She balanced herself as she walked into the adjoining chamber, only to come to a stop as she looked around the bulkhead at a little girl hiding there. The child stood in a pale nightdress just outside the dim amber light cast by a single sconce next to Christel's head.

"Are you an angel?" asked the girl in a small voice.

Christel stared at the small oval face looking back at her with wide, light-colored eyes. Black curls bound by a white ribbon reached down the length of her back. Her white nightdress topped her ankles just above her bare feet.

"An angel? The only angel I see in the room is you. You must be Lady Anna."

Christel knelt and placed her hands on the girl's narrow shoulders. "Look at you without slippers or a wrap. You are colder than an icicle."

"Hoarfrost," she said softly. "Mamma used to say I was colder than hoarfrost."

Christel gently touched the ribbon entwined in Anna's silken hair. She might have Saundra's delicate build, but the girl had her father's blue-gray eyes, fringed in his dark lashes, his sable hair, and his beautiful mouth. "Hoarfrost it is, then. Come." She led the girl to the bunk and pulled back the covers. "What are you doing out of your room?"

She wrapped Anna in the thick feather tick until only her delicate face showed in a fluffy mountain of white. She had aired the tick yesterday after the dog had slept on it.

"I woke up," the girl said. "I got afraid. Nurse Gabby did not light the lamp. I think she is ill."

Christel arranged the feather tick over the child's feet. "Does Nurse Gabby always take ill on rough seas?"

Christel would die if she had brought some plague aboard

this ship. But to her relief Anna nodded. "Red Harry *tells* her to eat the dry toast he brings for her. But she never eats toast without her butter and orange marmalade, and Red Harry said since we do not have our ship's cook on board, no one knows where anything is and she would have to eat the toast without butter and marmalade. I do not like marmalade. I like strawberries the best."

"I see."

"Nurse Gabby did not eat the toast."

"And now she is sick."

"Terribly so." Anna suddenly came to life. "Is that a *dog*?" She leaned over the side of the bunk and held out her small hand to the spotted hound. "I always wanted a puppy. Papa would never allow me to have a dog. What is its name?"

"I have not named him yet."

Anna's pale eyes widened. "Why ever not? Everything must have a special name so it knows 'tis loved."

Christel hadn't named it yet because she hadn't quite accepted the hound as hers, as if it had been a possession to be owned. Or perhaps it was more. Whenever she allowed herself to get close to something, it either died or ran away.

"Perhaps I have not known him long enough." Christel touched the dog's ear. "I met him on the docks when I arrived in London. He was hungry and I fed him. After that, he followed me everywhere and kept the tars and stevedores at bay. At any rate, any life in Scotland is far better than living on the docks in London."

A wave crashed against the ship. Christel looked out the window at the churning sea washing against the glass. With a sigh, the girl buried herself deeper into the blanket. "Papa would never let anything happen to his ship while I am on board. He told me so. Papa never lies. And Mama told me an angel would always watch over me and Papa."

Christel had had enough of this angel business. "My name is Christel, Anna. I am not the least bit celestial, I assure you. My Grams is your great-grandmother. I am returning to Scotland after being away a very long time. Your papa has agreed to take me. But if there is an angel watching over you and your papa, then 'tis your mam."

The little girl buried herself deeper into the blanket and looked away. Christel credited the response to the reality that a mother's death would be devastating to any child. "Cousin Tia said Mam is in hell."

Christel gasped, stifling her breath. She had not thought about her half sister in years. Tia had made her life a living hell even before their father had died.

"'Tis a cruel thing to say," Christel replied. "Why would Tia tell you such a thing?"

"Cousin Tia did not tell me. She told Grandmamma because Papa had to force a priest to say words over Mam after she died. Papa said if he did not bury Mama in the cemetery at St. Abigal's, he would see the kirk taken apart stone by stone and tossed into the sea. They think I am too young to know the hateful things people say about Mama and Papa. Some people blame Papa for her death."

"I am truly sorry, Anna."

"But I am glad to be going home. I dislike London so terribly much. If a lady is nice to me 'tis only because she wants to marry Papa. Not because she likes me. I miss my uncle Leighton the most. He always gives me the best presents," she said sleepily, burying herself in the pillows. "Even better than Papa's. Last year he gave me a pony. A real pony, but Papa says I am too young to learn to ride."

"Or perhaps your papa is protective of you."

"Grandmamma says 'tis because Papa and Uncle Leighton both loved Mamma and that they miss her, too. I think 'tis because Papa and Uncle Leighton do not like each other, though Papa would never tell me such a thing."

"Of course, he would not." Christel smoothed a hand over the comforter.

She had always cared for Leighton, even as he had changed from a friend on whom she could depend into a vice-seeking young aristocrat hellbent on defying his father at every opportunity. The elder Lord Carrick had expected him to join the service to the crown, as all St. Giles's men had dutifully done for centuries, but Leighton considered one brother serving enough for one family to sacrifice to England's colors. So he had gone to Oxford to learn law and had got himself involved in the war. They had always remained in touch through her uncle. During that time, he had never so much as written a word about Saundra.

"Have you eaten supper?" Christel quietly asked.

Anna wrinkled her nose. Christel smiled in sympathy. "You do not like cold herring and biscuits?"

"Nurse Gabby does not let me eat the biscuits because once a biscuit nearly cracked her tooth. She says they should be used only as weapons of war and shot out of a cannon."

"Poor Nurse Gabby."

The ship plunged feverishly. Soon it would be dark. Christel's gaze went to the door. "I need to check on her, Anna. I want you to remain here until I return."

The girl closed her eyes, seemingly quite content to remain beneath the warm feather tick, where Christel suddenly wished she'd been. She found the tinderbox and lit one of the lamps attached to the wall near the door, then tightened the belt around the robe she wore as she left Lord Carrick's quarters, feeling almost as if she'd been an escaped convict.

There were two other cabins off the companionway. One she knew belonged to Red Harry, as she had seen him retrieve a blanket for her from his room. She knocked on the adjacent door. When she received no answer, she opened it and immediately discovered that she was not immune to the effects of a rough sea when the smell of its effects flooded her senses.

After bracing something in front of the door to keep it open, she found Nurse Gabby tucked in her bunk, oblivious to the raging chaos around her. The elder woman did not even stir when Christel set the back of her hand to her cheek. She had no fever.

Nurse Gabby was a stout woman with round cheeks and steel gray curls sticking out of a woolen nightcap. A snore suddenly erupted, telling Christel that at least the woman still lived.

As was the norm in such cases, there was nothing to be done for the ailment but to ride out the weather. Christel made sure the slop bucket remained secured and that the woman was as warm as she could be. Christel would continue to check on her throughout the night. By the time she had finished, it was already dark. Looking around, she found Anna's blankets in her berth and decided to gather them up. A curly-haired doll tumbled to the floor.

Christel touched the faded velvet dress. She lifted it into the light spilling in from the companionway and stopped short with a gasp.

Lord Carrick stood on the threshold. From broad shoulders to booted feet, he filled the doorway with his tall form. He wore a black oilskin that went to his knees and dripped water on the floor. His hand scraped back his hood. The wind had torn most of his hair from its queue, and strands hung wet to his shoulders. The beginnings of a beard shadowed his jaw.

"My lord . . ."

He looked past her into the darkened room. "Where is my daughter?"

"In my quarters. *Your* quarters . . ."

But he had already turned on his heel. Leaving Nurse Gabby to sleep the rest of the evening away in unconsciousness, Christel rushed to follow him into his cabin, still carrying the doll and blankets.

Anna lay on her side already asleep in the bed, a barely visible lump beneath a rumpled feather tick. Christel could almost feel the tension leave the child's father. " 'Tis dark. I came down to make sure—"

"A lamp has been lit?"

"She is afraid of the dark."

Christel set the blankets and doll on a chair. "Aren't we

all to some extent? Her mother is dead. To be in the darkness is to feel completely alone. No one wishes to feel alone."

He turned, his legs braced apart. His eyes went over her, wearing only his robe. With its cinnamon brocade under weaving, the fabric seemed to flow over her like watered silk. She'd rolled up the sleeves to accommodate their length on her arms, and the effect only seemed to make her feel younger.

"I thought I told you to stay put in my quarters."

"Nurse Gabby is incapacitated with seasickness. Your daughter came to the door looking for you. I hope you do not think I would have harmed Anna. "

He took a step nearer and didn't seem to care that he dripped salt water all over the fine plush weave of a very costly Persian carpet.

"Nurse *Gabby*?" he asked with amusement.

"The woman in the other cabin. Your daughter called her Gabby."

"I see. Might I suggest you not call her Gabby to her face? Mrs. Gables is somewhat sensitive when it comes to etiquette and would be greatly offended by your lack of decorum. I would not want you to embarrass yourself."

"Ever the knight gallant. I will attempt to restrain my colonial impertinence in front of your staff." She followed the statement with a serene smile. "As much as possible. Seeing as how we are family and all. My embarrassment would be yours twofold."

His eyes narrowed. Another wave hit the ship.

Lord Carrick rode the movement, and she did not miss

the brief flinch in his expression as he put weight on his lame leg to catch his balance. Nothing else showed in his expression, and only his hand moved as he caught himself on the rafter above his head.

Christel never understood that kind of ruthless control. She was more like a cloud in the sky shaped by the wind and surrounding forces than like a rock, incapable of molding itself to its environment.

Still, as she fell against the back of the chair, there was something to be said for rocks and other immovable objects, and an ex-naval captain with the confidence not to think his ship was in imminent peril of sinking.

Closing the distance between them, England's former naval hero stopped in front of her. "Take heart," he said. "I have only lost one ship."

"Truly!" She glared. "I can think of at least two more pleasant ways to perish than having one's mortal remains consumed by starfish, crabs, and sharks at the bottom of the sea."

His blue-gray eyes were no longer disconcertingly direct. "Indeed."

"Aye. Being flattened on the cobbles by a beer wagon for one."

The corners of his mouth twitched, dispelling some of his sternness. "And the second?"

"Tucked in bed . . . alone, surrounded by a warm feather tick and a roaring fire sharing my last moments with a good book."

He laughed. A small sound, certainly nothing to celebrate,

but for one moment, she imagined him as he had been all those years ago when he had kissed her at the masquerade.

Not the man beneath the aristocratic façade that shaped him now and who was about as approachable as a growling dog. She had a feeling he hadn't laughed in a long time.

She found him watching her. "Which book?" he asked.

The question, like his nearness, startled her because she had not expected to feel anything and he had not allowed her to prepare a response. Then it occurred to her that he was a master tactician adept at war games that crushed enemies even if done delicately and without bloodshed. She might not have been an enemy, but he could crush her all the same.

"I would want to be reading Madam d'Aulony's folktales," she said. "Far more appealing than . . ." She scoured her memory for books she disliked and remembered shelves and shelves of such guilty tomes in his own library at Blackthorn Castle. " . . . the *Histoire et mémoires,* a collection of French language commentary and criticism on Greek and Latin classics. Give me the classics without the critique."

"And here I thought my grandfather had the only book in existence. You speak French, do you?"

"Oui, monsieur le comte. I noticed you have many books locked behind glass and filigree. Do you perhaps have a key . . . that is, unless they are not meant to be read?"

"The key is in the desk next to the gunpowder for the pistol. I believe you know where the drawer is."

He eased past her, hesitated, then stopped. His shoulder brushed hers as he turned and looked down at her, his expression bathed in amber from the light beside the door.

Raising her chin, she felt her heart slip into a thunderous rhythm she did not recognize.

"Red Harry said you asked to see me?"

Yesterday, but she did not point that out to him.

"I merely wanted to thank you for the clothes."

Lord Carrick slipped the hood of the slicker back over his head. "The garments belonged to Bentwell's daughter. You may thank him."

"Will the weather remain this wretched all the way to Scotland?"

"I am hoping it will not."

"Perhaps you should take hot tea. The cold cannot be good for you."

"Nor my crew. I am fine, Christel."

"My lord . . ." She squeezed past him, out of the room and into the companionway, then waited for him to shut the door, noting he was suddenly wary. "Perhaps when the weather is less demanding we could talk more. I would like to ask you about Saundra if it is not too painful."

She had a hundred questions, all of which began with who he believed had sent her that letter, culminating with Anna's statements about her mother. "I know very little of how she died."

The temperature in the companionway seemed to drop colder than the air outside. His pale eyes reflected the change. She was now aware that something terrible must have happened to Saundra.

Something that would make Lord Carrick want to leave Blackthorn Castle forever.

He moved to step around her, but she planted her feet against more than the turbulent toss of the ship. "You have to talk to me. You owe me at least that much."

She knew at once that she had said the wrong words. But she was Saundra's cousin. She had saved his life. Surely, that counted for something in his eyes. "Unless you truly do feel responsible for her death."

"Responsible—?"

The word stopped as if severed from his tongue by the drop of an ax. With an uttered oath, he looked away but made no attempt to defend himself. Of course, he wouldn't. He would not even defend himself against the charges leveled against him by the British admiralty for incompetence in command for losing his ship at Yorktown.

Yet uncertainty blossomed in her belly—and fear, because she had not expected to feel doubt. She had not thought that he *was* responsible. "She died from a miscarriage. You did not *cause* Saundra's miscarriage."

Her eyes raked his profile, searching for clues, dreading what she might find if she searched too long. "I . . ." She strove to keep her voice level. "There is a difference between guilt and responsibility, my lord. Whatever the course of events, you were not at fault."

"You have no bloody idea, Christel. You do not know anything."

"I understand more than you think—"

He braced a palm against the wall, trapping her, his jaw tense. They matched stares for several long seconds before his eyes narrowed slightly. He was behaving poorly and he knew it: she read it in the heavy weight of his gaze, felt it in the shift of his stance and the hard muscles of his chest as he moved his lips to her ear. Only his oilskin touched her, barely a brush against her arm, but it might as well have been his hand for the whisper of heat that warned her.

"Why have you really come back?" he demanded. "You have left your entire life in Virginia to travel across the world, and I doubt it was to be governess to my child."

"What do you mean?" She whispered the words.

"No one does anything unless something is in it for him or for her. Or she is running away."

"And you are not?" she accused him, feeling cornered by her emotions, daring him to defy the accusation, angry that he could turn this conversation back on her. He pushed himself away from the wall. Before he walked two steps toward the door, she said, "Do you have so little faith in humankind then that you could judge us all so harshly? What did Saundra do that no priest would say words over her, that you would threaten to tear down the village kirk stone by stone if she was not buried in the cemetery beside her mother?"

He wheeled around, but it was not anger she glimpsed on his face as he scraped back the hood of his oilskin with the sweep of his hand. "Where did you hear that?"

"Your daughter."

His eyes closed and he shook his head as he mouthed something that sounded like an oath. Suddenly beset by a terrible urge to touch him, she forced her hands into a fist. His defensive posture told her he would never have allowed it. "Please tell me what happened. I need to know. You were there."

He looked up at the rafter, his jaw tight. "Saundra climbed the stairs to the light tower overlooking the cliffs," he said in a colorless voice. "And then she jumped into the sea. We found her body the next morning washed onto the rocks."

Christel searched his face in utter shock. "I . . . I do not believe it. How can you be so sure she did not fall? How?"

"You have not been in the old light tower or you would not ask me that question. No one *falls* from up there unless they first climb out on the ledge."

Christel's eyes burned. "I . . . I am so sorry."

"Why?" she heard him rasp.

For assuming the worst of him. For not returning sooner. For staying gone too long.

"She has been dead almost two years, Christel," he said without inflection.

His hand suddenly came up, warm beneath her chin, turning her face into the light and returning her gaze to his. She had not expected his touch, much less to feel the gentleness behind it.

Another wave burst over the ship. Seawater dripped beneath the door seals into the corridor. He pulled away, then withdrew his gloves from beneath his slicker. He was not looking at her, and his unexpected vulnerability struck her.

"If you need anything, ask Harry. He will be down periodically to check on you throughout the night."

He shoved a shoulder against the door. It slammed shut behind him against an icy wind and a storm still lingering inside her that should have died long ago.

Chapter 3

D rawing in a deep breath, Christel set aside the remains of the blue-and-white striped feather ticking from Lord Carrick's bed and finished gathering up the last of the blankets in the master cabin. She had aired them and only needed to fold them. This she would do in the smaller cabin away from Mrs. Gables's stern eye.

Since Christel was the only other woman on board, she was duty bound out of common charity to assist Mrs. Gables, who continued to suffer bouts of seasickness. Christel hoped that by exchanging cabins, the light would help Anna's nurse recover. When Christel had returned to make up the bed earlier, Mrs. Gables had been sitting in a plush chair in Lord Carrick's cabin, her strength improved, if her curiosity about Christel and want of conversation had been any proof.

Christel welcomed the conversation if only because it gave her a chance to be with Anna. Mrs. Gables was not a completely unpleasant woman, and not without an interesting story. She had traveled extensively in her youth, and she'd borne and lost several children while serving with her husband in India. But, like most British, she had an acute dislike for the Irish, which meant she did not get along with

Lord Carrick's steward, for no apparent reason other than the fact that his cooking was wretched. Typically English to her core, much like one of those vexing types for whom Christel used to sew.

She was a woman who belonged to a circle of close-minded individuals set in their ways, perfectly oblivious to new situations or experiences, not because they did not know how to adapt but because they chose not to. Such persons could travel the world and be tolerant of nothing else outside their perfectly formed sphere.

Christel's dog fell outside that sphere. It was hairy and shed, lacked pedigree, tore up expensive feather ticks and enjoyed licking Anna's face. The dog had to be banished to the hold.

Even as Christel had listened to a steady barrage of gentle commands directed at Lord Carrick's daughter. *Don't gobble your food, Lady Anna. Hands in your lap when you sit at the table. Back straight. Sit pretty, dear.*

Anna seemed to take the instruction in stride. When not listening to her nurse, she kept herself occupied, diligently learning from Christel how to make a bonnet for her doll. She seemed like a practical girl, interested in the world about her, but content to remain on its fringes. In many ways, she reminded Christel of herself at that age. Perhaps that was why she felt drawn to the child.

Upon entering Mrs. Gables's former cabin, Christel did not at first note that she was not alone until she heard the creak of leather and looked over the tops of the blankets bunched in her arms.

Lord Carrick sat at the small table, his legs outstretched in front of him, a study of casual nautical sophistication. He wore a heavy dark blue seaman's sweater and woolen breeches tucked into jackboots that hugged his calves. Though he'd clubbed back his dark hair, strands had pulled loose in the wind.

She had not seen him below, and for some reason she almost tripped. "What are you doing here?" she asked, feeling ridiculous the instant the words spilled out.

He cocked his brow as if his thoughts mirrored hers. This was his ship; he could go where he chose. "Red Harry told me you had changed cabins."

She dropped the blankets on the berth and proceeded to fold them, not believing for one moment he'd come to see to her welfare. "There is no reason I should have remained in the master's chambers alone."

"You have an aversion to sleeping alone?"

She whirled to face him. But he was not even looking at her. He was looking at the comforter on the top berth.

"Tell me you are not planning to re-stuff that thing," he asked.

Her startled gaze swung to the berth where she had laid the tick, suddenly worried he might order it tossed overboard simply because it lacked perfection. She had salvaged the tick and most of the feathers. "And if I do?"

Smoothing her fingers over the fabric one last time, she carefully folded and placed it at the foot of the berth. Indeed, she had created a wedding gown less costly than this bed covering. But that wasn't why she wanted to save it.

"I would tell you 'tis not necessary, Christel."

Sitting forward with his elbows on his knees, he made no other comment, as if unwilling to argue the point, because either it was unimportant to him, or he sensed its importance to her. She was responsible for its destruction. She would see it repaired. She paid her debts. She would keep it that way.

"Do you have a place to stay once we are in Ayr?" he asked after a moment. "Have you been in contact with your grandmother?"

"You need not worry about my accommodations," she said. "I am returning to Seastone Cottage." The place where she had been born. Where she had lived for twelve years before her mother had died and Papa had sent her to stay with Grams at Rosecliffe. "I know the family my uncle hired to care for the place." Without looking at Lord Carrick, she said, "I am not returning to Virginia. My decision was made before I left Boston."

"Your uncle has been dead a year. Have you considered that you will owe taxes?"

She did not argue his point. His conclusion was true. Accepting employment with Lord Carrick had been as much a matter of economics as any other reason she had for returning to Scotland, but this too remained unsaid. Lord Carrick had wanted answers as to why she would accept a position as a governess for his daughter. He was intelligent enough to discern that her motivations were monetary without making her demean herself by spelling it out. Except now that she had met the child, even that point was no longer accurate. Anna was Saundra's daughter. Christel wanted to know her.

"I have no intention of remaining at Blackthorn Castle," he said. "Any governess I hire will have to accompany me back to London."

"I am sure you will find one in London to suit your needs, my lord. My home is Seastone Cottage."

He unfurled from the chair, his size shrinking the room by half in her mind. A wayward perception that she immediately decided was incongruous, for he was no taller or broader of shoulder than other men in her life had been.

She returned to folding blankets, listening as he walked past her to the port window, touching a hand to the washbasin as he bent at the waist and peered outside at the pewter sky. A quick glance and he continued his examination of the room, his restless pacing beginning to wear as her senses followed his movement to the cupboard. She could hear a limp in his step and caught the faint scent of liniment.

"Your hair is short," he said from behind her, giving her a start.

She shrugged a shoulder, indifferent as to whether her hair was short or long, and set the last blanket on the bed. "I sold the length to a wigmaker before leaving Boston. Better to salvage the coin than waste it on louse. Hair grows back . . ." *Unlike limbs,* she had started to say and had stopped herself, realizing at once that the thought had also been his. Just as quickly, she regretted the implication that her silence implied pity for him.

"You needn't fear speaking the truth around me, Miss Douglas. I am not made of eggshells."

"But neither are you forged from iron."

"Nor are you, Christel."

Dropping the blanket in her hands, she turned and placed her hands on her hips. "Is it to be Christel or Miss Douglas?" she queried. "Clearly, you cannot seem to decide."

"Which would you prefer?"

"That depends. Perhaps we should clarify our relationship to each of our satisfactions so that we can stop skipping about the other as if we are total strangers. For Anna's sake, we can certainly find a way to be friends. Can we not?" She smiled, aware that she was nervous, even more aware that he could sense it.

After everything that he had told her, she remained unsure of her place and of how much leeway he would give her. "Which means that I give you leave to call me Christel," she said decidedly. "I am family, after all. Indirectly, of course."

Folding his arms, he leaned a shoulder against the berth. She waited for him to invite her to call him by his Christian name. He didn't. He was still studying her, clearly unsure what to make of her.

"Though even if you gave me leave to call you Camden or St. Giles, I would not feel comfortable reciprocating," she prattled on. "To that point, I should speak my mind on another matter."

"By all means. Do. To remain silent or docile in the face of adversity only leaves the problem to confront another day."

"Well spoken," she agreed, even though she sensed amusement in his tone. "You shared a lot with me last night. Words are not adequate to state—"

"Then do not try. Some things are best left unsaid."

She nodded.

He remained silent. She drew in breath. "I also know that you have a certain noblesse oblige ingrained in you. You were born with it in your blood and you will feel obligated to protect me once we are in Ayr no matter what has happened in the past that might color your—"

"Are you *trying* to irritate me, Christel?"

"Who would dare, my lord?"

"Certainly not you."

Despite herself, she felt the corners of her mouth lift. "I only wanted to stress that I am quite capable of taking care of myself. I do not want you to think that you have to worry about me or think that you need to take care of me. When we get to Scotland, I do not expect charity from you. I do not expect, nor do I want, anything."

He returned to the porthole and stared outside, his seeming lack of attention to her allowing her to observe him unhindered.

The shadow of a beard marked the angular plains of his handsome face. He'd stepped from the persona once owned by the blue and white uniform of his naval rank into something inherently more predatory, always on guard, like a hawk that had suffered a broken wing, never to recover well enough to soar again. He wore his past like an unyielding mantle of iron. It weighed against him, and written deep into his posture was an inherent distrust of the world. Such men were dangerous and unpredictable, if only because they lived on the fringes of life and would defend their territory to the death. She thought of his daughter and wondered what it would be like to own that kind of love.

She had wanted it once. Not anymore.

Lifting her gaze, she realized too late that while she'd been assessing him, he'd also been assessing her, but far less subtly.

She looked into eyes the shade of the pewter sky churning behind him. Yet there was something else in his gaze.

Something that was not cold at all. She had thought the attraction between them gone.

She turned away from those penetrating eyes, aware of the burn in her cheeks as she resumed folding in an effort to pretend composure. She wished he would go now. She didn't understand his presence, especially after their conversation last night. He'd done his duty by her, had reassured himself that she had a place to go once in Scotland. There was nothing else to say. She had meant it when she'd said she wanted nothing from him.

"Why are you not married?" he asked.

It was an impertinent question and he clearly knew it. She presented him an offhand reply. "No man will have me, my lord. I have been quite happily on the shelf for years and intend to remain that way."

His mouth crooked slightly and his teeth shone white against the dark bristle on his face. "And what exactly is the age one is considered *on the shelf* these days?"

"When a woman learns how to use a saber as well as a man."

He looked mildly amused. "I should have guessed no mere colonial would have the bollocks to properly manage you."

"Pah! No mere Englishman had the bollocks to try, my lord. In fact, was I to pit the two factions 'twould probably end much like the war."

He surprised her by laughing. "A colonial to the core."

"I am half Scots." Her mouth curved up in a smug smile. "So are you, my lord."

Taking a step toward her, he stopped so near that she could feel his breath stir her hair. He smelled of wind and salt and an icy sea.

"Now that we have finally found common ground between us to both our satisfactions"—plucking something from her hair, he presented her with a feather—"I should return to my duties."

She took a casual step backward. "I could not agree more, my lord."

After he left, she shut the door behind him and leaned against it for solid support. She could credit that while she disliked her reaction to him, she could not deny the stir of long-suppressed awareness coming to life any more than she could deny his beauty, his height and heat that seemed to emanate from him.

She reminded herself to be more cautious. He had been Saundra's husband. Not hers. She thought she knew him. She did not.

But for now, they seemed to have struck a fragile truce.

* * *

"There she is again, my lord," Bentwell said over the lashing wind. "She's flying the revenue ensign and commission pennant."

Camden raised the brass telescope to his eye to see for himself. She was canted over steeply to starboard, every inch of canvas spread, giving him a full view of her profile against the churning sky. "The same ship just outside Dover?"

"Aye, my lord. She's been weatherin' on us. Dangerous at best in these winds. The captain is a fool to risk his ship in such a manner. But at that pace he will cross our path in the next hour."

There was only one reason a ship would weather on another, to maneuver into a superior position just before one initiated an engagement.

"Flying the signal flags of a revenue cruiser could be a ruse," Bentwell said.

"She's clench built. Typical British lines for a revenue cruiser. Probably constructed in Liverpool." Camden snapped the spyglass shut. "I would prefer she be French."

The crew of a naval revenue cruiser hunted and hanged smugglers pursuant to enforcing the navigational acts originally designed to keep the newly independent Americans out of the West Indies. Now the policy was enforced anywhere Britain considered her sacred waters. Camden was familiar with the fact that the captains of such vessels rarely asked questions before seizing a ship and pressing its crew into service. Pirates, privateers, and other ne'er-do-wells he could outrun and maneuver around to escape. The Royal Navy was another matter entirely.

His gaze swung upward. Visible just below England's bold red-and-blue standard, his own black-and-gold banner whipped above ice-encrusted rigging. The earl of Carrick was not an anonymous British entity. There wasn't a ship's captain in England who didn't know who he was. If that revenue ship had been shadowing the *Anna* since Dover, then the captain of that cruiser knew without a doubt this ship belonged to him.

"Do you think she was lying in wait for us?" Bentwell asked, clearly recognizing what Camden had already concluded.

"Only if someone knew the *Anna* was leaving London and tipped them off far enough in advance. Who delivered the message from the dowager countess Carrick three days ago?"

"The *Pelican*. The captain gave it to me himself. Said it came from your grandmother. The request seemed as dire as it did genuine."

The *Pelican* was a seal hunting vessel making its last run to market before winter. The captain had brought mail in from Blackthorn Castle while Camden had lived in London. But if for some nefarious reason that revenue cruiser had indeed been lying in wait, then someone had told them the *Anna* was carrying illegal cargo. That someone was playing dangerous games. The *Anna* was no smuggling vessel.

"Inspect the supercargo, then do a search of the hold," he told Bentwell. "If something is on board that should not be here, find it."

After Bentwell left the deck, Camden stood for some time with his wrists crossed behind him. He had already run out the weather guns to keep the ship on a more even keel, giving her a better grip on the water. Yet even he had his limits. He might know these waters, but in this weather, only a fool would test the limits of a ship when the wind could snap a mast and leave a ship floundering in dangerous seas.

"Helmsman, edge down to starboard. Keep her as near to the wind as she'll lie," he shouted, keeping his eyes on the distant ship.

It could be nothing, he thought, taking the most charitable view of a potentially unpleasant situation.

A view that was premature as he heard the lookout call, "She be signaling us to come about, my lord."

Chapter 4

The schooner flew the white ensign of the Royal Navy. It was all business as Camden waited on deck, watching the approaching jolly boat battle the swells. He raised his perspective glass to his eye.

A single officer stood at the bow of the small boat. A heavy military frock coat warded off the chill and whipped in the wind, revealing the crisp navy blue and gold braided jacket beneath. Two lobster-backs sat behind him. "Not exactly an armed boarding party," Bentwell murmured. "Are you going to let them board?"

"What do you think would happen if I did not?" Camden turned his attention to his crew. "Look lively there!" he shouted, sending them into action, up and down the deck and masts.

A lad lowered the rope ladder to prepare for boarding as the boat closed in against the hull of the ship. The officer swung himself up the ladder and clamored briskly aboard.

He was a tall man, in his thirties, square jawed and clean shaven in the way of a lieutenant who ran a strict ship. His cheeks were ruddy pink from the cold. Seeing Camden, he removed his bicorn and tucked it beneath his arm, revealing a helmet of burnished gold hair. It was unusual that a British naval officer would show that manner of respect to one suspected of smuggling, even more unusual that he would come aboard without escort.

Camden let his gaze slide over the blond lieutenant. "To what do I owe this signal honor, Lieutenant?" he asked, unimpressed and investing an annoyed air in his tone. All the while, his attention remained focused on the cannonades aimed at his ship.

"I am Lieutenant Ross of HMS *Glory Rose,* my lord. I was once the custom's agent assigned to the Tidewater region of Virginia. We have not had the pleasure of meeting personally. But I know who you are."

Camden heard a hint of admiration. "You were an excise officer in the colonies, and now a sailor?"

"I am from a family of seafarers," the lieutenant answered. "After Virginia, I returned to take a position away from the war and still serve England. You see . . . I married a colonial."

"I am sure you did not come aboard to share your personal history with me, Lieutenant." Camden tightened his mouth, though amusement laced his words. "You will not find me inviting you to tea. The seas are rough and I would like to be about my business."

Lieutenant Ross straightened his shoulders as if reprimanded. "The British navy has reason to suspect this ship of smuggling, my lord, a hanging offense—"

"So is stealing food in most parts of the world."

"Would you object if my men searched your cargo hold?"

"Would it make a difference if I did? Though if you believed I was smuggling, you would not be *asking* to view the cargo. My ship would be swarming with your men. As you can tell, this ship is riding high in the water. With the exception of a mangy dog and some livestock, the cargo bay is empty."

Lieutenant Ross withdrew a missive from inside his coat. "I was already on my way to London to find you when I received orders to intercept your ship. Someone informed upon you, my lord, and gave us information where you would be."

Aye, he had suspected as much.

Camden read the missive, signed by a former commanding officer in Bournemouth. "This communiqué gives you leeway to make your own decision about a search."

Lieutenant Ross took a step toward the railing, pulling Camden from earshot of his crew. "Aye, my lord. I wanted to discern for myself whether you would consent to be boarded. We did not see you flagrantly tossing your cargo overboard, so that either means you are not guilty of possessing contraband or you are too arrogant to think I would not find anything hidden on this ship. I do not see that you are arrogant, my lord."

Camden returned the missive to the lieutenant. "You were on your way to find me in London? Why?"

Ross straightened, his deep sense of duty evident in his posture, and Camden remembered a time when he had been such a man. But there was also something else in the man's eyes as well. "I am looking for a woman," he said. "Are you carrying passengers?"

Camden hesitated. "Do you want to explain to me what this is about?"

"Mrs. Claremont arrived from Spain some days ago. I was hoping she would have come to you. London is not kind to a woman on the streets—"

"Mrs. Claremont?"

"Christel Douglas Claremont," he said. "Your wife's cousin. She is my sister-in-law." The lieutenant turned. "Finding her means a great deal to my wife and her family. Enough for me to risk a career-ending formal reprimand from my superiors should anyone ever learn I stepped out of the realm of my job for personal reasons."

Camden faced the rail. "I was not aware that Miss Douglas was married."

"Daniel Claremont was . . . killed two years ago during the siege in Yorktown. She returned to Williamsburg shortly after that, where she managed a small dress shop, but she always kept in touch with my wife's family. Five months ago, she sold her shop and vanished.

"My brother-in-law, a former British naval commander, is an American frigate captain. He learned that the ship on which Christel left Boston was diverted for nearly three weeks to Lisbon for repairs after a storm damaged her severely. I missed her in Spain by days and was on my way to London when I received the missive that you were there. I was hoping she had gone to you. She spoke of your wife often, my lord."

Agitation stirred him. And something else. "If I see her, I will tell her you are looking for her, Lieutenant."

But Lieutenant Ross did not move away. Looking off across the choppy sea, he pressed his lips in a straight line as if he debated his next words. "You do not understand, my lord. Two years ago, during the Yorktown siege, seven British soldiers ransacked my wife's family home. Daniel was infirmed with a fever. Elizabeth—who was pregnant with my son at the time—as well as her mother, younger brother and sister, and five servants, were also in residence. The soldiers were hunting spies.

"Even sick as he was, Daniel fought the men. He killed four before they hanged him from the banister in his own house. They set the house ablaze. Christel defended the family against the attackers. Then got everyone to safety, hiding them in a root cellar behind the barn and keeping them alive for a week until my brother-in-law found them."

Camden felt his eyelids narrow. "What happened to the men?"

"Five months ago, the last man responsible for that murder was found dead outside Richmond. He had been killed in the same way as the previous two, a sword thrust through the heart. All were rumored to have been hunted down by a notorious Sons of Liberty leader called Merlin."

"You seem to doubt Merlin was responsible."

"Daniel Claremont *was* Merlin, my lord."

The implication sent a chill down Camden's spine. Surely, the lieutenant couldn't mean to be telling him that Christel was in some way connected . . . and yet . . .

"Let there be no mistake, my lord. Whoever it was who went after those men did the world a service. The three barbarians who got out of the Claremont farmhouse alive were not soldiers but criminals, in my opinion, though some would see it differently."

"If I should see Mrs. Claremont, is there a message you would have me give her, Lieutenant?"

Lieutenant Ross drew in his breath, and Camden knew the young officer would not search his ship, would not force him to betray Christel's presence even if he believed her to be on board. "Tell her that my wife and I now live in Bournemouth. Tell her she is not alone and we just want to know she is safe. We may not be blood kin, but she is one of our own. Family takes care of family."

With his bicorn tucked beneath his arm, Lieutenant Ross started to leave, but he stopped and looked out across the faces of Camden's crew. He then brought his attention back to the captain of the *Anna*. "In case you have not already deduced, my lord, someone wanted this ship intercepted. Perhaps even impounded. I would be looking to someone close to you and ask yourself who wants you destroyed."

Camden smiled mockingly. "I have considered that possibility, Lieutenant."

"I will bid you good afternoon, then, my lord."

Camden stood at the rail watching the lieutenant put off in the jolly boat. The sea swells were large, and returning to the cruiser would be rough going. But as Camden's attention absently wandered to the turbulent skies, he left it to the lieutenant's crew to watch out for their own men. He finally looked away, filled with a sense of foreboding.

Or perhaps what he felt was anger. *Why had Christel*

kept her marriage from him? Or the tragedy that had be-fallen her?

Could she have committed acts of execution in the guise of a once infamous highwayman?

"And what is the age one is considered on the shelf? Exactly," he had asked her earlier on the topic of marriage.

"When she learns how to use a saber as well as a man."

Slowly, becoming aware that the wind was shifting a point or two from the west to a northerly tack, he contemplated it with strong disfavor and ordered all sails trimmed, including the topmasts, which had been housed during the earlier heavier gale winds. Behind him, the ship's capstan clicked in a steady familiar rhythm as the boatswain was still shouting to raise anchor.

From his place near the rail, he caught sight of Bentwell talking to another man, who seemed to have just come from the hold and was gesturing with his arms like a broken signal line flapping in the wind. Bentwell's expression forewarned Camden that something had been found in the hold.

"Below the floor, my lord, between bulkheads," Bentwell informed him a moment later. Pulling his woolen coat collar around his neck, he opened the door leading into the hold and crews quarters. "A chest of rifles, cartouche boxes and brandy. Bigelow also informed me that the *Anna's* super-cargo is not aboard."

A supercargo was a merchant ship officer in charge of freight and the business dealings of the ship. In the navy, a yeoman held such a position.

"We are doing a run of the crew now to see if any others are missing." Bentwell lowered his voice. "But I will tell you, sir, nothing got on this ship while we have been in London. Whatever is here was put here before leaving Scotland."

"You are positive."

"I would wager my life on it, my lord."

Forcing himself into an attitude of composure, Camden nodded, aware that the only other person who had ever sailed this ship was also the bane of his life. With his left hand, he tapped his thigh impatiently. "Thank you, that will be all. There is nothing to be done for it now."

He would deal with his brother when he reached Scotland.

"One must never forget we are a civilized people no matter our circumstances," Mrs. Gables declared the next morning. "There is no substitute for a decent cup of hot English tea."

The pronouncement pulled Christel from her dire thoughts as she stood in front of the stern gallery window looking at the distant slip of land on the horizon. She didn't point out that the tea was actually from China. Unfolding her arms, she turned into the cabin.

Mrs. Gables sat at the table near the stove, warming herself, her fingers curled around a hot cup of tea. Along with breakfast, Red Harry had also proudly presented to them the rosebud painted teacups and matching pot on a tray earlier, just after the *Anna* had officially sailed into the Irish Sea.

"I do not know what could have got into his lordship. 'Tis not seemly for a young lady to be exposed to questionable elements aboard this ship."

"Perhaps he does not wish to tax you further with Lady Anna's care," Christel said.

But Christel had not voiced her real concern, that it was she Lord Carrick did not want around his daughter.

She had not wanted to consider that possibility, but the attempt to steer her thoughts from the idea failed. Yesterday, she had been concerned, nay scared witless, when the naval cruiser had signaled the *Anna* to stop and be boarded. But the ship had gone away.

That morning Red Harry had told her the *Anna* was still on course. Then he had told her Lady Anna's father wanted the child dressed warmly and that Lord Carrick would be taking her topside today.

The only thing that wasn't in order was her perception of the truce she thought she and Lord Carrick had struck. Had she expected too much to think that he would have said a few words to her this morning at least? That he might have explained why the *Anna* had been stopped? Or was she looking for shadows where they did not exist?

She finished straightening the cabin, carefully folding the blankets. "Would you care for more tea, Mrs. Gables?"

"You are a dear, Miss Douglas." Setting down the cup, Mrs. Gables pulled the blanket over her shoulders and watched Christel pour the tea. "Will you join me? One should never suffer cold tasteless porridge alone, if at all. I cannot stomach it myself."

Christel adjusted a blanket over the older woman's lap and put more coal into the stove. "You really should eat. At the very least if you intend to get sick again you will find yourself better served to have something cold and tasteless to be sick with."

Mrs. Gables reluctantly accepted the spoon Christel offered from the tray. "Pragmatic, are we?"

Christel set the orange marmalade beside the bowl, especially since she had gone to a great deal of trouble to find it. "I try to be," she said. "I ate earlier. Even coming from a family of seafarers, I am not immune to the effects of the sea. I know what tends to work."

"No one will ever accuse me of being a dainty eater."

But after a bite, Mrs. Gables's attention slipped to the window. She set down the spoon. "His lordship usually does not take Lady Anna on deck," she said. "'Tis not my place to question him, but her mother was such a delicate sort. What if Lady Anna should come down with a fever?"

"I am sure Lord Carrick has her safely tucked in the pilot house," Christel replied as she put away the sweater in the cupboard.

"Of course he would," Mrs. Gables agreed. Christel turned her head and found that Mrs. Gables was watching her. "You give my heart a jolt every time I look at you," she said. "You resemble her, but only a fool could ever mistake you."

Mrs. Gables's gown of black bombazine trimmed in white lace did little to distract from her stern visage, but on the rare occasion she actually smiled, her features softened to a motherly countenance. "Oh, my," she said. "There I go doing the same thing I detested others doing to me. I once had a younger sister that people always mistook for my twin. On closer inspection, most found *her* to be the one more beautiful. An annoying custom to have one's physical attributes compared to another and then to be the one found lacking."

"What happened between you and your sister?"

Mrs. Gables laughed. "I met my husband. *He* could tell us apart. To my sister's ever-loving chagrin, he fell in love with me. Of course, I had pursued him relentlessly. I knew his character. We were very much alike, you see. He would never have been happy with my sister. We were wed for twenty years." She smoothed her hands over her lap. "He died of the cholera while we were posted in India."

Christel lowered her gaze. "My condolences."

"That was ten years ago," Mrs. Gables said.

"Have you been in his lordship's employ long?"

"Eight years," Mrs. Gables said. "Lord Carrick's ship had been the one tasked with bringing back many of the wives and children from my husband's company after the cholera outbreak. One hot and humid night I found his lordship on deck pacing while we awaited the wind to freshen the sails. I guessed that he must have a young one on the way, as he was clearly most anxious to return to England. I had never seen a more restless papa-to-be than that one. He had seen me caring for the younger children on board the ship, some of whom were quite ill. He knew I had been hired as a nursemaid to the earl of Eastland's brood. He made an offer to me, I could not help but to accept, and he brought me up from London. We arrived some weeks after Lady Anna had been born."

Her expression fell subtly, and she turned her attention

to the teacup. "I am not a servant, so I am not privy to the gossip below stairs. But her ladyship was also most beloved to me. She was the truest of ladies . . . kind to everyone. I think I am correct in believing you are much like her, despite your desire to prove differently."

"Nay." Christel shook her head. "I am not like her. Much to Grams's disappointment." Christel started to smile, but the memory of Lord Carrick's conversation with her the other night sobered her. "I did not see my cousin in the nine years I was away. I wish I had returned sooner. She was like a sister more so than mine ever could be."

She had not meant to say the words, but there they were, out for a stranger to dissect. But as Mrs. Gables continued sipping her tea, her boot button eyes revealing no more than a gentle patience to listen, this woman, whom Christel had judged disparagingly for complaining about her dog, suddenly seemed understanding and selfless.

Indeed, with whom could she talk? She had no close friends to share her thoughts with. She belonged to no place and to no one anymore. Mrs. Gable's simple kindness enveloped her.

"Will you be staying in Scotland long?" Mrs. Gables asked.

"My home is there. Seastone Cottage is the most beautiful place in the summer," Christel said.

"Then Rosecliffe is not your home?"

"Rosecliffe is my grandmother's home. You have probably met Lady Harriet on occasion. I fear she and I did not leave on the best of terms."

"I would not presume to know Lady Harriet, but having another granddaughter home can only ease an old lady's heart. She has rarely set foot in Blackthorn Castle or seen Lady Anna in a year."

"Surely Lord Carrick would not keep her away."

Mrs. Gables shifted in the chair. "The fault does not lie with his lordship, no matter what you may hear, Miss Douglas."

Her answer, as cryptic as it was vague, was unmistakably colored by her loyalty toward Lord Carrick.

Loyalty that appeared to go beyond monetary dependence on him.

Christel was as bewildered by the woman's devotion and affection toward Lord Carrick as she had been by Red Harry's. She did not understand what could possibly inspire it, but she had seen it before when she had worked in the field hospital outside Yorktown and her uncle had brought in survivors from his ship. There had not been one single soul who had not inquired to the welfare of their captain.

The older woman leaned her head back against the chair and closed her eyes. "I should be awake when his lordship returns with Lady Anna, but I fear I am suddenly quite sleepy."

Christel rose and prepared the bunk for Mrs. Gables to rest. "I will look to Lady Anna. You need not worry."

Christel had no opportunity of speaking to Lord Carrick as it was Red Harry who brought Anna back to the cabin.

"The wind's picked up," he said. "Himself says to stay below."

"Mister . . . er . . . Red Harry," she called after him, pulling the cabin door shut behind her as she stepped into the companionway for a private word. "I know 'tis none of my concern, but I imagine it never bodes well when a revenue cruiser stops any vessel."

"Normally I would say you'd be right. But the cap'n of the *Glory Rose* knew his lordship—"

"The *Glory Rose*?"

"Ye are familiar with the ship, lass?"

"I am a colonial. I am familiar with revenue ships," said Christel. "But surely since Lord Carrick is a former Royal Naval captain—"

"A bloke's naval pedigree only means he can sail a ship, lass."

He seemed preoccupied with the ship's chores and was soon on his way.

The *Glory Rose*!

She knew the captain of that ship. One of her closest friends had married him three years ago. Her friend was a patriot and he a staunch Tory, and they had somehow found peace in a world that had seemed to have briefly lost itself. Peace that had forever eluded her.

All afternoon she paced her cabin, thinking about *him*. Yet as much as she wanted to avoid him, she had been bothered by the thought that it was the *Glory Rose* that had intercepted the *Anna*.

Later, Christel had been arranging the sewing box when she heard Lord Carrick's voice topside. She'd procrastinated long enough and now didn't have much time left before sunset swallowed the sea.

Restlessly, she returned to Lord Carrick's quarters for a cloak. Finding one in the armoire, she threw it around her shoulders. It was made of heavy wool and brushed the floor, but she welcomed the warmth even as she caught the faint scent of French perfume on the dark wool. She pressed her nose into the cloth. This cloak was the one he had been wearing when he had arrived on board. Not that it should matter to her with whom or where he spent his time. She hated that it did matter.

Pulling up the hood, she made her way out of the cabin, crisscrossing her way with the ship's movements in the corridor. She shoved her shoulder against the stout wooden door that opened onto the deck and stumbled over the coaming. The ship rose and dropped into a trough of sea, sending a rainbow of salt spray over the deck. The wind filled the sails and tore at her skirts and heavy cloak.

Clutching her hood with one hand, she stole a glance at the weathervane. Long spears of ice clung to the rigging and glittered amber in the sunset. With all sails braced, the *Anna* lay over steeply, plunging through the sea, sending spray aft in the sheets and making the weather rigging sing. The ship was running close-hauled before the wind, and the sight could not have been more beautiful.

"Our captain is very good at what he does." Mr. Bentwell stood near the capstan, holding a brass telescope. "That is why we are flying like a pretty bird over the waves."

" 'Tis breathtaking, Mr. Bentwell." Grasping her hood with one hand, she caught her balance on the door and looked around the deck, hoping to see said captain of the ship.

"If you have come topside to see his lordship"—
Captain Bentwell pointed behind him—"he is there in the wheelhouse."

She couldn't see him until she walked around the capstan. Her heart bumped against her ribs. For the briefest of seconds after she found him talking to the helmsman, she thought about abandoning her want to seek him out, but she hastily refrained from leaving. He stood over a chart with a sextant in his hand. When he saw her, he stopped talking, his hesitation barely discernable, yet blatant enough that the helmsman turned his head. Lord Carrick said a quick word to the man and he returned to the wheel.

The wheelhouse was sheltered from the brisk wind. He looked busy and, with his dark sweater and slicker, as unapproachable as the night.

"I hope you do not mind, but I borrowed your cloak."

He returned his attention to the sextant and the chart. "You could have asked Red Harry for something more suitable in this weather."

"Woolen breeches and underclothes would be the most suitable. I dare say women are at a disadvantage in the cold weather."

Her attempt at frivolity only made her reasons for being on deck more blatant in her mind. She pretended interest outside. "I have enjoyed the time I have spent with Anna."

"Is that why you came topside?" he asked while drawing a line from one place on the chart to another. "You could have saved yourself from freezing and told me tonight."

She gazed reproachfully at him, hardly realizing she was

staring until he lifted his head and their eyes met. Just that fast the rest of the world vanished and it was only them in the wheelhouse alone in the middle of the sea. Something hot and fierce settled in her chest. He gave instructions to the helmsman, then put away the sextant and took her arm, guiding her to the door. Holding the brass telescope in one hand, he waited like a proper gentleman for her to pass from the wheelhouse first.

The wind caught her hood and pulled it from her hair. "Have I done something wrong?" she asked after he came to a stop at the rail.

"You tell me. Have you?" he said, raising the telescope to his eye.

He could have been talking about the weather for all the inflection in his tone. She stared at his profile, lost momentarily between her heart and dread. "'Tis only that you seem . . . distant. I thought we had come to an understanding."

"Then why the subterfuge . . . Mrs. Claremont?"

Her hand came to rest on the rail, as if that would keep her standing. She was not interested in either defending herself or in lying, so she elected to say nothing of the turmoil roiling within. Yet another part of her was relieved that he knew.

"No denials?" His sober voice inserted itself in her thoughts, and she saw that he was not looking at her but north. "Are you not curious who was on that cruiser?"

"I know who captains the *Glory Rose* . . ." She suddenly lost the ability to think.

"Your husband's family is concerned about you. Why did you not tell me you were married, Christel?"

Anger flashed through her. She was weary of people interfering with her life, following her about as if she'd been a dog on a leash, trying to shelter or coddle her. "My reasons are none of your concern."

"I beg to differ. You sailed across the Atlantic under the pretense of accepting a position in my employment—"

"'Twas not pretense—"

"*Not* just any position but that of governess to my child. Your subterfuge is relevant to me and speaks to your integrity."

"My integrity?" To Christel, her honor and integrity were sacrosanct. "You know nothing about my life. Or me. Nothing."

"You are correct about that, Christel. And what I used to know had borne out to be a lie."

She stepped past him, but his hand snapped her around. Her hood fell down upon her shoulders. "Tell me who you are," he rasped. "I do not even know why you left Scotland, Christel."

The wind whipped her cloak around his legs. By nature, she refused yielding to weakness on any terms. It smacked of defeat and cowardice and all manner of vile emotions she'd buried for years.

She had no idea how the truth would serve her. Her reasons for leaving Scotland were as irrelevant to her current status as was the very question itself and were none of his concern. Her life was her own, bought and paid for with her soul. She had lost everyone she had ever loved, so she had ceased loving anyone. No softness was left inside her, no room for doubt. Yet she was terrified of cracking beneath the weight of his iron gaze, which bored into hers with a gentleness she did not expect.

"Please loose me now."

His iron-muscled grip on her wrist loosened but he did not release his hold, and she made no move to snatch back her arm. "Whether you like it or nay, you are my responsibility," he quietly said.

"I am no one's responsibility. I can take care of myself."

"Can you?" There was the hint of steel in his voice. He released her arm. "Like you took care of those who killed your husband?"

She snapped her gaze to his. "I am no murderer," she said softly, but fiercely.

But this time, the weight of his gaze was too much for her to hold. She looked past him and found the horizon her focus. "They died in a fair duel," she managed blandly. "Unlike the fight they gave Daniel."

"Fair? As in you allowed them the chance to kill you—?"

"Dueling is not illegal. They cannot hang you."

"What should I say to that, Christel?"

"Say that you will never question my integrity or honor again. Say anything except what is clearly in your thoughts."

She stepped backward to negotiate her path around him. But he moved nearer to her, blocking her withdrawal, touching her slightly, as if she was made from the most fragile glass. She reached for the railing and found his hand on her waist balancing her instead.

Their gazes tangled, locked and turned hot. Her lungs felt restrained by her bodice. She forgot where they were, forgot that they were in plain sight of his crew. Neither of them moved as his gaze lowered to her mouth and the whole world faded to the storm in his eyes and to the one possibility that he would kiss her, the way he had so many years ago when he had not known who she was.

Swallowing was hard. The frigid cold had finally found its way beneath her cloak and settled against her flesh. "If Lieutenant Ross told you to whom I was wed, you understand why I was reluctant to share. There are probably some in England who would gladly make a criminal of his wife. As the Etherton family's bastard daughter, I already have a controversial pedigree without adding this notch." Her chin lifted. "Not that I am ashamed."

His eyes narrowed slightly, but he looked out across the water before she could read his thoughts. "How long were you married?"

She swallowed with sudden difficulty. "Daniel and I were t-together for less than a year," she said, turning her head. "He was a g-good and d-decent man. He didn't deserve what happened to him. I had a fever a week prior . . . typhoid and dysentery ran rampant in the hospitals and among the troops. I became ill and he had stayed with me."

"That is why I never saw you at the hospital in Yorktown those last few weeks."

She nodded. "Daniel came home because of m-me and

became ill himself. If he had not been so weak . . . "

His expression told her nothing, while hers must have surely revealed everything. He pulled the hood back over her head. "Look at you. You should not be on this deck as ill-dressed as you are."

The wind pushed strands of her hair into her face. She didn't bother to repair them as she looked down to adjust the cloak around her and once again inhaled the faint scent of expensive French perfume.

"I am f-fine. I want to be here when we see the cliffs."

"Then turn around," he said, handing her the telescope.

She did as he told her, her gaze fervently glimpsing the magnificent windswept cliffs in the far distance. She raised the gold telescope to her eye and looked at a world encapsulated in ice, as if frozen in time, and naked fields made barren by winter's frigid kiss. The shoreline was as familiar as the back of her hand. She had forgotten nothing.

"We will be anchoring outside Blackthorn Cove near nightfall. At this pace, we should be on shore by nightfall."

She watched as he was called back to the wheelhouse.

Her pulse racing, she swung back around and raised the perspective glass back to her eye. She smiled pure joy.

Home.

For the first time since she'd left Virginia, she finally believed this was real. She could not see Seastone Cottage yet, but knowing it was out there, so close, quickened the blood in her veins and made her nearly dizzy with happiness.

Wrapping a palm around the gold coin warm against her breast, Christel shut her eyes.

It no longer mattered that she had traveled five thousand miles only to end up pleading for Lord Carrick's charity. Or that she was not the girl he remembered her to be.

When Christel had first received the coin a year and a half ago, Saundra's letter had merely read, *"Come home now. Please. I am in desperate need of a friend. S."* It was all the letter had said. The coin had been inside to pay her expenses home. But she had not gone back to Scotland, and then it had been too late. She had worn the coin around her neck, always hidden, but knowing it was there against her heart. Her link to home.

Daniel was gone. Her uncle was now dead. His death last year had severed her last reason to remain. She'd forced her grief into expectation—grief that there was no family left alive in Virginia to mourn her, expectation that she was returning to the place of her birth with a clean slate to begin her life afresh.

Someone had wanted her home in Scotland. Enough to send Saundra's letter three months after her death.

Wanted her despite what had happened in the past, despite who her mother had been, despite the pain Christel had caused her family.

If she believed in guardian angels, she would think it was Saundra watching over her, Saundra's arms she felt around her. Saundra, bringing her home for a reason.

Chapter 5

As Camden stood in front of the tall frost-covered window of his private dressing room, tying his cravat, he felt that same familiar edge he'd always felt when he was home. In the far distance, he could see the *Anna*. Too large to come into the shallower waters nearer shore except during higher tides, she was still anchored outside the half-moon bay and would remain there until morning, when Bentwell would do a final assessment of the damage she had incurred during the rough weather.

He had come ashore in a longboat earlier in the evening without the pomp and circumstance that usually occasioned his arrival. He had been welcomed only by a small party of retainers who had been alerted by those in the new watchtower. He had promptly learned that his errant younger brother was visiting with friends in the country.

After first seeing to the welfare of his daughter and Mrs. Gables and arranging rooms for Christel to stay the night, he had come to his own chambers to make himself presentable to his grandmother. Now, he looked out over the distant scenic cove.

Behind him, his solicitor sat on a chair in front of the

hearth. The older man was a faithful, stalwart figure. His reflection became Camden's focus in the window. Wearing a full-skirted orange coat with matching waistcoat and breeches, he was hard to miss in a room painted green and purple.

His grandmother had always been an artist at heart, though she would never admit to something so common. Her love for all the colors of the rainbow was quite evident in this wing of the house, from the green walls to the purple upholstered chairs to the emerald velvet hangings on his bed. She had shared these rooms with his grandfather when he had been alive, an uncommon achievement for a wedded couple—to actually share in love both physical and emotional.

"How long has my brother been gone?" Camden asked his solicitor, holding his arms back as his valet slid on him an informal black coat.

"A week, my lord. He does not stay away long. A month at most."

"He left while Grandmother remained ill?"

"She forbade anyone telling him the severity of her illness. But you are here now. Already there is color back in her cheeks."

Dismissing his valet, Camden poured himself a glass of port and finished dressing at the window as the solicitor caught him up on the news and business of the day. Camden gave the requisite nod and occasional grunts, signaling that he was listening.

The tall gilded clock at the end of the corridor bonged ten

times, dutifully reminding him of the hour, just as it had for all Blackthorn's occupants the last fifty years.

That his grandmother's illness had been a ruse to force him home still niggled at the back of his thoughts. But as he sipped his port, his mind remained wholly on Christel. Their conversation earlier that day still troubled him. It was not only that she had not told him she had been married; she had also betrayed herself to him with the onerous truth about the men who had murdered her husband, thus putting the burden of deciding what to do with such knowledge on *his* shoulders.

What bothered him most was that he recognized a part of something he once was that still lived in Christel: her idealistic belief in honor, her courage and her copious conviction that a single person has the power to right the wrongs of the world.

Her bravery in the face of adversity had unexpectedly affected Camden in a way he had not felt in years. He had not believed in anything for so long, and suddenly he found himself a taunting parody of his own importance.

Uncomfortably aware of the direction of his thoughts, he tossed back the glass of port, turning away from the window as he realized the solicitor was still speaking to him about Blackthorn's finances and the difficult times that had fallen on many.

"War has left many farmers unable to sell their crops," his solicitor said, "and the soil in some fields has not produced in years. Smuggling has become more prevalent, my lord."

"What has the provost been doing about the problem?"

"The prison is overfull. Transports are high. Perhaps if the people had another way to earn a decent—"

"Do not attempt to frame this issue in a charitable or moral light," Camden said, adjusting his sleeves. "I have no sympathy for a man who thieves for profit on the backs of others who work hard for their own bread. 'Tis not food these people steal." And what was Leighton's excuse? "Get a message to my brother that I have returned."

"Aye, my lord."

"And Smythe," Camden said as the man began gathering up his papers. "You did the right thing bringing me home."

Camden strode out of his chambers into the corridor, then through the portrait gallery. Passing generations of aristocratic Carrick royalty and decorated naval mariners, he looked up at none of them.

The processional route to his grandmother's quarters took him down the marble staircase to the apartments on the second floor, the click of his heels indicative of his want to get this meeting over with. This part of the house had been built around the central turret that formed Blackthorn Castle. Persian carpets in the corridor muffled his steps. Most were well worn, some threadbare, but they had been acquired by his grandfather on his travels and his grandmother had refused to part with them, moving them instead to a lesser-used part of the house.

As he approached, the door to the dowager's bedchamber opened and the physician appeared. He shut the door and turned. He had a crop of red hair and looked to be in his twenties—too young to know anything about medicine.

Camden had thought that when the man had also tended to Saundra.

Seeing Camden, he snapped to attention and hurried to meet him. "I have just been sent to fetch ye, my lord." He cleared his throat on a cough. "Not that I would presume to *deliver* ye anywhere. What I mean—"

"The dowager is strong-willed and, as such, easily riled to temper. Consider me fetched and delivered, Doctor . . . ?"

The young physician shifted the black leather surgeon's satchel he carried in his hand. "White. Doctor Stephen White," he said, following Camden to open the door. "I joined your staff six months ago, but I have lived here my entire life. No' here, per se at Blackthorn, but at Rosecliffe. Lady Harriet was my sponsor at University in Edinburgh. I have heard that her granddaughter, that Miss Douglas has returned."

"She has."

White's face reddened as he straightened. He looked uneasily at the door. "Despite what the dowager may try to tell ye to the contrary, she has been quite ill, my lord. I believe her prognosis to be a favorable one. She will most probably outlive us all."

Camden nodded, dismissing him, frowning slightly as he watched the younger man leave the corridor.

After a moment's hesitation, he entered the room. In the spacious bedchambers, firelight danced in the hearth, banishing the chill that had followed him into the room. Propped against a pile of cream satin pillows, his grand-mother awaited him as one who held court. She wore a white mobcap over silver streaked hair, neatly combed and plaited.

At sixty-nine, she was still a handsome woman, still in possession of her steadfast faculties and the kind of self-assurance that came naturally to those born and reared in privilege. His grandmother had lived her life by the mores of social convention. Even ill, she would never have considered receiving an audience without appearing her best.

She raised a lorgnette to one eye. "Do not look at me as if I am at death's door, young man! I have had enough of that these past weeks."

He greeted the dowager countess, a smile on his lips as he kissed the hand she held regally out to him. He possessed the greatest affection for his curmudgeonly grandmother, who had raised him after his gentle mother had died six months after giving birth to Leighton. An heir and a spare. His father had been satisfied with his mother's duty to the world and had promptly returned to the sea, leaving Camden and Leighton either in his grandmother's capable hands or within the walls of the various fine schools all British lads of aristocratic descent attended.

"I am relieved that you are too ornery to allow a small bout with pneumonia to crush your spirit, Grandmamma. Good evening to you as well."

She snorted as he sat on the edge of the mattress. "Good evening, indeed! You insult me coming to this room looking like a stable lackey. Can you not even dress properly anymore?"

Wearing a white lawn shirt and black buckskin breeches beneath an informal jacket, Camden might have been dressed unfashionably, but she could not accuse him of having forsaken a bath and a shave before requesting an audience with her. "I am not completely remiss." He opened his arms for her observation. "I bathed in your favorite soap. I smell like a spring garden. Just for you."

Her blue-veined hands shook slightly as she patted Camden on the forearm. "That is something, at least. I could use a dose of spring. Did you bring back my great-granddaughter?"

"She is in the nursery with Mrs. Gables. You can see her tomorrow after breakfast."

"I wish to see her now. I have waited too long. I could be dead tomorrow and you will have my disappointment on your conscience."

He held back a grin. "Nevertheless, you will see her tomorrow. She has had an exhausting week and needs her rest as much as you do."

"Pah! You have been listening to that young whippersnapper physician Lady Harriet had the audacity to hoist upon me."

"No doubt you have been belligerent and quarrelsome, with little regard for what advice has been offered you to aid in your recovery. I have been warned not to tax you."

"To be honest, Camden, I did not think you would come."

"To be honest, it had crossed my mind that this entire ordeal was a manipulative ruse to get me here."

She sniffed. "Indeed. If I had known a bout of pneumonia had the power to bring you back, I would have taken to my bed sooner. You have injured me greatly with your suspicions. Why would you think I would lie to you? Such nonsense."

"Because I brought along a visitor who arrived shortly before I left the London docks. She carried with her a letter of employment written by Saundra after she died. Or at the very least 'twas posted after her death. It bore the Carrick seal."

"I sent no letter to anyone. Who am I supposed to have hired and for what?"

"Christel Douglas returned to accept a position in this household as governess to Anna."

His grandmother's hand fluttered over her heart in what appeared to be a real expression of horror. "Oh, my. She has returned? And Harriet does not know, or she would have told me. Someone should prepare her for the shock."

Suddenly doubting the truth of his assertions, Camden stared without expression into eyes the same color as his own. He disliked uncertainty, especially since he had been so sure his grandmother's machinations had brought back Harriet's granddaughter. After all, his grandmother and Lady Harriet were closer than most sisters with a history between the two that predated even his father's birth.

"Maybe Lady Harriet needed to see her and you necessitated the events along," he suggested.

"Why would you suspect me of such a thing?" She settled back in the pillows. "That girl's mother ruined Harriet's family."

Camden silently swore. "Christel is hardly responsible for the sins of her parents." *Any more than Anna is responsible for the sins of hers.*

His grandmother observed him shrewdly. "Christel is it now? She has just returned, and you are already on a first-name basis. *And* you are *defending* her? Bother. I have not lived my life under a rock, Camden. That girl ruined herself gallivanting about the countryside barefoot and unchaperoned. Anyone who saw Miss Douglas could see that her face lit up whenever you were near. You were the reason Lady Etherton made Harriet send her away."

Sometimes his grandmother would say something that made a reply impossible. He was not pleased. "What are you talking about?"

His grandmother shut her eyes as if she suffered a headache. "Saundra's mother found out that Miss Douglas attended the masquerade. I do not know how. The particulars hardly matter. The family had already endured enough scandal with Harriet's eldest son, the girl's father. Lady Etherton wanted nothing to come between you and Saundra. But I could have told her you were head over heels for Saundra and that you would not have signed the contracts had you not wanted the marriage."

Camden rose and walked to the window. She held out her hand to him. "Camden, I want this to be your home again. The land needs tending. Leighton does his best by me and I could not do without him, but Blackthorn Castle belongs to you. If it means you will stay, I will give my blessing for you to wed your mistress for all I care."

The idea that the family's stoic matriarch would accept his mistress as a properly bred Carrick wife was laughable. "You are baiting me, Grandmamma," he said softly, catching sight of movement in the shadows on the terrace below, and something inside him loosened. "Do not. I will wed again. But on my own terms and without interference from you this time."

When Camden had left Blackthorn Castle a year ago, he had thought he'd never return. Now, while a part of him considered the need to deal with his brother, to see to the estate business and welfare of its inhabitants, another bit of unfinished business suddenly appeared in the courtyard. Her profile easily recognizable against the backdrop of a full moon, Christel turned away from the stone wall overlooking the cove and worked her way back to the terrace. Rather furiously, if the stiffness of her gait was any proof to her mood.

Watching her walk up the yard, he smiled to himself. He had set men at all points of the estate to see that she did not disappear in the night—as she had done all those years ago when all that he had found of her after the masquerade had been a golden slipper left behind on the beach. He had looked a week for her before the trail had taken him to Rose-cliffe and to Saundra.

He could still remember the first time he had met Saundra. She had been wearing a bright yellow muslin sprigged with cherries and a bonnet tied with red ribbons in a pretty bow at her chin, and looking lovely and serene as a portrait, sitting in a spot of dappled sunshine.

She had been nineteen, beautiful and gay, and so sure of her ability to charm that he had suspected at the time that it was taken for granted by her family that all men who met her fell in love with her. And he had.

And Christel Douglas had watched him court Saundra, never saying a single word.

Now, as the wind sweeping off the bay pulled at her cloak and tossed her hair around her face, he found she stirred his dormant senses in a way he had not expected.

He'd never thought Christel as beautiful as Saundra, yet the memory of her, like her laughter, was a portrait of color as bright as a Caribbean sunrise imprinted in his thoughts. For all her youthful annoyances, simplicity and imperfections, Christel Douglas was unforgettable, and it was as if she had just stepped through a window from his past to pick up exactly at the point where they had left off. Someone was responsible for bringing Christel home, and he wanted to know who and why.

Behind him, his grandmother heaved an audible sigh. "I have no wont to rehash the past when I want only to heal our family, Camden," he heard her say. "Blackthorn Castle belongs to you. Just tell me you will stay through Christmastide this year."

Letting the curtain drop, he turned back into the room. "I will stay into the new year, Grandmamma." He kissed her on the cheek. "And Grandmamma . . ." *if I ever learn that you lied to me about that letter, I will never forgive you.*

But he did not utter the words. If she said she did not write the letter, then he needed to believe her.

Instead of giving voice to his thoughts, he said, "I expect you will be well rested when Anna visits you tomorrow. She has missed you."

* * *

Christel was waiting forever for Lord Carrick to finally appear at the end of the corridor just off the gallery. He turned the corner and stopped. She barely noted his hesitation, if that was indeed what she glimpsed.

She pulled her cloak tight. "Why am I a prisoner?" she demanded.

His path brought her in front of him. Everything about him was sinfully dark from his neatly combed hair tied back at his nape to his clothing—everything except his eyes, which were like moonlight against a velvet sky.

"I thought you would have had better sense than to try and leave this estate at night. The landscape has changed since you were here last. The cliffs and beach are dangerous at night. Are you hungry? Come."

"Do you feed all your captives before imprisoning them?"

"Only the ones I find roaming my corridors at night."

He walked past her, leaving her no choice but to follow him down the stairs or stand there staring like a befuddled schoolgirl. "Are British nobles always so accessible to the common masses, my lord?"

He didn't answer. Nor did he betray any inkling of his mood. She followed him down another corridor into the dining room, stopping when her gaze fell on a tray laden with warm bread, cheese, and a glass of chilled milk. She could not contain a gasp of delight.

She picked up the glass as if it had been the food of the gods. "You have no idea how long since I have had a glass of chilled milk." The milk slid down her throat and left a mustache when she was finished. Peering up at him, she licked the white stuff off her mouth. "How did you know?"

"That you were hungry or that you like cold cow's milk?"

She picked up the bread and slipped it in her mouth. The slice melted on her tongue. She had been so nervous all day that she had not realized she was starved. "Both," she said over a mouthful, plucking a slice of peach from the plate and savoring it as well.

She took notice of the wavering shadows in the room. The empty chairs at attention around the long cherrywood table. Looking around at the oil paintings, the unlit crystal chandelier tinkling in the draft, she couldn't help but be impressed by the wealth displayed or how alone they were at this end of the house.

He leaned a hip against the table, watching her eat and survey her surroundings. Light from the candelabra washed over his face. "I knew that you had not eaten supper because I asked Smolich when I left Grandmother's chambers and sent him to the kitchen. As for the rest, if I remember your words correctly, you like the sunset over the sea after a storm and the way the air smells in spring. A glass of cold milk with warm bread. Roses and summertime. The smell of watercolors on canvas. And if you ever owned a horse, you would name him after the constellation Orion. You also like dressing up and attending masquerades and kissing strangers in dark, ivy-laden corners."

She swallowed the mouthful of bread. "You were not a stranger. I had been following you about like a puppy dog from the first moment I saw you riding your horse on the beach that summer. You were just too blind to notice."

The sudden mercenary flicker in his quicksilver eyes quelled her heart and sharpened her awareness of him. "Is that right?"

She picked at the bread. "Is my dog being cared for?"

"Stabled and fed."

She wrapped the warm bread in her napkin, aware of the lengthening silence. "Did you find out who sent the letter? Was it your grandmother?"

"She denied it. I am apt to believe her."

Christel paused her hands. "Why? Did she say anything else?"

He cocked a brow. "Anything else?"

"What I mean . . . did your grandmother mention Lady Harriet?"

"She thought I should warn your grandmother you were back."

Christel was not fooled. "And you are being generous to one of us, my lord. The dowager is not fond of me." She spread her hand over the napkin. "How *does* your grandmother fare? Mrs. Gables said that her ladyship was recovering from pneumonia."

"The physician thinks she will outlive us all."

Christel studied the crease around his lips. "You do not share his optimism? Are you concerned?"

The question appeared to give him pause, but she suspected not for the reasons it should. "Does no one ever ask how you feel about a matter, my lord?"

"No one but you knows me well enough to presume my feelings should be their concern."

She laughed, a full-throated sound, which she caught abruptly by sucking hard on her lower lip when she realized he seemed surprised by her reaction. Still, she could not contain her amusement at his expense. "I had forgotten how you British *toffs* cherish protocol. Stiff upper lip and all in front of the serfs." She leaned nearer. "Your upper lip was not always so stiff, my lord. I remember that it used to bend upward, ever so nicely into a smile."

Realizing at once the slip, she froze. *Good heavens! Was she flirting with the man?*

From the lazy-lidded look in his eyes, he was not entirely annoyed. He continued to behave every bit the gentleman, but there was an intensity about him now that belied his refinement and only seemed to make the candlelight more intimate.

Then the corners of his mouth curved. "You like my smile."

She glimpsed his interest, a mutual awareness that sent a rush of heat through her veins. "'Tis pleasing when anyone smiles," she said on a more sober note.

"Indeed."

She smiled benignly. "I know what you are trying to do, my lord. I am not the naïve girl I used to be. She is all grown up now."

She turned to leave. He blocked her as he pushed away from the table. Her eyes chased up to his. Her breasts brushed his arm and, without his sweater, she felt the hard muscles beneath his sleeve.

"A pity," he said. "I liked her the way she was. She was not so suspicious of the world."

"She could say the same of you."

He laughed and everything about him changed. He became familiar to her again as the sound softened the sharp edges of his voice. "I have always been suspicious of the world. 'Tis my nature to question. It was yours to see goodness in everything around you, even when it was difficult to see." Cupping her chin with his palm, he tilted her face into the light. "You may think that girl is dead, but she is not."

She jerked her face away from the gentleness of his touch. Hunger and doubt warred with resentment. He seemed to recognize something inside her that she had purposefully destroyed because it had made her weak and vulnerable.

He removed the napkin from her hand. "Have you been kissed so very little, Christel?"

"Have you not been kissed enough?"

His lips quirked upward in what might have been seen as amusement in a less guarded man. "Hmm."

Her eyes dropped from his, her uncertain gaze lowering without will to his lips. Then his finger beneath her chin tilted her face and, as if in slow motion, his lips covered hers. The breath froze her lungs.

He loved her mouth with exquisite tenderness even as he touched no other part of her. She raised her hands to ward him away, her conscience crying foul, but instead her palm pressed against the rapid beat of his heart.

She had not allowed herself to touch him since her return. She now knew why. Merely touching him felt as sensual an act as she had ever performed with a man.

The pads of his thumbs pressed gently against the corners of her lips. "Christel . . ."

He had pulled away slightly, but not so far that she couldn't taste him on her lips or breathe the air that he pulled into his lungs. Their breath mingled in a kiss that gave as much as it explored. He had made no other sound but her name. Brushing her hair from her face, he brought both hands to her cheeks.

Then he was deepening the kiss. She was cold, then hot and shaky. She was dead. Then she was alive and breathing for them both.

His heat bonded to the length of her body. Too long denied affection, she slipped her arms around his neck and leaned into his body. Her bosom crushed against his chest. And just that fast something elemental exploded between them. A moan formed in the back of her throat, a sound he swallowed. And she opened her mouth to kiss him back as deeply and as hard as she could, slightly desperate, but no longer innocent or untried, no longer caring if this might be a foolish mistake.

His tongue made a sweep of her mouth, dipping along the sensitive underside of her lips. Inside her, a new and silent storm raged past barriers and shattered memories.

Standing so close to him, she found she no longer cared

one way or the other what had gone before. What she did care about suddenly seemed infinitely more gratifying.

Too soon, his lips retreated, and his hungry gaze passed over her mouth in a way that made her feel ravished and naked. The predator inside him clearly recognized her desire for what it was, and she knew he was not opposed to taking advantage of it.

"Bloody hell." He buried his face in her hair.

She rose on the balls of her feet to kiss him again, to bring his mouth back down on hers and taste him. But he resisted. Still in a daze, she opened her eyes to find his gaze on her face.

His breath came rapidly. He braced both hands against the chair behind her. "What do you want, Christel?"

She swallowed the ball of fear that suddenly clogged her throat.

Losing Daniel had taken so much of her heart.

Now she and Lord Carrick were both free, and suddenly she did not feel the slightest guilt that she had kissed him, suddenly felt that not only would she let him touch her but she would welcome the contact. Nay, drown in it.

But what kind of person was she to want to forget Daniel? To wipe the last few years from her life as if they had never existed? "I want to go back to a simpler time."

When my emotions were pure, even if my thoughts were not.

He moved his lips to the shell of her ear. "If you are seeking oblivion, Christel, you will not find it from me. *This* will not be impersonal. It will be *my* eyes you are looking into when you come."

The crass words shocked her. And still she did not care. "Maybe 'tis you who is seeking oblivion."

He made a sound and turned his face into her hair. "Aye, there is that to consider, love."

She stayed in his arms, aware of his breath against the soft shell of her ear, the warmth from his body surrounding her.

She knew the implications of this moment if she continued. It was incredibly dishonorable of her to pretend otherwise, and she desperately tried to examine the emotions flooding her.

But in the darkness and without color, it was easy to fade into the shadows to become the chameleon, where one's differences blended into an homogenous swirling mist, where she did not stand apart. And if she clawed through the layers of shadows piled atop her, she might find the bright spirit of the girl she used to be. Here was her conduit.

Yet it was an eloquent demonstration of his knowledge of this hidden part of her that he did not seem willing to allow her entrance for the sake of her own deliverance or enlightenment.

"The hour grows late," he said quietly. "I suggest you go before I will not allow it."

Touching a hand to her swollen lips, she raised her eyes. "Why did you kiss me?"

"Why did you really leave Scotland?"

"I . . . I did not belong here."

"You are so full of blarney, Christel. What will you ever do with yourself when you can no longer play the martyr?"

Incapable of action or any thought, she stuttered, "I f-followed you around that summer like an adoring puppy," she said, pushing against the tightness in her chest. "And you never even guessed I was in love with you . . ." She no longer cared if he knew the truth of her child's heart. "You never saw me once you met her."

"You put me on a pedestal. You had no right. You set yourself up for everything that happened."

"I— I have no idea of what you are talking."

"All these years, I wondered why you did not come forward and tell me who you were. At least tell me that the woman I was about to wed was not the one who had so aptly intrigued me at the ball that night. 'Twas not a nobility-driven sacrifice. You were not afraid that if I knew, I would reject you, but that I might actually *choose* you despite your birth and background. Then where would your fairy-tale illusion of the world go? Where would your purpose be? Your sense of injustice?"

"How dare you!" she gasped.

"Tell me more about the man you wed," he said, advancing against her retreat. "Daniel Claremont. What was he like? Tell me."

"He was brave and courageous and noble. A hero to Virginia."

"No doubt another paladin in your eyes. But I will wager you did not love him any more than you believed you once loved me. 'Tis easier to place the men in your life on a tall pedestal than it is to stand beside him, stripped to your soul, annihilated by the force of his idea of you. You like wearing your inadequacies like a crown of thorns. 'Tis easier to accept that your circumstances allow you an excuse to never live up to anyone's expectations than it is to try and then fail."

Tears burned in the back of her eyes. His words rang with truth like a sword thrust through her precarious conceptions about herself. He was right. In so many ways, he understood her better than she wanted to understand herself. He understood because he had been living in hell these last two years.

"Our demons are not so different, yours and mine," he said, tilting her chin. "Only the means we chose to survive. We have fought for everyone else because 'twas easier than fighting for ourselves. But I, unlike you, who tends to blame yourself for all the ails surrounding you, I tend to blame everyone else. The least we can be with each other is honest with ourselves, Christel."

She yanked her chin from his hand. A door suddenly shut from somewhere down the corridor and she could hear the hushed voices of Smolich and another servant, the rattle of a tray in his hands. After their voices began to fade, she brushed the hair from her hot cheeks and straightened. "Goodnight, my lord." Her voice trembled.

"I will take you to Seastone Cottage in the morning," he said.

"I can find my own way home."

"Ten o'clock at the stables. I have to tend to business, but it should be sufficiently light when I return to safely negotiate the road. A lot has changed since you were here last."

"I do not intend to arrive at Seastone Cottage with you in tow, Carrick."

"Halfway then."

She drew in her breath, then nodded her head. It was a logical request. She walked to the doorway, stopped and looked over her shoulder. He was now sitting at the table, watching her, pretending nothing mattered to him, a devil atop a rock surveying his tedious realm. But something did matter. She had briefly glimpsed it in his eyes, but whether for his salvation or for hers he had gone no further than the kiss tonight. Aye, he was still her sin and her curse.

But when he had held her in his arms, she had felt a response inside her, when she'd thought she would never feel anything again.

Chapter 6

Christel awakened that morning with the remnants of a carnal dream that began to fade in the drowsy gray light of a new day. The bed covers were in disarray around her and, turning on her side, she touched her lips with her fingertips. More than Lord Carrick's words had had a profound effect on her.

There must be something terribly wrong with her, something reprehensible that she would have given herself to another man last night in an act that could be considered no less than emotional prostitution while her late husband's face was no more than a mere shadow in her memory. It could not be decent that she found her old childhood feelings bubbling to the surface when her own hands touched her body, Camden St. Giles's image in her mind.

Throwing her covers off, she crawled out of bed and welcomed the cold air against her. A pitcher of clean water and a bowl sat on the commode in the dressing room. She drew on her gown, then gathered together her few belongings, which amounted to what she currently wore, Lord Carrick's warm, costly cloak, which she considered a trade for the one he'd destroyed when she had come aboard the *Anna*, and Saundra's sewing case, which she had brought with her from the ship. Now as she looked she hesitated taking even that. But it contained thread and needles and important items that could be of use to her.

Someone rapped on the door. Christel cautiously answered the summons. A footman in black-and-gold livery, his hair beneath a powdered horsehair wig, stood in the corridor. "Her ladyship has requested your presence," he said. "I am to take you to her salon."

Unsure what would happen if she refused, Christel followed the footman past the same gallery in which she had confronted Lord Carrick last night. Her escort stopped at the end of the corridor and opened a gold-and-white-inlaid door. Half expecting to see the footman don an executioner's hood and ax, Christel paused uncertainly in the doorway. Lord Carrick's steel-eyed grandmother sat across the room awaiting her.

With a white lace mobcap perched atop her head like a crown, the dowager countess Carrick sat stiffly on a wing chair upholstered in bright yellow daffodils and violets. Beyond the tall windows, drizzle grayed the sky, but inside the room there was a feeling of perpetual sunshine and blue skies from the bright yellow walls, gilded scrollwork and the thick blue blanket spread over her lap. A chandelier above Christel's head captured light from the fireplace.

"Come inside, girl," the countess snapped imperiously, inspecting Christel through a lorgnette. "Let me see you."

As the door shut behind her, Christel hesitated. She

walked forward and stopped in front of the dowager. "Good morning, my lady."

"Good morning indeed. 'Tis dreary as watching dead leaves fall." Reaching behind her, the countess tugged on a bell cord. "Do sit down, girl. You are putting a crick in my neck."

Christel took the chair across from the dowager and lifted her gaze as a servant approached through a door in the wall, pushing a well-laden trundle cart in front of her. The countess motioned for the plates to be set out. "You have arrived in time for breakfast. Another five minutes, and I would have dined without you."

Christel sat in polite silence as the parlor maid removed silver lids from various chafing dishes containing eggs and bannocks, then carefully spooned out something from each dish onto porcelain plates. When the girl finished, she gave the dowager a brief curtsey and left the salon through the same side panel in the wall.

"You have filled out from the last time I saw you," the dowager said, having studied Christel while she had not been looking. "But the clothes will not do. You look as if you are wearing draperies from my boudoir."

As she lifted her spoon with a certain grim amusement, Christel contemplated the dowager and managed to keep her response polite. "Is there a purpose for which you have called me in front of you, my lady? For some reason this does not feel like a social invitation."

Delicately dabbing a slab of butter on her bread, the dowager sniffed. "You were always an impertinent one.

'Tis no wonder my grandson fancies an interest in you."

Without managing to choke on the bite of egg, Christel set down her fork. "I beg your pardon?"

"I saw him last night watching you out the window. Oh, I did not know what had grabbed his attention. Had to send Smolich to find out for me. Would you be a dear and pour the tea? At the very least, your presence has saved me the inconvenience of dining alone whilst my grandson gallivants off with that pirate crew he employs to sail his ship. 'Twould save us all trouble if it sank."

The dowager intently watched Christel pour the tea. Christel could be the lady of the manor when she chose, even if her hands trembled a bit with nerves. At twenty-six years of age, she should at least have been counted on to have some sense and decorum. After all, she had a grandmother who had tried diligently to train her in etiquette. She had learned at a young age how to pour and stir tea properly in one's cup, how to make a suitable impression.

She handed the cup to the dowager. "I once had a great-great-uncle the English authorities called Gray Beard," she couldn't resist saying. "He actually wore a patch over his eye because some Spaniard plucked it out with a cutlass. Mam oft spoke of him. He was hanged in Port Royal as a pirate."

Raising the cup to her lips, the dowager regarded Christel over its rim with her silver-blue eyes. Christel rarely spoke about herself. Few knew anything about her or her opinions, and she rarely found reason to share her thoughts. But she was awaiting the dowager to get to the point of her business, and she disliked being examined as if she were a butterfly with her wings pinned to a cork board.

"You have an interesting pedigree, Miss Douglas. Did he by chance spawn the colonial side of your family?"

The lightness in the dowager's voice caught Christel by surprise. She couldn't help that one corner of her mouth lifted in response. "To the best of our knowledge Uncle Gray Beard did not procreate, so the world is probably quite safe from his descendants."

"I do not care for the hoity-toity types that surround the gentry," the dowager said after a thoughtful moment. "The wealthy nabob title seekers. The ones that seem to fascinate my eldest grandson. I have at one time endured them all. But I have never experienced a colonial."

"I am half Scots."

"Hmpf. I know more about your family than you do. Knew your mother, too. Put a black mark on the entire Etherton clan and caused your father to break poor Harriet's heart. But he loved your mother as he never loved anything else," she said almost reverently before Christel's initial anger took hold. "One could almost forgive him his indiscretions for that alone. Almost."

"I do not understand. Why am I here, Lady Carrick?"

Turning her head, the dowager looked out the tall window over the pastures in the distance. Patches of dead brown grass stuck through the thin layer of slush. There was a sense of desolation in the empty fields that surrounded this estate that had little to do with winter.

"You will find much has changed since you went away.

Blackthorn Castle needs my grandson. Camden has a duty to the people of Ayrshire, his daughter, his family, and to himself to make this estate whole again."

Christel folded her hands in her lap, thinking that the dowager had another grandson, but she said nothing. Lord Carrick *did* have a duty here.

"Even if Camden feels no responsibility toward me, he owes it to the legacy left to him by his father and his father before him. He owes it to his daughter's future to remain, to marry again and to make his life here. He needs to find purpose again."

"Perhaps he has his reasons for wanting to stay away, my lady."

The dowager shot Christel a telling glance. Apparently, Christel's comment had not been what the older woman had expected. "That is the biggest mash of poppycock I ever heard. Of course he has his reasons. He is haunted by his wife's tragic death."

"I do not know what it is you think I can do, my lady."

"My grandson seems to hold a special interest in you. You resemble Saundra in some ways, but I do not think that is entirely it," she said consideringly as she examined Christel again through her lorgnette. "There is an air about you that speaks to him, I am sure of it. You might be the one who can entice him to stay."

Christel struggled not to laugh. "I am hardly the one to entice anyone, my lady. I have no wealth and no title. I do not even own what is on my back—"

"I will give you a thousand pounds sterling, Miss Douglas,

if you can help him find his passions again. Give him a reason to stay."

"Pardon?"

"I am old and weary, Miss Douglas. Is it too much that I want my eldest grandson and my only great-grandchild with me? Is it too much to want him to find his passion again?"

Christel stood. She was surprised her knees didn't fold. "You do him a grave disservice, my lady."

"But not you, I expect, Miss Douglas."

How *dare* her ladyship imply that by virtue of Christel's parentage she was so willing to be branded the village whore, as if being her mother's daughter predetermined her character. "I know *who* and *what* I am."

A sly look akin to excitement came from the dowager's eyes. "We can benefit one another. Your uncle mortgaged Seastone Cottage four years ago to pay for the muskets and powder that helped aid in your revolution. There are taxes that need to be paid. A thousand pounds is a fortune even by royal standards. 'Twill comfortably keep you for years. You would be dependent on no one for your survival, as your mother was. Is that not what you want?"

More than anything in the world, she wanted that kind of freedom. "You must truly be desperate to come to me knowing that it was my mother who ruined Lady Harriet's son . . ."

"I would remind you that you have no trouble returning to the cottage purchased by your father for your mother's . . . *loyalty* to him."

To the dowager's credit, she did not say "favors," though

that was exactly what Margaret Christine Douglas had done.

She had come to Ayr as the infamous mistress of a married man, then borne him a child. He'd given her the cottage by the sea, then given up everything, including his legitimate family, his reputation and his heritage to be with her and their infant daughter.

He had gone on to make a life for them, sailing for his brother-in-law, Christel's uncle, and they had oft gone back and forth to the colonies but always to return to Seastone Cottage. Until one day, shortly after her mother had died and Lady Harriet had entered her life, arriving at Seastone Cottage in her black lacquered coach, her father had sent Christel to live at Rosecliffe. Oh, how she had begged him not to send her away, to take her with him. But he had not.

Through the years there, she had joined Saundra and Tia in dance and music classes and worn pretty dresses, only to learn that hypocrisy and class went hand in hand.

High Society preached a good show about charity and tolerance for the unfortunate as long as those unfortunate souls did not sully the hallowed halls of the aristocracy's stately estates. Christel had never been invited or allowed to attend balls or soirées. She, who had been dearly loved by her parents, had learned about the fate of bastard children. If not for Saundra and Leighton, she might have perished from loneliness during the months her father had been gone, until one day he had not come back at all.

She knotted her hands in her skirts. "I loved her, but I am *not* my mother."

"We are all our mothers in some way, Miss Douglas."

*   *   *

Camden reached the crossroads that dissected the edge of his estate, where the trees had thinned and the wind sweeping off the white-capped sea had grown increasingly brisk. The stone remnants of an old castle made a somber landmark against a pewter sky.

He saw her in the distance, and something that had been tight in his gut unclenched. But his stomach pitched oddly, the sensation without reason or cause except that he was cold and impatient. Moreover, he had worried that he had somehow concluded wrongly that she would be walking the five miles to Seastone Cottage via the beach or that he would not find her if she chose not to be found.

He reined in at the top of a knoll. The horse pranced in a circle until Camden stayed its movement with a squeeze of his boots against its girth. A gust pulled at the heavy folds of his cloak and almost tugged off the tricorn that covered his head.

As if recognizing his master's impatience, the horse sidled in agitation as Camden took one more moment to watch her trek across the carpet of grit and sand. He loosened his grip on the reins and allowed the horse to work its way down the steep rocky path to the beach. They had left behind the higher cliffs a half mile back. Once on the sand, he nudged the gelding into a gallop. Christel turned, a hand tented over her eyes. She lowered her arm and awaited his approach.

He reined in beside her. Foamy fingers of seawater splayed the sand near her feet then disappeared.

Christel's infernal hound bounded past him, nearly unseating him from the horse. Camden tightened his grip on the reins to keep him from bolting. "Easy lad." He patted the gelding's neck with a gloved hand.

Her cheeks were red, and the damp air had plastered her hair against them.

He slid to the ground, catching himself on the cantle to keep from stumbling. The muscles in his thigh had cramped painfully. "In case the notion has skirted past that intelligent brain of yours, you could freeze out here."

"The temperature has warmed since I left Blackthorn and the walk is good for me," she said. "There is a pub not a mile from here. I used to know the owner. I thought to borrow a hor—"

"The pub burned to the ground years ago. The owner is dead. This is a desolate area frequented by scoundrels and smugglers and an occasional revenue cutter." He tipped back the tricorn with his finger. "What did you and dear Grandmamma talk about that made you bolt like you had the devil on your tail?"

" 'Twas after ten o'clock. You were late."

He had been less than fifteen minutes late arriving home. "You could have asked my driver to take you wherever you wanted to go, Christel."

"Would that have prevented your riding after me, my lord?"

"Aye," he snapped in irritation, leaning heavily on his elbow against the saddle. "I could not sleep tonight worrying if the *Haggis* or *Wulvers* had dragged you off into their beds, never to be seen again by mortal man. I promised to get you home. Remember?"

"Wild Haggis live in the Highlands. Werewolves are from the Shetlands. I think I am safe on a beach in Ayrshire."

Drawn by the urge to brush the moisture from her cloak, he started to lift his hand. The dog growled, and having momentarily forgotten the cur, Camden glared at it. "I trust that if that fanged beast were to go for my throat you would call it off?"

"Mayhap 'tis your temperament and intent with which he disagrees. Next time, try coaxing him with a bone. I have discovered he *can* be bought with food."

"You mean he can be bribed by a pretty face and food." His eyes were warm as they encompassed her.

"A matter of perspective. Sometimes kindness is the best bribe."

His gaze ranged the length of her. "I had expected to see you passed out on the beach two miles ago."

She turned and started walking. "Not all women are maidens in distress, my lord. I have two feet. I am capable of using them. I hope your business this morning was not too taxing."

"Among other things, the *Anna* has damage to the rigging. Bentwell will be taking her to Glasgow to be refitted." He grabbed her elbow and turned her to face him. "Tell me what my grandmother said to you."

Christel peered ahead of her. "We chatted about the weather, dead leaves and you. Then I left. How did you know where to find me?"

"'Tis low tide. You spent a lot of time down here when you were younger, collecting your treasures. The beach takes you home." His voice softened. "Do not allow anything she said to upset you. She is old and set in her ways about certain things. I am afraid she is very much a snob."

Christel started walking again but not so fast that he could not keep pace. He stepped over driftwood. "Anna missed saying good-bye."

She remained silent. He didn't understand why he felt as if he'd been talking over a tied tongue. "I am saying that you are family, Christel. You are welcome at Blackthorn Castle to visit her while we are in residence," he said.

He didn't think she had heard. He realized she had when she turned her head and nodded jerkily, as if she hadn't been sure what to say.

"Why do you not love it here?" she asked after a moment. "How could you ever leave?"

The whisper of the waves breaking against the beach filled the silence between them. Then he looked down to adjust his step. Water dripped from the rim of his tricorn onto his shoulders. "I found the open sea more to my liking. Out there, a man lives or dies by his own wits and actions. I felt as if I made a difference."

"A man in command of his world."

He laughed. The horse nudged his shoulder. His hands went gently over the bay's long muzzle, and he soothed the animal with a word. "I was in the service of the king. I lived my life being told what to do by some higher authority. I was adept at following orders."

Aye, he had followed orders all the way to hell.

Her eyes squinting, she cast a sidelong glance at him. "So you think I have an intelligent brain?"

"Did I accidentally say that? I take it back. If you were smart, you would be sitting in front of a fire warming your hands." After a moment, he said, "I should not have kissed you last night."

"In that we can stand in agreement."

Imprisoned by his imagination, and the manner of unfinished business between them, he found himself smiling. "However, I did not say that I did not enjoy kissing you. Or that I would not do so again. Indeed, I am lost as to what overcame me that I should have stopped."

She turned, her narrowed eyes accusing him of being blatantly ungallant. "Is that right?"

"God's truth."

"Do you want to know my theory?"

He dragged his gaze from her mouth, then met her eyes again, the heat from his skin pressing against her own. "You have me intrigued."

Folding her arms beneath her cloak, she gave him her first real smile that day. "My first thought would be that you were entirely too shocked by my response. But clearly, unless a lightning bolt struck you, I can see that not much of anything is shocking to you anymore."

"And your second thought?" he asked.

"Perhaps you knew if you continued, it would mean more than mere intimidation on your part."

His brow shot up. "Intimidation?"

"Aye. Men are notorious for coercion tactics against the weaker sex. 'Tis a way of putting us in our place."

He made a scoffing sound protesting her description of females. "And where might that place be?"

Except beneath a man, he thought with little temperance.

"Last night, you attempted to prove to yourself that you were no longer attracted to me. When that failed, you resorted to following me today to prove to yourself that *I* was still attracted to you."

This time he laughed, and he admitted she was partially right. He *was* attracted to her.

He took a step nearer. "I kissed you last night because I thought you were the most beautiful thing I had seen since moonlight."

Her mouth dropped open.

"You had that red mouth of yours so near mine, so tempting that a damned monk would sin just for a taste. So I took advantage of your lack of defenses to claim what I wanted. Admittedly, I did hesitate when you threw yourself in my arms and kissed me back, because, despite what you think, I *am* still capable of feeling shock."

"You mock me, Carrick."

"'Tis not my intention." He didn't have to lift her chin very high before their eyes met. "The truth is I *want* you. More of you. But if we ever go farther than a kiss"—his gaze traveled the length of her body, pausing on her breasts in a way that made her skin flush—"both of us will be naked and in a warm bed. That I promise, my pretentious flower."

And it *was* a promise, deep and dark as sin, dangerous stuff as he bent his head slowly to kiss her, allowing her room to back away, to escape now if she so chose. He would walk away no questions asked and accept last night as a one-night memento of his time spent here.

He leaned his hands against the horse, trapping Christel between his arms. "Ah, I have succeeded in leaving you speechless. And you have given light to this dour day, when I did not think either was possible on a cold December morn as this."

With a small turning of her head, she managed to avoid the kiss. "Pretentious flower?"

He flicked at her beautifully disheveled bun. "Weed then."

She studied her toe, drawing circles in the sand. "Then I will be your lady bird of convenience while you are in residence?"

The soft-spoken words did not disguise the steel in her tone. Still, some last shred of desire warred within him. "There is nothing convenient about you."

Her ire awakened, narrowed her eyes. "What is to be my worth then? A hundred shillings? A pretty gown? A town house in Mayfair? Is that not what you give your mistresses?"

This time he was the one to laugh. "I did not say I wanted a mistress."

"Then I am not worth a pretty gown or house in Mayfair?"

His smile was subtle and warm. Deliberately, he lowered his head until his breath caressed her temple. "You told me you did not want to go to London."

The muffled rattle of a carriage sounded from up the seacoast road some distance away. A black, stately coach and matching black horses came to a halt at the road juncture some distance away.

Her attention snapped back in accusation. "I thought we agreed to keep my arrival inconspicuous."

"The carriage is for me, not you."

"I . . . do not understand."

"Unlike you, I do not have the ability to walk miles." He wrapped his hands around her waist and lifted her into the saddle, then adjusted the stirrups to fit the length of her legs. "After making inquiries this morning, I learned Seastone's caretakers are still living at the cottage. They have been informed of your arrival." He did not allow his hands to linger before he straightened. "I promised you I would accompany you halfway. I am a man of my word. Go home, Christel."

Tears welled up in her eyes. He stepped back.

Until this moment, he hadn't thought her capable of tears. He'd only seen her strong and determined. "Thank you, my lord."

"You may return the horse at your convenience."

The wind plucked at her hair and the fastenings on her cloak. Then she nudged her heels against the side of the horse and the gelding shot forward like a ball from a cannon, sending a flock of standing seagulls fluttering into the air with flapping wings.

At once, she reined the horse around. The color high in her cheeks, she pranced the horse sideways, holding his gaze. He watched as her smile of gratitude changed into something more pensive before she swung away again, leaving him alone once more.

Chapter 7

Christel awakened with a start. A feral growl from deep in Dog's throat brought her abruptly out of a deep sleep. The coals in the brazier provided the only light and warmth in the room. She could barely make out Dog's shape against the low-burning fire in the stove. He stood at alert, his hackles on end, his tail extended straight as an arrow as he faced the window. Yesterday, Blue had told her they had spotted wolves in the area. But this seemed different.

Working a sash around her waist, she stood and peered through the darkness at the bedroom door. The hound emitted another low growl. "What is it, Dog?"

For lack of anything creative, she had finally decided to name the hound "Dog" since he seemed to respond to that name best.

Her room was on the second floor. She drew aside the curtains. To see out, she had to scrub a circle through the frost on the glass. Seastone Cottage squatted on a rise overlooking the sea. Snow had been falling for most of the day, leaving a blanket of white covering the rolling hills. A forest of beech and chestnut trees once stood grand on the land, shielding the cottage from the ice and the wind sweeping off the sea. But the timber had been taken and sold years ago. Directly south, on a clear day, she could see the dark towers of Blackthorn Castle. But tonight heavy clouds enshrouded the coastline.

Christel dropped the edge of the curtains and turned to the smoldering fire burning in the stove.

Two weeks had passed since her return and the weather had done little more than sleet or snow.

A tap sounded on the door, causing her to start. "Mum," she heard Heather rasp on the other side. "Ye be wanted downstairs."

When Christel opened the door, Dog whipped past her. Heather held a candle in one hand. She was a young girl and married to Seastone's caretaker. "Blue says the horses in the barn be throwin' a raucous. He be concerned and is going out there."

Christel swept past the girl and down the stairs. Blue was standing at the back door in the kitchen, wearing heavy jack-boots and winter garb, attempting to stuff wadding down the barrel of a long rifle using only one arm. He lifted his head. A heavy woolen scarf covered his thatch of straw-colored hair. "You are not going out there alone," she said.

She was reaching for her cloak when Dog started claw-ing at the door. "Mum," Blue said looking out the window. "We have visitors."

Christel stepped in front of him and looked outside. Three men on dark horses were in the yard. One dismounted, hand-ing the reins to the bulky rider on his left. He stood for a second, staring at the cottage while saying something to the men. He then trudged forward through the drifts. He wore a tricorn and a heavy cloak that scraped the tops of his boots. But even after nine years, Christel recognized him.

She flung open the door. "Put away the rifle, Blue." She could not contain her excitement as she watched Leighton St. Giles push through the snow toward her. He picked up his pace and met her at the door.

"Leighton!" Laughing, she pulled him inside. "What ever are you doing here this time of night?"

"Christel!" He brought her hands to his lips. He was still tall and golden, with wheat-blond hair clubbed at his nape and light brown eyes that danced with merriment as he held her at arm's length. No one ever smiled quite like Leighton. "Look at you. No longer the skinny waiflike creature in breeches I used to tease. A comely lass all grown up."

She tested his upper arms and shoulders. "As have you. I feel real muscle, not bone."

"I had heard you returned," he said.

They shared a smile. He reached down and petted Dog. "A family pet?"

"He came with me from London. He was a stray. What are you doing here?" she asked again.

He removed his tricorn and used it to brush snow from his cloak. "I am duty bound by family obligation to appear before Blackthorn's dark ruler. My illustrious brother summoned me home from a delectable month at a friend's estate near Kilmarnock."

He looked around the mud room, his gaze touching on

Blue McTavish and his wife standing in uncertainty in the kitchen. "Is it just the McTavishes with you?"

"You were expecting a crowd?"

He looked around the small kitchen. "You do not mind if I stay until morning? I should be able to continue on to Blackthorn Castle at first light. The weather is a damnable inconvenience."

"Of course you will stay. What about your friends?"

"They are on their way south. Pressing business. Unlike mine, theirs cannot wait. I will tell them I am remaining here." His gaze touched Blue standing in the kitchen still holding the long rifle. "My horse needs tending," he said. "Have you grain?"

Blue hastily set aside the rifle. "Oats, Lord Leighton. I will see to your horse."

"Take the dog, Blue. He probably needs to go outside," Christel said, then asked his wife to ready the other bedroom on the second floor. Blue and Heather shared the room downstairs off the kitchen.

"Aye, mum."

Watching Heather go, Leighton drew back on his leather gloves. "If you have mead or ale or any *hot* fermented beverage, I would not mind a cup. I am frozen to the bone."

He went outside into the blowing snow. Christel shut the door and pulled aside the curtain to peer out the window. Leighton approached the other two men. Both had remained atop their horses. Of the riders, she could only make out their heavily cloaked bodies and the tricorn hats. One swung his horse away, and she glimpsed the scabbard he wore. The other continued speaking to Leighton before he, too, followed the first rider into the night. Leighton trudged back across the yard. She opened the door for him and he blew in with the wind and snow.

"It is still blowing hard out there," she said. "Perhaps you should have offered the stable loft to them."

Leighton removed his tricorn and gloves. "They will be well enough. There is another inn in Maybole if they choose to bed down before dawn."

A whisper of fabric turned her toward the kitchen. Heather stood in the doorway. "The second bedroom upstairs be prepared, mum."

"Will you make warm mead and bring it upstairs?"

"Aye, mum. The fire on the stove is still warm. I will tend to it."

Christel grabbed a lantern. Leighton followed her up the stairs to the room tucked at the end of the corridor down from where she slept in her parents' old room. The ceiling slanted low, and Leighton could not walk halfway into the room and stand straight. He looked around at the bare walls before settling his gaze on the box bed. She set the lantern on the scarred maple dresser.

"The room is free of dust at least," she offered in way of condolence, as the room would not be anything to which he was accustomed. "But I am afraid your feet will overhang the bed. I outgrew it myself when I was twelve." Before she had gone to live at Rosecliffe.

Leighton was looking at her standing in her robe with

the light in the corridor behind her. "It will do, Christel. Thank you."

She walked to the doorway. "It is remarkable that you made it this far in the storm. The road to Seastone Cottage is quite out of the way."

Leighton leaned an elbow against the dresser. "Not if you miss the detour to Blackthorn Castle," he said.

"Who were your friends?"

He suddenly laughed. "Suspicious of everything, are you?"

She returned his smile. "The past few years have taught me to trust my suspicious nature."

"They came with me from North Ayrshire. We missed the road to Blackthorn Castle and ended south quite by mistake. I had heard that you returned and guessed that if you were anywhere at all in Scotland, 'twould be here." His smile momentarily faded as he studied her. "You are looking well, Christel. I like your hair."

"Liar," she said. "Men do not like short hair. They find it uninspiring and shocking."

"Aye," he said consideringly. "Short hair does make it rather difficult to conk you over the head with my truncheon and drag you by your tresses to bed for a lusty night of entertainment."

"Only if I am not willing," she teased with a flavor of steel behind her words. " 'Tis a way to find oneself gelded otherwise. Tresses or nay."

"Ahh, little Christel, you have not changed a bit, have you? Still the firebrand. What does my brother think about your return?"

She was suddenly glad for the dearth of light, for she felt her cheeks warm. She had not seen him since the day at the beach when he had given her his horse. "He has been kind."

"Kind?" Leighton scoffed. "He is in a perpetual state of annoyance with the world, at war with himself and his own demons. 'Kind' is not a word I would use to describe him. But Grandmamma is fond of him, so for her sake I will pretend to be glad to see he returned. I will be just as content to see him leave again."

"An English revenue ship stopped him on his way here," she said after a moment. "Would you know something about that?"

The grin fell from his face. "The English have been boarding everyone these days. They are a suspicious lot."

"I am no longer in the business," she said. "I have a chance to begin afresh with my life, Leighton. So if you are still involved—"

He set a finger against her lips. "That war is over for me. You will understand that I would prefer my brother never know my loyalties on the matter. Treason is a serious stain on my honor."

"We made you rich, Leighton," she said. "You had no honor."

"Aye, there is that."

"It would hurt your brother to learn the truth about his family," she said. "I would never be the one to tell him how deeply you were involved with the war against England."

"I doubt it would help your cause with him either."

An invisible band squeezed her chest. "He knows about

me. Lieutenant Ross was the one who intercepted the ship."

Leighton scratched his stubbled chin. "Interesting. And then my brother calmly questioned you about your family's illicit activities with the Sons of Liberty and the smuggling empire your uncle and in-laws built and left it at that?"

"My in-laws are decent people. We all did what we had to at the time. *I* did what I had to." She lifted her chin. "I meant it when I told you the war is over for me. I have a chance to begin afresh with my life. I have no secrets from your brother."

"We all have secrets, whether we want them or nay." Leighton turned to the window and edged aside the curtain. "Did he talk about Saundra?"

"He told me . . . what Saundra did."

"I guarantee, imp. My big brother did not tell you everything."

By morning, the storm had moved east, leaving behind a rare blue sky and a rolling landscape glittering white. Not a cloud marred the sky.

Christel had overslept the dawn by at least three hours if the position of the sun was any indication. She washed and dressed, then went downstairs to total silence. Slipping through the doorway at the end of the corridor, she entered the warmth of the kitchen.

Blue's young wife turned from the countertop, where she was pounding bread dough. "Good mornin' to ye, mum," she said cheerfully. "Ye gave me a start."

Christel looked around her. She reached for a mitt and

lifted the tin coffee pot from the stove. "Where is every-one?"

Heather turned the bread dough over on a wooden block and began beating the other side with equal intensity. "Blue went with Lord Leighton to the barn. They have no' re-turned. I gathered eggs. Breakfast be ready for ye." She di-rected Christel's attention to the table in front of the hearth. "I made scones."

With a mental groan, Christel calculated the supplies used to make scones, then walked to the table and picked up a small cut-glass bowl filled with what looked like rare strawberry preserves. "What is this?"

"Why, 'tis strawberry preserves, mum."

"I know 'tis strawberry preserves. Where did this come from?"

Christel had made an accounting of all their supplies in the larder only three days ago. Strawberry preserves had not been among their supplies.

"Lord Leighton presented us with a jar of strawberry preserves in exchange for your hospitality, mum. From the French court of Versailles, he told us. Versailles is where the kings and queens of France reside."

Christel tamped down a surge of irritation. Strawberry preserves, like brandy, tobacco and chocolate, were staples of the smuggling trade this time of year, commanding pre-mium profits from the rich. How had Leighton happened upon strawberry preserves? He had sworn . . .

"Good morning to you, Lady Sunshine," Leighton said from the doorway. He leaned a shoulder against the doorframe and smiled at her. "A simple 'thank you' will suffice as my reward before I bid farewell."

He wore his cloak partially open and over his shoulder. He was clean shaven and fashionably turned out in a smart riding jacket, waistcoat, and buff riding breeches, as if he'd had substantial practice making himself presentable in a lady's cottage. She didn't remember seeing a satchel with him, but he must have had one on his horse, for he had changed his clothes.

Christel directed her gaze to Heather. "Have we cream in the cellar?"

The young woman looked at Christel as if she expected it was a trick question. "Aye, mum. Ye put it there yourself only yesterday."

"I would like some for my coffee. Thank you."

Heather startled at the request. She wiped her hands on her apron, then, with a backward glance at Leighton, hurried away.

Christel set down the bowl of preserves. "The gift was very magnanimous of you."

"I thought so, too. The jam is Anna's favorite and quite rare to come by. If you want more, I can direct you to the bakery in Prestwick that sells the stuff. For another bucket of silver, he will also sell you hot bread and butter." The lift of his lips became a trifle self-mocking. "I have a soft spot for my niece."

Guilt assailed Christel. She had no right to be suspicious of him or his motives for everything he did. He had been her uncle's ally during the war.

Perhaps that was the problem. He had been so quick to betray his brother. But even that was not a fair assessment. There were many in Scotland who'd fought on the side of the colonists; they either held the same political aspirations for Scotland as the colonists held for America, or they held a vengeful grudge against England. They were Highlanders mostly, but they did not fight the British in exchange for silver and gold.

"Thank you for the strawberry jam."

Leighton scooped up her hands and pressed the backs of her fingers to his lips. "You are most welcome. As always, I am your humble servant. However, I now need a favor. My horse has run into a lamentable spot of bother and has come up lame. I need to take the other horse—"

She pulled her hands from his. She *needed* that horse. It was her lifeline into the village. Lord Carrick *trusted* her with the horse.

Outside, the commotion generated by the barking dog drew their attention. "Mum," Heather said in a slightly breathless apology from the doorway. "You have a visitor coming up the road."

"A visitor? Here?"

"Blue says it be his lordship hisself, mum, from Blackthorn Castle."

A moment later, Christel stood in the salon at the front of the cottage, staring out the window. The rider was still far away, but she had no doubt as to his identity.

With an uncharacteristic consideration of female vanity, Christel barely quelled the impulse to check her reflection in the looking glass as she turned into the room and leaned flat against the window.

Leighton's silence drew her gaze up. He stood in the doorway. "And here I was hoping that you and I might grow to share a *tendre* for the other."

"When you were outside, you must have seen him coming. Why did you not tell me?"

Leighton didn't even have the grace to look contrite. "I was curious. 'Tis as simple as that."

"Nothing is ever simple with you, Leighton. You need to go."

Looking for her cloak, she edged past him into the corridor. He grabbed her arm, turning her. "I know his heart better than you do, Christel. He might be free of his marriage, but he is not free of the past. He has never been the man you believed him to be—"

"Candor has always been your one *honest* quality, Leighton. But you do him an injustice." She pulled her arm from his grip. "'Tis up to you whether you tell him you slept here last night. But I do not want your reunion with him to take place in my cottage. Now take the horse if you must and go."

He adjusted the brim of his tricorn and regarded her with a glance that was at once cool. "Before you decide to take him beneath your wing, Christel, ask him why Saundra walked up into that light tower and jumped. Dare him to tell you the truth."

Christel was shaking in fury when she walked to the front door a few moments later. She drew in her breath as much to calm her nerves as an excuse to look down at her dress. Her navy serge might have been worn and a bit out of date, but it was well cut and altered from her mother's old things to fit her perfectly. No one could find fault with her looks. She pulled open the front door with a screech of rusty hinges and walked out onto the porch into the sunlight.

Blue exited the stable carrying a halter, looked to the road then at the cottage. Christel waved him back to the stable. Beyond the paddock, the morning light touched the sea visible in the distance. The same brisk wind that made distant whitecaps slipped beneath her skirts. No cloak, gloves or bonnet protected her against the cold gust pressing her skirts firmly against her legs.

As Lord Carrick brought the horse to a halt outside the picket fence that had once guarded the yard from rabbits, he raised the collar on his cloak. He tipped his French cocked hat with his finger. "I hope I have not come at an inopportune time. Anna and I thought we would check how you weathered the storm."

"Anna?"

Christel realized suddenly that he was not alone. Anna's small face peeked out from inside the folds of his cloak. She smiled brightly at Christel. "Papa asked if I wanted to come see you. I said yes. It has been ever so busy at Blackthorn since Sir Jacob arrived. He has *both* of his daughters with him." She wrinkled her nose. "Miss Catherine stares at Papa and blushes too much, and Miss Ruth cannot talk at all."

The sound of barking signaled Dog's approach, saving Lord Carrick from a requisite response. "Oh, let me down,

Papa." Anna wriggled out from beneath his cloak. "Let me down. Hurry!"

He lowered her from the horse before she fell. A moment later, Dog skidded around the corner of the dilapidated picket fence, scrabbling in the snow for purchase.

Anna giggled as Dog greeted her with sloppy kisses and a wagging tail. She knelt down in the snow. "Is he not the best dog, Papa? Have I not told you so?"

Lord Carrick eased off the saddle. "All the way here."

"Hold out your hand, Papa." His daughter giggled. "That is how you greet dogs. Is that not right, Miss Christel?"

His reluctance to offer his hand made her laugh. "He does seem to like everyone except you."

Lord Carrick quirked his lips. "And you would have me risk my fingers?"

"If one truly likes a dog, I find 'tis important to try. Sometimes past experiences have taught them to be cautious."

"Indeed."

She felt herself blushing, and it was suddenly being borne home to her that in not wanting to bring attention to her thoughts, perhaps she was doing just that.

Aware that she was leaving them in the cold, she said, "I am afraid I was not prepared for guests. But please come inside."

Snow crunched beneath Lord Carrick's boots. He stopped at the bottom of the stairs, his breath visible in the crisp air, his eyes no longer shaded by his cocked hat. "We are not expecting tea and crumpets," he said almost gently.

A hint of citrus touched her senses as his cloak brushed

her arm. "Would you prefer instead tea with scones and strawberry jam?"

Anna clapped her fur mittens together. "How did you know? Strawberry jam is my favorite, Miss Christel. Oh, Papa, may I?"

He nodded and she ran inside with the dog barking at her heels.

Christel turned to Lord Carrick. Beneath his cloak, his fitted riding jacket opened slightly to reveal a cream waistcoat. "You have guests at home?" she asked. "What do they think about your leaving?"

Stomping snow from his boots, he followed the swing of Christel's arm through the door. "I did not ask their permission to go, so I would not be privy to their thoughts."

Unexpectedly she smiled. She took his cloak to dry in the kitchen and found Heather coaxing a fire to life in the hearth while Anna stood next the table holding a scone and telling Heather how much she liked strawberries. Leighton was not present. Christel took a moment to enjoy Anna's enthusiastic reception of the scones before asking Heather to bring tea to them in the salon.

Since her return, Christel had been cleaning the cottage. Against the wall she'd moved everything she would eventually sell. A bifold door had closed off the room from the rest of the cottage.

She hesitated in the doorway. She watched as Lord Carrick took a turn around the cluttered space, his eyes touching on items that had belonged to her mother and father. Light barely sifted through the crack in the heavy curtain. Satins, silks, and half-made bodices draped the chairs and table. Her mother's old dress dummies still wore remnants of costumes and clothing faded by dust and time. "My mother was a seamstress for many of the gentry in Ayrshire."

"I know." He picked up her old drawing tablet on the desk in front of the window.

She slipped the tablet from his hands. "Has anyone ever told you it isn't polite to rummage through another's possessions?"

His mouth crooked in a lopsided grin. "As a matter of fact, no."

A small oval portraiture on the wall was his next point of interest. He peered more closely. "Are these your parents?"

With the stroke of her hand and her mother's encouragement, she'd captured that long-ago image on canvas. "Aye."

"The artist has some talent," he said.

She drew open the curtains. "I thought so as well at the time."

"Are you the artist?"

She tied back the curtains. "I painted that portraiture on my first trip to America."

Christel remembered sitting on the shores of the River York and watching the wind ply the sails of the tall-masted trading ships. She would paint them, too. "My mother used to tell me that I had the ability to create something beautiful from nothing and give it color and life and a story filled with passion." She turned into the room. "It did not matter whether the painting or drawing was any good. Back then it had never occurred to me that my own worth should be measured by another's approval."

She looked at the discarded tablet on the desk. "I owned a small dress shop in Williamsburg," she said, lifting her gaze to his. "But I have not drawn anything in a long time."

"Perhaps you should start painting again," he said.

Candlelight flickered in his eyes. And she could not stop the seditious catch in her breath. His was not the presence of authority but that of a man who—for one instant, one tiny instant—made the whole world go away.

Heather appeared from the kitchen just then. She glanced at Christel, then set down the tea tray on a gateleg table that sat in front of a threadbare settee.

Heather had arranged the tray with porcelain cups rimmed in violets, plates and silver flatware. It included scones, seedcake, a square of sugar and the strawberry preserves. Nothing matched, but together the chaos worked to make an appealing setting. Heather arranged the cups with nervous hands, nearly dropping the creamer filled with milk. The poor girl spared Lord Carrick a cautious glance and a hasty apology.

Christel stepped forward to save her from herself. "That will be all, Heather. I will pour the tea."

"Is Anna still in the kitchen?" Lord Carrick asked.

"Aye, my lord."

Heather shut the bifold, leaving Christel alone with Lord Carrick.

"She has never been in the presence of such an esteemed peer," Christel explained as he sat next to her on the settee and watched her fingers test the teapot before she lifted it to pour.

"That might account for *her* nerves, but I am not sure what accounts for yours."

"Mine?"

He leaned forward. "You have not asked me why I am here."

"You mean you are not here to reassure yourself of my health after the snowstorm?" Thrumming her fingers, she pondered him. "If your intentions were of a lascivious bent this day, you would not have brought your daughter. Though I am not sure if she is here as your chaperone or mine. You cannot have come for my tea, yours is far better." She studied him. "My conversation is witty, but hardly worth traveling five miles in the snow for. Alas, I am stumped."

A half smile played on his lips. But rather than answer, he sat back, completely at ease, making her uneasy. "Have you contacted your grandmother?"

No, she had not. Twice in the last few weeks she had ridden the horse as far as Maybole, but she'd turned back before she'd reached the road to Rosecliffe. She folded her hands in her lap, feeling much like she'd felt in the interview with the dowager countess. "Why *are* you here, my lord? I thought you would have left Blackthorn Castle by now."

"The *Anna* is in Prestwick being refitted. I will be here through next month."

"The dowager should be pleased that you will be here for Christmastide."

"You could seduce me into staying longer," he suggested.

"My grandmother's offer was a thousand pounds, I believe."

Christel almost choked on the tea. He raised a brow at her. "Ooops," he said.

"She *told* you."

"Grandmamma is a known meddler into all things that are not her business. But she does not stand up to torture."

"You *tortured* her?"

"Aye," he said readily. "A game of chess has that effect on her. 'Tis notoriously slow, and she has the endurance of a week-old kitten. And here you were being so honorable not to tell me what you and she discussed that morning in her salon."

"Maybe I did not tell you because I *was* planning to take her up on the offer? A seduction takes time."

He chuckled. "Aye, that is why you flatly turned down my overture on the beach, impugning my honor and injuring my sensibilities beyond repair."

She looked at him, unsure if he was joking. His eyes were on her, hooded like a hawk's. "Have you already prejudged every facet of my character and condemned me to the gallows, Christel?"

His words served to remind her that she had treated him as people had treated her in the past, and the reminder shamed her. Still, she was not sure what she had said that morning on the beach that was not true. "Do you *not* buy your mistresses town houses in Mayfair?"

"It is not the statement to which I took exception. 'Twas the implication that I had mistresses while married to Saundra. Where else would you have heard the gossip?" He raised a brow, daring her to refute him. In fact, his assertion was correct. "I was guilty of a lot of wrongdoing in my marriage," he said, "but adultery was not one. Unless you count the sea as my mistress. Believe it or nay, I do have some honor left."

"I never thought you did not."

He cast her a sidelong glance. "Thank you for that bit of confidence," he said in chiding self-mockery. "I thought I would have to spend more time convincing you, and here we are only a half hour into my visit."

She scrubbed her thumb over the faded rose motif on the cup. "Did you love her?" she found herself asking.

"Aye, in the beginning perhaps. When I first met her at Rosecliffe."

"Did she love you?"

"Maybe," he said. "Once."

His gaze went to the bifold door as the sound of Dog barking came to them. He leaned forward and rested his elbows on his knees. "I do not hold to the expectation that little girls need begin social training at eight years of age, and I loathe the idea of turning her into a society darling. But perhaps in my distaste of society, I am doing her a disservice. Maybe Saundra was in the right of it when she reached out to you to be Anna's governess. Anna is fond of you."

"More like she is fond of my dog. You have an entire staff at your beck and call to help you do right by her."

His attention shifted to his gloved hands rather than her, and at once, he seemed more vulnerable. "I know you are in debt and that you returned to Scotland with the intent to use your employment with me as a way to help restore Seastone Cottage. I could still make that work for you. You can come two or three times a week to Blackthorn Castle . . ."

She turned her face away and stared, unseeing, at the floor. Her hair fell over her chin, and she brushed one side behind her ear. She doubted that he'd ever allowed more than a handful of people into his life, and it seemed as if he was allowing her a foot inside.

"I can think of no better way to enlist you in her life," he said after a moment, "than to ask you to teach Anna to paint or sing or to play the pianoforte, whichever you think she will enjoy best." He stood and walked to the window, staring outside with his hands clasped behind his back. "You do not have to give me an answer today."

"What will be my other duties, my lord?"

"You will not be required to *perform* any other duties, Christel."

She studied her hands. "And should I *want* to take on additional duties?"

Leaning with his back against the window, he folded his arms. "As I see it, you are bound only by your imagination."

She joined him at the window. "Then if I wish to do painting *and* needlepoint you will pay me accordingly."

"Draw up a contract if you wish," he said with amusement. "My intentions are noble."

Noting her hesitation, he dipped his head to peer into her face. "So what is bothering you? I thought I was doing the right thing coming here, and I find I have still managed to insult you."

"You have not insulted me. I am honored by your trust . . ." She glanced at him, tried to read his mood and could not.

"What else do you want?" he asked.

"I would not miss this answer for the world."

She and Lord Carrick turned at the same time. Leighton was leaning against the door, his arms folded beneath his cloak.

Lord Carrick swung his gaze from his brother to her. That one cold glance told her more than words could have that the olive branch he'd just tried to extend to her had not only snapped but had also been pulverized into mulch.

"I was on my way out," Leighton said to her. "And would have made good my escape, except I thought it judicious to warn you that you are about to have company. A platoon of dragoons is headed this way."

Chapter 8

Christel stood inside the stable while a sow of a sergeant, his spurs clinking with every deliberate step, walked around a high-stepping mare his men had pulled from the last stall. The icy draft coming in through the stable door battered the horsehair crest on his helmet as he turned from his official inspection of the horse. He wore the green uniform of a dragoon, but he was missing one button on his waistcoat, which became more evident as he held his hands behind him and rocked back on his heels.

"Where did you get this mare?" he asked her like a turnkey she had once met in a gaol in Williamsburg.

Conscious of Lord Carrick standing behind her, she felt humiliated that this oaf was quizzing her like a criminal, when all she was guilty of was allowing that scapegrace Leighton St. Giles to seek refuge from the storm.

Leighton was still inside the cottage, having informed his brother as the dragoons thundered into her yard that it was best he remain inconspicuously out of sight. Heather continued to occupy Anna in the kitchen, where Christel had also locked Dog out of the way.

The uniformed man beside her holding the bridle waited for her to respond, his glance briefly touching on Lord Carrick. It was clear that these men had no idea who he was, or no one would have dared round them all up like criminals.

Lord Carrick could have halted the interrogation at any time. Even as she understood why he didn't—he was clearly furious and intended to allow this charade to go forward if only to discern the purpose of the dragoons' visit—she felt as if she'd been walking off a plank into the cold sea, except that she also felt hot. And nervous. As a rule, she disliked British dragoons.

With a deep breath, Christel looked at the horse for the first time. She was nearly black and silky smooth, with a coat that glistened in the sunlight filtering through the wooden slats above her. The animal looked exactly like the horse Lord Carrick had given her on loan.

"The horse was stolen last night from the Blue Moon Inn outside Dunure," the sergeant informed her. "The husband of the lady who that there horse belongs to declared it stolen by a thief that he found in his wife's chambers. And what escaped through a window."

"Truly, Sergeant," Christel snapped. "Do I look like I would be visiting a young lady in the middle of the night? And Mr. McTavish's wife can vouch for *his* presence last night. As you can see, a shod is missing. Clearly that horse has been nowhere."

The observation forced them to look. "We followed tracks here."

"We did have a disturbance last night. The dog awakened

us with his barking. We have had wolves harassing our horses."

The sergeant's gaze rose to Blue standing near the stall. A man stood at his back, ready to spear him at the slightest provocation.

"We have answered your questions," she snapped. "You have found naught amiss. Now if you have concluded this ridiculous interrogation, you may now go."

The sergeant chuckled. "Men, I be thinkin' we got us a true Boudicca in our midst. Maybe someone should frisk her for weapons."

She tilted her chin. Let them try. "If you knew anything of Boudicca, you would know that fighting a coward who threatens women would be like stepping on a bug to her."

The sergeant's hand snatched out to grab her cloak. Lord Carrick intercepted his hand. The five men standing in a circle around them raised their long spontoons. Even she froze as his eyes locked on the sergeant's with deadly intent.

"The interview is over," Lord Carrick said. "Your questions have been answered. Whatever happened at the inn, the lady and this man are not involved."

The sergeant's eyes narrowed. "And who might you be, guv'nor."

"The name is Carrick," he said. "*Lord* Carrick. I own the land you traipsed over to get here."

The blood seemed to drain from the sergeant's bristly face. His gaze flickered nervously back to Blue, then to her.

"You have already made one enormous mistake," Lord Carrick said. "Do not make another."

The click of two pistols sounded loud in the ensuing frozen silence. "'Tis true, Sergeant," Leighton said from the doorway of the barn. "His lordship is who he says he is, and nothing in this barn is stolen."

The sergeant yanked his hand from Lord Carrick's ruthless grip and adjusted his coat. "I am only doin' my job, guv'nor."

"Indeed. What job is that?"

"That horse was at the Blue Moon Inn last night with others suspected of bringin' in a shipment of brandy."

"That horse belongs to me. If someone wants to claim it stolen, then you send him to Blackthorn Castle."

The sergeant looked to the men who had been searching the grounds and the house. "Did you find anything stowed away?"

They shook their heads.

"Then get out," Lord Carrick said.

After the group mounted and rode away, Christel chanced an uncertain glance at Lord Carrick. He was looking at her, his eyes as still as an underground pool, their touch so impersonal that she felt it like a bruise against bone. "Thank you," she found herself saying, hating that he had come to her defense yet wondering what would have happened if he had not been here.

Gone was the camaraderie they'd briefly shared.

Gone was the man who'd solicitously cared about her welfare. She felt fortunate she still had her freedom if he thought she was involved in smuggling along with Leighton.

His face did not change expression as he turned to Blue

and gave him the reins of the horse. "I will send someone to shod the mare and get her back to Blackthorn as soon as possible," she heard him say.

"I will do it, my lord," Blue said. "I may only have one good arm, but I am no' a cripple."

"This is not her fault," Leighton said, stopping his brother as he walked out of the barn.

"You had to involve her in your sordid affairs. You could not wait!"

"Stop!" Christel set her teeth to prevent her jaw from clicking in the chill, afraid that the two would suddenly kill each other.

Whatever was between them went far deeper than what had just happened today and had little to do with her.

"I am not without fault, my lord," she said. "I did not want his reunion with you to take place at the cottage. I could have told you he had come here last night and that I gave him shelter against the storm, but I did not." To Leighton, she did not even know what to say, she was so angry with him for dragging her into his disreputable life. "Were you at the Blue Moon Inn last night?" she asked.

"Aye. But I did not know she was married."

Lord Carrick swore. "You went too damn far, bringing gougers here, Leighton. What the hell were you thinking?"

Leighton's eyes flashed hotly for a heartbeat before his gaze went dead and flat, as if an artist had wiped the life from his eyes. "Does this mean I am no longer welcome at Blackthorn Castle, *brother*?"

"Fook you, Leighton. You have been scraping bits of flesh

off my bones for years. I do not even know who you are."

"I am Grandmamma's other grandson, Anna's uncle, and your heir, *brother*."

Lord Carrick stepped back, his boot crunching straw. Then he turned and stopped. Anna stood in the middle of the snow-packed yard between the cottage and the barn. The wind was quick and salty. It fluttered the ribbons on her small bonnet and her cloak. She had stopped and was now pressing her hand to her mouth.

Lord Carrick swore.

He strode out of the barn and through the snow, his heavy cloaked form bending as he scooped her into his arms. "Come, Anna."

"No, Papa!" She stared in confusion over his shoulder. "But I want to see Uncle Leighton."

He tried to soothe her. "Let us go home, Anna."

"No, Papa! . . ."

The rest of her cries were lost as Lord Carrick strode with her in his arms across the snow-packed yard. He mounted his horse.

Christel returned her attention to Leighton. "She talked so much about seeing you. You are a fool, Leighton."

"Camden?" The dowager stood in the doorway of his private study, backlit by the light from the corridor. "Are you in here?"

He stood in the darkness at his window, staring outside. The snow was falling again. He quaffed the last of his scotch and, surrendering his concealment, moved into the light surrounding his desk. He turned up the lamp and said lightly, "And what brings you into the lion's den, Grandmamma?"

She negotiated a path around the leather chair to the desk. "What the devil has got into you and Leighton? He barely spoke at supper." Lifting a carafe of whiskey into the light, she gave Camden a careful look. "Drinking alone? That is unlike you."

He wore no jacket or waistcoat, just a white shirt with sleeves shoved carelessly to his elbows. He set the glass on the desk.

"Anna is finally abed," she said. "She was too upset to eat much supper. What happened at Seastone Cottage?"

"Did Leighton send you in here to fight his battle for him?"

"Nonsense. As if he would allow it. He is as stubborn as you are when it comes to allowing others to defend him. But I would have you consider Anna's heart in this matter between you."

"Do not ever accuse me of acting injudiciously when it comes to Anna, Grandmamma."

"Leighton is not who he wants you to think he is, Camden."

"He has proven to be exactly who he is."

"Are you angrier that he spent the night at Seastone Cottage, or that you believe his character corrupt?"

"Grandmamma," Leighton said from the doorway. "Camden is not interested in anything you or I have to say." He walked into the room. "Of course he thinks I am corrupt. Go." He kissed their grandmother on her cheek. "Camden and I need to talk."

Leighton reassured her they would be fine—that no one had any weapons. Though that was not true; Camden had a pistol in his desk.

"Are you responsible for the rifles on the ship?" Camden asked the instant the door shut behind his grandmother. "For informing the authorities that I was carrying illegal cargo? Did you hope to see me arrested? At the very least, my ship would have been confiscated. Blackthorn depends on the revenue the *Anna* generates to survive."

"Then why would I sabotage you, Camden?"

"Because watching me fail seems to be your forte. Because you have an acute dislike for high-minded society. Because you have never forgiven me for what happened to Saundra."

"You are correct on that score, brother, and I do have a massive dislike for authority, particularly that which robs its citizenry. But that war has never been aimed at you."

"'Tis always been easier for you to steal what is not yours."

"You have chosen to bury your head in the sand, and it does not change the fact that you care as little for Blackthorn and the people here as you did for Saundra. Christel may not believe it now, but I did her a bloody favor today if it keeps you away from her."

Camden opened his fists. He stepped away. "Oh, aye, you are a ruddy saint, Leighton. I had forgot how well you care for your fellow man . . . and woman. Did you or Christel consider her reputation when you spent the night there? And naturally, a platoon of dragoons will be as discreet as a bevy of fishwives drunk on ale. What were you doing in Dunure?"

Leighton cracked his rake's smile. "Other than enjoying the favors of the sauciest wench this side of Prestwick? While Westmont's men were chasing me, *my* men took twenty tons of tax-free brandy from a broad-beamed beauty of a schooner beneath their very noses just three miles away. I was a-smugglin', brother, a proud tradition in these parts."

"I do not know you anymore," Camden whispered.

"I am the spare. A useless one at that, as Papa used to remind me with the back of his hand across my face. Left to my own devices and amusements, I chase gold and women and enjoy both. I admit fully to my faults. You, on the other hand, hide behind the biggest lie of all—"

"Leave Blackthorn Castle, Leighton. You will not involve me in your vices and your crimes any longer. You will not see my daughter again. You will not step foot on these grounds. If you ever show up here—"

"You will have Westmont or the sheriff arrest me?"

"I will shoot you myself."

Leighton gave a deep bow. "Aye, I believe you would at that."

Camden was still standing at the window when he heard the sound of a horse riding away.

"Sir." Smolich stood in the doorway, carrying a silver serving tray. "With the cold and damp, your leg must be bothering you. I brought a cup of chocolate. They say chocolate does wonders for one's spirits."

"Thank you, Smolich. You may set the tray on the desk."

By the time Camden left his study and walked the corridor to his daughter's rooms, the tall clock down the corridor had long struck the hours of midnight. He quietly edged open the door and stepped inside. A lamp burned on the dresser, casting an orange glow over the pillow, where he could see Anna's dark curls.

He sat on the edge of the bed. All he could do was bury his face in his hands.

"She is gone, Miss Douglas!" Mrs. Gables told Christel two days later, near hysteria. "No one has seen the child since tea yesterday afternoon. I must have dozed for only moments. I did not mean to sleep. But I am not as young as I used to be. When I awakened, she was gone."

"What happened, Mrs. Gables? Why would she leave?"

"She must have heard her papa and Lord Leighton arguing." Twisting her hands, Mrs. Gables paced back and forth. "The dowager has taken to her bed ill again. And all this happening just before the holy day of Christ's mass."

Christel took her hands. "There is a storm surge coming in on the beach. Do you know if Lord Carrick has thoroughly searched the cove?"

"Lord in heaven, mum. He has people everywhere, searching every tunnel and crevice in the house, every shadow and beneath every rock in the parkland surrounding Blackthorn Castle. He has not discounted the possibility she may have been kidnapped."

"Kidnapped?"

"I heard him send for the sheriff. He wants Lord Leighton

found. There be bad blood between the two brothers. One will kill the other to be sure." She buried her head in her hands. "This be just too horrible, mum. And 'tis my fault. How can a child survive in the cold?"

"Do you know where Lord Carrick is now?"

"He be in the library, mum."

Christel broke away from Mrs. Gables, found the library downstairs and knocked on the door. Lord Carrick called sharply to enter.

She found him, palms flat on the desk, leaning over a stack of papers. He had not shaved, the first thing she noticed. He wore his cloak as if he had only just come in from outside. Water had beaded on his shoulders, and the papers on the desk were wet. His tricorn lay on a chair beside the desk, tossed aside. A single lamp cast light on his hands and face, and he straightened as if to move away from light.

She hesitated as she spied two other men near the fireplace. "I was not aware you were in a meeting."

"What are you doing here, Christel?"

"I only just found out about Anna. I came to help. . . . But—"

One of the men came forward into the light. He wore a tidy wig queued at the nape. His light brown eyes seemed cordial but attentive as he briefly inclined his head. "Stay, Miss Douglas. I am Sir Jacob Westmont, the provost."

The provost was the chief magistrate in Ayrshire, one of the most powerful men in Scotland. He then introduced the sheriff. "We were told Leighton was at your cottage," Sir Jacob said.

"She has nothing to do with Anna's disappearance, Jacob," Carrick said.

Any softness she had briefly glimpsed in Sir Jacob's eyes was gone. "Are you willing to stake Anna's life on that?"

Lord Carrick's gaze touched hers. Her breath quickened. A muscle in his jaw clenched. "If she knew where Anna was, she would tell us."

Sir Jacob considered her. "Are you in the habit of letting strange men spend the night at Seastone Cottage?"

"Enough, Jacob."

Christel lifted her chin. "I have known Lord Leighton most of my life, Sir Jacob. He is not a stranger to my family. I was not alone at the cottage."

She stepped aside to allow Sir Jacob and the sheriff to leave the room. Sir Jacob's cloak whipped against her skirts as he stepped past. When she blinked again, she found herself in Lord Carrick's gaze. The tightness in her chest compounded. For several seconds neither of them spoke. "The provost and the sheriff?" she asked.

"Jacob is here as a friend." He began pulling on his gloves. "What are you doing at Blackthorn, Christel? Did you come alone?"

"Blue shod the mare. We returned the horse to your stable. You cannot believe that Leighton had anything to do with this."

"You are naïve to think he was ever worthy of your loyalty. Stay out of business that does not concern you."

The insult bristled over her nerves. But he was right. This

wasn't about her or her feelings. The only important person in this entire ordeal was Anna.

" 'Twas not my intent to defend your brother or myself," she said. "Please tell me what I can do to help."

He dragged his hat from the chair. "You can go back to Seastone Cottage." He walked past her. "I will send word when we find her."

If Leighton *was* responsible, she had harbored him. "Did I do this?"

"Go home, Christel," he said simply.

While standing in the foyer awaiting Smolich to bring her cloak, Christel heard the sound of voices, female, subdued by somber emotion, familiar. No one had lit the lamps. A wedge of light from an opened door down the hall spilled across the polished marble floor. Christel followed the voices and paused abruptly in the doorway of the drawing room.

No one saw her. Her sister, Tia, sat on the window bench, gazing out at the remains of a bleak day. Wearing dull yellow silk, she looked as pallid as her gown. Her hands tightly clasped in her lap, her head was bowed. The other two young women, with their white-blond hair and identical sober expressions, were silently working on needlepoint samplers. Lady Harriet, with one foot propped on an ottoman, sat on a plush blue damask sofa surrounded by pillows.

Grams.

Christel and she saw each other at the same time.

The part of Christel that had been strong cracked like glass exposed to cold for too long and dropped into a kiln.

"Grams . . . ," she heard herself whisper, aware of the subterranean stirrings of her heart.

Everyone's head snapped up, as if they'd been expecting a messenger bearing ill tidings, and all eyes fell on her.

"You!" Tia was the first to find her tongue. She came to her feet. "This is your fault. Lord Carrick and Leighton were arguing over *you*."

Already on her feet, Lady Harriet pointed the tip of her cane at Tia. "Enough, Tianna Faye. We've had enough venom spewed without adding yours to the pot." To Christel she said, "You merely brought their long-standing enmity for one another to a head a little earlier than it would have eventually arrived. Come," she said, as if nine years and an ocean had not divided them.

With a last glance at her sister, Christel followed her grandmother out of the room. Clearly familiar with Blackthorn Castle, Lady Harriet escorted her to a smaller, cozier room, where a fire burned in the hearth. The dark velvet draperies had been pulled against the drizzle. Heavy furniture gleamed in the firelight. Gold-bound classics, maps and sea charts filled the polished teak bookcases that lined one wall. A globe framed by an ornate wooden trestle sat near the desk and gave some evidence that the masculine owner of this room was a seafaring individual. The faint familiar essence of tobacco, whiskey and a hint of sandalwood touched her senses. She closed her eyes.

"I do not think his lordship will care if we use his private study," Lady Harriet said as she shut the door. "This is the only other room I can tolerate in this drafty castle. At least 'tis warm." At that moment, she seemed to run out of words. Then she snorted. "You look exhausted, child. Come closer into the firelight. Let me see you."

Her throat tight, Christel moved nearer to her grandmother. Lady Harriet was shorter than Christel, but one never felt her lack of size when sharing the same room. Quite the opposite. Her grandmother had always been a giant in Christel's mind. She was shocked, seeing Lady Harriet's physical frailties.

"Do not look at me as if I am in the grave, young woman," Lady Harriet snapped. "I was ancient when you left. I am no more so now."

Christel touched Grams's powdered cheek. "You look wonderful."

Grams tilted Christel's chin in the light, then lovingly cupped her cheek in her palm. The gesture was faint and lasted no longer than a second, but Christel felt it to her core. "And you look like one of those tragic heroines from those silly blue books I used to catch you and Saundra reading. I wish it had not taken *this* to bring us together, but here we are. On neutral territory. 'Tis better, I say."

Lady Harriet stepped backward to observe her granddaughter. "Your hair has only grown to your shoulders. Do not tell me it has never grown out. I have never heard of such a thing."

"I cut it, Grams." Christel wiped at the moisture beading in the corner of one eye. "You know how I dislike all that long hair in the way."

"Posh! You and Saundra loved long hair. How many hours

did you both spend brushing each other's hair? Before you went and cut it all off to purchase those silly gold slippers." Grams lowered herself into the chair next to the hearth. "I heard that you arrived with Lord Carrick on the *Anna*. You have met the child then?"

Christel turned away in the pretense of studying the books and to reframe her thoughts. Or to contain them. "The first time I met Anna she asked if I was an angel. She told me that her mother had said an angel was coming to watch over her and her papa. I feel responsible—"

"Nonsense." Grams's soft voice penetrated Christel's grief. "Have ye not watched over your cousin's husband, gel?"

Christel turned.

"Your uncle told me that after the disastrous conflict at Yorktown, you sat at Carrick's side while he lay unconscious from his wounds."

Christel looked at Grams with wet eyes. Her grandmother merely sniffed. "Did you think I made no effort to keep up with your life for all the years you were gone?" she said. "You are my granddaughter, every bit as important as Saundra and Tia."

The last of Christel's composure fled. Her throat tightened. She could no longer contain the horrible swell of tears.

Grams patted her knee. "Come sit beside me for awhile."

"Oh, Grams . . ." Christel dropped to her knees beside her grandmother and let the soft, leathery hands cradle her head.

"You loved him when you were a child, I know." Grams's whisper reached Christel's heart and held.

Christel thought she had grown up and moved on with her life. She thought she had forgotten the foolish emotional side of her that had reared itself so unmercifully. "How did you know? I told no one."

"I think most who knew you could see how ye felt. Dear me, lass, he was always trouble for you. Your uncle did you a favor taking you to Virginia before ye got your heart broken over his marriage to Saundra."

Put bluntly, Christel had made a spectacle of herself. In truth, she no longer knew how she felt. Except she felt helpless and angry. Helpless for Lord Carrick. Angry that she could not do more to help him.

Where would a confused girl angry with her father go?

"I will not believe Leighton has taken Anna," Christel said.

"Who is to say? Leighton was like a father to that girl while Carrick was off fighting the king's war. He may not have taken kindly to being told to stay away from the child."

"What happened between Leighton and Lord Carrick, Grams?"

Lady Harriet inhaled a deep breath. "Saundra happened between them. Leighton was here. Carrick was not. And when he finally did return, he was . . . scarred. The war had changed him. No one was prepared for the scandal that followed his defeat at Yorktown. Saundra least of all. Two months after his return, she came to me, begging me to help her leave Scotland with Anna. I would not. At the time, I did not know she was four months gone with child."

"Come home now. Please. I am in desperate need of a friend." Christel closed her eyes. "Four months?"

"Shortly afterward, she lost the child and her health began to fail. Carrick was taking Anna and leaving her the night she walked up into that tower. Leighton blames Carrick for her death."

Christel glanced up, her eyes full of tears. "What do you believe?"

"That Leighton was the father of the child she carried. I suspect Carrick knew that and will take that knowledge to his grave."

Christel folded her hands tightly in her lap. For a long time, she was unable to speak.

"I truly believe that for all her faults, Carrick loved Saundra," Lady Harriet said. "I understand why he has chosen to leave Blackthorn Castle. But 'tis human nature to come back to what is most familiar. He needs to heal. He can only do so here."

A deep inhalation strained Grams's bodice. "And I have no doubt Anna will return safely to her father when she is hungry enough," she said, a staunch believer in the power of positive thoughts. " 'Tis cold outside. The child has no place else to go for food and shelter."

Except perhaps somewhere familiar to her, where the fire was warm and she could eat her fill of strawberry jam with her scones.

The early evening air was cold and thick as pease porridge by the time Christel and Blue reached Seastone

Cottage. She was glad for the heavy gloves and bonnet that Heather had found for her that morning.

Christel could see no farther than the cold landscape of her yard, which was dappled with chunks of snow that had slid from the roof to form mounds on the ground. The air smelled heavily of seaweed, and the crash of waves on the beach was louder than normal tonight.

No one greeted her at the door, and as she ran inside, she felt a strange silence engulf her. Removing her cloak, she hurried into the kitchen to hang it near the hearth—only to come to an abrupt stop.

Leighton stood near the fireplace. His blond hair hung loose and wet over his nape and ears. His wet frock coat was spread over a chair. "She is upstairs with Heather," he said.

With his white shirt, buckskin breeches and jackboots, the man's appearance was as stark as his expression. But not nearly as severe as Christel's anger. She spun on her heel and started for the stairs.

"I did not kidnap her, Christel." His voice trailed after her as she ran up the stairs to the bedroom he had occupied a few nights before.

Heather was coming out of the room, an empty tray balanced against her hip as she turned to shut the door. She startled. "Mum!"

"How is she?"

"The Lady Anna be a wee bit bumped and bruised when Leighton found her on the beach. I be looking for more blankets."

"Thank you, Heather."

Christel stepped around her and into the room. Anna was sitting up in the bed, wrapped in blankets, her hair soaked. She was talking to Dog, lying with his head on her lap. She and Christel saw each other at the same time. Anna grabbed a gulp of air, her big blue eyes swelling with tears.

Christel rushed to a seat on the edge of the bed. "Are you injured?"

Anna wiped the tears from her eyes with the heel of her hand. "Only a little when I try to walk." Gulping over sniffles, she wrapped her arms tighter around Dog. "He fell on the rocks, Miss Christel."

Dog's tail wagged as Christel slid her palm delicately over his wet fur. He whimpered when she touched his back leg, but it did not feel broken. She gently scratched between his ears and accepted two licks to her cheek. "You were on the beach?"

Anna's pudgy cheeks firmed a little. "I was hiding in the caves below the rocks. The tide started coming in and I could not get out. I was scared, Miss Christel. Dog heard me shouting and barked and barked until Uncle Leighton came. I was so dreadfully cold, Miss Christel."

Christel shoved away the wet folds of Anna's skirt and ruffled petticoats to examine the child's injuries.

Anna's ankle was swollen. The cut on the left side of her knee was an inch across and deep enough that she might need sutures. *Please, no.* Someone had already cleaned it up and wrapped a bandage around it. They would need a doctor. Anna's exposure to the cold had left her pale white. "We need to get you out of these clothes."

Heather entered the room carrying blankets. "I am heating water for the lass, mum. I warmed these on the hearth." She laid one over the dog. "He was on the ridge barking for most of the afternoon. He would no' come down. And a storm be coming. I did no' know what to do. When Lord Leighton rode into the yard, I told him about the dog. Lord Leighton found them both trapped near a tidal pool with the tide coming in around them. The dog's barking took him to her."

Christel's dog had been gone from the yard when she had left earlier that day. At the time, she'd thought he'd been off foraging for food, and she had been in too much of a hurry to think anything of it.

Christel cupped Anna's pale wet cheek and found it ice cold against her palm. "The least you could have done if you were going to run away is to dress for the weather. How long have you been outside?"

Anna gulped. "Most of the day. Yesterday, I waited until Mrs. Gables thought I was napping. Then I escaped through the servant's door and hid 'til this morning. I know all the places to hide, and I am *not* afraid of the dark. I am not, no matter what Papa says."

"He is very worried about you."

"I will never go back. Ever! I hate him. I do! He made Uncle Leighton go away! I never want to see him again."

"You do not mean that."

"I do!"

The child fell across the pillow crying. Christel bundled her in her arms. She knew nothing about children and didn't know how to console a distraught little girl, so she let Anna weep hot tears against her bodice.

"If you take me back to Blackthorn Castle, I shall only run away again." She looked down at the dog crushed in her arms. "He is my only friend in the world."

Lady Anna might have been Lord Carrick's daughter, but she did not possess his usual knack for hiding emotions, and she displayed them with a melodramatic flair. Everything in her thoughts showed on her face. Confusion. Love. Fear. Anger. All of it flickered in her wet eyes as she wrapped her arms tighter around the dog.

"Where do you think to live, Anna? Your home is Blackthorn Castle. Your papa loves you."

"I want to live here with you and Dog and Uncle Leighton."

Christel sensed a presence and turned toward the doorway. The object of the little girl's affection stood in the opening. He held up his hands. "Do not look at me," he said. "I never told her I lived here."

Chapter 9

⌒◯◯⌒

Christel rose from the chair she had pushed flush to the bed where Anna lay sleeping. "She has a fever," she said to Leighton, who stood at the end of the bed, his hair and shirt rumpled. Until a few moments ago, he had been sleeping downstairs on a pallet in front of the hearth.

She had sent Blue to Blackthorn Castle four hours earlier to inform Lord Carrick that his daughter had been found safe. Blue should have already returned, bringing Doctor White. *Four hours!*

Somewhere a shutter banged. The wind moaned through the cracks around the window. A cold draft touched Christel's slippered feet. "Where is Blue?" she muttered, more to herself than to Leighton.

"The beach is closed off due to the tide. It could be dawn before anyone gets here coming from the road," Leighton replied.

A fire burned in the stove next to the wall where he stood. Christel stared at the light that flickered on the floor and ceiling. In her exhaustion, the somber dance of shadows began to haunt her. Doubt plagued her, and she hated it. "Maybe I should have waited until daylight to send Blue to Blackthorn. His horse could have fallen in a hole."

"'Twould be an ignoble end to a fine steed," Leighton said lightly. "Let us hope for better than that."

She stopped and looked at him squarely. Everything Grams had told her yesterday returned to her with the force of a slap. Christel wrapped her arms around her midriff. "What are you doing here?"

"I gave Blue my horse, remember?" He leaned a shoulder into the door. "I cannot very well ride the cart pony, as my feet would drag on the ground."

Christel cast a worried glance at Anna, then settled her gaze on Dog, at her feet. His head lifted in interest. After scratching him between his ears, Christel stepped around Leighton, forcing him into the hallway, and pulled the door shut behind him.

"I am asking again," she said in a low rushed whisper, "why are you here? At this cottage? I am grateful that you *were,* since you probably saved Anna's—"

"But you would prefer that I not be here."

"I would prefer to know the truth."

"I am homeless," he said, obviously avoiding the question.

She brushed hair off her cheek. "Then you intend to be here when your brother arrives?"

"I intend to be here until I can retrieve my horse. Unless you know of someplace else I should wait." His mouth crooked, but no amusement touched his blue eyes. "Little momma bear," he said softly, "big brother does not need your protection from me. When he returns to his castle on the hill overlooking his kingdom, you and I will still be here. Still alone. Maybe not at this cottage . . . but *some* place."

Christel picked disapprovingly at a patch on her plain woolen gown. She had changed out of the other dress after returning, as it had been soaked. She hated feeling as if she was wandering in a mist, running from whatever it was hiding inside her. Angry at Saundra and Leighton, yet knowing this was not the time or place to say anything.

After a pause, she said, "You were close to my uncle. Did you know he mortgaged this cottage?"

"What is it you want me to tell you?"

Heather appeared at the top of the stairs with a tray in her hand. "My lord," Christel heard her murmur.

Leighton turned on his heel. "Get some sleep, Christel," he said.

Heather dipped slightly as he passed her. Heather then turned her attention to Christel, her eyes shyly downcast. "I heard ye up and talkin'. I thought the tyke might need a bit of warm liquid and biscuits. She did no' eat much at supper."

"Thank you, Heather. I will take the tray," Christel said, and two cups chinked together as she accepted it.

"Mum." Heather stopped her as she helped Christel open the door. "After your uncle passed, it be Lord Leighton what has kept Seastone Cottage from the excise men. He has helped many people."

"How?"

"I . . . I really cannot say, mum. But I just did no' want you to think poorly of him, as some do."

"Thank you, Heather."

Once inside the room, Christel leaned her head back against the door, closing her eyes. The cottage creaked against the wind gusts that continued to race off the sea like a hungry banshee clawing at the cracks and crevices in the walls. She walked to the nightstand, moved aside the candle and set down the tray. She moved the candle until the circle of light touched Anna's flushed face. Her lashes slowly lifted. Christel dropped in the chair beside the bed and took the child's hand.

"I do not feel so well," Anna whispered. "My leg hurts."

"I know." Christel wiped the hair from the girl's smooth brow. "You are running a fever."

Anna pulled fretfully at the quilts. "But I am so cold."

Christel gave the child warm tea and helped her drink. When they were done, Anna's hand again found hers. "Miss Christel? I want to see Uncle Leighton. . . . Will you tell Papa not to send him away? Uncle Leighton tells me stories. He bought me a pony for my birthday. You do not think Papa will take her away from me. Do you? Because I was bad?"

"Your papa loves you. He will not take away your pony."

"Promise you will not leave me."

"I will not leave you."

Christel's throat tightened and a great anger that any child should suffer swelled inside her. But it should have been the girl's mother holding her hand, not a stranger to her life.

How could Saundra, who'd had everything in the world, have foolishly thrown it all away?

Anna's fingers touched Christel's hair every so often, as

if the gesture could reassure her that Christel remained. But after awhile she slept again.

Christel had just started to drift on a dream when she awakened to the sound of a door slamming and muffled voices downstairs. Heavy-soled boots marked someone's approach. The door opened, spilling in candlelight from the hallway. She brought a hand to her forehead to rid her temples of the piercing intrusion to her senses.

Lord Carrick's cloaked figure stood in the doorway.

Anna opened her eyes. "Papa," she gulped, holding out her arms.

Christel rose from the chair and stood aside to let him take his place beside his daughter. His shoulder brushed hers. He'd brought in the scent of the sea and the wind.

"Shh, little one," he said in a low, tender voice, gathering his daughter into the protective folds of his cloak as he sat with her in his lap. "I am here now."

"I am sorry, Papa," she wept against his cloak. "Truly, I am."

"Hush now." Scraping his palm gently over her forehead, he pressed his lips to her temple. "You are safe. Nothing will happen to you."

Christel watched the hushed exchange, aware that others were gathering in the narrow hallway behind her. A tightness squeezed her chest, squeezing and squeezing. She backed out to go. He turned slightly, his daughter in his arms, and looked at her from over the top of Anna's head. The shade of his dark woolen coat blended with his hair and his eyes, which were so deep as almost to be black in the dull light.

His gaze touched hers. And held in the taut silence. Then Anna made a sound and pulled his attention back.

Christel quietly withdrew from the room and shut the door, pausing to draw a deep breath. The doctor stood uncertainly in the corridor, wearing a wooly cloak. His wild red hair stuck up in uncombed dishevelment, and he was attempting to clean his fogged spectacles with the tail end of his loose shirt. He bore the indignity of one who had been dragged from his bed.

"Miss Douglas." His brown eyes peered with uncertainty from behind spectacles too large for his red nose. "Ye might no' remember—"

She recognized him the moment he spoke. His mother had been the housekeeper at Rosecliffe. Stephen used to work odd jobs about the house and stable. Christel had taught him to read and write.

She took his hand. "Stephen White."

He adjusted the leather bag in his other hand. "Thanks to your grandmother's patronage, I am now a physician."

"Please tell me you are a good one." She patted his arm and told him to go inside. "There is a father in there who needs to be reassured that his daughter will be all right. 'Tis good to see you."

He walked past Heather and Blue. "Boil water," he said to Christel.

In the kitchen, she found Leighton, leaning with his back against the wall on the other side of the door. He wore his cloak and held his hat and gloves.

"Is she all right?" he asked.

"Anna is still feverish," she told him. "Your brother needs to know what you did for her."

"I am here because I want to know that she will be all right. I did nothing for Camden's sake."

"What about for my sake? I know you have kept Seastone afloat."

"Your uncle made me profits. I owed it to him to keep this cottage in his family for as long as I could. Call it a debt paid."

He bent his head until his lips touched her temple. "Now I shall leave your life and your problems in your own capable hands. Guard your heart well, Christel."

Too late, she thought.

Later, wiping his hands with a rag, Doctor White went to his bag, clicked the lid open and pulled out a brown bottle the size of his palm.

"This is for pain," Christel heard him tell Lord Carrick, setting it on the stand beside the lamp. He unrolled first one sleeve, then the other, then pulled his coat off a hook on the wall and shrugged into it. "She will be asleep soon, my lord."

Lord Carrick sat on the chair beside the bed with his elbows resting on his knees. He pressed the heels of his hands against his forehead, as if he'd been kicked in the head. Christel could still hear Anna's cries in her mind, and her father must have felt like a heartless bastard for holding her, nay cradling her small body, while Doctor White had sutured her leg.

Ignoring the tightness in her throat, she continued to sit at the head of the bed, Anna's head in her lap. Anna's sobs had turned into small hiccoughs as Christel had gently stroked the girl's hair and hummed a lullaby.

Doctor White showed Christel how to mix the herbs he had given her for the tea that would help Anna rest. Christel nodded as he spoke. The light framed the child's tear-streaked face, and Christel gently dabbed the sheet against her pale cheeks.

"Thank you for everything, Stephen. If you need a place to sleep, Heather can fix up a pallet near the hearth downstairs," she told him.

He told her he had rounds to make at the orphanage and couldn't stay. He would be back in the evening to check on Anna. Christel looked out the window. She had not realized it was already dawn. After Doctor White left, she returned to the lullaby, gently stroking Anna's face. Christel's mother used to sing to her. She remembered many of the songs that she thought she had forgotten.

When she finished, she looked up to find Lord Carrick watching her. A lock of dark hair had fallen across his brow.

For an instant, something showed in his eyes that touched her bone deep and reminded her of all the reasons why she did not allow herself to need anyone or to be needed. The responsibility was too much. It always led to trouble. She had learned not to let people get close. It would be so easy to let him inside her. But with him, no reserve would be possible, no concealment for the sake of self-preservation.

He must have read her thoughts. His mouth crooked slightly as if to tell her he understood the feeling well enough. Then his gaze dropped to the hand gently stroking Anna's hair.

Christel looked away. He knew it was Leighton who had found Anna on the beach, that Leighton had come to the cottage first before he had followed Dog's barking to Anna.

Whatever the reason, Leighton had most likely saved Anna's life—and certainly complicated hers. She also knew one decent, unselfish act would not erase Leighton's reservoir of sins in Lord Carrick's eyes. He must have questioned why his brother had been twice to the cottage. But he said nothing, and somehow she didn't think he would. Everything had suddenly become complicated. She had not asked to be put in the middle.

But as the wind continued to gust off the sea, whipping the eaves of the cottage, Christel pushed aside her concerns.

She remained with Anna all that day as the child slipped restlessly in and out of slumber to settle finally into peaceful repose near nightfall.

After supper, Lord Carrick went below to retrieve a bag sent over by Mrs. Gables. Sir Jacob and the sheriff arrived to talk. Christel finally fell asleep in the chair Lord Carrick had vacated. She awakened briefly when he lifted her and carried her to her room.

No man had ever carried her so intimately against him, her legs dangling over his arms like some damsel in distress.

She didn't like the feeling. "Put me down," she murmured sleepily.

Surprisingly, he did as she asked. They stood alone in

her bedroom. He was in his shirtsleeves. He'd removed his neckcloth.

"How long have I been asleep?"

" 'Tis past midnight. Blue and Heather retired an hour ago. Your dog is lying asleep at the bottom of the stairs. Anna is resting peacefully. I checked the horses in the stable and banked the fire."

Scraping the hair from her eyes, she held his gaze. "You did a brave thing with Anna last night," she said, "holding her in your arms while Stephen sutured her leg. You may think she will hate you for it, but she will only remember that you comforted her when she was afraid."

"I am not good with comforting little girls." He walked to the bedroom window and, pulling aside the curtain, peered outside. He kept his voice low as he spoke. "I know you and Leighton were . . . are . . . friends," he said. "But I need to know if 'tis more than that, Christel."

They had edged into fragile territory, a place she had not wanted to go. But she'd had enough of the past. Tonight, she wanted the ghost that was standing between Camden St. Giles and his brother to stay away.

"There has never been anything physical between us. Perhaps he only wanted me to know what had occurred between the two of you."

"He is dangerous, Christel—"

She put her finger to his lips. "So are you, my lord."

"Where was Anna found?" he asked.

"There is a partial cave on the beach," she said. "Leighton followed the sound of Dog barking and found her."

"Anna ran from me," he said. "She could have died. And it would have been my fault." He closed his eyes, weighing more than his words. "After being an outsider in my daughter's life for so long, there must be a better way to go about knowing her."

"Anna is fortunate to have you for her father."

"Do you think so? She might argue that point when I get her back to Blackthorn Castle and throttle her. I can sail a ship across seas, stand at the helm in the face of a full broadside, but I have scant knowledge of little girls and pet hounds. Of how to be the kind of father mine could never be. More than a stranger to his children. 'Tis something Leighton seems to have mastered in my absence . . ." His voice faded, as if he recognized where this conversation was leading. "I have spent years letting others monopolize her heart to the exclusion of my own. I am precariously perched between my desire to protect and shield her and the need to allow her the freedom to be a child without the burden of my problems."

"You do not have to explain yourself to me."

"I do. God help me, but I do. You do not know me. I am not a nice person. I have seen and done things that will send me to hell a thousand times over. Anna is the one truly innocent person in all of this. You asked why Saundra went into the tower the night she jumped. I cannot tell you her heart, but I can tell you mine. We had argued. I had told her I was leaving her and taking Anna. If I could change that night, do it over again . . . now Anna will forever pay the price of her parents' sins."

He proceeded to step past her. Desperate to touch him, Christel wrapped her arms around him and pressed her cheek against his chest. She only wanted to do the right thing and protect him. "Do not go."

For most of her life, it had been easier to run from the frailties of her heart than to confront her own vulnerability, but there was something fragile about a man of the world who suddenly did not seem so worldly in all things. A man who loved his daughter and wanted to know his child better, who had been betrayed by his wife and brother and—if Christel really wanted to list all the evil culprits in his life—who had also been betrayed by the Crown he had served so loyally for so many years.

He was a man who'd used every situation to his own advantage, a strategist who'd played life like a game of chess or one of his naval sorties but who had suddenly found the new territory he was now sailing unnavigable.

In a week or a month, he would be back to his old self, fighting his current battles in a state of reckless surrender. He would leave Blackthorn, return to London, and resume his life where he had left off.

"Camden has a duty to the people of Ayrshire, his daughter, his family and to himself to make this estate whole again," the dowager had said. *"He owes it to the legacy left to him by his father and his father before him. He owes it to his daughter's future to marry again and to make his life here. He needs to find purpose again."*

But most of all, he owed it to himself to find the place where he belonged. Even if it was not here.

"Christ . . . do not do this, Christel."

She touched her fingertip to his lips, then fanned her fingers over his cheek, as if by virtue of her will she could pull the tension from him.

For several heartbeats, they remained in each other's gazes, no longer caught by the past but by something less adversarial and more intimate. On impulse, she gently pressed her lips to his and kissed him.

She felt his hesitation and knew a flash of uncertainty just before he pulled away. Her stomach kicked in warning as he raked her face with eyes that burned all over her. At first, he made no effort to embrace the contact between them, as if caution bid him to test the waters to regain his bearings and understand the direction of hers. Impossible, since she did not understand herself. This was not about Saundra. It wasn't about loneliness or the past or even the future.

Whether with animosity or something else—she couldn't tell—his callused hand slid beneath her hair to splay her head. His loose hair cloaked her face as he crushed his mouth against hers.

Then she was reaching for him as he thrust his fingers through her hair, his lips prowling through her senses, taking more and more of her response the same way he conquered his foes, one battle at a time.

He groaned and shifted his body, holding her wedged between him and the door. She clung to his shoulders, her fingers digging into his rigid flesh.

His palms followed the arch of her back. Then he gripped her bottom, lifting her off the floor until she was pressed flush against his body, and like a wanton, she raised her legs and wrapped them around his hips. His hand fisted in her hair, pulling her head back to expose her throat to his sensual assault. He turned with her in his arms, her knees pressed against his hips and on the edge of the bed with her still straddling him. Her urgency matching his, she moved her hips against him. He was being too rough and fierce, but she didn't care. It mattered little that tomorrow would come, and the storm would be gone, the sky would be blue. Now there was only the sound of the wind.

"Look at me."

She squeezed her eyes shut. She felt suffocated with yearning. "I do not want this to be a dream."

He made a sound like a laugh. Cradling her face between his palms, he stared into her eyes from beneath heavy eyelids. "I have never been accused of being a woman's dream."

All ten of her fingers traced the shape of his face. "Then you have not known the right woman, my lord."

Their breath mingled with whispered words. "Lord . . . Christel." He stroked her hair and brushed his lips against hers. "Where did you learn to sing the way you do?" he asked softly.

"My mother used to sing to me as a child."

"Your voice is like your name. Beautiful."

Her body shuddered with desire. His words pulled at her heart. He cradled her, whispered her name, then kissed her with a hunger that she knew now was not hers alone.

It was a kiss as she had never experienced. He sipped her lips. He indulged himself in her mouth, as if taking pleasure in the taste of her. He took her down to the mattress, the weight of him offset by the angle in which he lay, the steady suck of his mouth like a pulse against her heart. He took her mouth again and again and again, engaging all of her senses, focusing her desire, ravishing her without quarter. In giving, he was taking. Mutual consent. Need. Her fingers caught in his hair and her mouth found the rapid pulse at his throat.

Her breasts seemed to swell. She whimpered in frustration when he cupped her in his palm. He lifted his head only briefly while his hand tore at the laces on her bodice and drew the neckline of her gown off one shoulder and then the other. Cool air touched her breasts a moment before his lips replaced his hand. She arched, wanting him to take more, and he plundered her with his mouth, drawing her nipple between his teeth and lips, then giving his attention to the other. A groan vibrated deep within his chest. Stubble teased her tender flesh, arousing wondrous sensations.

She had wanted this for so long. Turning her head, she opened her eyes and absorbed the night. A wedge of light lay on the floor in front of the partially opened door. They were moving shadows on the bed, alive in the darkness, their breathing hot rasps. She relished his touch even as a part of her listened to the wind and the faraway sound of a shutter banging against the house.

His body lifted slightly as he raised her skirts and shift. He laid his palm above one garter and slid the stocking down, then moved his hand up the back of her naked thigh to the curve of her bottom, warm, possessive. He slid his hand across her hip and gently urged her legs apart, his palm lingering on that most intimate part of her. She was panting now in anxiety. His mouth returned to swallow the small sounds she made, and at the same time, he cupped her mons and slipped one finger inside her. When he inserted a second, her body contracted.

She could not see all of his face in the shadows. Her fingers curled in his shirt till the starchiness of the fabric surrounded her senses like the wind and the sound of their breathing. Citrus mingled with the redolence of hot, male sensuality and a musky scent she vaguely recognized as hers. A soft groan tore from him as he straightened and rose up on one knee. He still wore his boots. Neither of them was undressed, and she did not care.

His hands fell to his waist and she heard him tear at his breeches. He did not give his own clothing the same care as he had hers. His ragged breath, husky with want, whispered over her as he leaned his knee on the bed, bent and lifted her bottom with one hand.

Words were not needed. Only urgency defined as much by the absence of dialogue as the presence of desire. She bit back a sob of pleasure as he entered her. His lips found the curve of her neck. She relished the sensitivity of her skin. She wrapped her legs around his thighs, wanting all of the hot, pulsing length of him.

Bracing his palms on the bed, he moved against her, his powerful body rocking slowly at first, as if savoring the sweet ecstasy like one savored the rare taste of rich chocolate.

Then they were moving together. Their palms touched and she laced her fingers with his. Her breathing fragmented, an incoherent moan lost between their lips. There were no other sounds outside herself. She heard only her own body, the roar of the blood in her ears, the sound of her breath against his cheek. Glad for the darkness that kept him from seeing her face, she turned her head and kissed him and then he was kissing her deeply, catching her trembling cries until she was drowning in his arms.

Release consumed her, wrenching a cry from her throat. He left no part of her body or mind untouched, branding her senses, even as he pulled out and spilled himself beside her.

He lay in her arms with only the sound of their heartbeats between them. Now she knew what it was like to lie in his arms.

He awoke to daylight in her bed. He lay on his stomach, blankets entangled around his hips, one arm flung to the side, the other hanging slightly off the bed. He still wore his clothes, minus his boots. Twisting around, he looked outside. The wind still blew, but only an occasional gust tweaked the old bones of the cottage. Frowning, he rose and padded to the door to look into the hallway. Heather was coming up the stairs with a pitcher of water in her hands.

"My lord." She dipped. "I was just bringing this to you."

He started down the hallway to Anna's chamber. "Miss Christel has been sitting with her, my lord. They ate breakfast. The child be sleepin' comfortably."

"You should have awakened me."

"Miss Christel told us no' to. Most stern aboot it, too. Said you needed your rest. Doctor White was here earlier and said Lady Anna can travel. Miss Christel said to tell ye that she sent him back to summon your carriage so that the two of ye can join yer family for the Christ's Mass celebration tomorrow."

This was not a conversation he expected to have the morning after he made love to a woman. It sounded to him as if Christel was sending him home by way of her servant. Suddenly amused, Camden plowed his fingers through his hair. "Where *is* Miss Christel?"

"She be up on the hill overlooking the cottage. Her mam is buried there near the oak, my lord."

"You may put the water on the dresser," he said as he continued down the hall and edged open the door to Anna's chambers.

The curtains were opened slightly. Anna slept soundlessly, the sleep of health and not one influenced by opium. He eased the door shut and returned to Christel's room to wash and straighten his clothing.

Standing at the window as he laced his shirt and shoved the tail end into his breeches, he espied the oak on the hill some distance away.

A knock on the door signaled Heather's return with his other clothing, including his cloak and hat. If she suspected that Christel had been in here with him last night, her expression gave nothing away.

As he waited for her to lay his belongings on the bed, he could not help but notice a patch on the girl's threadbare sleeve. His glance took in Christel's room, the faded lace pillows and counterpane on the bed. Everything, from the wardrobe to the washstand, needed refinishing. He had noticed the same throughout the cottage, from the moth-eaten winged chairs to the wooden floors that needed a new coat of varnish.

"Heather?" He startled the girl as she started to scurry from the room like a mouse in the sights of a cat. "How is Miss Christel surviving here?"

Folding her hands, she lowered her eyes. "Miss Christel's uncle took care of the business. Ye would have to be talkin' to her—"

"I am talking to you, Heather. Captain Douglas has been dead nearly a year. Who has been paying the upkeep? Did Captain Douglas have a trust that a solicitor manages?"

"Aye, he did until the funds run out. It be Lord Leighton what has taken care of us, my lord. Takin' care of the cottage, that is."

"Leighton? In exchange for what?"

Bewilderment touched her gaze. "On account that he and Captain Douglas were friends, my lord."

"Does Miss Christel know?"

"Aye, my lord."

When he said no more, she dipped and shut the door.

He finished dressing and, after checking on Anna, left the cottage. He walked out of the yard, past the barn and paddock. His leg began to ache halfway up the snowy incline, and his boots had no traction in the snow. He stopped to catch his breath, at once hating his clumsiness.

He looked up at the blue sky. He could hear breakers crashing against the shoreline as he continued up the hill, grabbing onto a scrub bush for leverage before finally reaching the spreading oak tree on top. He looked around at a crumbling crofter's cottage nearly buried beneath a century of dead wooden vines and weeds. Christel stood on the other side of the cottage near the rock ledge overlooking the beach. She was staring out at the seagulls.

The banshee winds coming off the sea whipped her hair and cloak. She clutched it tightly beneath her chin. For centuries, such a vision had crowned the bowsprit of great ships.

He moved forward. Upon hearing his clumsy step, she turned suddenly. Sunshine had warmed the color of her hair to soft butter.

"My lord."

If he had thought today would bring shame or embarrassment to her, he'd been wrong. Her mouth lifted into a smile, and he felt something like a low current of electricity go through his veins, similar to what one felt standing on the deck of a ship in a storm. He had not felt its power in some time. To feel it now was almost like learning to walk again.

Aware of the atypical bent of his mood, he concentrated on reaching her side without slipping. But she quickly joined him beneath the naked limbs of the oak.

"I thought you would sleep longer," she said.

"The room was cold."

"I see." Again, that brilliant smile. "I thought it circumspect to let Heather find me sleeping in Anna's room this morning when everyone awakened," she said.

"Aye . . ." He tucked a slip of soft hair behind her ear. "We would not want to be plagued by gossip."

A distant church bell rang for the morning service and he looked past her. "Heather said your mother is buried up here."

She pointed to a granite marker twenty feet away. A portion around the headstone had been cleared. "'Tis fitting Papa buried her here." She looked toward the whitecapped sea. "Especially since he died somewhere out there. I do not feel she is here alone."

All his life, he had never truly understood death, except that it treated all men equally without regard to religion or class.

His fingertip slid down to her chin, urging her face up. They stood, cloaked in shadows of a passing cloud, serenaded by gusts of wind. He had forgotten to put on his gloves, and his flesh was exposed to the elements. He felt chafed, inside and out, not only by the events of the last few days but also by those of the last few years.

"I need to say something," he said.

"If 'tis an apology about last night, then I assure you the only thing you will be apologizing for one minute from now is the apology itself. I would think that last night is the sort of thing that should be normal for you," she said with a casualness he did not reciprocate.

"Define normal."

"You have mistresses—"

"Had. Singular. Not plural. Not you."

"I am not your mistress. Or lover. What happened last night was truly wonderful, *truly* remarkable, but 'twas a onetime occurrence."

He tipped her chin, trapping her in his gaze. There was nothing tranquil about him as he lifted one finger to her cheek. "Ask me to stay through spring or summer."

She pressed her lips to his chin. "Nay."

He lowered his hand, niggled by an annoyance he could not place.

"I like you," she said. "Very much. I always have. 'Tis true, you have your faults. You do not get along well with people or dogs. You tend to flee the difficulties in your life rather than conquer them." She folded her arms. "And you have sometimes shown a great deal of arrogance when it comes to your view of events. But you are a wonderful father, kind to horses, and you are an excellent sea captain."

His lips quirked. "If that is a compliment, I have suffered kinder at my own admiralty board."

Her lips softened. "Does *liking* a person not count for a start?"

"To what end? A long, enduring friendship?"

"Aye," she said quietly. "What else can there be between us? You are lord of Blackthorn Castle. I . . . I am me."

As he started to reply, she held up her finger to stop him. "You can have no true interest in me beyond the physical and you need not pretend there is more between us. Despite the fact that Lady Harriet is my grandmother, you and I will never visit the same circle of friends. I am not your peer or of your class or even a friend to your friends' friends. You will wed someone who is suitable to your rank because your title expects it of you, and I will never submit to being the mistress of a married man."

Camden stared at her. His initial impulse was to argue, especially since he had no plans to marry anyone anytime soon. But her passion-filled eyes intrigued him, and he enjoyed watching her even if she absolutely believed in her heart everything she spouted—a telling point that enabled him to consider her sentiment with remarkable patience and curiosity. He had not seen her sparked with fervor as she was now.

"Last night we needed each other," she continued, barely pausing for breath. "I admit I took advantage of the situation, but regardless, neither of us can continue with the nonsensical notion that we should do this again."

"So 'tis best to end it now."

"Aye!" She seemed impressed that he got it. "Which brings me to my point. If I asked you to stay, I would only be forcing you to confront a choice too soon and you will either come to regret the decision or your answer will be no. Either choice is a detriment to me. If you stay, I do not want it to be because of your friendship to me. Therefore, I will never ask and you will never have to tell me nay. I shall leave your future to fate."

He worked at keeping his expression unchanged. Despite her oratory on the virtues and vices of his character and relationship to her and on allowing fate to shape her life, she did not like it when she was not in control. *Too bad, my sweet*. Sometimes in battle, the only offense was an attack-and-run strategy that left the enemy confused.

"The same fate that put your uncle's ship in the bay outside Yorktown and you in the field hospital when he brought me in that day? That sent you the letter that brought you back to Scotland? The same fate that kept me in London just long enough for you to find me? Fate brought Anna to Seastone Cottage and put me alone with you last night. Seems to me fate has shadowed us for years and that last night was more an act of fate than your belief that I am so feeble that I succumbed to you out of weakness."

Her gaze was now watchful as his own assessment lingered, and he could see she was suddenly wondering what he saw beneath the surface. Past her barely combed hair pinned atop her head and sprouting short unruly curls flirting with the wind. Past yesterday's brown woolen dress, one that she had not yet altered from wherever she had procured the thing, for it was much too tight across her bosoms. Tighter now as she found herself short of air, as if wanting to breathe deeply.

He pinned her between the tree and his arms, his mouth curved into an unholy smile. "Fortunately for you, I have to return to Blackthorn Castle," he said.

"I know. 'Tis the beginning of Christmastide and Anna needs her family. I sent for your coach."

"You can join me."

She made an exasperated sound. "I am spending Christmas with Blue and Heather's family. They have already invited me."

He took a moment to assess the statement. Despite what she thought of him, he did understand the social impediment she faced. What she did not understand was that none of that mattered to him. But her grandmother would be in Prestwick, where she'd spent most of her time these past years at the orphanage she sponsored. Blackthorn Castle would not be free of guests, some who might not welcome her.

He lifted his gaze and hers followed to the mistletoe hanging from the branches above their heads. "Tomorrow is Christmas," he said.

"My lord . . ."

"Camden," he said against her lips. "My name is Camden."

He bent his head and kissed her, her lips still so unfamiliar yet so completely intimate, so flagrantly carnal they left his limbs weak. With the light weight of his thumb, he rolled her lip down, suckling lightly, and the sensation of her washed over him, unhampered by self-censure.

Then there was nothing but Camden St. Giles kissing her, slipping his tongue between her teeth and feeding her groan with one of his own. He plundered just as he had last night and she let him, allowing his caged emotions unfettered rein—if only for now, for this minute.

Time would have spun away if not for the intrusive sound of an approaching coach, still some distance away, but close enough to bring reality back into play to remind him where they were. With reluctance, he lifted his head. But this time he could read much more than his own desire reflected in her eyes. There was yearning there, the unfurling of passions awakened. He could feel the beat of her in his blood. He was already hard and, inwardly groaning, he found he wanted more of what she had given him last night.

His hands lowering to her skirts, he felt her shiver and

move against him, and he felt the primal thrill of it rise in his veins. "I . . . I do not want to need you," she said against his ear.

"I know." His words were gravelly, his breath hot against hers. He was already unlacing his breeches, insensible to the cold, wrapped as he was in her warmth. "I do not want to need you either."

He lowered his head and she raised on her toes to meet him halfway, pressing her soft lips to his. "This is good-bye, then," she said, stating that everything would return to the way it was between them.

"Aye."

His hands were beneath her cloak and he touched her through the thick fabric of her gown, pushing her backward with the slightest pressure, all thought beyond this moment disappearing from his mind as she slipped her tongue against his.

Then he was lifting her, holding her with the weight of his arm, bending his legs to enter her, her back against the tree. Fighting the staggering impulse to sigh in pleasure, he moved against her, inside her, filling her, forcing her entire weight upward. His mouth closed over hers with self-indulgent temperance he was unused to feeling, and he could not slow the rhythm of movements. Yet her passion equaled his and she held him tightly, her ragged breaths beside his ear, consuming him, until he let satiation claim them both.

Chapter 10

⟨❧⟩

"**Y**ou are out of practice, Carrick. I have outscored you twice."

Camden's expression remained sober behind his leather-and-mesh mask. He sliced the air with his foil. "Are you telling me you are exhausted, Westmont? One more go-round. Supper is not for another hour, my friend."

"Friend, indeed," he replied. "What kind of friend am I to kill you twice in one day?"

Camden laughed. "Merciful."

His riposte drove Camden back and around the floor. Yorktown might have left Camden less agile, but he had not lost his reflexes. At the very least, he had mostly held his own for the last hour, and it was all he could expect against a master like Jacob.

Tempered by a capricious mood since his daughter's return to Blackthorn, Camden had thrown himself into physical activity. Anything to alleviate the restlessness that seemed to have been driving him these past weeks since his return from Seastone Cottage. Sweat trickled from his brow and he welcomed the cold breeze as he passed an open window. Outside, snow had started falling again. Jacob and his family had arrived last night to celebrate Twelfth Night as he did every year. With the exception of last year, Jacob had been coming to Blackthorn Castle for over a decade.

A man in his midforties, he was a mentor, as well as a longtime friend and business partner, a Loyalist to the core of his being, a magistrate, and a political ally, one of the few who had remained steadfastly at Carrick's side for most of the past ten years.

"I understand Anna is recovering from her ordeal," Westmont said.

"She is up and out of bed, wreaking havoc with the servants, who have spoiled her mercilessly."

"I heard Miss Douglas has visited here twice since Anna's return," Sir Jacob said too casually. "Are you sure that is wise?"

Camden missed his timing, parrying too late. Westmont nicked him again in the chest. Fortunately, a protective leather vest covered his white shirt. "Unless your heart is made of stone, Carrick, you are dead a third time."

Camden slid off the mask. "Aye, Jacob. The match is yours." He tossed the foil to a footman standing on the floor's perimeter. *But stone his heart was not.*

"Your leg has been troubling you?" Westmont asked as Camden limped to the table where the other fencing gear lay.

Camden tugged at the laces on his leather vest and removed it. Sweat dampened his shirt and hair. The footman brought him a ladle filled with ice water from a pitcher, and he drank.

"More so in this weather," he said over the rim of the

ladle, then tipped it back as if it had contained a needed draft of whiskey.

"Count yourself fortunate you have both your life and your limb. You could easily have lost both."

"Ahh. Ever the optimist to see the bright side of everything." Camden dabbed his brow with the back of his arm and studied his friend. "Why the interest in Christel Douglas, Jacob?" His tone was cool.

"I do not need to remind you that her uncle was a blockade runner. Many here were loyal to the colonial cause. Just because that conflict has ended does not mean illegal activities have ceased."

"Her uncle is dead."

"But your brother is very much alive. He is running with a rough crowd some years now and is still a suspect in the gold theft three years ago that left six of my men dead. Rumor is that Christel Douglas was his contact in the colonies. They are closer than she lets on, Carrick."

Camden leaned against the table. "As much as my brother and I disagree on certain issues, he did not murder those men, Jacob."

"How can you be so sure in light of the recent events?"

"Four of them were Scotsmen. One was a friend."

Westmont dropped his towel on the table beside the water pitcher. "Your judgment has already been thrown into question by many in Parliament, Carrick. You do not want to find yourself defending the wrong sort of people."

Camden swore. "I am not defending Leighton's character.

But he is no murderer, and Miss Douglas has no connection to him here."

Westmont raised his hands palms out. "If I did not trust your integrity, I would not be in business with you. To that point, I have been able to arrange for you to meet with a dozen wool merchants next month in Glasgow. Your ship is there being refitted. It will give the investors a chance to view what you have to offer."

He wanted the shipping contracts. "This could be a boon for Blackthorn. I need this."

"Have I told you my eldest daughter will be traveling with us?"

Ah, Camden thought. *The crux of this conversation emerges.* Sir Jacob's wife had passed some years ago, leaving him with two pretty daughters, the oldest of marriageable age.

"Catherine is twenty and beautiful," her father said. "She still has all her teeth and she comes with a plump dowry. She would make a suitable Carrick countess."

"Jaysus, Jacob, you sound like an old horse trader."

The smile Westmont offered was faintly rueful. "Have pity on me. I will spend my afterlife in purgatory if I do not find suitable husbands for my daughters. Do you know there is a shortage of decent candidates in all Britain? Think of it. Their dowries are the land my family owns. Not many appreciate the value of good Scottish earth."

Camden knew that Westmont wanted a match between his eldest and a Carrick lord. The marriage made sense, as it would bring a large chunk of pastureland into the Carrick fold, something the estate needed if it was to remain economically viable into the new century. It was the reason why Camden had decided to go to Glasgow next month.

It was not that Camden disliked outright the opportunity for another sort of alliance. Westmont's daughter was petite and unassuming. Eager to please because it was expected of her.

Yet, strangely, her biddable nature held no interest for him. She might have possessed the necessary background required to make an admirable Carrick bride, but Camden found marrying merely to produce an heir distasteful. Perhaps because he still held to the old-fashioned notion of fidelity and honoring thy vows—honoring vows was what he did best, after all—he could not see himself spending his life with her.

But a part of him knew that he needed to either break free of the invisible chains drowning him or go down with the proverbial ship and accept his life as it was and live within the strictures and duties required of him. Except he had already tried that route and failed.

Perhaps that was why something inside him responded to Christel. She stood outside the circle of society. Even as a young girl, she had been independent and possessed an ability to poke her thumb in the eye of society. Of course, one is freest when no one holds expectations of you. He wondered what life would have been like living if he'd been *that* free.

"There are more laudable gentlemen than I," Camden

said, "who can appreciate what you are offering. But I am not ready."

"You are not in a position to sit idly by and leave Blackthorn without an heir. Unless you count Leighton in that category. Saundra has been dead over a year, Carrick—"

"*Christ*, man. If you value the tenuous ground on which you stan—"

A rap on the door mercifully halted their conversation. Camden's butler entered, appearing harried. Behind him, Lady Harriet, Christel's spry grandmother, appeared.

"My lord, Lady Harriet requests an audience—"

"He knows who I am, Smolich," Lady Harriet said, edging the butler aside with her lethal cane. "You may dispense with formalities. We are all family here."

Smolich puffed his chest, looking much like an angry penguin, dressed as he was in formal black with a pristine white shirt beneath his jacket. "I asked that she await you in the drawing room, my lord. She refused."

"The drawing room is much too drafty to await your convenience, Carrick. I would die of lung fever 'ere you ever found the time to grace me with your presence."

Camden nodded to the butler. "You may go, Smolich. We are well armed enough in here to protect ourselves if the need should arise."

"Indeed, Carrick!" Lady Harriet snapped, glaring at the butler. "Do not encourage the man's impertinence."

With a smug glare at Lady Harriet, the butler turned squarely and strode from the salon, leaving the door open behind him.

Lady Harriet opened her mouth to speak. The sound of water being poured into a cup interrupted her, and her gaze homed in on Sir Jacob standing casually at the table. "'Taint the done thing to eavesdrop on a private conversation, Jacob. Shame on you."

"Aye, my lady," he deferred with a bow of his head. "I was thinking the very same thing."

Camden gave Westmont a brief nod. "We can conclude our business later."

Camden followed Westmont to the door, shutting it behind the provost. Putting Jacob's conversation to the back of his mind for now, Camden leaned against his palms as he considered his grandmother's longtime friend, and Christel and Tianna's grandmother.

Even leaning on a cane, Lady Harriet was a formidable woman, with a shock of henna-dyed hair and diamond-hard eyes that seemed their sharpest only when she looked at him. She wore black bombazine, a monument to her widowhood, as if she thought anyone around her could forget the undying love she bore her husband. More often than not, Camden suspected it was she who needed the reminder. As if moving on with her life was akin to a sin, and that moving forward meant forgetting the past. He could have told her that assertion was wrong.

He walked to the table and took up a cup and the water pitcher, wishing he'd had something stronger to pour. "Lady Harriet," he said, lifting his cup in salute to her, "to what do I owe the pleasure of your visit today?"

"You are an impertinent one, Carrick. I just had tea with

your grandmother, and she said that you asked Christel to be Anna's tutor. Why is she not here, then?"

He scrubbed a hand over his face. "I have no control over your granddaughter, my lady."

"She would rather live at that cottage alone in a state of destitution rather than live here or at Rosecliffe?"

He studied the clear liquid in his cup before taking a draft. "She is not alone. When Heather and Blue McTavish are not there, she has a dog with her. A vicious dog with snarling yellow teeth. He is protective of her. *I* cannot even go near her without fearing for my life."

Lady Harriet eyed him over her powdered nose. "Because he does not like you only makes him smart."

"I cannot agree with you more," he said, "which is why I did not throw the mutt overboard the first time he curled his lip at me."

Obviously studying him, Lady Harriet laid both her gloved hands over the polished wooden hook of her cane and held it tightly, despite the fact that one hand was bent and gnarled with rheumatism. "Surely, there is something that can be done for her," she prodded.

"What is it you expect me to do? I cannot help her if she does not ask, and she will not take charity. If you know her at all, you would know that she would hate me and you for it."

Lady Harriet's mouth tightened, the first hint of real emotion he had glimpsed in her. "We have not got along for some time now, Carrick," she said. "'Tis not easy to undo what has been said between us. You have not even attended church since Saundra died."

"I am not seeking any absolution, my lady," he said without inflection. "I found my closure months ago."

"Pah! Emotions are not candles that can be snuffed out at one's convenience. She is the mother of your child. Do not tell me she did not break your heart. Or that you did not break hers."

"I doubt you have come in here to lecture me about my heart or lack of soul. I get that from my own grandmother."

Anna's voice sounded from the hallway just before the door flung open. "Grams! You have finally come to see me!"

A winded Mrs. Gables appeared behind Anna. Holding a hand to her ribs, she leaned against the door frame, red-faced and huffing from exertion. "My apologies, my lord," she gasped. "Lady Harriet. The child heard you were here and escaped the nursery."

Lady Harriet held out her cane to stop Anna from flinging herself forward. "Let me see you. Goodness. I thought you would still be abed."

Anna held out her pink dress as she demurely curtseyed. "Good afternoon, Grams. I am much better."

Lady Harriet's gaze took in the bare feet. "Running about barefoot. I should have known. And after your accident, too. Where are your shoes?"

"Papa said if I do not wish to wear shoes, then I do not have to. Is that not correct, Papa?"

"Truly, Carrick. 'Tis not the done thing for a growing girl, running about like a hoyden."

Anna flung herself against Lady Harriet. "I know, Grams.

But I wanted to see you. I *had* to see you. It has been ever so many days. Did you bring my surprise?"

Lady Harriet's arms went around Anna. "Dear me. Of course." Withdrawing a tin from a pocket within her skirts, she smiled. "I brought your favorite gumdrops."

"Has she eaten her supper?" Camden asked Mrs. Gables.

"Cook served brisket, Papa. I dislike brisket. Mrs. Gables said I was to eat it anyway so as not to hurt cook's feelings. But I did not want to."

"I will see what cook can do about the matter," Lady Harriet said before Camden could respond. "But first we will return to your rooms for your shoes. You are like ice."

Camden let them leave together before turning his attention to Mrs. Gables in the doorway. "Last week she wanted nothing but brisket," the nurse said in apology. "Cook made brisket."

"If she does not want to eat brisket, I see no reason to force the issue. Have cook make what she wants."

"In my experience when giving in to children's demands—"

"She needs to eat," he said. "Surely, it cannot be too much to feed her something she likes."

"If you wish, my lord. Be there anything else?"

He came to his feet. "You visited Miss Douglas yesterday," he said. "Did she accept the blankets and foodstuffs you brought her?"

The color rose in Mrs. Gable's cheeks. "She told me to take everything to St. Abigal's, where it was needed. I meant to tell you—"

"Was she angry?"

"I attempted to inform her that you had nothing to do with the donation, but she would not believe me."

"Hmm. And the horse left in her stable?"

"I believe she just gave up trying to return it, since she had already done so twice before."

Little steps, he thought with some satisfaction, that he could find even a minute way to make her life a bit easier. At the very least, every time she returned the horse, she gave him an opportunity to see her, and her presence lightened Anna's face.

He stepped through the door into the corridor, then turned on his heel to face the nurse. "I have known you for eight years. I trust your judgment when it comes to my daughter. I did not mean to imply otherwise. If cook made brisket for Anna out of kindness to please my daughter, then Anna should appreciate the gesture."

"Thank you, my lord."

Camden retired to his private chambers to bathe and change out of his sparring attire. Later that evening, dinner was served promptly at eight. Sir Jacob's daughters, Lady Harriet and Tia were in attendance, as was his grandmother.

He barely remembered the last occasion at which his entire family had spent time together, except when Saundra had been alive and had been able to get him and his father and brother in the same room together.

It had been her gift to bring cheer to a room full of people, he realized.

He lifted his gaze past the pianoforte to her wedding

portrait. It hung in all its golden glory above the marble fireplace, her grace and beauty forever immortalized in a tapestry of oils and canvas.

Lady Harriet's words scrolled through his mind. *"Do not tell me she did not break your heart. Or that you did not break hers."*

Aye, Saundra still haunted him in ways he would have never thought possible. She had ripped his heart from his chest and died with it clutched in her fist.

And had left him with a little girl, one who would soon be waltzing on the cusp of womanhood, that misunderstood age between childhood and motherhood. God forbid that she should experience the latter before finishing the former. Or that he would fail her as he had his wife.

Indeed, there were a hundred reasons why he spent so little time at Blackthorn Castle, why he did not want to be around come spring, when the earth came back to life and the weather warmed and his soul would begin to thaw in places he wanted only to keep frozen.

But there was only one reason why he would stay.

By the time Christel found her father's old solicitor in Maybole, she thought her feet and hands might drop off from the cold. Even wearing gloves, her hands were frozen. With the dog following on her heels, she pushed aside the gate into his yard. She had spent time here when she was a little girl. The house was smaller than she remembered and needed a new coat of whitewash. The path leading to the front door was in want of crushed stone, and she stepped over a rut. But the porch was solid and the door was oak. Using the knocker, she made her presence known.

A gray-haired man appeared in the doorway. A broadsheet tucked beneath his arm, he peered over his spectacles at her. "May I help you?" The door opened wider. "Miss Douglas?"

Christel stood with her cloak tightly clasped to her. "I am sorry to bother you, Mr. McGinnis. I was not sure if you would know me."

"Aye, lass. Look at ye, a young woman now, but I would know ye, Miss Douglas. You have the look of your dear mam in your eyes."

"Thank you, Mr. McGinnis."

"Come, lass. Come inside. Standing out here in the cold." Holding the door open, he stood aside. "May I get you hot tea?"

"Nay, that is not necessary."

He closed the door, inviting her into his library. The room smelled of musty tomes and cigars. Mr. McGinnis had been her father's solicitor in charge of the trust that had been set up to manage Seastone Cottage. From what she remembered, he had also been a trusted friend. "I thank you for seeing me."

He walked around the desk. "Will you sit?"

Christel sat on the chair facing the desk. He settled in his own chair and waited for her to speak her business. She withdrew a placard from her reticule and spread it on his desk. Today it was this tax notice nailed to her front door that had brought her to Maybole. "I am in need of funds,

Mr. McGinnis. I know Papa had a special trust he specifi-
cally set up for Seastone Cottage. I came today in hopes
that something might still be available." Christel closed her
hand around her necklace chain. "I did not know where
else to go."

"I am sorry, lass." He pushed away from the desk and
went to a shelf at the back of the room, returning with ledger
books. "I have kept records of all transactions. I paid out the
last of the monies six months ago. I am sorry I could not
give you better news, Miss Douglas."

This was not the visit she had wanted to have when she'd
left Seastone Cottage this morning. Her hands tightened on
the necklace. She had spent a week tabulating figures, deciding how much longer she could live at Seastone with no
viable income. If she could not solve this problem herself,
she would be forever dependent on the charity of others for
her survival.

Clearing her throat, she forced her fingers to relax. Circumstances bid her to go forward. "You were a good friend
to my father. He always trusted you."

"I would like to think I served him well."

Making a decision to trust him, too, she reached behind
her and unlocked the clasp on her necklace, letting the gold
coin drop into her palm. "Can you tell me what this might
be worth?"

She slid the coin across the desk. He took it to the window
for better light. A frown formed between his brows. He
looked back at her.

"Where did ye get this, lass?"

"Is it valuable?"

"Its value is twenty-five shillings per coin, the same as any other gold coin today. Still more than most people here earn in a month, to be sure. But 'tis not why this coin is unique."

Christel stood as he invited her around into the light. He scraped his thumb across its face. "The millage was changed to produce the shape of a chevron arrowhead. This coin has the mark of the East India Company still visible. The last of these old hammered coinages were melted down a decade ago. This is a rare coin. Rare enough that spending it anywhere in Ayrshire will bring the provost's dragoons to your doorstep, lass. You best be able to tell him where that came from."

Her mouth went dry. "The coin was sent to me in a letter from a friend."

He sat back behind his desk. "Some years ago a shipment of old gold coinage vanished from one of His Majesty's ships in Prestwick. By anyone's estimates the stolen gold was worth twenty thousand pounds. Every so often a coin like this one surfaces and raises questions."

"Twenty thousand! But if anyone here had that kind of money . . ."

"A person can no' hide that manner of wealth unless 'tis literally hidden in a cave somewhere and forgotten. But I have always been under the notion the coins were melted down to bullion."

"Then 'tis possible the coin is merely random. Sent to me for funds. There must be some still in circulation."

He slid the coin back to her. " 'Tis possible. But the crime is still unsolved."

"Mr. McGinnis, I do not know what this coin means, if it even means anything. But twenty-five shillings will purchase enough feed and supplies to last the winter for me. At least until I can find employment. I was a rather good seamstress in Williamsburg." She slid the coin back to him across the desk. "If you can help me cash this, I will give you—"

"Nay, lass." He laid his hand across hers. " 'Tis dangerous times. An accusation of sedition has hanged more than one man. Smuggling rum is seditious activity these days. Your uncle was an enemy of England. You are his heir. I would have to explain why I had the coin, and we could both be arrested."

"I need the money, Mr. McGinnis. Is there someone you can trust?"

He shook his head. Christel understood fear of authority better than most. But his fear went beyond the mere possibility of being interrogated by the provost and his men. She laid her gloved hand across his. "I thank you for seeing me today, Mr. McGinnis. Please believe me when I say that I did not mean to upset you."

His fingers closed around hers. "This is no' the same place in which ye grew up, lass. Much has changed since the provost has come into power. And Lord Carrick be his friend, mum." A warning?

After wrapping the accounting ledgers for her, he walked her into the foyer and helped her into her cloak. "I am sorry I could not be of more use."

As he opened the door, her gaze fell on the portraiture of an older woman she remembered was his wife.

"She died two months ago." A smile tipped the corners of his mouth. "We were married thirty years, Miss Douglas."

"My condolences on your loss, Mr. McGinnis."

"We had no children," he said, gazing at the image, as if his world lived inside that painted piece of canvas.

"Maybole is not so far from Seastone Cottage," she said. "If I may, I would like to visit here on occasion." To reassure herself that he had someone to look after him. "Perhaps you would allow me to go through your broadsheets. I noticed you had stacks of newspapers against the wall. 'Twould give me a chance to catch up on the news of the area."

"I would welcome the visit, lass." Hands sliding into his pockets, he said, "Ye might get three guineas for that gold chain in your hand. I know 'tis no' much, but it can get ye through the next few weeks. A jeweler could help ye. There be one in the square." He glanced over her shoulder at the sky. "Ye best be headed home soon, though. A storm is coming."

Christel thanked him with a kiss on the cheek. As the door closed shut behind her, she tucked both the gold chain and the coin into the pocket she'd sewn into her skirt, wondering what madness Saundra might have got herself into. If Saundra had been involved in a gold theft, Christel was sure Leighton had to have been involved. She was also sure she needed to visit Blackthorn Castle for answers.

Christel slipped past the picket fence to where her scruffy hound sat on the road. His tail thumped the ground as he glanced quickly at her, but turning his head again, he resumed his vigilance, as if something up the crowded street had grabbed his attention. Kneeling beside him, she followed his gaze. "What is it, Dog?"

His tail thumped faster and he barked. She glimpsed a black lacquered coach sitting in front of the notions shop. Anna and Mrs. Gables had already descended. Christel started to stand when another woman briskly alighted from the coach. *Tia*.

Christel rose to her feet. A large leghorn straw hat sat prettily over her sister's sable curls, its wide brim blocking much of her profile. Festooned with pink ribbons, the hat made her look all sweet and innocent, like a character straight from *Little Red Riding Hood*. Her rust-red redingote and the basket she carried over her forearm did much to enhance the image. Holding Anna's hand, Tia smiled down at the child as they moved toward the shop.

Dog barked and whined. Before Christel could grab his scruff, he launched himself across the crowded street, barely missing being run down by a beer wagon, with Christel running after him. Even as she called to the errant hound, she could hear Anna's squeal of excitement. Pulling from Tia's grip and ignoring Mrs. Gable's horrified warnings, Anna ran forward, and, dropping to her knees in unladylike abandon, opened her arms to the hound. Dog licked her face and hair.

Anna raised her head at Christel's undignified approach and smiled brightly. "He looks much better than before, Miss Christel," she said approvingly. "I think he has been eating well. I can no longer feel his ribs."

"Fortunately for him, Seastone Cottage has an abundant rabbit population."

Adjusting her bonnet, Christel greeted Mrs. Gables and, as Anna's reunion with Dog continued undeterred by the cold wind or curious onlookers, faced Tia. Christel's uncertain smile of greeting went unreturned. Very well, she thought. So be it. Though she had once held out hope that they could be like real sisters, Tia clearly had no want to share that desire, and Christel did not have the stamina to try.

Doctor White approached from the carriage. "Miss Douglas." He carried his black leather physician's bag beneath his cloak. "Have you walked to Maybole?"

"I have a horse at the livery down the street. I should be leaving." Looking down at Anna, who seemed content enough in the brisk cold as she rubbed Dog's tummy, Christel wanted to inquire about the child's father.

"You *must* bring Dog to Blackthorn more often," Anna said. "Especially since Papa is leaving next week for Glasgow."

"He is going away?"

"For a while."

Tia readjusted her redingote against the cold breeze. Christel realized she was keeping them all outside.

"Snow is coming," Mrs. Gables said, stomping her feet for warmth, and taking Anna's hand.

Christel tweaked the pink bow on the girl's bonnet. "I shall visit soon. I promise."

Anna's face brightened, and she looked to a place behind

Christel. "Did you hear, Papa? She has agreed to visit."

Lord Carrick stepped onto the cobbled walk behind her, the force of his presence filling the air like the gathering clouds above her. Her heart flip-flopped against her ribs. He had not been present a moment ago, so he must have just crossed the street. He wore a heavy cloak and tricorn, and his cheeks were ruddy from the cold. He carried packages, which he gave to an attending footman even as he kept a red tin box in his hand.

"Miss Douglas," he said in greeting.

"Papa! You visited the candy shop."

Stepping around Christel, he lifted Anna so she could procure the anticipated treasure in his palm. "I could not find gumdrops, but I did find horehound on my way back from the warehouse."

Looking perfectly at ease in his daughter's company, surrounded by her laughter, he flipped off the lid and revealed six large pieces. "Oh, Papa! Thank you!" She placed a piece of candy between her lips, then gave one to Mrs. Gables, Tia, Doctor White and Christel. "One for you, too, Papa."

"Hmm." A dimple creased one side of his mouth as he sucked on the drop. "Bitter." He looked curiously from Christel to Tia. "We are having a reunion? Outside in the cold?"

"I was just taking Anna inside the shop, my lord," Tia said.

"I was on my way to the livery," Christel said at the same time.

He said something to Mrs. Gables, then set Anna down. "Now, off with you, pup. Find something for your great-grandmamma to appease her while I am away." His gaze touched the darkening sky. "You have about an hour left before you need to be back in the coach."

Without looking at Christel, Tia took Anna inside the notions shop. Mrs. Gables smiled kindly at Christel and followed. Doctor White bowed to her. "If I may, I have a patient to see and will escort you to the livery on my way, Miss Doug—"

"Unnecessary, White," Lord Carrick said before Christel could respond. "Make your rounds. If you wish to return to Blackthorn Castle, you need to be back to this coach before the snow begins."

"Aye, my lord."

Clutching her accounting ledgers tightly to her chest, Christel watched him leave. Almost reluctantly, she lifted her gaze to Lord Carrick's. "You are presumptuous, my lord."

"Aye," he agreed. "I am. Did you come to Maybole alone?"

She pivoted on her heel. "Nay, I did not." Christel called Dog and started walking to the livery.

Lord Carrick hooked his arm around hers, turning her. "The livery is this way."

Of course it was. She drew in her breath and changed direction. "You are leaving soon?" she asked after a moment. "Will you be returning?"

"I am leaving my daughter behind. What do you think?"

"Then you will be staying or returning to London?"

He chuckled. "Are you asking as my *friend* or my future lover?"

She glared at him. Touching her elbow, he shouldered his way across a busy street, stopping once as a coach thundered past. Warmth from his fingertips seeped through the fabric of her gown.

"That depends on why you are traveling to Glasgow."

"Strictly a financial endeavor. Business."

At the edge of town, the population had thinned and she slowed their pace. "I never gave you an answer when you asked that I tutor Anna," she said. He stopped, forcing her to stop as well and face him.

Her arms tightened around the ledgers. She felt uncertain because of what she had learned about Saundra and the gold coin.

"The offer is still open," he said.

She sensed restraint as he awaited her reply. His nearness made her uneasy, but only because he made her aware of herself. These past weeks, since their meeting on the hill above the cottage, she had thought of him constantly. He came to her in her dreams when she slept and her thoughts when awake. She did not want her reasons for going to Blackthorn Castle to be only so that she would be nearer to him. Taking a job also gave her purpose. She desperately needed the income.

"I pay well," he finally said.

She narrowed her eyes. "How well?"

"The deed to your cottage. Something to consider."

"I should have known that you cannot help but be deliberately provocative."

"Aye." His fingertips came alongside her cheek and,

exerting only the slightest pressure, he tilted her head to meet his gaze. "But an honest provocateur."

He smelled a little like citrus, too, warm like sunlight, and a pleasure sharp and sweet sliced through her. "Lord in heaven, you are an ass," she rasped.

He laughed. "I am not going to kiss you," he said. "I would hate to make you suffer by actually enjoying it. You will have to wait for me to return from Glasgow."

Two hours later, Camden watched from a distant hill as Christel reined in the black gelding at the top of the rise overlooking her home. Heavy clouds shrouded the coastline. Snow had begun to fall, leaving a blanket of white covering the windswept landscape.

Seastone Cottage squatted on ten acres below her, a small piece of paradise her mother and father had carved out of the land. The cottage was a pretty house, with its stone walls and thatched roof, three stories if one counted the attic rooms. A garden once stretched along the southern exposure. On a clear day, a person could look north and see the dark towers of Blackthorn Castle. He watched as she looked that way now, toward him, and he felt a visceral tug the moment her gaze touched his.

Silhouetted against the turbulent sky, Camden sat astride his horse. A black cloak twined around him and draped his mount. As he saw her pause, his horse pranced sideways. He was too far away for her to see his face or for him to see hers.

He did not remain long in his vigilance of her. He reined his horse around, and now he needed to reach Blackthorn

Castle before the storm. But he caught himself hesitating, pulling at the reins of the horse, at once stirred by the primal power of the world laid before him.

The same way he felt when on the deck of his ship, drawn to the view, to the raw elemental sensation that came as he looked out over the sea and drank in the sheer incredible beauty of it. And in that moment, he knew why she loved it here.

This place. This land. It was in his blood, too.

He had just forgotten.

Chapter 11

─────◯◯◯─────

Lord Carrick had been gone a month when a rare bout of winter sunlight took Christel and Anna to the ballroom, a beautiful empty place with tall windows and glass doors. After an attempt to teach Anna needlepoint had met with dismal failure last week, Christel hoped to impart upon her young protégée the art of watercolors.

"Why can't Dog come inside?" Anna asked for the second time.

Christel leaned on a tall painter's stool, her gown protected by a smock and her vision partially obstructed by the canvas in front of her. A bowl filled with plump fake apples, grapes and oranges shared a display with one of Anna's curly-haired dolls.

"Dog is in the barn, Anna. He cannot come inside because the last time he did, he broke a valuable vase chasing after you. I warned you he would be the one to get into trouble if something untoward occurred."

"What if Dog freezes and we do not find him until spring?" Anna asked. "Will you not be sad?"

"Aye," Christel agreed, smearing her brush in red and orange pigment. "I would be horror-struck."

Anna thrust out her bottom lip, a gesture that Christel was fast coming to recognize as a pout. She ignored it and without rebuking the girl said, "I promised your grandmother I would not allow him anywhere near *anything* that is of value, which includes everything at Blackthorn Castle. Your behavior has consequences, Anna."

"When is Papa returning?"

Swishing her paintbrush in water, Christel swiped the loose hairs from her face with her free hand. "How many weeks are in a month?" she asked, bringing in a hated arithmetic lesson. Mrs. Gables had informed Christel only last week that Anna was refusing to do her lessons, which was one of the reasons Christel had decided to come more often to Blackthorn Castle.

Awaiting a reply, Christel lifted her head and peered at Anna, who stood momentarily defiant. "Four weeks are in a month," Anna said. "Except in February, which is shy four weeks by two days."

Anna had her merits, to be sure. She was excellent with numbers.

"Your papa is due back the last week in March. If three weeks and five days have passed since your papa's departure, what does that leave before his return?"

Anna rolled her eyes. "Three weeks and two days, Miss Christel."

Christel resisted a smile. "Now tomorrow, when you are bored and ask me when your papa will be home, you will already know the answer."

"But I shall perish of boredom before he returns."

The child was still young and tender and full of her own self-importance, and not used to being told no. But Christel knew Anna pushed because she could, and Christel had definitely worked up a tolerance to the patter of young angst these days.

"Perhaps I should set you to the task of writing a novel," Christel said without looking up. "You have a definite flair for large words and drama. I am impressed. Truly."

"Papa does not force me to do anything I do not wish to do."

"Methinks sometimes Papas spoil their daughters too much."

"But I do not *like* watercolors."

Folding her arms, Christel walked behind Anna and observed the girl's work with a critical eye. "That is unfortunate. Especially since you are quite inventive with your lines and rather creative with your colors. I have never seen such a unique apple."

"Grams thought it was an orange. And Grandmama said 'twas a croquet ball."

"Hmm." Christel managed not to laugh lest her reaction be misconstrued. "It *could* pass for a croquet ball, I suppose. But most definitely 'tis not an orange."

Anna suddenly giggled. They shared a smile. Christel went back to her own canvas.

"Do all ladies have to know how to paint and sing and dance and do needlepoint?"

"Yes."

"Were *you* a lady?"

"When I was your age, I wanted to be a lady more than anything in the world."

"Why?"

"Because only a real lady could marry a prince."

"What happened?"

Christel lowered her paintbrush and found herself remembering this ballroom in its golden glory days. She could almost hear the music. The unfinished chapter in her life had suddenly become a book that she had yet to close. "The prince married someone else, and I knew I had to find a way to take care of myself."

"Truly? Were you sad?"

"To grow up? Who does not want to believe in fairy tales forever?" Christel turned. "I know 'tis hard, Anna, but you cannot let yourself quit every time something becomes difficult or does not go your way. How will you ever learn to believe in yourself?"

Anna picked up her paintbrush. "Miss Christel?" she asked after a long moment. "Am I bad?"

"Absolutely not. Why would you say such a thing?"

"Because Uncle Leighton has not come to see me. He was not here for the Christmastide supper. He has not been to church with us. He did not say good-bye, Miss Christel."

Christel swished her brush in water. "He had to go away, Anna."

"Did Papa make him go just like before?"

"Your Uncle Leighton is a grown man. Wherever he is, he is fine. In fact, he has probably written to you, but the post just has not arrived."

The corners of Anna's mouth turned up as she considered this. "'Tis only that I miss him. He plays marbles and jackstraws and takes me ice sliding with skates. He tells me the best bedtime stories. I want him to teach me how to ride my pony."

Christel gently wiped the hair from Anna's cheek, but she made no reply, though she was wont to do so with anger at Leighton. 'Twas a simple matter to win the affection of an eight-year-old child when all a person had to do was play games and bring presents. He had been quick enough to disappear without saying good-bye or sending a note to the girl.

"I *do* know that your papa loves you," she said quietly. "He allowed you to stay here with your great-grandmamma, did he not? When he returns, ask *him* to read you a story. If he does not know how to play jackstraws or marbles, offer to teach him. Tell him you want to learn how to ride your pony. What did he say in his letter to you?"

From the outset, Christel had not inquired after Lord Carrick because such an inquiry would have demonstrated an unseemly interest in the master of the manse. She still managed to learn by listening to others talk, but this time she found herself wanting to ask Anna about the letter the girl had received yesterday.

"Your papa must have said a lot. The letter was quite long."

Anna shrugged a thin shoulder. "Papa mostly wrote that I was not to give you worry wrinkles and gray hair, but that if you asked what he wrote to me in my letters that I am to tell you that he would think you are very pretty even if you *did* have gray hair."

Christel felt heat crawl up her neck. Anna cracked an impish smile. "I think he likes you, or he would not have told Grandmamma to allow you to come here." She studied Christel with earnest blue-gray eyes. "Are you my governess?"

Christel set down her paintbrush. "I am only your tutor, and only until your papa returns. I stay here when the weather or time of day does not allow me to walk home. But my home is Seastone Cottage."

"Cousin Tianna said that she is your half sister. If that is true, why do you not live with Grams and her at Rosecliffe?"

"Seastone Cottage is my home, Anna."

"Will you live at Seastone all by yourself *forever*?" Anna asked. "Why can you not live *here* forever and be my governess?"

"Because nothing lasts forever. What I mean . . . is that one day, you will be all grown up and have a family of your own. You will not need me anymore." She tipped her chin at Anna's watercolor. "Now put a stem on that apple so I can teach you something much more fun."

Anna looked uncertain. Christel placed the watercolors back into their tins. "In the real world people learn skills to survive."

"You mean like learning how to shoot a pistol and to fish?"

Christel laughed. "We can do that when the weather warms. How would you like to design and make a real dress for your doll?"

Making doll clothes would involve not only learning how to sketch creations from one's own imagination but also arithmetic to properly measure and make patterns. And Christel had gotten the urge to draw again.

Anna's blue eyes perked with interest. "Can my doll be a real fairy princess?"

"She can be whatever you want. That is the beauty of using your imagination. Your dreams become real."

Christel's chambers at Blackthorn Castle were on the third floor at the opposite end of the sprawling estate where she had spent her first night. The room was in the same wing but one floor up from the chambers that Lord Carrick had once shared with Saundra. The corridor joined to his floor by a garret staircase near Anna's nursery, which the child shared with Mrs. Gables. One window at the end of the hall overlooked the cove and a crow colony that had taken nest in the old battlements.

Every day as she passed the nursery, Christel stopped at the window to look out at the cove. Tonight clouds drifted across the sky, blotting out the stars. Water and sky blended as one, and she could see nothing in the darkness. She had just left Saundra's bedchambers, having searched drawers and cubbies, beneath the bed and in her armoire. The room was empty of most everything, so Christel had had no high hopes that she would discover anything significant that might shed light on Saundra's activities or troubles. She'd found no correspondence or journal.

Christel entered her chambers and closed the door. She

had left a fire burning in the hearth when she had taken Anna to her rooms and put her to bed. She stopped. The dowager sat on the green damask chair in front of the hearth, looking more genial than she had before. She held Christel's drawing tablet, which contained all the fashion plates on which she had been working these past evenings when she'd been alone in her room.

While designing the wardrobe for Anna's favorite dolls, Christel had gotten the idea to expand the concept. After all, what were doll clothes but miniature versions of adult attire? Though wonderful for little girls to indulge in, dreams did not put food onto one's table or pay one's bills, and if Christel had become anything these past few years, it was realistic about her circumstances. She had once owned a successful dress shop in the heart of Loyalist Williamsburg that had catered to the former lord-governor's wife. Someone would be lucky to have her ideas.

"These are quite acceptable," the dowager said without looking up.

She continued to thumb through drawings depicting polonaise-style overskirts looped back and pinned behind, revealing an underskirt, or open-robed higher-waisted gown with no trained overskirt. "A bit of Parisian finesse to add a worldly flair to the styles. Not what I expected from someone just come from the colonies."

"Thank you, my lady. Your praise warms me."

"*Hmpf.* Always a cheeky one. Are any of these Anna's ideas?"

"The dress that is made of ruffles, gauze and a bounty of

glittering jewels, feathers and seashells is hers. Her doll is a fairy princess, you understand."

The dowager's mouth turned up slightly at the corners. "She has told me so on occasion."

The last drawing was of Lord Carrick. But before Christel could remove the tablet from the dowager's hand, she turned the page, and Christel had a sudden wish for the ground to swallow her.

She had drawn Camden's hair slightly shorter than it was in reality, and she'd streamed it like a shadowy cloud behind him. His eyes were a pale reflection, like moonlight. She had sketched him wild and shameless, the way her mind had captured him on the deck of his ship with the storm clouds behind him.

"Does my grandson share your fantasy of him?"

"All art is fantasy."

The dowager folded up the portfolio and set it on the small round table at her elbow. The candle flickered with the draft of the movement.

"'Tis only a drawing, my lady," Christel said.

The dowager rose with a rustle of black bombazine and glanced at the sparsely furnished room. "You have been spending much of your time with us of late. Are you comfortable in this room?"

"Why are you here, my lady? Have I committed some crime?"

"I came to give you this," the dowager said, offering Christel a folded length of vellum.

Confused, Christel popped the seal and leaned nearer to the candle.

The dowager walked nearer to the hearth, where she stood within the radiant warmth of the fire. "Seastone Cottage is yours," she said. "No lien. No mortgage. No taxes due. As of today, everything is yours."

Heat burned across Christel's cheeks, as if she stood within reach of the flames in her hearth. She closed her eyes.

This was what she had wanted after all. Did it make a difference how the gift had come to her? Was her heart not as mercenary as any man's? Had she not proven that over and over again throughout the war? Had a part of her *not* wanted the thousand pounds the dowager had offered to her to *entice* her grandson to stay? This was far less. Christel refolded the vellum with a calm she was far from feeling.

"My grandson pays his staff well," the dowager said. "In a year, you will have earned enough to make your work here a trade for the taxes on your cottage, at least."

"A year?"

The dowager faced the hearth. "My grandson hired you to be Anna's tutor. But I wish that you be her governess. She needs you. You are very much earning your keep. I have been told that you have already taken over many of Mrs. Gable's responsibilities."

"Only until her gout subsides. Doctor White has tasked me to keep an eye on her."

"Is that why you visit the kitchen daily to prepare her meals?"

"Your cook is already busy enough. Mrs. Gables requires special meals. She has no one else to do it, my lady."

"Then you will find no problem taking on the responsibilities of Anna's governess full time."

Only when it was time for Lord Carrick to take a wife. But it was more, Christel realized. For as uncertain as she was about mothering another woman's child, she was less certain about living for a year in the same household as the child's father. Her solitude had always kept her heart safe. Nor was she drawn by a desire to be more than who she was. She was not always comfortable in her own skin, but it was her skin and she had accepted the fit.

So far, Christel had been able to resist getting too involved in this family's life, but little by little, she had already begun to spend more of her days and nights at Blackthorn Castle, especially as it had become apparent that Mrs. Gables was having difficulty caring for an energetic eight-year-old. The nurse had admitted such to Christel, afraid that once she could no longer do her job, she would be of no use to anyone and turned out. Christel had reassured her that was not true but that she had taken on more of Anna's care and education so Mrs. Gables could rest, though she'd had no idea why she was confident of such.

Aye, the impossible thing about emotions was that once out of the bottle, they could not be easily poured back inside and corked. Attempting to do so was like trying to catch smoke with one's hands. In the end, it was all Christel could do not to kiss the dowager's powdered cheek for bringing her the deed to Seastone Cottage, and out of relief or gratitude, tears welled in Christel's eyes. "I will do my best by Lady Anna, my lady."

"I know. You will also remember your place when it concerns my grandson's future. When 'tis time for you to go . . . you must go."

Christel nodded. She dabbed away the moisture from the corner of one eye. She had no delusions concerning the earl of Carrick's responsibilities and future. Christel would never be mistress to a married man. Would she?

"You trust my judgment concerning Lady Anna?" Christel tentatively asked.

"Only as long as you understand that my granddaughter is a precious, beautiful wee gel. I will not have her spirit stomped from her."

This was a new face from the dowager. "Nay," Christel agreed. "I will not do any stomping. *However,* if she is going to be given over to my care, I will ask that you no longer indulge her every whim. In fact, you and Grams have set no boundaries for her, and I wish to rectify that beginning tonight."

"I beg your pardon."

Anna's obvious loneliness reminded Christel of herself as a young girl after her own mother had died. "If you have ever been a recipient of spiders in your bed or molasses in your shoes, you would understand that she is a very bored, but creative, little girl. When she is out of the nursery, 'tis akin to giving her the keys to the castle."

Indeed, Christel had already spoken to Smolich and later the housekeeper concerning some of Anna's antics. "Your servants already spoil her. She is allowed to jump on beds.

She rides the banister down the stairs, raids strawberry tarts from the kitchen and spends a great deal of time reorganizing her menu so as *not* to eat anything that might be good for her. Everyone here allows her to do what she wants."

Evidently, by the pinched look on the dowager's powdered face, no one had ever dared tell her that her precocious great-granddaughter had a propensity for creating havoc to keep herself occupied.

"Humbug. She is a lady, the daughter of an earl—"

"No one *expects* anything from her, my lady. 'Tis not fair to her. She needs boundaries and purpose."

Surprisingly the dowager made no other protestations. Instead, she raised her lorgnette to her eye and peered closely at Christel. "You will need a new wardrobe more fitting of your position," she said briskly. "Shall I hire you to be your own seamstress as well?"

Christel smiled. She had not thought of asking. But truly, it was an excellent idea.

Two evenings later, the sound of soft footfalls awakened Christel. She sat up in bed. A storm was moving inland from off the sea. Wind gusts whistled through the seams in the sash. Christel eased out of bed, walked to her door and cracked it open to peer into the corridor.

Realizing at once she must have been dreaming, she returned to bed and pulled the blankets over her head. This was how rumors of ghosts began, she thought, listening as a chime banged against a stone wall somewhere in the courtyard below.

Thunk.

She lowered the blankets and stared up at the plaster ceiling. Wind gusted against the window. The sound could have come from outside. Yet at once, she rose again. She drew on a heavy wrapper, then left the room to make sure Anna was asleep.

A lamp burned on the dresser near the child's bed. For a moment, as Christel stared down at the little girl, she realized a fierce want to protect her. She covered her more securely against the cold before drawing away.

By the time Christel returned to her room, dawn had begun to spread a thin gray line across the horizon. She washed and, throwing a black shawl over her shoulders, went below to the kitchen to secure a breakfast tray for Anna and Mrs. Gables.

"What is above the nursery?" she asked Smolich when he came down to iron that morning's broadsheet for the dowager.

He peered over his nose. "You mean other than the roof?"

"I thought I heard something up there last night."

He considered this. "There used to be servants' rooms up there, but they were closed when the new part of this house was built around the old castle," he said. "Other than cats or occasional rodents Mrs. Gables has heard on occasion, no one has lived up there in decades."

A week passed before Christel heard the sound again. A *thump* and a *creak,* as if the planked floor protested the tread of a heavy boot. This time Christel was sure she had not imagined the sound. She flung off the covers and rose, drawing on her wrapper as she eased her door open. She listened and heard another creak above her head.

As was her custom since the last time she had heard the sound, she kept a sconce lit in the hallway beside her room. She lifted the glass, grabbed the candle and quietly paced herself beneath the muffled sound above her until she reached the end of the hallway, where it dead-ended into a brick wall. The candle fluttered, but she could find no crack.

An old servant's corridor must have serpentined through these old walls. Her breath suddenly caught. She blew out the candle.

Someone was on the other side of the wall, she realized, afraid to move lest the floor creak and give away her position. Footsteps continued past her and down a stairway. She had no idea about the layout of the inner hallway between the walls, but she did know that the kitchen was directly below this area of the house on the bottom floor. If the rooms above this floor had once belonged to the servants, it made sense that this corridor would take them directly below stairs.

Whirling around, she retraced her footsteps to the stairway. She had no sword or pistol in her possession. She imagined that, depending on the intruder, she could scream, but something about the cadence of the steps as they had walked past seemed familiar. Since Lord Carrick was not in residence, that left one other who would know the inner meanderings of this house.

She found Leighton coming out of the pantry carrying a wedge of cheese and bread in one arm and a bottle of wine in his hand, like some recalcitrant adolescent stealing food and drink after sneaking into the house after curfew. Surprise etched itself briefly on his handsome countenance. He was still wearing his cloak. Mud caked his boots.

"What are you doing here?" she demanded.

His mouth cracked into a smile. "Until your return to Scotland, I had resigned myself to utter boredom. Now everywhere I go, you seem to be there awaiting me." His eyes slid the length of her in masculine appreciation. "And in your nightclothes, no less. Are you Blackthorn Castle's new gatekeeper?"

Aware of the firelight behind her, Christel moved to the side of him. Still, she felt undressed as she clutched the neck of her nightdress. The hesitant movement raised his eyes to hers.

"Pity my brother is not here to see you," he said.

Tucking the bottle of wine beneath his arm, he proceeded to walk past her toward the back wall. She followed on his heels. "Is stealing food and drink not stooping to new lows for you?"

"Big brother told me to stay away from Anna and so I am. But I will not stay away from Grandmamma. Sadly, I have arrived too late tonight and will have to make it up to her. But now I am off to sleep. I will be gone in the morning."

"She knows you come here?"

"Aye, she is more tolerant of my faults than my dear brother."

"Does her tolerance extend to your bedding your brother's wife and getting her with child?"

Leighton stopped dead on the stone floor, his action so unexpected that she walked past him. His fingers wrapped around her arm, spinning her around. His silver eyes flashed. "What did you just say?"

"You heard me."

"Oh, aye, my hearing is excellent. I just did not *understand* you."

She dropped her gaze to the hand still latched onto her arm. "You are hurting me, Leighton."

"Where did you hear that accusation? From Camden?"

"Does it matter? Tell me you did *not* bed Saundra? Ever?"

"*Ever,*" he said flatly. "I defy you to tell me who would say I did. I will ask you again. Was it my brother who accused me of such?"

Christel studied him. Leighton was a rake, a bounder, and most likely a liar, but no one could fake the pain she'd briefly glimpsed in his eyes—raw, honest emotion.

"I did not hear the accusation from Lord Carrick," she finally said. "But he must believe it of you. Why else would he hate you?"

"I can name a dozen reasons, starting when I was five when he took a strapping for me for a transgression he did not commit. But to my credit, I did try to correct the matter. Our good papa only then took the strap to my backside, thus convincing me that great pain comes from taking responsibility. 'Tis better to lie. My brother, on the other hand, prefers pain."

"You are despicable."

"Aye, I am," he said readily. "I am a thief, a pirate, a

libertine and plagued by a general lack of morals. I dislike our government to the point of subversion. I am not averse to stealing what my brother thinks belongs to him as long as he is not wed to it. Sleeping with my brother's wife is low, even for someone like me."

He was being honest with her. Why admit to treason and lie about this? "Are you telling me that you and Saundra never . . . ?"

"If she was guilty of adultery, 'twas not with me, Christel. She and I . . . were always *only* friends."

"Then why would people suspect such a thing?"

"Because of who I am. Because when Saundra needed a shoulder to cry upon, I was there. She cried a lot. Camden was . . . *is* a bastard."

"You are as wrongheaded about him as he is about you."

"Am I?" His eyes narrowed. "They argued fiercely that last night. Three people saw him go up into that tower just before she jumped. By the time the rest of us reached the tower, 'twas too late."

"He did not push her or cause her to jump."

Leighton clenched his jaw, looked away, then brought his fierce gaze back around to her. "Neither did he try to save her."

"You are a fool."

"He wanted a divorce. He was taking Anna from her. The proud Carrick name would better stand the scandal of her death than the scandal of adulterous affairs and divorce."

Christel whirled on her heel, but he grabbed her arm,

and this time his touch was not so gentle. "Who told you I fathered her child?"

"If you touch me again, I will lay you flat on the floor, Leighton. And I will *not* be kind about it."

He lowered his arm and adjusted his load. "You do not have many friends, Christel. I now see why. You are about as soft and gentle as a quill-stuffed bed." Leaning nearer until they were nearly nose to nose, he said, "I know things about you, too, *Madam* Claremont. And I do not play nice any more than Camden does when angry."

"Do not threaten me. You are not going to do anything to me. Anyone who has spent the past year keeping Seastone Cottage afloat because of your loyalty to my uncle is not going to suddenly murder his niece."

"You put too much faith in people, Christel. You always did."

Leighton attempted to leave, but Christel stepped in front of him. "Did Saundra ever tell you that she was trying to leave Scotland with Anna? How could she have supported herself on her own?"

"Are you asking if I was helping her? No, I was not. Nor did she ever ask for my help, financially or otherwise."

"Surely someone must have known her heart."

His mouth crooked. "You were the only one she ever truly trusted, Christel. You would know more about her secrets than I."

He stepped past her and continued his way across the kitchen. "Leighton . . ." She stopped him as he popped open a hidden panel door near a breakfront filled with white and gold porcelain plates.

"Write Anna a letter. Tell her you miss her and that you are visiting France or Italy or Africa. I do not care where, as long as you make it convincing. You can slide it beneath my door or leave it on the desk in the library. Please," she added in afterthought. "If you do this . . . I will not tell anyone that you are visiting here."

"Blackmail, Christel, me gel?"

"I would rather think you would write the letter because you love your niece, my lord Leighton."

Chapter 12

~~~~~~~~~~~~~~

Potholes rutting the narrow drive made Camden's approach to Blackthorn Castle excruciatingly slow.

Leaning nearer to the window, he looked toward the distant meadow as the coach passed beneath the imposing stone watchtower on the drive that opened into the parkland. The morning was fresh and pure. Yellow gorse hugged the ground, scenting the air with a honeyed coconut aroma. In the distance, sunlight turned the front of Blackthorn Castle golden.

When he'd left here almost seven weeks ago, the trees had still been brown, the roads frozen. Only that morning, he had docked the *Anna* in Prestwick. In another week, the ship would be sailing without him, her hold filled with goods.

"You have not taken your eyes from the window for the past hour," Sir Jacob remarked. He sat in the seat opposite Camden.

Jacob's coach had been waiting in Prestwick that morning, and Jacob had offered to deliver Camden to Blackthorn Castle, where they would conclude their business. "One would think you are actually glad to be returning home," Jacob added with amusement.

It wasn't the sight of the estate that lent impetus to his impatience, Camden realized. The moment the coach stopped and the step lowered, he opened the door and climbed out. None of his footmen or groomsmen greeted the coach upon its arrival. As he approached the stone portico, the door opened and the staid butler appeared, red-faced and breathless. "My lord!" he said as Camden walked past him into the house. "We did not receive a message that you were arriving."

Making a perfunctory comment, Camden removed his tricorn and gloves, and peered up the winding staircase. "Where is everyone?"

"Most of the servants are at the old gardener's cottage today."

"Indeed. And why would they be at the gardener's cottage?"

"Oh, 'tis no longer the gardener's cottage, my lord. Miss Douglas and Doctor White have renovated it and 'tis now the new surgery."

Camden's hands paused over his gloves. "Miss Douglas?"

"Aye, my lord. Blackthorn Castle has been without a physician since the last one was lost in the blizzard of eighty and fell over the—"

"Smolich."

"Aye, my lord. Miss Douglas thought that Doctor White should be available to the servants and tenants' families. The dowager agreed, and they found the old gardener's cottage unused."

"Are my grandmother and daughter upstairs?"

"Oh, nay, my lord. They are also at the cottage."

Camden held out his hand to retrieve the cloak Smolich had just taken. "Is there anyone *not* at the cottage besides you?"

"The cook, my lord. Supper is at eight." Smolich's gaze settled on Sir Jacob. "Will we be having guests overnight?"

"Aye, Smolich. See that he is settled."

Camden's first glimpse of the old stone cottage stopped him. He vaguely remembered that the place had gone neglected for years, its thatch roof one with the brambles that had overgrown this section of the estate. Not so any longer.

A slew of people worked on what used to be a yard overgrown with prickly gorse. Furniture sat outside in the sun while the floors were being varnished, the roof and windows replaced, and the chimney flues cleaned.

Wearing a double-caped military cloak, Camden was hard to miss, and people stopped working when they saw him. One of the men oiling the door hinge spotted him. "My lord!"

Snow melt had made the ground wet. Camden was careful to remain on the flagstones, but his shoes were no longer spit-and-shine black by the time he crossed the yard. "Are my grandmother and daughter inside?"

"The dowager has gone to the herbal with Doctor White. Lady Anna is upstairs with Miss Douglas."

Stepping past him, Camden said over his shoulder, "Send word to the dowager that I am home."

The man dropped the rag in his hand. "Aye, my lord. At once."

Pausing in the doorway, Camden looked around. A new coat of whitewash had already dried on the walls. The room held a pungent, though not unpleasant, scent of varnish and beeswax.

As he walked inside, Christel suddenly came into view on the landing above him. She stood on a spindle back chair before the tall window, her arms outstretched, struggling to hang a length of drapery. A blue kerchief wrapped her hair. An apron covered the front of her dress but did little to hide a shapely backside and two perfectly formed ankles. He stood transfixed, his head brushing the beam that ran the length of the ceiling.

With muted anticipation and without taking his eyes from her, he climbed the stairs, and he wondered in the next thundering beat of his heart if she had thought about him as much as he had thought about her. The stair creaked beneath his step. She looked over her shoulder, seeing him at the same time that he reached the second-floor landing, and her smile was so powerful that it was like a physical force against him.

"My lord . . ." The chair wobbled. "You have returned!"

He caught the back of the chair and steadied her with a hand on her waist. "'Twould do me no good if you broke your neck because of it."

He possessed a profound desire to kiss her. Picking a cobweb off her bodice, he lowered his gaze to her mouth. "Only you could look carnal covered in dirt and grime."

"What are you *doing* here?" she whispered. "Your staff received no word of your arrival."

"I believe I live somewhere on this estate, though I cannot be sure this is the same place I left in January."

And there was nothing civil inside him as his gaze went over her face, her breasts, the curve of her waist, traveling lower. He had no need to stretch his memory to recall the promise of what lay hidden beneath her clothes.

His arm was already behind her back, dragging her off the chair and full against him. He surveyed her with a slow smile, an action as indicative of his current unreserved mood as it was of something else he could not define.

She might have glimpsed the maelstrom of emotions that broke within him, but he also bore witness to hers. Her sigh touched his ears. "I have missed you," she said as her feet finally touched the floor.

"Papa!" Anna's voice came from the hallway behind Christel, startling him to step away and turn.

Anna came running toward him, the green ribbon in her hair trailing after her. Dirt smudged her nose and apron. With his leg, he could not lean down on his knee, but it didn't matter to his daughter as she flung her arms around his waist.

"Oh, Papa! I am ever so happy you are back."

He laughed, and because it was already too late to save his clothes, he lifted her in his arms. His daughter smelled of grown-up things like sandalwood and talcum, as if she'd played with Christel's personal effects. "Your words are music to my ears, pup." His eyes drifted upward, and from over his daughter's head, his gaze touched Christel's. "I have missed you, too."

* * *

"How is it you could allow the niece of a known smuggler and blockade runner to take on the job as Lady Anna's governess?" Sir Jacob asked from the doorway behind Camden. He had already changed for supper.

Camden stood in his dressing room, his hair still damp from a bath. With a word, Camden released his valet and finished tying his own cravat. "We have already discussed Miss Douglas, Jacob," he said, an edge to his tone.

"Aye, but the last time she was not Lady Anna's governess."

"No offense, Jacob . . ." Camden slapped his friend on the shoulder as he snagged his dinner frock from a plump upholstered chair near the window. "You are thinking like an officer of the Crown," he said, sliding his arms into the sleeves. "Always suspicious."

"Does she know that you are the one who paid the taxes and the note on Seastone Cottage?"

Camden yanked the cuff of his shirt from beneath the coat. "I would like to know how *you* know that."

"Then your solicitor neglected to inform you that I *own* the bank that held the mortgage on Seastone Cottage. I am apprised of all business of import."

Camden walked to the door and edged it shut. Out of courtesy for their long-standing friendship, he tempered his agitation as he faced the only man who had never turned his back on him. "Then you must have known that bank note was due soon. If I were not such a trusting friend, I would believe the only person inconvenienced by her presence is you?"

"Bloody hell, Carrick," Jacob snapped, his temperament equally volatile. "Why do you trust her? She is rumored to have been wed to one of the most notorious spies in the colonies during the war. She is alleged to have been one herself and is suspect in the deaths of three of our men in Virginia."

Camden tightened his jaw. He knew the story. Lieutenant Ross had related it to him in a more sympathetic version, considering the three had murdered her husband in cold blood. "Only three men? Why not make her responsible for the loss of the war as well?" He hesitated, choosing his next words carefully. For whatever the matter was between him and Jacob—and Camden suspected it had much to do with Jacob's desire that Camden wed his daughter—they were in bed financially. Camden needed Jacob's political and monetary support to bring to fruition his plans for Blackthorn. It was one of the reasons he had gone to Glasgow. Why he had remained an extra week.

He also knew that Jacob had always been a devout loyalist, while Camden had already begun to see beyond the symptomatic blindness that had come with his own oath to the Crown. He was by no means a Whig, but neither was he blindly loyal to any man's cause, not any longer.

"Whatever happened, the war is over," Camden said. "Most certainly, 'tis finished for me. I have given all but my life and my daughter to Crown and country. You will afford me my indulgence when it comes to the feminine company I keep."

This seemed to pacify the worst of Jacob's concerns. "If our positions were reversed, Carrick, as a friend, would you not ask me these questions concerning your new governess?"

Maybe. Perhaps. But Christel's presence at Blackthorn was not open to discussion. Camden's smile was brief but unapologetic. "I know what I am doing." He stood at the door, inviting Jacob to leave. "Now go. I need to say good night to Anna."

Only after Jacob's departure did Camden feel his fist unclench from around the doorknob.

Brushing her hands down her skirt, Christel walked into Anna's room to make sure she was dressed. The purple draperies were still open. A hint of coral-and-crimson-tipped clouds was all that remained of the sunset. Christel drew the curtains shut and turned into the room. Bright yellow and lavender wallpaper matched the tiered yellow fabric draping in swathes from the canopy around the bed. It was a beautiful room, and when Christel had left it an hour ago to change her clothes, the chamber had been in pristine condition.

Christel now confronted a disaster.

Blankets had been dragged off the bed and were now draped over a dresser and a rocking horse. Evidence that Anna had raided the kitchen pantry lay in an incriminating trail beneath the blankets. Amidst this wreckage, her hair a wet tangled mop, Anna, wearing only her shift, was jumping on the bed, ignoring Mrs. Gables's attempts to entice her into her stockings.

When she saw Christel, Mrs. Gables straightened. "She will not listen to me, mum. Perhaps you will have more luck."

"But I wish to stay up and play!"

"Not tonight, Anna," Christel said.

"Yes. Tonight." Anna suddenly stopped bouncing. "Papa!"

Lord Carrick stood in the doorway behind Christel, a silver-eyed aristocrat, looking immaculate, dressed formally in a dark blue velvet dinner frock, black breeches and a white waistcoat. This was not how she had expected him to see her in her role as governess.

"My apologies, my lord," Mrs. Gables said as she failed to contain Anna's wriggling. "I have been trying to dress her for bed."

"But I do not wish to go to bed."

"I do not blame you. Come." Lord Carrick held out his hand. "Let me see you."

Anna jumped off the bed. Christel stepped between Anna and her papa. "What did I say earlier, Lady Anna?"

She lowered her blue eyes contritely. "You said a lady never runs in the house barefoot or climbs trees in dresses or bounces on beds. But I do not *wish* to be a lady anymore if I cannot have any fun!"

Lord Carrick coughed over what sounded like a laugh. He hastily looked over at Mrs. Gables, now standing next to the rocking chair. "Come, Anna." He lifted her in his arms. "You will need to dress for bed. Your hair is still damp and your feet are like ice. No more trouble."

As Anna turned her attention to Mrs. Gables, her small mouth tightened.

"Tomorrow I have a surprise for you," he added.

"Do you, Papa?"

"I do." He set her down. "Now off with you."

Without arguing, Anna accepted Mrs. Gables's hand. Together they disappeared into the dressing room.

Whatever else Lord Carrick might have been to the rest of Britain, beneath that hard masculine shell, the great Barracuda was naught but mash in Anna's hands and she well knew it.

Perhaps he did as well, as his expression signified. "What does it matter if she breaks routine this one time? Or jumps on the bed?" Amusement-laced words lightened his tone but did not dispose Christel to humor. "I do not remember you being so rule-oriented and ladylike when you were younger," he said.

"I do not recall your having a breadth of fondness for unruly young ladies, either," she replied, noting that his slight smile no longer held humor. "It matters not a whit to you that I have been working with Anna these past weeks," she continued, "making a concerted effort to do my best by you and your grandmother."

She did not mention the deed to the cottage, and neither did he. There was no need for the reminder.

"I am pleased that you want to please me, Christel."

"And I am torn between wanting to give you a facer and kissing you."

Pressing his advantage, he took her hand and pulled her outside the room and into the hallway, cradling her face between his palms. Then she was reaching for him as he was easing his fingers through her hair, and, in a moment, everything changed with the force of his touch.

He deepened the kiss, each thrust of his tongue joining hers, and she found a need equal to her own. He groaned and shifted his body, holding her wedged between him and the door. A part of her disliked being trapped. There was a certain helplessness that came with the feeling, but before discomfort began to rise and take hold, his kiss turned from an intensity that suckled the core of her being to one more defined by leisurely enjoyment. His palm glided from her breast to the curve of her hip. Lingering just one more heart-beat, he pulled away, but only far enough to look into her eyes. His heart pounded against her palms.

"I have truly missed you," he said.

Smolich was suddenly standing at the top of the stairs. Christel saw him first and barely restrained a gasp. Lord Carrick looked over his shoulder, his forbearance more re-fined than hers as he straightened. "What is it, Smolich?" he asked, as if it had been commonplace to be caught in the hallway kissing his daughter's governess.

"My lord . . ." The man cleared his throat. "The dowager sent me up to tell you supper will be served in a half hour. She asked if Miss Christel will be joining you in the dining room."

Lord Carrick said, "I will be down momentarily. How-ever, Miss Douglas will join us another time."

Smolich momentarily looked as startled as she felt. "Aye, my lord."

After the butler left, Lord Carrick returned his attention to her. "You need not concern yourself," he said, misread-ing her expression as shock. "Smolich will say nothing."

"You need to attend to your guests," she said before his mouth could touch hers again.

He put the side of his thumb to her cheek and turned her face. "They can wait another five minutes."

"Nay."

"Christel." His thumb brushed over her mouth. " 'Tis only supper."

She toyed with the soft edge of his clubbed hair. "If it eases you, I had no desire to join you and guests for supper tonight."

He leaned his palm against the wall. "I have my reasons for not including you tonight. In this you must trust me."

"There. You see?" she said.

Recognizing a challenge when he heard it, he raised a brow. "You think I am concerned by what family and friends will see?"

She let out a soft laugh. "You blanched. I think you are wondering how best you can retreat from this conversation with your fortitude intact. I assure you, you have paid me well to do your bidding, my lord."

Drawing her close, he stood for a space of time with her body touching his and gently said, "You misread my intentions, Christel."

"If you say so, then I will believe you," she said.

"Listen to me well, love. I only know that somehow away from the rest of the world, we have a chance to find something that is ours alone. Something we cannot have in the public eye." He took her face between his palms. "You must feel the same desire for me, or you would not be here no matter what it is I paid."

"No guarantees or expectations. No promises."

"You mean you will expect nothing from me, so nothing is lost when I disappoint you." Teasing mockery underlay the deference in his tone. "Do you expect disappointment, then?"

He was still perfection to her, and she was tipsy with desire. "Nay, my lord." She stood on her tiptoes to reach his mouth and smiled against his lips. "I expect nothing less than paradise."

The vibration of his chuckle made her want to hum in tune. "I do not think anyone has ever held me to such a standard," he said.

"And I have never been anyone's illicit lover."

"Ah, Christel . . . I am glad to hear that, love."

With a twinge of illogic, she found herself jealous. He could not say the same. He was suddenly the Barracuda, the consummate hunter, and she the prey.

And he had her pressed to the wall, his arousal hard and explicit against her stomach, and she was stretched taut against him, like some carnal offering on the altar of pagan sexuality.

The vague scent of soap, sea and salt mist enveloped her senses. His hand slid around the slim column of her neck, feather-light against her throat, and he marked the race of her pulse against his fingertips. His other hand moved to the back of her waist, his thumb brushed her breast. Her senses seized, nay exploded. He couldn't have been clearer what he wanted from her, and she didn't know if the sharper edge of desire now coloring their exchange was his or hers.

"Perhaps . . . you should return to your guests now."

The sharp, rasping sound of his breath touched hers, mingled and burned. "Perhaps I should," he agreed.

Rationality did not seem to sway either of them. And they remained thigh to thigh, neither willing to move first.

She felt the rise and fall of his chest against her breasts. The thrum of her pulse in her ears as he slid his lips to the soft shell of her ear. "But you and I both know I will not."

He sealed his words with a kiss, acquitting himself well as his masculine strength overwhelmed her, and because they urgently longed for each other, the kiss quickly turned into something more. Akin to the sensation that came from stepping off a ledge into a black bottomless chasm that had both the depth to swallow her and the width to allow her to spread her wings and fly.

Somehow, they kissed the whole way to her bedroom. He shut the door behind him. Paused as his hand turned the key with a click. His waistcoat was already undone. She had not lit a candle, but her room was not so cluttered with furniture that she felt in danger of colliding with any unmovable object. He dropped his frock on the way to her bed.

He had already begun to work his shirt out of his breeches. Christel busied her hands over the laces of her dress. Soon the rest of their clothes lay in a heap at their feet next to their shoes. He took her down to the bed, turning her in his arms so that she sprawled on top of him and became a part of him, her response in tandem to his. His hands gripped her hips, forcing her down as he thrust upward, a perfect fit. Her fingers closed on his hair. They were neither gentle nor patient, but with pain came searing pleasure. He increased the rhythm of their lovemaking and she felt the first small convulsions deep within her build. Her lungs grabbed onto his name. She clutched at him to hold him deep inside, and the long weeks of wanting him ended astride him in a violent shuddering climax. He poured himself inside her, and she collapsed against his chest with the sound of her own sated heartbeat loud in her ears, feeling drowsy and heavily content.

His big hands cupped her bottom. The house itself seemed to stretch and sigh with her contentment. He finally turned her onto her back and eased from her. She could feel his eyes on her face in the darkness. He touched her jaw gently, letting his hand slide through the cloud of her hair and down her throat to delicately cup her breast, then lower still to rest against the curve of her thigh. A cool draft played against the hot wetness between her legs, warming as his fingers touched her intimately. Primal. Possessive. Her soft moan slipped into his mouth. An unmistakable heat still lay between them.

He reached behind him and pulled the blankets over them. "Did I hurt you?" he asked, the words vibrating against her lips.

"I have never felt better." She tugged his lip between her teeth, then joined him in another kiss. "Will they not miss you at supper?"

"Probably."

She snuggled against him. "I will not be offended if you choose to leave now."

He chuckled against her hair. "I would as soon stop breathing than leave this bed. Do you not have a stove or candles up here?"

"I have both. But who needs either when I have my own warm luminary in bed with me."

She lowered her gaze over the corded muscles on his shoulders and arms, the dark shadows of hair at his armpits. He was on his back, his forearm resting across his eyes, and she visually traced the perfection of his silhouette. With his dark hair and the refined detail of his severely classical features, made more evident in his long-lashed eyes and delicate mouth, she wondered if somewhere in his ancestry he did not have a Roman general's blood running through his veins.

The thought struck her that she had never spent the night with any man but her husband.

She laid her cheek against his heart and splayed her fingers across his hip, touching the runnel of a scar that stretched down his thigh. His head turned on the pillow, his features lost in the shadows cast by the moonlight coming in through the window, but his breathing had changed. He moved his hand over hers, as if to cease her exploration of that most private to him, and set it on his stomach.

She swallowed. "You have not told me if Glasgow was a success."

"The *Anna* is now part of a three-ship fleet that will be transporting wool goods from Glasgow to Flanders and other ports of call on the continent. Our first consignment will be just after the midspring sheep shearing," he said.

"*Our*? Do you mean yours and Sir Jacob's?"

He pressed his lips to her hair. "One does not acquire contracts of that magnitude without having ships. One does not acquire ships without investors. Aye, I mean Sir Jacob. The contracts are a necessary hedge against the possible failure of crops over the next few years."

She traced the ridge of muscle across his stomach.

"Talk to me," he said after a moment.

"There is so much about you I do not know. I never knew anything about your parents, except that your father gave me my first unpleasant glimpse of an aristocrat."

"My father preferred to be feared rather than loved. He was an autocrat, master in his kingdom. He wed for political power. He bred the required two sons, then left. When I was nine, he came back for me. Despite what you may think, I have always been an outsider here."

"What happened to your mother?"

"I was a child when she died. Even when she was alive, I was never privy to her thoughts or her heart. Stiff upper lip and all that. Unlike the Scots, who bleed passion, we Brits find any display of emotions coarse. Neither parent was alive to see my disgrace after Yorktown. I almost wish my father had been."

"I am sorry."

"You mistake my sentiment. My father would have preferred me dead than to know that 'twas an American ship that pulled the survivors from the water. That your uncle saved our lives." His finger traced a path up and down her arm. Her cheek still pressed atop his heart, she sensed a subtle change in him. "I remember . . . waking to the darkness," he said. "*You* beside the cot talking to me as you are now."

"I worked at the camp prison hospital," was all she could manage to say. "The doctors were always short of help and supplies. I oft cared for most of the British prisoners. I read to them, composed letters to their families. That is why I was there the day you came in."

He turned her onto her back and looked down at her. "Is that all you did at the hospital?"

She began speaking because she had to talk, because the burden weighed so heavily on her heart she thought it would be crushed. Even if he hated her, he had to know what kind of person she was.

"Daniel and I both were involved with the Sons of Liberty," she said. "I carried missives from camp to camp. I owned a popular dress shop in Williamsburg. Therefore, I could travel easily into places where no one else could. He was part of an underground printing press run by his older sister. I oft brought . . . information to them and they printed it."

"Information that you sometimes received from British households and prisoners?"

She nodded jerkily in response. "If I thought anything I learned could save lives, I reported it. I became very adept at what I did but not adept enough to know when my cover had been compromised. The men who killed Daniel . . . found him because of me . . . I brought those men to my husband's house. He died saving me. I had never even told him that I loved him."

Turning away, she tasted the tears she did not want Camden to see. Her greatest fear was not that he would revile her as a spy and a thief but that he would know her as a faithless wife and find her *truly* undeserving of anyone's love.

He pressed his lips against her cheek gently and without expectation that his overture would be returned. Expecting censure, she was struck instead by compassion. She couldn't fathom why it set her emotions into a state of chaos.

She was afraid of the strength in him. Afraid that it made her feel helpless in a world that had rarely been kind to her.

When he drew back, it was to adjust his position so that he could settle her head on his shoulder and carefully arrange the blankets so that they protected her from the night and the cold. He couldn't know that the darkness had always been her friend more than the light.

She kissed him first.

Part of Camden hesitated. Not because he didn't want to indulge his own carnal need but because he was still capable of considering his own moral boundaries when it came to life and the choices he made. He had listened as Christel's tears had subsided. Listened as her breathing had softened. Knowing he should say something. But in many ways, they were a matched pair, a combination of personalities refined by guilt.

He kissed her back, pressing her into the pillows, and lost himself in the sensations that came with her touch in the darkness.

Tomorrow would be soon enough to contemplate the ramification of her revelations this night.

Yet, with sudden tenderness, he shifted his arm to bring her nearer. The movement stirred the scent of him on the sheets and between her legs. Then his mouth slanted across hers and he wasn't thinking about anything outside this room.

He made love to her with exquisite slowness. It was a softer coming the second time for them than it had been earlier, no longer rushed, as if the world would end tomorrow. Their whispers like the brush of soft blankets were hushed and mixed with the occasional squeak of the ropes beneath her mattress.

Later, even as she lay quiescent in his arms, he was too aware of her to do more than fitfully doze. He felt every small movement of her muscles and he sensed she was likewise aware of him. Every time she moved, his arm tightened as if to keep her near him.

Camden must have finally slept, for he came awake with a start, his senses alert. The squeak of a floorboard came from outside the door. He felt Christel stir in his arms. She remained spooned against his chest, and he smoothed her hair from his face as he looked over her head.

No candlelight wavered beneath the door. A light tap sounded. The doorknob turned slightly. He had locked the door earlier.

Camden eased his arm out from beneath Christel's head and slipped out of bed. He fumbled on the floor for his clothes. He was as practiced at dressing in the dark as he was at dressing in the middle of a hurricane, and he did so now with economical ease.

When he opened the door, only the acrid smell of a recently extinguished candle marked the intruder's passing. Tension remained tight in his body as he checked on Anna, and it wasn't until he returned to Christel's room to have her lock the door behind him that his foot brushed a letter that must have been slipped beneath the door. He walked to the window and held it in the waning moonlight. After reading it, he refolded the letter and stuffed it in his frock.

A quiet dangerousness touched, then filled, him as he found himself sitting on the edge of the bed looking down at Christel. His gaze fell on the pale curve of her profile, the bow of her full mouth, the gentle wing of an eyebrow. His palm cupped her cheek, turning her face toward him. She was a conflicting blend of virtue and vice. And not for the first time as he found himself staring at her did he know that in some indelible way, she was dangerous to him. Jacob did not trust her.

When was the last time Camden had trusted another human being?

She stirred and smiled into his palm. "What is it?"

He sank his hands into the mattress on either side of her shoulders. "Nothing that cannot wait until the morning."

And then he laid claim to her lips.

She made a soft sound in the back of her throat, wrapped her arms around his neck and pulled him closer. His blood raced through his veins like a potent aphrodisiac. His mouth trailed down her neck and lingered on her collarbone.

Somewhere in the tempest of his mind that separated her pleasure from his, reason failed to rear its head. And he didn't care. He slid the blankets down her body so that he could lift her, and with his other hand he loosened his breeches. She was already wrapping her palm around his erection and guiding him between her thighs.

Chapter 13

The next morning, Camden was gone from the room when Christel awakened. Gone but not absent. His scent remained on her sheets. He'd left his mark on her body in the way his stubble had rasped her breasts, and her insides were tender in more places than where he had touched, every inch bearing some mark of his possession. Pulling the sheet to her chin, Christel smiled at the play of light on the ceiling. For the first time in so long, she was almost afraid *not* to be happy.

After washing, she took extra care with her appearance, dressing in a practical soft gray linen gown with a white collar befitting her station but far nicer than the gowns she had originally brought here. Her fingers smoothed with a conscious gesture over her skirt.

She walked to the classroom and gathered up the canvas and watercolors to take Anna outside to paint the sea. Normally, Christel ate upstairs with Mrs. Gables and Anna. But today no tray had been brought, and Mrs. Gables and Anna were not in their rooms. Nor was Anna in the dining room or the ballroom.

Christel finally found Mrs. Gables below stairs, sitting at

the table with four servants and the butler, the staid bewigged Mr. Smolich, who had come upstairs last night. Upon her entrance into the servant's dining room, her smile slipped as everyone stopped talking. Smolich diligently dispensed with a glass of chilled milk, then took his dishes and utensils to the scullery. In similar silence, the upstairs chambermaid and underbutler followed.

Christel set her hands on the back of a spindle chair and caught them trembling as she turned aside and watched them leave. The elderly housekeeper remained at the back of the room, brushing out a jacket. "Did he force ye, lass?" the housekeeper asked when the others left.

"Hush, Mrs. Redding," Mrs. Gables snapped before Christel could think past her shock to reply. "When has his lordship ever *forced* anyone to do his . . . bidding?" She was also gathering up her teacup and plate.

Christel hadn't known what to expect today. In a house filled with servants, she had never been under the illusion that she could keep everything secret, but the ignominy of feeling unwelcome by those who had been friendly to her these past weeks stung. Coming from Mrs. Gables, it made her ache with embarrassment and regret.

Christel helped clear the dishes and take them to the scullery. "I have been searching for Anna," she said. "We are late for our lessons. I thought she would be with you."

"His lordship brought home a saddle for her pony. He came upstairs this morning and asked if she wanted to learn to ride. They are presently at the stable."

The saddle must have been the surprise he had told Anna

about last night. "She wanted to learn to ride. I am pleased to see that he is endeavoring to teach her." She set the dishes in the wash bucket. "Have his lordship's guests departed?"

"I was told Sir Jacob was called away last night just after supper. The dowager and Doctor White will be off to the orphanage later today. His lordship's grandmother asked if Anna would be permitted to come and go with them to Rose-cliffe for a few days. He agreed and will take us this after-noon. Lady Anna and I are to be packed to leave after lunch."

Mrs. Gables walked past her. Christel folded her fingers into her skirt in an attempt not to stop her from leaving. "Mrs. Gables . . . ?"

The woman turned. "His lordship's affairs are his own, mum. I have no doubt he will be generous with you. But you will understand that Lady Anna is my only concern. I do not want to see her hurt."

"Neither do I," she said and wondered how the day could go downhill so quickly.

Sadly, Christel watched Mrs. Gables go.

"Miss Douglas is here to see you, my lord." Camden's valet set aside the boots he had been polishing. "Shall I tell her . . . ?"

"Nay." Gripping a towel around his neck, Camden left his valet behind him in the dressing room. Having just come from the stable, Camden was neither presentable nor ame-nable to visitors, especially this particular one, when he was required to be downstairs in less than an hour.

Christel stood in front of the large picture window

overlooking the drive, her hands clasped in front of her. He watched her with a strange sort of possessive energy as she turned and her blue eyes went over his bed and the deep blue velvet curtains that draped the canopy before her gaze fell on him standing in the doorway.

"I knocked," she said when he didn't move any farther into the room. "The door was open."

He shut the door to the dressing room behind him. "I can see that you took care to fix the oversight, as the door is now shut."

"Why am I not going with Anna?" she asked, visibly upset.

"I think she can survive a few days with Mrs. Gables. Anna has thus far done so for almost nine years."

"Does this have to do with . . . last night? Us? Have I done something wrong?"

"I do not own you, Christel," he said softly. "If you wish to visit Rosecliffe, I am not stopping you. But Anna does not need both you and Mrs. Gables escorting her to an orphanage tomorrow. Take a holiday."

"A holiday?"

"Grandmamma has told me you have spent nearly every day the last two months with Anna or Doctor White, working on Blackthorn's new surgery, and every Wednesday at Seastone Cottage renovating your home. You have been tireless. Do whatever you wish for the day," he suggested. "Borrow a horse if you want. The stable is at your convenience."

Shaking her head, she backed away. "I do not need a horse to go home. Nor do I need a holiday."

Even with his lame leg, he managed to beat her to the door. "'Tis not my intent to be standoffish," he said quietly, aware of the high color in her cheeks, aware that he had hurt her. He used his index finger to raise her chin. "'Tis merely that I am due downstairs."

She peered over her shoulder at the large, mostly unused bedchamber. His own gaze took in the Chinese hand-painted wallpaper that brightened the walls in a gilded production of exotic vines and flowers, and he knew he had found no pleasure here in years.

"I am sorry, Christel." This was all new to him. This wanting.

Her smile was a mixture of compassion and affection. Unexpected. "I do understand that this is your personal sanctuary and you wish to keep it separate from me."

Perhaps. "I have not *shared* anything personal in years." *My private sanctuary most especially.* "My heart," he wanted to add. "My life," he said instead.

She stepped against him and laid her cheek against his heart. "Strangely . . . I understand that sentiment most of all, my lord."

Her touch gilded his senses in fortitude-melting heat and blew his self-control all to hell. "Do you?"

"This is new to me as well."

He stepped aside and opened the door.

"I will see you this evening," he said.

Nodding, she stepped past him and turned. He slowly shut the door. Turning back into the room, he leaned against the door and momentarily shut his eyes.

That morning after leaving her chambers, he had taken his daughter to the stables to clear his head and to rid himself of the anger he had felt after realizing that it had been Leighton outside her door last night. If he could not trust her then he might as well send her away now, for there would never be a tomorrow between them.

"Shall I have her followed, my lord?" he heard Smolich say.

Smolich stood next to the panel door in the wall. Earlier that morning, he had come to Camden with more letters that Leighton had written to Anna and information that Smolich had intercepted after seeing Christel in the library. He'd pulled the letters from the basket where invitations were delivered and placed on his desk for his grandmother's attention; the letters had been placed there as if they had been delivered in the same way.

Letters that had been written on paper from Camden's own library. Camden had read them. They were benign enough, clearly written to assuage a little girl's feelings. Camden had elected not to confront Christel, though it was obvious she was involved in his brother's subterfuge, especially when he suspected the culprit might also include his grandmother.

No, he would not have her followed.

The sun had nearly gone from the bloodred sky by the time Christel passed beneath the weathered arch that separated the cemetery from the old stone kirk. Leaving Dog outside the back gate next to the horse she had borrowed from the Carrick stable, she found her way among rows of lonely, lichen-blotched gravestones as she walked toward the enclosure at the far end of the hallowed grounds. A low mist lay thick beneath the boughs of two huge oaks. Stopping to find her bearings, she clutched her cloak tightly beneath her chin, as if that alone could ward off the chill. The land sloped and curved so that some of the stones lay toppled or bent sideways in a hollow.

Christel meandered through the markers looking for one that was not yet stained green by age or rounded by weather. A few early spring flowers mingled with grass and twigs, giving shape and muted color to the shadows. This patch of consecrated land belonged to the Carrick earls, their wives, sons and daughters who had lived and died in Scotland for the last two hundred years. With the exception of the unfortunate earl beheaded for serving on the wrong side at Culloden some fifty years ago, all of them were buried here.

Since her return to Scotland, Christel had not visited Saundra. As a rule, she disliked cemeteries. She was not one of those romantic figures of lore who, with sword raised aloft, could march courageously into the jaws of death. She was not Lord Carrick.

She found Saundra's headstone just then, a tall obelisk barren of angels or hearts or any of the other sentimental carvings that marked the other stones. It read simply:

IN MEMORY OF
SAUNDRA ETHERTON ST. GILES, COUNTESS CARRICK
MOTHER OF ANNA
JANUARY 9, 1756–APRIL 30, 1782

A sudden gust lifted dead leaves around her half boots. Only the wind and a crow sitting in the tree above her were her companions as she stood in the silence of a fading day.

"They say no one comes to a graveyard after dark," Christel said.

Unable to fight the tightness within her chest, she tucked the cloak beneath her and sat on the ground with her back to the headstone. "I imagine 'tis what we cannot see that we fear the most."

She let the sounds of the approaching dusk fill her. The *caw* of a crow. The wind in the grass.

"How could you climb to the top of a tower and leave this world as you did? How could you leave your husband and daughter?"

She closed her eyes. "How could you, Saundra? You, who did not like heights and could not even take the goat path down to the beach. Oh, Saundra. I want to understand," her mind whispered. She pulled her legs to her chest and leaned against her knees. "Camden is a good man, Saundra. He is battle-scarred like the men and boys I used to read to at the field hospital. But he is a good father. I cannot believe he was not a good husband."

Leaning her head against the cold stone obelisk, Christel felt her anger fade as quickly as it had come, and she let her heart move elsewhere for now. Her gaze riveted to the darkening sky.

"Tia and I still have not spoken," she said after a moment. "Perhaps I have not tried hard enough. It was different when you were alive. You always knew how to buff away the scrapes and edges. You were good with people. What happened to you?"

Christel shut her eyes. "I wish I could understand everything you did. I wish I knew if you were trying to tell me something with the gold coin you sent me. I wish I could find the answers. I wish you would give me a place to start."

Somewhere a door slammed.

Christel's eyes popped open. Her cloak was damp from the mist. The moon was higher in the sky. Realizing she must have drifted asleep, she turned her head toward the kirk. Headstones protruded from the rising mist. The vicar's house sat behind the copse of trees.

She climbed to her feet and ducked into the shadow of the tree next to the shoulder-high stone wall. Pale moonlight revealed a cloaked shadow, head down as if watching for obstacles in the path. Whoever approached, either a child or a petite woman, walked directly toward Dog.

The shadowy figure stopped on the path. As if recognizing the hound, her head snapped up and her hood slid from her head.

Tia!

As Christel's half sister looked toward the Carrick family plot, Christel caught only a glimpse of her. Her hair, much darker than Christel's and no longer pulled from her face, fell in waves over her shoulders. Christel's obscure thought in the midst of her shock was that Tia was quite pretty with her hair down. Tia took a step backward, spun on her heel and ran. At once, Dog started barking furiously. Christel called sharply to him, then gave her own chase.

"Tia!"

Giving up, her sister turned. Her hood having fallen to her shoulders, she stood in the open between the stone kirk and the vicar's residence, with the thatch-roofed stable some distance behind her. Her breath steamed with small puffs in the chill night air.

Out of habit, Christel made a study of the surrounding shadows.

"What are *you* doing here?" Tia demanded, as if Christel had been the one running like a mad banshee across the mist-shrouded graveyard.

"I am visiting Saundra. Fancy that we both had the idea at the exact same time. Unless you were walking someplace else."

Though Rosecliffe sat only three miles northeast of Blackthorn property, Christel could not believe Tia had walked here, though her muddy half boots told a different story. Nor did she believe Tia was here to visit the cemetery, certainly not at night and alone. And weren't Anna and the dowager at Rosecliffe this evening? Lord Carrick had escorted them earlier and had not yet returned when Christel had left Blackthorn.

Christel looked over Tia's shoulder toward the darkened stable. "There would be only one reason you would not be on a horse," Christel said. "You did not want Grams knowing you had left Rosecliffe."

Tia laughed. "Truly? Are we suddenly friends that I should be sharing confidences with you? In case you did not know, the only horses we have left in our stable are used for

Grams's coach. 'Tis none of your concern why I am here."

Christel walked after her. "Tia—"

A hand suddenly covered Christel's mouth. Followed at once by a whisper that brushed her ear. "It's me, Christel. Do not fight."

Leighton.

"You will not scream or hit me?"

She bit his hand. He yanked it from her mouth. "Bloody hell, Christel! That hurt."

"You should be so lucky to die of blood poisoning."

"We can trust her, Tianna."

"Bother, Leighton, why would you trust her?"

Oddly, Christel also resented the notion that Leighton trusted her. His words by their very meaning drew her into a conspiracy with them.

He lowered his voice. "Would you rather I kill her? Now that she has found us out?"

Christel folded her arms over her chest. "Tell me you are being facetious."

The argument stopped. Leighton took her arm and turned her toward the stable. "She has worked in a field hospital. She is a seamstress. She knows how to use a needle and thread."

In the shadows, three soot-faced men slumped against a water trough, muskets braced between their knees. Two more stood near the paddock, another in the doorway of the stable. All wore dark clothing.

Leighton took her into the stable. Someone lit a lamp.

Her gaze fell on Blue slumped next to a bail of hay. Blood covered the lower side of his shirt. Christel dropped to her knees.

"Blue!" She removed the soiled rag someone had already placed on his side.

"It hurts only a bit, mum," he said.

A smooth slice in his flesh just above his hip oozed blood. She looked up, into the farmer's eyes. "Blue, this is a saber wound . . ."

Tia knelt in the straw across from Christel and presented her with a small surgeon's kit.

"He needs a real doctor," Christel said.

"Doctor White is being watched," Tia said. "Sir Jacob and his daughter are dining at Rosecliffe tonight. Otherwise he would be here rather than me."

"Will you not be missed?"

"I fell down the stairs this evening and sprang my ankle terribly." She held up a small brown bottle. "Doctor White gave me laudanum and put me to bed. I will not be missed until morning."

Tianna opened Blue's big hand and set the bottle in his palm. "You may need this before the night is through," she said gently.

Dipping the rag in the water and wringing it, Christel pressed it to the wound in an attempt to gauge its severity. "How did this happen?" she asked Blue.

"Me an' Heather were visitin' her kin near Maybole last night. The gaugers knocked on the door near dawn wantin' to search the place for contraband. When they dragged us out of our beds and set the place afire . . . weel, I did no' much like the treatment, mum."

Gaugers—preventive men, custom officers of the Crown: they were as hated as the plague.

"Who else is injured?" she asked.

"The family inhaled smoke, but everyone be otherwise safe. Heather be with her sister and the wee lads in the rector's cottage."

"Why would someone do this?"

Blue looked up at Leighton, clearly passing the responsibility of answering the query to him.

"That is what Westmont's men do with conspirators," he said. "Your cottage is burned and your lands confiscated. If you are unfortunate enough to be caught, sedition is oft added to your list of crimes so his magistrates can more readily hang you."

Christel's gaze touched the shadowy shapes lingering beyond the lamplight. "You mean that is what his men do to people *caught* smuggling."

"They will be hangin' my brother-in-law in the village square in two days," Blue said.

Numbly she shook her head as she tried to think. "This wound has bits of cloth inside. If I stitch it now, it will only putrefy."

Leighton knelt beside her. "Unfortunately we do not have the luxury of a surgery, and we have already been here too long."

"He be right, mum," Blue said.

"Blackthorn Castle has a surgery, I can see to the wound there."

Blue shook his head. "I will no' leave Heather and the bairns. I will no' have them defenseless should a patrol come here."

"You will die if I cannot dig the scraps of cloth from the wound, Blue. And trust me, 'tis not a painless way to go. You need—"

"I will no' leave those bairns, Miss Christel."

She sat back, more frustrated than furious. "The only place any patrol will not check is Blackthorn Castle. Maybe we should take all of your family there."

"Aye," Leighton scoffed. "You will hide a family of fugitives under my brother's nose. Too dangerous, Christel. If anyone suspects you are involved . . . hell, Westmont and my brother are close friends. Camden will not compromise Blackthorn's security for a bunch of tenant farmers."

"You do not know him, Leighton. He would die fighting for what is right. If you think there is some grave injustice about, *you* should have gone to him long ago."

"He will not die fighting for these people, Christel. He would not even die fighting for England if you asked him now. He is not the same man he was. Ask Tianna."

Tianna was watching Christel. "Maybe she should ask him," Tianna said to Leighton. "I do not see that we have a choice. *You* cannot stay here on guard, and she needs the use of the surgery. 'Tis logical that we take Blue and Heather's family to Blackthorn. Who would think to look there?"

"*Logical!*" Leighton rasped, keeping his furious voice low. "What is logical about getting hung?"

"Hanged," Tia corrected. "The proper word is hanged."

"*Fook* the proper word. I will not have her risking—"

"*Her!* You were not worried that *I* risked a great deal coming here."

Christel watched the hushed verbal skirmish, a little awed to discover Tianna had a temper. Growing up, she had always been so pale and balmy in comparison to Christel and Saundra. More than that, she clearly had a *tendre* for that rapscallion libertine towering over her.

"Hush! Both of you," Christel snapped. "'Tis a moot point. We need the surgery. And Tia is correct. No one will look for the family there."

The lamp suddenly whisked out with a hiss. "*Dragoons!*"

Christel could hear the soft rasp of movement as men took up positions outside behind bushes and trees.

"Get down," Leighton whispered. "Cover your hair. Especially you, Christel. Your hair is like a light beacon in the night."

"And what is mine?" Tia whispered. "Mud?"

Christel knelt next to Blue with Tia on the other side, her sister's breathing staggered in the darkness. Tia wasn't used to the terror of being hunted by soldiers. Christel breathed slowly, calmed by the stable's fecund smells.

"Concentrate on the smell of the stable," she whispered to her sister. "Inhale."

She thought Tia coughed behind her cloak. "It stinks!"

"I know." A sliver of moonlight wedged between the slats. "I think your hair is more like sable," Christel whispered, her gaze holding Tia's, "not mud."

Silence fell between them.

"Have you done this before?" Tia asked.

Christel nodded. They both turned their attention to the doorway. A man with a perspective glass stood inside the shadows and quartered the hill at the back of the cemetery. "Six dragoons," he said. "I do no' think they are alerted to us or they would no' be sitting like pretty ducks in a row for us to pick off."

"Then why are they no' movin'?" someone whispered.

"They could no' have seen the light."

Christel's heart leapt and she struggled to stand. "My horse and dog are still at the cemetery—"

But even as she said the words, a man's distant shout alerted the other soldiers, and they headed down the hill.

Chapter 14

~~~⟡~~~

When Camden left Rosecliffe near nine o'clock, the night was cold and clear. Even this close to spring, the threat of snow lingered until May. Moonlight reached across the ground in pale fingers, sifting through tree branches that had not yet budded with the first breath of spring.

A tap on the small port above the forward seat alerted Camden just before it slipped open. "Riders approaching, my lord," his driver said. "A full half dozen at least."

Camden leaned to the window to see the oncoming riders directly on the road in front. Even though he was on Blackthorn land, he never discounted the possibility of being robbed on his own road by overambitious highwaymen bent on their own self-destruction.

As the coach slowed, Camden reached beneath the cushion of the opposite seat and withdrew two pistols already primed, setting both next to him. "Can you tell yet who they are?" he called back.

"Six dragoons. A woman and a dog," the driver said. "They are hailing us."

Camden's heart dropped into his stomach. As his coach

slowed, he dimmed the interior lamps and returned to the window. "Stay armed and alert," he said to both men up top. Two others rode the boot. All were well armed.

When the coach came to a rocking halt, the footmen hurriedly set out the step. Camden opened the door and descended before the riders reined in their mounts in front of him. Camden refrained from leaning heavily on his cane to work out the cramp in his thigh.

The first thing he noticed was that Christel rode side-saddle, her cloak spread around her skirts, revealing a glimpse of half boots laced over her ankle. Her hood had fallen across her shoulders and, even in moonlight, he could see that the wind had reddened her cheeks and her pale hair lay in windblown curls around her face and shoulders. His first thought was that she possessed a graceful seat on the saddle. His second thought was territorial, primal in nature as he shifted his attention to the dragoon sergeant holding the reins on Christel's mount. He had met the man once before in Christel's stable.

"We found her in the cemetery," the sergeant said without sliding from his horse. "She claimed she was there visiting the late Countess Carrick. I am not of a mind to disbelieve her, my lord, seein' as how they were related. But 'twas past dark—"

"If I am not mistaken, St. Abigail Kirk belongs to Black-thorn Castle," Camden said tersely. "What are you doing on my land without permission, Sergeant?"

The man straightened in the saddle. "We have Sir Jacob Westmont's warrant, my lord." He fished out a folded document from deep within his waistcoat but was forced to dismount when Camden made no effort to step forward and retrieve it. "We have been cleaning the spiders from their nests," he said. "Ridding Ayrshire of its criminal elements."

Camden walked nearer to the interior of the coach and read the decree with a frown. *Damn, Jacob.*

Adjusting his tricorn, he turned his head. Christel sat atop the horse, watching the proceedings. "My horse bolted, my lord," she said. "The good sergeant thought I was attempting to escape him."

The sergeant shifted uneasily. "One of my men was seriously injured earlier this morning near Maybole during an altercation with dangerous blackguards, who have since eluded capture. After I informed the woman of this, she became frightened and begged us to escort her to you directly. She said you were dining with Sir Jacob at Rosecliffe."

Christel smoothed her hand through the gelding's mane. "Before they arrested me for seditious activities, they needed to confirm with you that I had legitimate cause to be at St. Abigal's, my lord."

"Are you all right?" he asked her.

"Aye, my lord. Who am I to argue with six dragoons when they offered me the protection of their services?"

He could not see her face in the shadows, and he was glad, because he knew she was no damsel in need. She was the most capable woman he had ever known. She was lying.

"The men you seek, are they the same responsible for the sinking of the merchant ship outside Troon three years ago, holding, among other goods, gold that was supposed to be going to the royal coffers in England? Am I not mistaken?" Camden asked.

"Aye, my lord."

His eyes returning to the document in his hand, he said, "Six men died."

The sergeant concurred that this was the same lot.

"Did you search St. Abigal's?" Camden asked.

"We saw nothing amiss. But . . . then Miss Douglas's mount bolted. We were a mile gone before we finally caught the horse."

Camden returned the warrant. "Miss Douglas is in my employ, Sergeant, and has leave to go wherever she chooses on my land. Next time you want to visit St. Abigal's for whatever reason, come to me first." He kept his voice calm. Only someone who knew him well would have guessed his anger.

He was furious.

Once in the carriage, Christel bundled in her cloak and attempted to relax against the velvet squabs, listening as Camden barked orders to his driver to tie her horse to the coach. She whistled softly and Dog bounded into the vehicle, exuberant with joy at her invitation. After she finally stopped him from licking her face, he circled around the squabs, turned three times and plopped next to her on the seat, clearly finding the prospect of traveling in royal style preferable to running another three miles. "I am sorry you were run so hard tonight, boy."

His red and white tail thumping, he settled his head in

her lap, gave a great heave of his chest and was asleep. She reached up and extinguished the light at her head, preferring the darkness.

The coach dipped with Camden's weight as he shut the door. Dropping onto the seat across from Dog, he braced one arm along the back of the squabs. A crack of the driver's whip roused the four horses and the coach jerked forward. She and Camden remained in silence each in their corners, like two pugilists awaiting the bell to ring for the first round.

"Why were you at the cemetery?" he asked.

"I thought it prudent to visit your wife . . . now that I am sleeping with her husband." Tears sprang to her eyes. She bit them back. "I am sorry. That was a horrible thing to say."

"I am relieved that you recognize it."

She smoothed her cloak over her skirt and found it damp from the evening mist. "I did not go to the cemetery tonight with any intent but to visit Saundra. I have not done so since my return."

"And somehow during the course of that visit you came across the blackguard spiders the sergeant is hunting." He leaned forward, his elbows braced on his knees. "I did not tell you that Jacob Westmont would be at Rosecliffe tonight. I can only guess you found out from someone who knew he was there. The only person not present at supper was Tianna. So I will merely speculate 'twas she you met at the cemetery. And if there was trouble in Maybole this morning, then Leighton was no doubt involved."

With half-angry discontent, Christel rubbed Dog between

the ears. Camden had most everything figured and she had barely said a word.

Leighton would have gotten Blue and Heather's family to Blackthorn Castle by now, she thought. How could she possibly broach the topic of their needing shelter? Her heart shivered in her chest.

"You would not have asked those questions about the merchant ship if you did not want me to hear the answers," she said.

"I want you to know the kind of people you are defending."

"Leighton would not . . . he would not condone murder."

Camden dragged off his hat and tossed it on the seat. "And I am finished with your defense of him."

"The dragoons burned a house that belonged to Blue's brother-in-law. Blue was seriously injured defending the family. The children's father is to be hanged in two days."

"I know," he said.

"You know? You *know*?"

"I found out tonight over a glass of port."

Christel waited for him to say more. He didn't.

"There were women and children inside that house," she said.

"There are sixty-two men imprisoned at the military stockade in Ayr. Should I fight to have them all pardoned? Or merely the ones for whom you care? Does being a father make a man less a criminal?"

He leaned forward and tilted her chin. "Look at me." Even in the darkest of nights there was always some light.

Moonlight came into the coach via the windows. She could probably see Camden better than she could have had he been shadowed by lamplight. "If anyone ever learns that you had contact with Leighton tonight . . . or in any other way—"

Turning her head, she dislodged his grip.

"I know about the letters he has written to Anna," he said. "He would not have done that on his own accord—"

"The fact that he did write the letters at all should mean something. Anna misses him terribly. She is a child and does not understand the world."

"Then I am thankful for something," he said.

Christel could only gaze at him in the darkness as a tumult of emotions coursed through her. "I am glad you know," she finally said.

"Indeed," he said doubtfully.

"I meant it to be no secret. They were not hidden."

The mood in the carriage shifted like currents in the sea, the ebb and flow of a tide, the sky just before the sun dipped into the sea.

Christel did not have to light the lamp to know that his eyes were as grave as his mood. A chill went over her. "Whatever you think of him . . ." *He is not the one who fathered Saundra's child.* "You both are blaming the other for something . . ." Shaking her head, she didn't know what to say. "Something that was neither your fault nor his. Talk to him."

Numbly, she lingered in the silence growing heavier between them, then she heard his quiet laugh. "We do not need you to save us from each other, Christel. What is between us has nothing to do with you."

"Talk to Leighton."

"Why? Because you have affixed some moral aura around my heart that gives off the delusion that I am somehow of different temperament than other normal men? Or from the man I have always been? What makes you think we would not kill each other?"

"Oh, yes. I forgot. Much of the world once feared the Barracuda. Your accolades reach to all shores of the Atlantic. You built wealth and rank as thick as the stone walls of Blackthorn Castle. You filled your world with beautiful things and a beautiful wife who gave you a beautiful daughter. Now you are battered by your own insignificance in an attempt to find relevance in your life again. And all I can do is be a spectator."

"Do I detect a hint of scorn in your opinion of my character, unworthy as it is?" he softly asked.

"Nay," she said just as softly. "You do not. I think you are one of the bravest men I have ever known."

"I would rather be scorned by you, Christel."

She drew her cloak tighter. "Too bad," she sniffed. "If you were not an earl, I would probably fall in love with you; maybe even settle on being your mistress."

"Come here." He opened his cloak. "That dog in your lap has hair all over his body to keep him warm. You do not. Your teeth are chattering."

She thought about refusing him. The words were on her tongue. But then she eased Dog's head from her lap. The hound protested briefly with a sleepy groan that ended as he stretched out on the velvet squabs. "Thank you for allowing Dog to ride in the coach," she said.

Camden gripped her waist and pulled her across his lap; even through the layers of their clothes, she felt him hard against her.

After a moment, he pressed his mouth against her hair. Her breasts brushed his arm, and she felt the hard muscles beneath his sleeve. "No one has ever believed in me as you have, Christel. No one has ever had more cause *not* to believe in me."

"You are wrong. You have just forgotten what it's like to believe in something again."

"Leighton and I were not always adversaries," he said.

The vulnerability in his voice lifted her chin. He was looking out at the night and she knew that he was thinking about Saundra.

"I know."

He touched the strands of her hair as if her presence became something greater in his thoughts. Something he did not comprehend. "Leighton was with Saundra when Anna was born. I had tried to get back but missed the event by a few weeks. In the fourteen years I served the admiralty, my brother buried our grandfather, father and cousins. I missed every special occasion, every important event in my family's life except Saundra's death. I was the last person to be with her before she died. Had I been more of a husband . . ."

The edge in his voice became even more perceptible.

"All of my life I have played hero to a cause that was more important to me than my own wife and family. I did everything duty bade me to do.

"In the end, nothing mattered. Not wealth or prestige or honor. I never questioned my responsibility before, but I find myself questioning it now. I do not want Anna growing up thinking her father a cripple who failed his country. Even more so, I do not want her dishonored because of something I did or failed to do right by this family."

His deep sense of duty, which was evident in every nuance, every word he spoke, made Christel's throat tighten. "Whatever happened, you did not kill Saundra. She was a fool."

His hand tilted her chin. "'Tis not my intent to make you feel pity for me, Christel."

She dabbed a knuckle at the corner of her eye. "I fear I have harmed you."

"How so, *a leannan?*" Amusement laced his words.

He had called her "darling" in Gaelic. She had thought he did not even know the language.

"Blue needs help," she whispered.

"I will find a way to get Doctor White to him, though that in itself poses risk. Westmont is watching him."

"I know."

"Where is Blue now?"

She pressed her cheek in the loose cloth of his neatly folded cravat. "If all went as planned, he is in your surgery at Blackthorn Castle, waiting for me."

* * *

Just after midnight, Christel found Camden standing in front of the tall window in the library. The curtains were open, but a thick mist outside pressed against the glass. A fire burned in the hearth. He had removed his dark jacket since leaving the surgery. Firelight favored the pale gray breeches and the silver threads in his waistcoat. His inordinate self-possession made her cautious as she stepped into the room.

"I wanted to thank you for allowing Heather and her family to stay," she said to his rigid back. "I cleaned the wound. I think I found all the cloth caught inside. I stitched it. Doctor White should find my efforts passable."

She stood just over the threshold. He still had not turned. She could envision him on the deck of his warship right before he blew his enemies out of the water, wearing the same captain's façade he wore now.

"Where is Leighton?" he asked.

"I was told he left almost as soon as he settled the family. Probably to spare a confrontation with you."

"I doubt it."

A spurt of anger grabbed hold and she choked it back. She would have preferred rage to this calm, cold man standing at the window looking out across a world blanketed in mist and darkness.

"What am I to do with you, Christel?"

She caught his gaze in the window and realized then he was looking at her reflection in the glass. "Do you want me to leave Blackthorn Castle?" she asked.

For a moment, he said nothing. "I want you to go back to the surgery." He tipped the goblet and finished the drink as he turned. "Tend to Blue. See that the Ferguson children are warm and fed. I will talk to you tomorrow when I have found out what chargers on which Reginald Ferguson and Blue are being accused."

Her head throbbed at the effort to stay stone-faced. "You are not . . . you will not turn their families over to Westmont?"

He narrowed his eyes. "I will not be turning women and children over to the provost to be judged like criminals and indentured for crimes that are not their doing. I may be cold-blooded, but even I have my limits."

She pulled the shawl closer around her shoulders. "I do not think you cold-blooded."

"Forgive me, Christel, but at the moment, I am not interested in what you think."

He had a right to his anger, she told herself. She'd violated his trust and burdened him with the task of protecting people wanted by the Crown. Even aristocrats were not immune to the laws of the land. She had put his honor on the table to be sliced and diced for public consumption should he ever be found out, but in the end, he must see that he was doing the right thing in protecting these lives.

"I understand your anger—"

"Oh, aye! You are the expert on my character. Anger does not equate to what I feel."

"You detest liars."

"I detest deception."

"And people who would use you for their own ends."

"You know these things and yet you still chose to involve Blackthorn Castle in a conspiracy with my brother."

"What if it had been Anna in that house when they'd set it afire? Would you not have defended your family and your property?"

"Anna would not have been in that house because I would never have involved her in my criminal activity. Do you want to know what they found in the hidey-holes beneath the Fergusons' house besides brandy?" he said in a voice that challenged. "They found rifles. The same brand that were hidden away in my ship, which Lieutenant Ross from the *Glory Rose* would have found had he decided to search that day he stopped us. Along with a cask of illegal brandy. Do you want to know what would have happened? The government would have had every right to confiscate or burn my ship and take me into custody. Sedition hangs people."

"Then why are you not handing them all over to the authorities and cleaning your hands of the matter? Why are you allowing them to remain here?"

He crossed the room and stopped in front of her. The light from a single taper lit the dark walnut corridor behind her, yet it was enough to see his face. "You cannot guess the answer to that?"

She blinked, and he seemed to welcome the uncertainty in her eyes. "I am doing it for you, Christel."

Chapter 15

The next morning Christel learned from Doctor White the details and circumstances behind Reginald Ferguson's release.

"Four men were slated to be hanged with Ferguson," he told her, "and no' a single deposition for a one of them and no evidence to be found."

She learned that last night, after she had spoken to Camden in the library, he had gone to the bailiff in Ayr. Rousing him from bed, Camden had demanded to see the depositions from Ferguson's tribunal. When none had been found, his lordship had told the turnkey to bring Ferguson from his cell. After spending a half hour talking with Ferguson, Camden had ordered Ferguson and three others released, then he'd gone to see the provost himself.

Nothing was said of what Sir Jacob Westmont and his lordship had discussed behind closed doors.

Later, Christel listened as Doctor White spoke to Heather, instructing her how to care for Blue. Christel learned that Camden would be sending the family to Carlisle to an old bosun mate of his in need of drovers and weavers for his farm.

Christel remained with the family, but by dawn the next

morning, she walked with them to Blackthorn Cove, where a jolly boat was moored to take them all to the *Anna*. With a heavy heart, she bade Heather and Blue good-bye. She remained on the beach until the *Anna*'s masts faded in the sunrise.

Christel returned alone to her room. Wrapping herself in a blanket for warmth, she sat on her bed, exhausted and embattled. Knees drawn up to her chin, she tried to come to terms with her heart.

She did not feel any older or wiser a person than she had been at seventeen, when Camden had been her Prince Charming.

She could love him 'til the cows came home and it would make no difference in a culture that held to such staunch elitist segregation formed by mores and faith and, yes, honor.

Logic and prudence told her that every thought and fear she felt was true. But logic did not work against solitude. Logic didn't renew the body's spirit or nourish the soul, or take away the yearning to mother a little girl.

Logic certainly did not keep her from worrying about him.

Who had ever championed him? Or protected him?

Camden had not sought her out, so after breakfast and a change of clothes she went in search of him.

She found him in the ballroom practicing his fencing. No draperies marred the wall where a long row of glass doors looked out onto the terrace. He stood alone in the room, framed by the advent of a new day, no footmen on guard, the ever-present Smolich nowhere to be seen. Foil in momentary riposte, he paused, lunged and retreated, crossing his back leg over the other, only to turn and begin the master's wheel again, the hushed silence broken by the sound of his breath. By the sweat on his brow, he looked to have been at it for some time. He stumbled, and swore, resting one palm on his thigh. Then he picked up the pace again with the clear resolve to finish the master's wheel.

His movements might have lacked perfect physical grace, but he did not lack strength or perseverance as he pushed himself to exhaustion. Then the exercise was suddenly over and he walked to a table, tossing down the weapon as if he could have rid himself of all life's discomforts with such ease. He drank from a pitcher, lowering it from his mouth when he spied her. He wiped his forehead with a sleeve of his billowy white shirt and set the pitcher back on the table.

"You are quite skilled with the blade, my lord."

Thick dark hair fell over his brow. His dark lashes added to the stark effect of his silver-blue eyes as she approached. "I endeavor to do my best," he said.

He smelled salty from exercise, and hot, dispelling the chill surrounding them. And she felt that familiar spark inside her grow and grow and grow until she grabbed onto it with every ounce of her being. If she could not fight for him and for herself then what was worth fighting for in this life?

"I wanted to thank you for what you did for Heather's family. I do not know how you did it or why, but I am truly grateful."

"I did not do it for your gratitude, Christel."

"I know, but I am grateful all the same. No one else could have accomplished what you did."

Christel lifted a long-bladed foil from among the half dozen laid out on the table and tested its weight for balance. She stood in momentary riposte, foil extended, and slashed the air. She peered at him from over the protected tip.

"I am not sure what I accomplished."

"You found a place for them to go. I know 'tis none of my affair to ask—"

"But when has that ever stopped you." Despite the humor in his eyes, Christel suspected that his mood was serious beneath his words.

"What happened when you went to see Sir Jacob?"

"Westmont is proficient at mopping up before the game is over," he said after a moment. "'Tis well-known Scottish justice to hang a man first and then try him."

She whispered, "Sir Jacob will not arrest you?"

"Nay, he will not arrest me. But neither will he forgive me for interfering."

Nothing was ever that black and white. He and Sir Jacob were friends.

"What about Leighton?"

"My brother is fighting on the wrong side. I intend to destroy the lucrative smuggling trade," he said. "I intend to take my place here as earl and lord of Blackthorn Castle. To wed and have many sons, and I will not have them trading in black market brandy or whiskey."

"Then why did you save Reginald Ferguson and protect Blue?"

"Because if a man is to hang, then let it be through a just

process, not a tribunal more corrupt than those it condemns to die."

She suspected Camden could be every bit as ruthless as she was when it came to protecting those he loved. But he'd had no connection to Blue or Ferguson. He could have walked away.

"Are you up for a game of skill and sport, my lord?"

He raised a brow. She smiled. "You have your limp. I have my skirts. I figure that will make us even."

He scratched the stubble on his chin. "Is that right?"

Again, she smiled in reply and began tucking the hem of her skirt into her waistband, leaving her legs visible just below her garters at her knees. His tall calf-hugging boots gave him the advantage of another inch of height atop his own six feet, so tucking her skirt in merely evened the odds.

He slid the protective leather vest over his head and settled the mesh mask around her face. She did the same and tightened the leather ties at her waist. He took up his foil.

"What are we playing for?" he asked.

"If I win, you will sit down and talk to your brother about everything—and I do mean everything. If you choose to continue to hate each other, then the loss belongs to you both, but hate should be based on truth."

"And if you lose?"

"Then 'twill be a first."

He barely deflected her attack. Behind the mask, his eyes narrowed. Clearly, he hadn't considered that she might actually have been equal in skill to him.

He tapped the blade to his forehead. "No doubt there is much we can learn from each other about swordplay."

"On your guard, Carrick."

He parried with a single swift blow that sent a fiery jolt up her arm. Behind his mask, he grinned. "Is it your intent to let me win so easily?"

She waggled the foil tip in front of her nose. "Arrogance is one of your less-appreciated attributes, my lord."

"Camden," he said, his blade tapping hers. "My name is Camden Augustus James St. Giles."

He stepped forward and took up the position. She took up hers and their blades crossed, her eyes on his through the mesh.

She had never heard his full Christian name. "Augustus?"

He grinned. "My grandfather had a fondness for Roman history. He named me after the first emperor of Rome."

"I see."

She liked knowing his full name. The *click-click* of foils marked the beginning of the contest.

She drove him back two steps, then three before the fight was on. Their clicking foils eclipsed the sound of their breathing as they crossed the floor, making bold use of the space. Her steps close to the ground, she moved like an acrobat, all limber grace as her uncle used to tell her. She parried his riposte slashing her blade up against his. He stepped aside as she swiveled with the foil extended ready to impale him through the heart. They were both breathing hard when they stepped back from the first round with no points scored.

Like cats, they walked a slow circle around the other, flexing their claws, studying the other for weaknesses. "Where did you learn to fight?" he asked, clearly impressed.

"My uncle was a pirate, a coastal raider who survived not only the Spanish but also the Dutch and English."

Camden swished his foil with two cutting strokes to the air. "Your uncle was a thief who stole from others what he did not earn for himself."

Violence surged from deep inside her. "What do you know about what it takes to survive in the real world? You live in a castle."

"I know that it takes more courage than sense to remain honorable to your principles. I expect from others no less than what I expect from myself."

"Perhaps that is your problem. How does anyone live up to your standards?"

"I could ask the same of you?" His foil glided across her blade until they were hilt to hilt. "What are we fighting for?" he asked, their fists touching. "Your honor or mine, *a leannan*?"

What had begun as a fencing match quickly degenerated into a sword fight. Christel ducked beneath his blade.

"Not bad, my lord. But you still will not win."

He laughed. "I do not have to win to beat you. I only have to stop you from gaining a point."

She was too lost in her own reaction to take measure of his. She could not look away. She mustered her skill, keeping her movements close and quick. But she worried that she had lost her rhythm, that her emotions had been let loose from their cage and ran amok in her head. Her ribs ached. Her lungs burned. She crossed-over with her foil and might have scored a victorious point had he not skillfully countered the move like the blade master he was. When they broke apart for the third time, her lungs heaved with the exertion. She removed her mask, as did he. Neither had yet to strike a point.

The restraint she'd sensed in him until now had been replaced by something far more dangerous. "Enough games, Christel."

Her chest tightened. But before she could question his fury, he stepped against her. His heat infused her. His fingers pressed into the thick waves of her hair, closing possessively on her nape.

"Let me inside you, Christel."

Then his mouth covered hers.

She had no thought but the shameless taste of him in her mouth. No want but the feel of his arms around her. Her splayed fingers curled then climbed around his neck to entangle in his hair. Then with a groan that resonated against her chest, he was pressing her onto the table with a possessive urgency as powerful as her own.

There was no tender melding of lips as he tore away her protective vest and his hand went boldly to her breast, the curve of her waist, her bottom. No gentle wooing of her soul as he plumbed the depths of her mouth. Something inside her rebelled.

She knew some part of him was asking for more than her surrender. This was not about lust or desire but yielding to what lay between them. Everything inside told her to break the kiss. Spoke to her even as she started to fragment.

Like a flooding eddy, blood lapped through her veins feeding the fire in her loins. Another deep groan joined his.

All the while, she gripped the foil as he gripped his, and it occurred to her they had merely moved their duel closer to the other. The kiss turned hotter.

With one arm, he lifted her against the table and stepped between her legs, following her down to the table and catching the palm holding the foil against the polished wood at her back. He edged one hand beneath her skirt. His want explicit as he reached between her legs and parted her, sliding his finger inside her. She felt something primal claw at him as he inserted another and pushed inside her.

"What is it you want, Christel?"

She wanted never to be responsible for another person's pain again. She wanted to live free. She wanted him forever.

"You," she whispered. "I want you."

His warm mouth moved downward until it closed over the turgid hardness of her nipple. A shiver passed over her and his lips became a brand on her heart.

She was liquid. "Open your eyes." The words feathered across her face. "Look at me."

He pulled back and looked down at her, moving his palm between her thighs to nudge her legs apart. Then he was a part of her and held himself hard against her womb.

Before she caught her breath, he began to move as if driven. He made love to her with his body, his lips, his tongue, and the softly whispered word that was her name.

Dragging her head back, he trailed his mouth over her jaw, down the smooth column of her throat as if to taste her lifeblood. She melded against him as his lips suckled the pulse beating wildly at her throat. He had undone the laces of her gown. Her breasts strained her chemise that had at once become an erotic and sensual barrier to her skin. Her wild pulse tattooed against his lips.

Her breathing quickened. Her grip on the hilt of her foil slackened.

His mouth, his warm breath and tongue followed the rhythm of his body, and through heated lips, he whispered, "Say my name."

The pressure built within her. "Caesar Augustus," she rasped.

She thought she felt his smile against her lips. "God, I should not have told you."

He gripped her hip hard in his palm, and loosing himself in his own climax, swore like a true Scotsman, the heat of him pouring hot inside her, before he collapsed on his elbows, weak as she.

She stared in wonder at this rare glimpse of him—so unexpected even to him. She smoothed the hair from his face and kissed him. How could anyone have married him and not loved him so completely?

"I think I am in heaven," Christel said, a wine goblet in her hand as she sank lower in the hot scented water with Camden at her back, both of them watching firelight dance with the other shadows on the walls of the small kitchen at Seastone Cottage.

They had been coming to the cottage for a month. Christel returned to feed her chickens and tend to the small vegetable garden Heather had planted before she and Blue had left Scotland. April had exploded with a rare blast of sunshine. Bluebells carpeted the meadows for as far as the eye could see, transforming the brown terrain into a kaleidoscope of color and scent. The cottage had become their private Eden, always beyond the shadows and the darkness, away from the past and the future. Somewhere safe. A place that was totally hers and Camden's alone away from society's strictures and the weight public censure carried, especially for her. At Seastone Cottage, the earl of Carrick belonged to her and not to the world.

She recognized now what her mother must have felt for her father, deeply in love and sharing blissful solitude in the cottage by the sea, a world apart from his responsibilities at Blackthorn Castle.

"What will happen between you and Sir Jacob Westmont?"

Camden had made no mention of his old friend since he had interceded for Reginald Ferguson and Blue. Sir Jacob had not visited Blackthorn Castle since.

"I do not think he is a nice person to blame you for what happened under his own purview. If he receives a royal reprimand, it serves him right."

"Do you see this scar?" Camden placed her hand on the

puckered and purple scar on his thigh. "I have little memory of the battle itself. Even to this day, I do not know if the stories people talk about are true."

The stories being the battle itself: that a storm had separated two ships from the British fleet, leaving one severely damaged. Camden could have saved himself, but he had stayed behind to cover the second ship's retreat. He had faced five French warships that day, sinking two before his own had gone down into the churning sea. He had been hailed as a hero by those who had survived, and a scapegoat by an admiralty who had failed to prevent the French from coming to the aid of the colonists.

She became at once protective. "I do not know how you survived."

"If not for Jacob, I might have never learned to walk again," he said. "After I had been back a month with no desire to even feed myself, he told me that I had been waited on enough and that if I wanted to eat, then I could bloody well join my grandmother and my wife downstairs at mealtime. He would not allow people to feed or bathe me any longer. As you can imagine, I learned to walk again if only to go beyond the walls of my room before I starved."

He seemed to contemplate the wine before drinking. "Jacob returned me to fencing to help condition my mind and leg. He got me back on my ship again as a partner in business. You ask how I survived. Jacob Westmont."

Chapter 16

$\sim\!\!\curvearrowright\!\!\sim$

Bumpy and nearly impossible to travel even on horseback, the road to Rosecliffe wound through whin and heath and sandy, bent hills interspersed with once grassy hollows where cattle would return to graze in the summer. Christel finally drew rein atop the crest of the hill overlooking her old home. The house faced south. She had come in from the backside, and with the afternoon sun high in the sky, the leaded glass windows beneath the gabled roof were awash in cold. The horse did an impatient turn before she rode through the dilapidated iron gates and continued down the long, winding slope.

She'd left Blackthorn Castle early that afternoon after she'd finished her lessons with Anna. The complexity of her emotions exasperated her. Forcing her hands to loosen their grip on the reins, she took a deep breath. This meeting with her sister was long overdue.

She found Tia on her knees digging in the garden near the old garden wall in the same place Christel used to come to be alone or to hide in the beds of flowers when she had gotten in trouble. The garden had changed in nine years only in that it had been transformed into earthen mounds overflowing with wintergreen, yellow dock and wild carrot, mixed among a colorful array of daffodils and tulips.

Tia saw her enter through the gate and sat back on her heels. Her chestnut braid spilled over one shoulder to her hips. Dirt streaked a white smock that framed her simple woolen serge. Her narrowed eyes were a stark contrast to the black fringe of lashes that only served to intensify the angry spark in her blue eyes. A breeze whispered through the blanket of leaves overhead, touching Christel softly as if to calm her.

Christel motioned at the stables behind her. "I left the horse in one of the stalls. I didn't see a groomsman."

"We had to sell off most of the stock years ago."

"I did not know."

"Why should you? You have been gone."

"Is that why you are involved in . . . whatever Leighton is involved with? Do you need the silver?"

"He said that we owe you for what you did when ye drew away the dragoons from the kirk yard, so I will give you your due respect for that bit of heroics, but I will not say anything else."

Christel stepped past Tia and looked around. "You have done an incredible job."

Tia climbed to her feet and shook the dirt off her skirt. "Grams is not here. The Mayfest fair is arrived in Prestwick. You know how she and the dowager enjoy the fair. Oh!" she said. "I forgot. You would not know that since you have not lived here in almost a decade."

Christel looked up at the stone house. The casements

needed painting. There was just enough of a neglected feel that made Christel sad. But the garden was magnificent. Ignoring Tia's surliness, she walked between the mounds, impressed by the amount of work someone had done to create this. "These are mostly medicinal herbs and flowers."

"Aye. This is my garden. I have managed to make myself useful to the shire folk. I am an herbalist," she said.

"I think that is . . . quite useful actually," Christel said, more than impressed.

Tia removed her soiled gloves. "What are you doing here?"

"I thought it was time that we talk."

"Is that a joke? We have not talked for most of our lives. So you are welcome to go now."

"What did I ever do to you, Tia?"

"Do?" Tia flung out her hand. "Look at you. Riding a fine horse from Blackthorn stables, playing governess to Saundra's daughter. All your life, you have managed to do what you wanted. Say what you wanted. Dressed as a boy, you wandered the ranks of deprivation with complete freedom," she said. "You got away with it because no one ever had any expectations of you. You have no idea how I have envied that about you. How I *hated* you."

The words hurt. Christel's first instinct was to walk away. It was what she had always done in the past rather than engage her sister in an unpleasant argument. But this afternoon something stopped her.

"How can you have nothing and still manage to have everything?" Tia said.

Christel stepped nearer. "And how can you have everything and think you have nothing? Do you have any idea how I have envied *that*? You had your debut. You have waltzed and worn your pretty dresses. Lived at Rosecliffe. Papa's ancestral home. Have you ever had to sleep on a straw pallet? Been hungry? Watched your friends die while the world exploded around you? Have you ever been alone in the dead of night? Truly alone?"

"How have I ever been able to be alone? I have always been the staid one. The one who remained behind. *I* was the one who tried to comfort Grams after Grandpapa died and after Saundra died, and now 'tis *you* Grams talks about. *You* that Grams visits at Blackthorn Castle. Even Anna spends these days talking about that silly dog you named *Dog*." Tia rolled her eyes. "When she ran away, she ran to you."

"You have Grams and Rosecliffe and respectability—"

Tia folded her arms. "You had Papa and two parents who loved each other. Then after he left and returned to the sea, Grams brought you here and expected that I should tolerate you because you had nobody. In the beginning, I thought your heartbreak was justice. I reveled in it." Tears filling her eyes, she looked away.

Tia's emotion shocked Christel. "But not anymore."

Tia studied the toe of one wooden patten. "I ceased reveling the night Saundra was betrothed to Lord Carrick . . . and I came to your room and heard you weeping. You thought no one was there, but I was. I had won. Yet, I sat outside your door wondering how I could talk to you because your pain was my fault and I could do nothing to make it go away for both of us. It suddenly was not important to hurt you anymore."

"Nothing was your fault, Tia. He chose her."

Tia shook her head. "He found your golden slipper on the beach the morning after the masquerade. I know because I heard Grams and the dowager talking about the mysterious woman seen with his lordship and how she had vanished in the mist. I sent him an anonymous note and told him he would find the other slipper at Rosecliffe. He went to Rosecliffe looking for you."

Shaking her head, Christel could only look up at the sky and wonder why she did not ball up her fist and give her sister a facer. "It matters little," she finally said, because in truth, the past no longer mattered. "I could never have wed him. I still would have been sent to Virginia."

"But maybe we would not now be strangers. So much has changed."

"Do you miss her?" Christel asked.

Tia nodded. After a moment, she said, "I remember when Grams nearly had an apoplectic fit after you removed the draperies in the salon and made clothes for all of our dolls."

"If I remember the incident correctly, *you* were the one who told me Grams was putting up new draperies in the salon."

"If *you* remember correctly, I told you the green salon, not the blue. Grandpapa strapped my backside for that and sent me to bed without supper. He thought I had lied to you."

The incident had occurred a month after news of Papa's death had reached them. Her father's world had still been so new to her. During those months, she had lived in continuous fear that her grandparents would send her away.

"'Twas Saundra who defended us both."

They were both silent for a moment. Tia lifted Christel's hand to peer at her right index finger, where a ring used to be—a gift her father had once made to Christel on their thirteenth birthday. He had given one just like it to Tia for her thirteenth birthday the year before Christel's.

"What happened to it?" Tia asked.

With its tiny emerald and ruby cabochons, it had helped finance her trip to Scotland. "It paid for my passage here." Christel noted Tia no longer wore her ring. "And yours?"

"I lost it years ago. I remember when Papa gave you that ring. I was so angry."

"I felt cheated, too. I only wore mine in front of you because I knew you had one just like it, and I wanted you to see that I was special, too."

The corners of Tia's mouth lifted. "Me, too."

Discovering common ground between them was much like discovering the glint of a penny in the grass. One could leave it or pick it up.

"Would you like some tea?"

"Perhaps you can invite me in."

They had spoken at the same time. The shock of it was enough to startle a laugh from both.

"Only if you tell me about you and Leighton," Christel said lightly, aware that she might have been tramping on sensitive ground.

But Tia sighed. "There is nothing to tell. He hardly knows I am alive. He does not want me involved with what he is doing."

"Then why are you?"

Tia shrugged. "He needs me. I do not want to see him killed."

"You are in love with him."

"I suppose I have been since we were children. But he only had eyes for Saundra."

Christel shook her head. "How pathetic does that make us?"

And from the bleakness in Christel's own heart, a sense of camaraderie with her sister was born.

Christel stayed late at Rosecliffe that night. It had been a long time since she had traveled anywhere alone at night. She reached the edge of the woods two miles from Seastone Cottage and reined in her horse. A ribbon of moonlight cut a narrow swath through the meadow spread out before her. Wrapped in her cloak, she leaned over to pat the horse's damp neck and listened to the night sounds. Camden had gone into Prestwick that morning. Rather than return to Blackthorn Castle, she decided to go home.

She smelled the smoke first.

And then she saw a strange orange pall shimmering against the velvet sky, burning like dusk.

By the time she crested the distant hill, Seastone Cottage was already full ablaze. Terrified by the fire, the horse reared. She jumped but hit the ground hard, rolling to get away from the horse's hooves. Heedless of rabbit holes, she scrabbled down the incline and reached the yard in a full run. The thundering hooves bore down on her as another horse and rider skidded to a prancing halt in front of her, a dark ebony silhouette against the flames licking at the sky.

"Christel!" Camden shouted over the roaring of fire. "Get back!"

He held the reins of his horse tightly clenched in his gloved hands. Then he, too, slid from the horse and let it go, taking Christel by the arm and leading her away from the sparks and embers floating on the air above them. Her bedroom, the room where her parents had lived, was now a flaming pyre. Glass began to shatter as windows exploded all over the cottage. Her ears hurt from the roaring noise the fire made, as if it had been a living, breathing beast, a fierce dragon of lore.

Where was Dog?

A part of her mind grasped that she had left him at Blackthorn Castle that afternoon.

She stumbled, too shocked to fight the grip on her arm. Too numb to protest as she felt herself lifted and carried into the cooler breeze of the night, but not so far that she could not hear the cottage dying. He held her close to him, and together they watched the fire consume all that remained of her childhood. The walls collapsed inward, sending sparks roaring into the sky. The portraitures she had made of her parents. Her mother's costumes. Her father's saber. Everything that was her past.

Gone.

Dawn had yet to burn the night away, and the sky still glowed. Camden had taken Christel to the beach, where he waited in hopes that someone from Blackthorn Castle would see the ethereal glow of the fire and come.

He'd seen that kind of orange pall against the sky many times in his life during night battles that had sent ships to the sea floor. The ship could burn for hours, her timbers crackling with flames before finally surrendering to the sea.

Waves broke over the sand. He turned. Christel sat with her legs pulled to her chest. She had not spoken, as if she was determined to keep whatever was inside her there. He laid his cloak over her shoulders.

"It's cold," he quietly pronounced, sitting down beside her and pulling her against his shoulder. In a detached sort of way, he noticed he was trembling.

There was nothing he could do until daylight. If no one came, he would make the trek back to Blackthorn Castle himself, unless he could find the horses. He tightened his arm around her shoulders.

After awhile she gave up the struggle and sobbed as though her heart would break. Then, curling into a tight ball, she laid down and wept, as if letting the years fall away in a river of grief that suddenly seemed to overwhelm her. He wanted to lay her on the beach and kiss away her tears, as if he'd had the power of God to heal anything. She was bleeding inside, and he wanted to love her in the sand.

There was a copper taste of fear in his mouth that mingled with smoke. He would not have even been here tonight if he had not arrived home earlier than planned from Prestwick and found her gone. He hoped to God that whatever had started the fire had been a candle left burning or a spark from the hearth. He didn't know why she'd not been in bed when the fire had begun, but by whatever providence, she hadn't been.

He held her tightly and her sobs weakened. The sound of approaching horses came to him above the crash of waves on the beach. He had left his pistol in the saddlebag on his horse. He had no weapon. But the pace of the horses did not imply someone who was traveling in stealth.

A rider came out of the salt sea mist. It was Leighton. He held the reins of the two horses trailing behind him, heads down. He stopped a few feet away. "I saw the fire," he said as if it had only been yesterday that he had left Blackthorn Castle.

"Which direction did you come from?"

"South. No one came that way from this direction."

Christel had not stirred, and Camden realized she was asleep.

"I have to get her back to Blackthorn Castle," he said.

But his leg would not bear her weight if he tried to stand with her in his arms.

Leighton dismounted. For a moment, they faced each other, then Camden let him take Christel from his arms. Camden stepped into the stirrup and settled in the saddle. Leighton handed her up.

"I will remain here and see who might come," Leighton said. "See if anything is salvageable come daylight."

She awoke to find herself in a clean, white nightdress. The sleeves encompassed her arms in petal-like softness.

Sitting up in bed, she shoved the hair out of her face and glanced around. A great weariness weighed down her limbs, and she lay back in the pillows. She felt as if she had fallen off a cliff and bounced against every rock on the way down. A whisper of movement turned her head.

"Grams," she rasped.

The mattress dipped. Grams fanned her fingers through Christel's tangled hair. "How do you feel, dear?"

A frown served as a reply before Christel's gaze moved searchingly around the room. She lay in a large tester bed. The curtains were drawn around her except where Grams had stood in front of the richly draped window framed by the soft morning light. Christel placed a hand on her brow. The light hurt her eyes.

"Where is Lord Carrick?" she asked.

"He stayed with you until I arrived this morning. He returned to the cottage. He did not want to awaken you."

"He should have. I am not injured."

The strength of Grams's gaze held her immobile. "Ye will remain in bed. You have had a terrible upset. Doctor White gave you something to sleep."

Christel's strength ebbed as quickly as it had flowed. She found she did not want to get out of bed. Indeed, she wanted to bury herself in the pillows. She felt as if someone had died and had ripped a hole in her heart all over again. The pain was almost unbearable.

Christel curled closer to Grams's warmth, the familiar scent of citron, and wept. "'Tis gone, Grams."

"I know, dear."

Had she left a candle burning? Unlikely. If she had, it would have burned down to a nub hours before she'd arrived home last night.

It was just a cottage, she told herself.

But it was not just a cottage. Seastone was her home. Her sanctuary. Papa's gift to her mother. The destruction of something sacred. She had nothing left of her parents.

When she awakened again, the sun was lower in the sky, and she found Anna spooned next to her on one side.

Camden was lying atop the covers next to her on the other side, her back to his chest. He still wore his cloak, and it felt cool, as if he had just come from outside and lain down. He raised his hand and smoothed the hair from her cheek with infinite tenderness, and she turned against his shoulder. Fully dressed as he was, he did nothing more than hold her. It was everything for now.

Three days later, Camden, Christel and the sheriff went to what remained of Seastone Cottage. "Don't see what could o' caused the fire, my lord," the sheriff said, mounting his horse as he prepared to leave. "Candle, maybe. A fire still burning in the hearth. Seen many a fire caused by carelessness—"

"Like Ferguson's cottage?"

"You think the fire could have been deliberately set? Why?"

"I do not discount the possibility."

Earlier, Camden had watched as Christel had walked through the soot-covered debris. All that was left of Seastone

Cottage was the tall chimney stack thrusting up among the blackened beams and charred rubble.

But without witnesses or proof, nothing more could be done, so the sheriff rode away, leaving Camden with the hound. Dog had tagged along with Camden this morning, but the object of the hound's loyal heart stood on the hill staring out at the sea. He could see the resolute set of her shoulders, traces of defiance in her expression, as if to say she was finished mourning. He noticed that about her. Christel did not just turn away from pain; she ran with heart and soul tucked deep inside an armored breast plate and then sometimes vanished across an ocean.

He would remain to sift through the debris and then send someone back to retrieve the cow and chickens still alive in the barn. He would probably be here the rest of the morning.

Christel turned at his approach, and the wind caught her dress. She wore no cloak. The front of her blue woolen serge clung to the high curves of her breasts, tight at her small waist. Raw, hot sensations were like a potent fuel rushing through his veins.

"Are you trying to catch your death?" He unlatched his heavy woolen caped cloak and laid it over her shoulders, drawing her to him. "It's too chilly for you out here."

She seemed diminutive beneath its bulky weight. Where the cloak went just below his knee, it dragged the ground with her.

"I want to thank you for coming with me to the cottage," she said.

She rose onto the balls of her feet and pressed her lips

to his cheek. It was such a spontaneous gesture that when she drew back, he felt suddenly dizzy, the way he used to feel when he climbed the main mast of his ship and looked out across an endless blue sea and saw only water and sky.

The way he had felt the night he had gone to the surgery—the night Blue had been there and Camden had seen her with the little Ferguson boy and girl on her lap, comforting them with a lullaby, and he'd felt raw with a sudden sharp stab of longing, the way he had when she had held Anna.

She had not known that he'd been there in the darkness and that he had watched her through the windows, knowing as he'd done so that he could believe in something bigger than himself with her so near.

Maybe he didn't give a damn what anyone saw.

He bent his head and kissed her, pulling her into his arms, holding her pressed against him with his hand to the small of her back. She accepted the hot suck of his mouth. Then slowly he pulled away and she accepted his fingertips smoothing the hair from her face.

"I wish to walk for a while," she said. "If you do not mind."

His thumb traced her lower lip. Wind whipped his hair and caught the sleeves of his shirt. "I expected you might," he said. "Stay on the beach."

She was too distracted to note the order and comment. But as long as she remained on the beach, he could see her up until she reached the crumbling basaltic cliffs.

Christel's hound remained sitting beside him, its tail thumping against the sand. Camden squatted on his haunches and offered his hand for a friendly sniff. "You are about to become a permanent resident at Blackthorn, boy."

The dog rolled over and gave Camden his belly. He scratched the hound's pale pink tummy, his black-gloved hands stark against the hound's skin. Something in Dog's guarded brown eyes reminded him of Christel's eyes. Not their color, for Christel's were a Caribbean blue, but they both held the same cautious scrutiny of the world.

Then he released the dog and, bracing one elbow on his knee, watched the hound chase Christel down the beach.

The current path of Camden's life left little room for ruminations. Yet here he was, hunched on the ground, watching the spotted hound flit about Christel, listening to the sea and the wind and wanting to do all in his power to protect her.

He was about to impale himself on the staff of shire politics, but he realized now that getting more involved than he already was had been as inevitable as the sunrise, from the very beginning.

She had a way of making him look deeper into himself and not only asking questions but also seeking the right answers. Nothing as complex as the meaning of life, which he had always left to the clerical philosophers and dreamers of the day, but complicated all the same.

It was time he and Leighton sat down and had a talk.

Chapter 17

~~~ ∂∞∂ ~~~

St. Abigal's vicarage lay fifty yards behind the old stone kirk. Tianna brought Christel to the door and knocked.

Surrounded by a trimmed box hedge, the house was an old stone two-story dwelling with sash windows on the second floor and a quaint box bay window overlooking the drive and a small thatch ice house. Smoke snaked out of the chimney, and the warm scent of almond pastries lingered in the air.

Carrying a wicker basket large enough to fit Dog, Christel's sister looked every bit like the fabled Red Riding Hood on her way to Grandmother's house, all the way down to the rust-red redingote she wore. Tia had come out of the woods earlier as Christel had been leaving the kirk. "I was not sure you would be here," Tianna had said when they'd met each other on the path. "Lord Carrick came to Rosecliffe tonight looking for you."

Christel was unused to having to account for her whereabouts to anyone, and it both startled and annoyed her that he had gone all the way to Rosecliffe looking for her. But strangely, it wasn't on her account but his that she worried. "Was he all right?"

"I sent him off to Dunure."

Dunure was a known smuggler's nest! "Truly, Tianna. Do you want to see him injured or killed?"

Tianna laughed and grasped Christel's arm, leading her up the path to the vicarage. "If Leighton is there, he will not let anything *much* happen to his lordship, though I would not worry. Lord Carrick can take care of himself. Besides, Leighton knows that you have been spending time here. Their ride back will give them a chance to commune."

The door suddenly swung open and a little girl and boy flung themselves against Tianna. The girl spoke in French, telling Tia how glad she was to see her and that they had almond pastries awaiting them. "Very nicely spoken," Tia said.

The girl curtseyed and primly recited, "*Merci beaucoup, Mademoiselle Etherton.*" Her wide-eyed attention turned to Christel as Tia introduced her as her sister. The child leaned up and whispered something in Tianna's ear.

Tianna's eyes smiled into Christel's. "She thinks you have the most beautiful hair."

"Thank you."

"I come once a week to teach them French," Tia said. "But today"—she kissed the top of the child's head—"I have come to eat pastries."

"You are late, Miss Etherton," a gruff voice boomed from the doorway.

Wearing a woolen priest's robe, a silver-haired man wheeled on a chair into the room. His bushy, gray-streaked brows arched as he looked at Christel. "This must be Miss

Douglas. I have heard much about you." He held out his hand for her to take. His palm wrapped around her fingers. "Believe me when I say I am sorry for the destruction of your cottage."

Her throat tight, Christel nodded her gratitude for the words.

Tia warmly touched the man's shoulder. "Christel, meet Colonel Reverend Nunn. He and his wife tend to the business of the kirk. That includes making the best almond pastries in all Ayrshire. How else could he get me here as often as he does?"

The reverend laid his hand over Tianna's with fatherly affection. "She comes three days a week to make sure I work these old legs."

"He fought with the Highlanders in North Carolina," Tia said.

"Even reverends are not given divine protection from mortars. I grew up here," he said. "A year and a half ago, I replaced the former rector after his lordship, for a better term, broke with canon law and lost support of the religious council. He was excommunicated."

"Because he demanded that Saundra be buried on consecrated ground."

"His lordship will not even follow God's law if he thinks 'tis wrong." Reverend Nunn cleared his throat. "Miss Etherton said that you are Lady Anna's governess."

"Yes," Christel said without preamble, looking past the reverend to see his wife and four towheaded children, ranging in age from four to ten, standing at their mother's side.

"Come all of you," his wife said. "Dessert is ready."

Screaming children scattered into the adjoining room.

"I was about to begin my coffee without you," the reverend told Tia.

Pushing the wheeled chair into the next room, where a stove emanated warmth, Tia smiled at Christel. "I indulge him because his wife pays me in delectable pastries," she said.

"Do not let her fool you. She comes every Monday and Thursday evening and lets an old man win at chess—"

"Don't believe it. I cannot play."

The children had vanished from the room, leaving only the three of them at the table. Tia poured coffee into porcelain cups, their flower motifs faded with age, and sat next to Christel.

Reverend Nunn offered her a cigarette from a green tin box, then winked at her. "Have you ever smoked, lass?" His eyes twinkled.

Smoking was one of the first vices she'd indulged upon in her life after she'd snuck pipe tobacco from Papa's stash in his drawer. She wrinkled her nose. "I find tobacco to be positively revolting."

He chuckled, and the conversation turned to the weather and the planting that had begun on time this year. " 'Tis only unfortunate that he and his brother cannot work together, since they are both on the same side when it comes to the welfare of Blackthorn Castle and its tenants. Still, this is the first year Carrick has remained through spring planting. The dowager is beside herself and in high enough spirits she has filled my donation plate for the last two weeks."

Christel wrapped her palms around the coffee cup and raised it to her lips, looking away from the scrutiny of his gaze. She was living at Blackthorn Castle now, practically sleeping in his room. When she was with him, the rest of the world ceased to be.

They sat at the table quietly eating almond pastries, drinking coffee, and talking. Christel watched as Tia set out tins of herbs with instructions on their use, made a visit to the children, and took a list of families that might be in need of a doctor or supplies.

"Tia is our lifeline," Reverend Nunn said after an hour, when Tia stood to leave.

"Thank you, Reverend." Tia held out her hand and he took it. "Please give my gratitude to Moira and thank her for dessert."

Christel bid him good-bye as well, and she and Tia left the vicarage. A soft, misting rain began to fall. Christel and Tia both pulled their hoods higher to cover their heads.

"I thought you could use something positive in your life," Tia said when they reached the yard that opened into the cemetery.

Christel had never seen her sister in this light, and it gave her a new perspective on her older half sibling. "Thank you, Tianna."

"These were the people you were helping that night in the stable, and we wanted you to know that none of us had anything to do with what happened to Seastone Cottage."

Seeking warmth, Christel tucked her shoulders deeper

into her cloak. She suspected the cottage had been torched in retaliation for her helping Blue and Heather.

Christel stopped. She faced her sister. "Did any of your people have anything to do with possessing stolen rifles and attempting to frame Lord Carrick on charges of smuggling?"

Tia's mouth tightened. "Leighton told us what happened on the *Anna*. I assure you, we had naught to do with it. Those rifles are kept at the armory in Ayr. Anyone in power has access to them. The ones in the Fergusons' hidey-hole came from a contact three years ago while Leighton was still running guns with your uncle during the war."

"What about the sinking of the merchant ship outside Troon three years ago and the disappearance of the gold?"

Tia lowered her head. "That was a terrible, terrible incident," she said quietly.

"Were you and Leighton involved?"

"None of our people are responsible for the deaths of those men. Four of them were Scotsmen from Prestwick. The officer in charge had been Leighton's contact at the armory. They were friends."

"And what of Saundra?" Christel found herself asking. "Whose side was she on during all of this?"

"Lord, I do not know. She changed. Something happened."

"Do you believe she killed herself?"

Tia looked up at the sky and into the fine mist, as if it could cleanse her. "Perhaps some things are better left alone for all our sakes, Chrissie."

The use of her old childhood nickname caught Christel's

breath, and it was she who looked away. "What about for Anna's sake?"

"I will not stop you from hunting the truth," Tia said. "All I can say is that I am sorry you became involved. I would rather it have been Rosecliffe burned than Seastone Cottage. You did not deserve it."

"I want to be involved," Christel said. "I want to find the people responsible . . . for everything. Whoever is behind this burned my cottage and is a threat to Lord Carrick. You tell Leighton I will be involved in finding the truth."

The sound of horses came from beyond the trees, distant at first, then louder as the horses approached the kirk. Tia and Christel smiled as they saw Camden and Leighton rein in. The horses stomped and puffed steam into the cold chill of the night, and they looked to have been ridden hard.

Christel felt the silliest thump of her heart, as if she'd been an adolescent schoolgirl all over again, and not four years away from the ripe spinsterish age of thirty. Still, she could not help her smile as Camden nudged his heels and sent the horse to where she stood, all flushed and glittering inside like a warm star awash in the night.

The cowl from his cloak lay around his shoulders. "Madam," he said. "Are you ready to go home?"

Christel turned to her sister. "Good night," she said, pressing her mouth into her sister's hair and whispering, "Talk to Leighton."

Christel stepped away and lifted her arms toward Camden as he was leaning down. He deftly plucked her off the ground and set her across his lap. His arm tightened around her waist as his other hand gripped the reins.

"I am ready to go, my lord."

Then they were galloping the gelding past the cemetery and down the backside of the kirk yard. She could feel the tenseness in his muscles and knew he exercised restraint as he drew her into the curve of his arm and covered her with his cloak.

This morning, standing in front of Seastone's charred skeletal remains, helpless and in pain, she had panicked. Less restless now, her reasons for leaving Blackthorn today no longer drove her to want to run away.

"Are you and Leighton friends again?" she asked after she adjusted her bottom to fit more comfortably in his lap.

"We will never be friends," he said flatly, but there was something unfinished about the statement. "But neither do I have the urge to do him great physical harm."

She pulled in breath and drew on her newfound respect for Tianna. "Sometimes we think of people as being a certain way . . . and 'tis not the way of it at all."

Christel allowed a measure of happiness to invade her heart, as though she could gauge Camden's. He had come after her. "Did you think I had gone to Leighton? Is that why you went to Dunure tonight?"

"He knows the people here. I thought you might go to him for answers, the same reason I wanted to. I would have tried to talk to him had I not been bloody concerned about you."

She laid her head against the warmth of his shoulder. "I have not asked for your concern, my lord."

"Nay, you have asked me for nothing except that I *give*

you nothing. And now, the one thing that is yours is gone. You have yet to talk about Seastone Cottage with me," he said. "I do not want to awaken tomorrow and find you gone from Scotland."

"You have an image of my character firmly planted in your mind, then?" she demanded because he had guessed her nature with such ease. When life got tough or frightening, she had a tendency to either rebel or run away as far as she could go, as if by escaping she could flee the pain.

He reined in the horse. They sat atop a knoll. The mist had faded, though there was the usual dampness, mixed with heather and pine resin and a faint scent of kelp from the distant shoreline. Familiar smells that should have been comforting. A full moon broke through the scudding clouds, backlighting him and shining on her face.

"Do you know what I want?" He kissed her, then all pretense of gentleness was gone. "I want to find that elusive flame inside you, the one that burns in passion. The one you are afraid to show because it hurts like bloody hell. The one you are afraid others will douse before it has a chance to catch and burn bright and hot in your heart. And aye, it hurts like hell in the beginning, but there is nothing that feels better than to know you are alive."

She wanted to understand herself when she was around him, or perhaps she understood herself only too well as he lowered his head and kissed her. Their breaths mingled, and he pulled back, leaving her wanting more. "I think . . . I do not like you anymore, Englishman."

He chuckled softly. "Aye, you more than like me. Admit it."

Her arms raised to encircle his neck. "You are conceited, my lord."

"Tell me you were not thinking of leaving Blackthorn Castle."

"I cannot leave. I am in debt to you. You paid off the mortgage and taxes on Seastone Cottage. But I still have the land. I can rebuild. Can I not?"

"Then I will help," he said. "If that is what you want."

"Do not offer to purchase me anything. I am more worthy of your respect than that . . . and you are more worthy of my heart than to insult me by asking. Besides . . ." She cupped his check. "When I have bored of your *boorish* company and want payment for abiding you in my bed, I will help you find a bride and take the rest of the thousand pounds your grandmother offered me to keep you in Scotland."

He smoothed his hand over her hair. "I appreciate your candor on the matter. Do you have a bride in mind?"

Jealousy was a strong rival to love. "Someone with no teeth and a penchant for eating garlic and onions will do."

He laughed. "I, too, am a possessive man, love." He traced the curve of her spine with his fingertip. "I am trying to tell you that you can trust me," he declared softly. "You do not have to be afraid to be vulnerable. Let me love you, Christel." What he was proposing frightened her, and he seemed to know that. "Let me help you. I will not allow anything to hurt you."

"Unless of course a rabbit bolts and throws us from this horse."

He captured her laugh against his mouth, then pulled

away slowly, lingering. "Indeed. My ardor is such that it makes it dangerous to be on this horse."

His lips touched hers, feather light, undemanding, yet filled with promise. Then, with desire a living thing between them, he turned the horse to go home, cooled only barely by the crisp night chill.

For a long time, as Christel sat spooned against his chest, with his arm around her waist and his words returning fresh in her mind, she realized that not only was he asking her to trust him but the very request was a sign of good faith and proof that he trusted *her*. But then she had already known that, or he would never have allowed her near his daughter. He knew her better than anyone did, and still he trusted her.

She also knew a little something about him. Camden St. Giles possessed a deep sense of responsibility for what he considered the sins of his past, his part in the failure of his marriage and the part he believed he'd played in Saundra's death. Nothing would ever make up for what he'd lost at the hands of those he'd trusted, but she would try.

The steel-gray sky had not yet colored with the sunrise as Camden opened his curtains and looked outside into the mist of a new day. He leaned a shoulder against the window and raised a cup of coffee to his lips as he observed Christel in his bed. He'd not shaved. He wore a silk robe tied at the waist. He'd been unable to sleep. He'd spent too many years of his life possessing no heart not to realize that something elemental had shifted inside him. She made him feel things he'd thought gone forever, and now he found that he wanted to protect her.

"You look like a pirate prince, m'lord." The sleepy voice came from the bed and arrested his hand as he started to take another sip of coffee. "Lord of the manse, ruler of the world."

He sat on the mattress beside her. "I *am* ruler of the world, at least the one visible out this window."

She sat up and took his coffee to her lips. "Am I your concubine then, and is this room your seraglio, m'lord and master?"

He smoothed the tangled hair off her face. He wanted her as more than a concubine, as more than a lover or a mistress. "I could not manage a harem. You are enough concubine for me."

She blew on the coffee. "That is good"—she sipped, her eyes smiling—"because I will not share you either." Her gaze touched the window. "I need to return to my room."

"I will take you." Although the kiss he gave her mitigated his words. He wanted to keep her in this bed. But soon his staff would be stirring, and she did not want people to find her in his bed.

He rose, found her clothes and helped her dress. Then he kissed her, inhaled her softly into his senses and let her go.

The next few weeks progressed without incident. The investigation into the fire went nowhere. Camden knew that in Christel's mind, the cottage was gone and it would do her no good to mourn its loss. He also knew it was a lie; though she never let him see her tears again, he sometimes heard her weeping silently in her pillow.

She spent her afternoons in the classroom with Anna, and as the days warmed, she took Anna's lessons outside.

To Camden's surprise, Tianna came often to see Anna and Christel. They spent time together in the woods, and Tia taught Anna how to collect herbs and other medicines for Doctor White. Christel absorbed it all like a dry sponge in need of water. On occasion she followed Tia and Reverend Nunn when they went to visit some of the tenants on Blackthorn land.

Sometimes when Camden returned late, he would go to Christel's room and hear Tia and Christel talking into the early morning hours before falling asleep. He knew that Tia had stayed over and he would not be able to see Christel until morning. Christel had told him that she and her sister had made a pact not to talk about Saundra or Leighton or him, but that still left a lifetime between them. She told Camden everything.

Tia hadn't ever married because she'd wanted to be a doctor and help those who needed help, though she would have married Leighton had he ever asked.

Christel told Tia about her own marriage and a little about the war. They talked about their father and the fact that, in his way, he had abandoned them both. Camden sensed the sisterly bond forming and welcomed it for Christel, and only hoped he was not making a mistake in trusting Tia not to hurt her. He didn't know Tia well enough to know her character. She had always been the plain brown mouse in the room when Saundra had been present, doing little to make her presence known. But if she was a friend to Christel, then he welcomed her in Christel's life.

By the end of May, the fields were plowed and planted, and the business of being a landowner occupied his time. He began to receive a slew of invitations, from teas to balls hosted at neighboring estates, debuting young daughters coming of age. The mamas were out in droves, and those who had not gone to London for the Season stayed to pursue him.

On the days when Camden was not in Prestwick on business or tending to some judicial matter with one of his tenants, Christel would find him in his library, bent over paperwork or accounting books or merely reading about animal husbandry, which was very different from tactical naval warfare.

They managed to carry on their relationship outside Blackthorn Castle at night, sometimes in the day, finding ways to be alone on the beach, the pagoda, the stable, anywhere no one else was. Occasionally it was too much for them to wait, and, impatient, they made love on the desk in his library or the Persian rug in his small, secluded salon, where he oft went for solitude. More and more, he found his mind drifting to her when he should have been working. Found his thoughts pulled by the primal realization that he wanted her to belong to him.

She had told him it no longer mattered to her that people suspected they were lovers, but she would not flaunt the relationship, certainly not while she was Anna's governess.

But like him, she was restless. She found him once on the lower terrace, smoking a cheroot and holding a glass of whiskey, standing in almost the exact place she had come across him the night of the ball nine years ago.

Only this time, rather than kiss her, he backed her up against the ivy-encrusted embankment and made love to her.

"Are you happy with our life the way it is?" he asked with a restrained violence he did not recognize in himself.

"Aye," she said, holding him to her trembling body. He was still shimmering from an organism that had left him weak-boned and feeling more alive than he had ever felt. "I am happy."

He wanted to disagree, but then she kissed him in that perfect way she kissed, her lips warm and shaped to his, inviting him to dance with her. And raising her arms around his neck, she led with uncurbed pleasure. Her back against the cool stone, surrounded by pungent juniper, she led him all the way to the stars.

He was in love with her.

He had known it for some time. The feelings were so strong, so overwhelming, that they were like a vise tightening around his chest.

At times, when his grandmother entertained guests or when he visited neighboring estates, he would find himself standing apart, listening to the chatter that inevitably came with such visits. He would imagine what it had once been like for Christel when she was younger and living at Rosecliffe, when she would watch such functions, hidden on the staircase, believing, as she had told him, in fairy tales, wondering what it would be like to walk among them as equals.

Then he would listen to the gossip and look at society all bound up by their silly rules and stringent etiquette, and realize why Christel once chose to live in breeches and climb trees rather than take part in the lives of the fashionable set.

For all of his desires to make her part of his life, she was still who she was, part American, part Scottish, neither rich nor exceedingly worldly, the bastard daughter of an illicit union. And though his own heart would no longer be confined, more than his whimsy shaped her future. He knew that when a year was up and Christel had repaid him, she planned to find a way to support herself, independent of her life with him.

He didn't know at what point in the last few months he had decided that he would take Christel as his wife, but he suspected the idea had always been there in the back of his mind.

He also knew that with her sense of societal mores and need for independence, she would reject the idea forthright. But he was patient, perusing her slowly, chipping away at the glass walls she'd erected, which skewed her view of the world. She might not have intended to live at Blackstone Castle forever, even if he was determined that she should.

Chapter 18

❧❧

It was a warm sunny day in June that brought Christel and Anna to the Fountain Court. The court took its name from a pleasant marble fountain complete with white horse statues and continuous running water. It opened into an area fronting the terrace on one side and an ornamental outer portal on the other, with full view of the sea. Their day started with a watercolor session and lunch and ended when Anna found a baby bird hopping through the grass.

A pile of white and gray feathers scattered nearby gave evidence that a hawk had most likely eaten its mother. Anna became upset and began to cry. "But what will it do without its mother, Miss Christel? 'Tis not fair that a baby has no mother. She will die."

Christel removed the contents in the wicker basket and placed the baby bird inside. "I do not think its wing is broken. I think all we have to do is put it someplace where it can grow just a bit more."

"What will it eat without its momma to feed her?"

Mrs. Gables came outside to see what the commotion was. As the baby bird continued to hop in agitation, the consensus found that Christel should find Doctor White for a prognosis.

Christel took the basket. Dog leaped up from his place in the sun and followed closely on her heels, interested in the squeak coming from inside. After much searching, Christel finally found Stephen on his knees, doctoring a pony's cracked hoof. He was quite a distance from Blackthorn, in the older, unused area of the estate that used to house the stable near Ghost Rock, so named for the howling sound heard when the gale wind whistled over the cliffs. She had not been in this area since her return to Scotland.

"What are you doing out here?" Christel asked.

He peered up at her from beneath the rim of his tricorn. "I was on my way to Dunure to see a patient. Not anymore, 'twould seem."

Christel knelt beside him and shouldered Dog away from the basket. "I have another patient for you."

He examined the bird by delicately poking his finger at the wings. "Barely a week old. I do no' feel any broken bones."

Christel looked toward the nearby tower, its walls glowing gold in the warm sunlight. Stephen tented a hand over his eyes. "'Tis been out of service for a decade."

"That is the old lighthouse."

"Aye, it once served to keep incoming ships away from the shoreline during rough weather. The new one south of here was built to replace this one. Even before . . . Saundra . . . even before she took her life here."

This was the tower from which Saundra had leapt to

her death. There were two on each corner of the estate that overlooked the sea. "I always thought it was the other one," Christel said quietly.

Stephen shook his head. "Nay. She came here that night. 'Tis dangerous enough with much of the cliff having fallen away years ago. I suppose if a person wanted to end her life, this would be the place to come."

Christel covered the basket with the baby bird inside. Leaving it beside the horse, she walked to the old structure.

A tall stone archway opened to an enclosed courtyard. The open space connected the old stables on one end with the coach house, where the drivers and coachmen used to live, on the other. A locked iron gate blocked access. Christel gripped the rusted bars and peered inside. Weeds and thorny vines grew in the stone courtyard.

"This is part of the original castle," she said. "Built in the time of William Wallace."

Stephen stood next to her. "Aye."

It was a lonely, silent place in contrast to what it once must have been. She stood back and let her eyes travel upward to the lighthouse tower belfry. Even the slitted windows had been plastered over.

"How do I get up there?" Christel asked.

"You cannot. He closed off this place forever after the accident. No one comes here."

"Accident?" Christel asked, turning her head to peer at him. "Why do you say that?"

He shrugged lightly. "I would prefer to think of Lady Carrick's death in that way."

"You cared for her."

He nodded. "She was always kind to me growin' up. We were friends."

Christel faced him.

"When she spent time at Rosecliffe, she spoke often aboot ye," he said. "Months after she died, I found a letter in my belongings with a note that I mail this to ye after she was gone. She wanted you to raise Anna."

"You sent the letter?"

"I was not sure that you received it. I am guilty of having read some of it and writing the rest myself. She wanted ye here. I considered it her dying wish."

"Do you believe it was a suicide note, then?"

"All I know is she wanted ye to be here, Miss Douglas."

Christel walked to the lower rock wall that looked out over the cliff. A breeze tugged at her hair and skirts. At least it was warm for June, which allowed her to be out here. She stepped back and saw a faint boot print almost directly next to her foot. She knelt and ran her fingers over the hardened ridges in the mud.

"Someone still comes here," she said. "This print was made after the last rain, when the ground was soft."

How many days had that been? Two?

Doctor White walked to where she stood. "Could be Lord Carrick, for all we know. The size boot is near the same. There is no crime comin' here," he said, leaning his hips against the wall and looking out across the sea. The Arrann Isle was faintly visible through the heavy sea mist. "As you can see, there is no better view of the world than here."

"What happened the night she jumped?"

"I was no' living here yet, but from what I know of the story she had had something of an argument with his lordship. There was a lot of screaming and shouting, she accusin' him of hatin' her and tryin' to destroy all her happiness, him tellin' her he was leavin' and takin' Anna and she'd not be seein' the girl again."

Folding his arms, Stephen leaned a hip against the stone wall and peered up at the tower. "No one knows why she ran up there. There would be only one reason, I suppose. The place has been crumblin' into the sea for centuries and no' been in use for years since they built the new stables and carriage house on the south side of Blackthorn Castle. I had heard that his lordship had always planned to be tearin' it down. But that his mam had apartments here and he used to spend a lot of time with her when he was a lad."

Brushing specks of dirt and brick mortar from his hands, he turned. "I should be goin' back to our feathered patient before Dog figures out how to nose open the top of the basket. I will attempt to make that wicker basket into some sort of cage for now."

Christel thanked him for taking the bird. "I would like to stay a little longer," she said.

After he left, Christel walked along the wall and peered over at the rocks below. A chill went down her spine.

The old lighthouse tower had been built into the face of the basaltic cliff. Centuries ago, the cliff had crumbled enough to form a pathway down to the beach. She could see the old goat trail, the one she used to use to sneak up from the beach without being seen. A person on foot could follow the trail up or down the side of the cliff, which was why when she was a little girl she had always worn sturdy shoes and breeches when she'd gone treasure hunting in Blackthorn Cove. She knew the trail well. From up here, debris blocked the descent so that she could not climb down the lower tower wall, but she could certainly climb up from the beach.

Christel returned to the lower terrace and took the cart road down to the beach. From this end of the cove, the entrance was only accessible during low tide. The water looked to be coming in. Tucking the hem of her skirt into her waistband, she barely evaded a crashing roller. She worked her way around the tidal pool and up onto the higher rocks. The old goat trail was five feet across in places and as narrow as two in others.

A freshening breeze carried with it the high-pitched whistle that came from the wind screaming through the cracks and crevices in the rock. She followed the path up the cliff to where it had crumbled around the backside of the tower. She found a window, covered only by ancient wooden shutters. She grabbed a rock and broke the latch.

Christel wrapped her fingers around the ledge, scrabbled up the stone wall, and promptly fell over the sill, nearly landing on her head as she tumbled into the stairwell. She felt a bright bolt of pain as a finger jammed back, then her elbows hit, then her chest. She gasped in air thick with the reek of mold and sea kelp. Braced against her palms, she sat, collecting her wits and her breath. Finally, brushing the hair off her brow, she looked around, grateful for the sunlight coming in through the window. Streamers of dust marked its path.

She climbed to her feet. She disliked the narrow walkway. The damp stone walls enclosed her like a tomb. But she walked up the curving stairway past the main floor where the doorway into the courtyard had been bricked over. She followed the wall until she reached the top and came face-to-face with a heavy oak door slightly off its hinges and ajar. The belfry was open to the sea. Bats and seagulls nested inside and on the stone ledge. Guano covered the floors and walls.

She hesitated. Then, wrapping the bottom of her skirt over her nose and mouth, she gingerly stepped over the disgusting mess as she made her way to the high ledge. A three-legged stool lay overturned in the corner. She stood on it and leaned out. Camden had been right when he'd once told her a person could not fall from inside. A person would have to climb out onto the ledge and then walk out another four feet to jump.

She leaned out to look left and upward. Steps led from the crumbling stone ledge to the cupola. Glass enclosed the old lantern room that had once housed the lard oil fires used to warn off ships. She turned inside to look at the walls. The door to the lantern room looked to have been sealed decades ago as well, when the lighthouse went out of use. One could still reach the cupola by accessing the stairs from the ledge, probably once used by workers to clean the glass.

There would be no reason for Saundra to go up there,

Christel thought. She could find no hint of conspiracy afoot, no reason to doubt the facts as they seemed laid out before her.

Christel remained on the stool a moment longer. The sun was lower in the sky than it had been and threw vibrant light against the wall. With one last glance, she started to turn away when the glint of something gold caught her eye. She pushed up on her arms and leaned out to reach the bottom stair. The flash of gold was lodged in a crevice half covered in the remnants of an old bird's nest. She would not have seen it at all had it not been for the position of the sun. Christel worked it out from the crack.

The gold had long since tarnished. The ring itself was made with tiny emerald and ruby cabochons—the gift her father had once made to her and Tia on their thirteenth birthdays.

The ring belonged to Tia.

"I am glad you know," her sister said from the doorway. "You have no idea how hard it has been carrying everything that happened that night on my shoulders."

Heart pounding, Christel climbed down from the stool. They faced each other from across the filth- and offal-ridden room.

"I have no intention of harming you if you are concerned," Tia said.

"Did you kill her?"

Tia's eyes shone with tears. " 'Twas a horrible accident."

"Then if you do not mind, I would prefer to get out of this room."

* * *

They made it back outside. Christel used the stool to climb out the stairwell window. Once outside, she dropped to the path and sat. She wanted to tear off her shoes and clothes and throw everything into the sea. Far below her, down the goat path, waves crashed high on the rocks, blocking her escape. She could wait twelve hours for the tide to recede again, or she could try to climb over the crumbling debris and go up. She remained sitting as Tia dropped from the window and fell next to her.

Neither spoke. They sat with their backs against the rock wall. The goat path stretched out unevenly in front of them. Christel leaned back her head and shut her eyes.

"You were on the ledge that night with Saundra."

"I did not murder her," Tia said. "She . . . she fell."

"Why were you both up there?"

Tia shook her head. "Saundra was going to destroy everything. She wanted to leave Blackthorn Castle. She wanted the gold. I could not let her take it. If Sir Jacob found out . . ."

"The gold?"

"There is twenty thousand pounds' worth of gold coins sitting in the lantern house. Leighton, Saundra and I are the only ones left who know the truth. We made a pact to tell no one it was there." Tia struck out at the tears on her face. "If Sir Jacob found out . . . he would have us hanged."

Everything began to pour out.

"It had all been so noble in the beginning. The gold was headed to royal coffers in the war effort against the colonies. Leighton had friends on the inside. Everyone involved had agreed that it would be used for the good of those around here. Something happened. Men were killed that night. But not by Leighton's men. They were alive when Leighton left the ship."

"Do you believe Sir Jacob executed his own men?"

"We could never prove it, any more than Westmont could prove it was Leighton who took the gold, and without proof, he could not search Blackthorn Castle outright. But Westmont was around here a lot. Saundra had already fallen in love with him before Lord Carrick returned from Yorktown. She kept it a secret from everyone, and when Lord Carrick came home, Westmont broke it off with her.

"She was distraught. Later, when she told Westmont she was with child and begged him to take her away, he would have none of it. He took her to a woman who could rid her of the babe. She came to me shortly afterward and told me everything because she was afraid of what she had done. Shortly after that, she started to bleed and Lord Carrick learned she had been with child."

"What happened the night Saundra died?"

"She and Lord Carrick argued. I do not think he realized how sick she had already become or I do not think he would have said the things he did. She ran away and came up here with the intent of taking as much gold as she could. I think she was desperate enough to take it to Westmont if he promised to take her back. She had no business coming up here. The weather was dangerous that night. I followed her. I begged her to consider what she was doing. But she was blind and deaf to reason. Nor did she care that if Westmont found the gold, 'twould be traced back to Blackthorn and to Leighton and me. I would not let her take it.

"She jerked away from me. The ledge is four feet wide. But that night, she could not stop from sliding on the damp stones, and I could not stop her from dying. I tried to grab her hand. She pulled my glove off and went rolling down the stairs and over the ledge. If it had not been wet that night . . . she might have been able to stop herself."

Tia looked up and blinked back tears. "I was so terrified I hid in the lantern room for a day. No one ever came up to the cupola. Why should they, when everyone thought she had been distraught and jumped? I let Leighton . . . I let everyone think she had killed herself because of Lord Carrick."

Christel turned her head. The backlash of wind caught her hair. "Saundra wrote me a letter asking me to come home and care for Anna as her governess. She had asked Stephen to mail it after she was gone. She must have written it that night."

"'Twould make sense. She wanted you to care for Anna."

God. "Have I always been such a naïve fool?"

"You have always been generous and unspoiled and loyal to those you love. I know that she loved you. She had no intention of ever returning. Maybe she was trying to do one decent thing for you before she left Blackthorn Castle, and that was to bring you together with Lord Carrick." Tia inhaled and leaned her head back against the rock. "Now you know everything."

Christel wished she hadn't. Lord in heaven, she wished she hadn't known any of it.

She gave Tia the ring. "This belongs to you."

Tia studied the filigree gold band. "I thought I had lost this forever." After a moment, she asked, "What will you do now?"

"Lord Carrick has a right to know. Anna has a right not to live with the stigma of her mother's suicide." But was it better to learn that Saundra was trying to run away with stolen gold, and that she was an adulteress?

Christel drew her legs to her chest. "If I tell Carrick the truth, he will hunt Sir Jacob down. But if I say nothing, Sir Jacob lives free. If I say anything at all, you will be implicated in her murder. And what about the gold? You could be accused of murder. At the very least you could be transported.

"I do not know what to do, Tia. How could you put your life in my hands like this? Why would you do it? You could have told me Saundra stole the ring from you. I would have believed you!"

Tia's wet gaze went to the sea, where salt mist was forming over the blue-gray water. A bank of white clouds was building over Arrann. "We have no cloak, and it gets cold up here at night," Tia said. "I do not think either of us wants to go back into the tower, and we can't leave by way of the beach until the tide goes down."

Christel leaned out and looked up the goat trail. The ledge was a natural funnel for the wind. What was left of the path extended thirty feet in an inward slope that tapered to nothing before falling off into open air. The trail itself was a mix of crushed rock, clumps of grass and bird droppings.

"If I give you a boot up over there, can you reach the wall?"

Tia shuddered but nodded. They walked to within a few feet of the drop-off, standing on five feet of ledge and needing only to climb four feet to the top. Christel knelt and linked her palms for a step. Tia stepped into her hands and Christel boosted her up. In moments, Tia scrabbled over the side, sending a shower of loose pebbles down on Christel's head, causing her to choke and cough. Tia stuck her head over the ledge.

"I made it," she said unnecessarily and held out her hand. Her long chestnut hair had torn away from the pins and hung over the ledge like the flowing mane of a mermaid. "You will have to climb a little to the left. I see a foothold."

Christel drew in her breath. She stepped into the crevice as she pushed off and grabbed Tia's hand. The rock beneath her shoe broke. She slipped and clawed for a handhold in the loose rock. She began to slide backward. For a terrifying moment, one foot dangled above empty space as she sought a foothold in the rock.

"I need your other hand!" Tia was shouting. "Take my arm so I can pull you up!"

Grabbing Tia's outstretched arm with her second hand meant letting go of the only grip she had on the rock face. With all her strength, Christel reached for Tia's hand and latched on to her arm. Together they worked to pull her over the ledge and to safety. Breathing hard, Christel collapsed on all fours. Tia sprawled on her back and found herself staring up at the cloudy sky. They were both suddenly laughing.

Christel lifted her head and found her sister. "You could

have dropped me," she said seriously. "Then your secret would have been safe forever."

Tia sat up. Her bodice was ripped at her shoulder. Her knuckles were scraped. "And lose my only sister when it has taken me this long to find out that I *like* you? I would rather die myself."

Christel looked over Tia's shoulder at the old tower courtyard. Thick growths of alders, larch and birch blanketed the landscape. They would have to walk around the high stone wall to get back onto Blackthorn Castle grounds. Christel stood and helped her sister to her feet. They had walked a hundred yards when the sound of horses approaching alerted Christel. She pulled Tia into a cove of alders.

A half dozen riders approached at a gallop, Camden in the lead. He saw the two sisters and swung his horse in their direction.

"His lordship looks angry," Tia said.

He was dressed in nondescript homespun with a coat over plain brown breeks and hose, as if he had been called from the sheep pens. He reined in beside Christel. Thick clouds flew overhead, driven by the wind, and battered her hair as his gaze dropped down to her soiled skirts. She saw it was taking him a moment to assemble a frown as he looked from Tia to her.

"Doctor White was concerned when neither of you returned to the surgery."

"I went to the Lighthouse Tower," Christel said.

"He told me."

"You never asked me not to go," she said.

"I never asked you not to walk along the edge of the cliff either, and still I had thought you would have the sense not to. The tower is dangerous. I should have torn it down years ago."

"You should have, but you have not."

He motioned for a rider to come forward. "Take Miss Etherton back to Blackthorn so that she can clean up and change."

Tia gave Christel a shaky smile. Then Christel watched Tia mount and ride away with the other riders, leaving Christel and Camden alone.

"What was all of that about?" he quietly asked. "I have no idea why you would come here."

"This entire area is dead. You have closed away the tower courtyard, encapsulated the tragedy in time. This place stands as a shrine to the heartbreak of that night, a rock headstone as if you need more self-flagellation—"

"Enough, Christel."

"What happened that night was not your fault. She failed you."

He crossed his hands over his reins and looked toward the sea.

"Marry me," she said. "I want to be your wife."

He slid from the horse and stumbled. She caught him by his shoulder. He hated his weakness. Hated the constant reminder of his failure. Still, she moved against him.

"What is this really about?"

"Justice," she whispered. "The future."

His fingers speared through her hair, pulling her head

back. His sex stirred against her belly. It was thick and hard, and she could feel the heat of it through her clothes.

She took his palm and placed it against her heart. "Tear down this place or make something good of it, Camden. Go visit her at the church. Say hello. Say good-bye. Tell her she was a fool. Tell her anything and let us be done with it."

She looked into his eyes, her own clear and unshielded from his. He touched the end of her nose with his fingertip, kissed her deeply, then wrinkled his nose. "You will forgive me, my love, but you need a bath."

She leaned against him, holding him tightly. And did not disagree.

Chapter 19

Leighton listened to the subtle swish of fabric and the soft tread of slippers pacing back and forth on the oak floor. Opening one eye, he gave his trespasser's back a frown even as he admired the way her skirts flared from her hips.

As he pushed himself up on an elbow, she lifted her head. Upon meeting her gaze, his first thought was to check his weapons. His second was less refined. The simple cream linen dress matched her hair. With her wealth of butter-soft curls pinned atop her head, she looked refreshingly virginal—quite different from the women with whom he'd been acquainted of late. Until this moment, he had always considered Christel sensible.

Coming to his senses, he asked, "How did you find me? Hell, did you come to Dunure alone?"

"Luck. And yes."

Leighton slept naked. The sheet covered the lower half of his body, but that was all the modesty it afforded him. "What are you doing here?" he asked, at once suspicious. "I thought my brother would have you on a short leash by now."

"You thought wrong, Leighton St. Giles."

Watching her approach, he considered telling her that

she was playing a dangerous game coming to an inn filled with disreputable blackguards, looking like a lovely swan among geese.

"I want you to testify against Sir Jacob," she said. "Stand as witness against his crimes. I want everyone to know the kind of man he is."

He sat with his back against the headboard, leery now as he narrowed his eyes. "I would like for everyone to know the kind of man he is, too. But that will not happen as long as he is provost."

She opened her palm to reveal a shiny gold coin.

He sat up as a cold chill went over him. "Where did you get that?"

She tossed it to him. His reflexes keener than usual despite the night of drinking, he caught the coin.

"Saundra sent it to me before she died. Sir Jacob fathered Saundra's babe, then sent her to a butcher. He betrayed Camden and hurt Anna. I want him . . . gone. He is evil." Her eyes shone wet with passion.

"What are you talking about?"

"Tia told me about the gold in the tower. She told me everything."

With a quiet oath, Leighton flipped the coin back at her. "Where is Tianna now?"

"Why do you care?"

He threw his legs over the side of the mattress and stood, grabbing a sheet as he did for modesty's sake, though he didn't know why he bothered.

He took two steps and came face-to-face with a pistol.

"Do not think I will not use this if you threaten me," she said. "There are places I can shoot that will not kill you but will hurt like bloody hell."

"All right." He returned to sit on the edge of the mattress. He had no wont to hurt or scare her, but he was suddenly furious. "Camden will not appreciate that you have come here on his behalf, Christel."

"But you loved Saundra, too."

"Camden has a right to know the truth. Saundra was his wife."

"But he could kill Camden. He is already a criminal!"

He stood. "Aye, so am I and so are you if one looks deeply enough into your past. Do you have proof of his crimes?"

She drew herself up.

"I did not think so."

She lowered the pistol. "I should have known you would not help your brother or me or Tia."

He grabbed her arm. "What are you talking about? Is Tianna in trouble?"

"Talk to her yourself."

"I am talking to you."

"Leave off, Leighton. I should have known you were incapable of helping me." She flung open the door and stopped dead on the threshold.

Camden leaned against the wall in front of the door, his boots crossed at the ankles. The dark woolen shade of his cloak blended with his hair, and only the cutlass he wore was visible in the dim corridor light. His predatory stance told Leighton he'd been listening a long time.

No one moved.

Camden's pale silver gaze shifted to Christel. "You certainly make my life more interesting, love," he said. "I have been searching everywhere for you. Worried as hell."

"I can see that, my lord. I am found out."

He pushed away from the wall. Entering the room, he shut the door and faced her. "So you would duel with Sir Jacob for my honor."

"I would duel him for your life. Your honor has never been in doubt."

Camden looked past her at Leighton, standing in a sheet. For once Leighton had the good sense to keep his mouth shut. His eyes narrowing slightly, Camden held out his gloved hand to Christel in a silent command for the coin. She gave it to him. He turned it over in his hand and raised his head.

"I would never have forgiven you if you had done something to cause yourself harm."

He opened his arm. Christel stepped against him, pressing her face against his shoulder as he held her against him. "Do you understand?"

"How did you know where to find me?" she asked.

Camden looked pointedly at Leighton. "Tia came forward this morning and told me everything. She has made a confession to the sheriff for her part in Saundra's death and implicated Westmont in more than the murder of those men who died guarding the gold."

Christel shook her head. "Nay, she should not have. How could she? Why did you allow her to do so? They could hang her."

"Because she loves you, Christel. And she would not see you do anything that would jeopardize your future. She could not save Saundra. But she believed she could save you and Leighton." His next words were for Leighton. "She took full responsibility for everything."

"Where is Tianna now?" Leighton asked.

"She is at Blackthorn Castle for now. We are looking for Westmont." Camden tossed the coin in the air and caught it. "Shall we go down and spend this?" he said to Christel. "See what sharks we can dredge up from that cesspool downstairs?"

The dowager snorted and thumped the ground with her cane. "Who'd have thought England would ever see the day when Sir Jacob would be wanted for questioning in a crime."

"Who would believe it of him," Grams said.

Christel's gaze went to Tianna, who was sitting quietly on the settee at the back of the drawing room, reading to Anna. By the look of the girl sleeping on Tia's lap, Anna had lost interest in the story. Dog had been allowed inside and lay on the floor near the settee.

Christel walked to where a circle of light separated her sister from the shadows of the night. Tia was staring outside.

"How are you doing?" Christel asked.

Tia folded her hands over Anna's shoulders. "Leighton came to see me this afternoon. He was furious. He tried to step forward and take responsibility. He must have been eating mushrooms, I think. Either way, he is quite mad."

"We are all worried."

Tia's mouth softened. "I could not let you ask him to find Sir Jacob alone. I know you wanted to protect Lord Carrick. But I needed to protect Leighton."

"They will find Sir Jacob." Christel wrapped her hand around Tia's. "You need not be afraid. Camden is not without power, Tia."

"I know." Tia's gaze lifted to encompass Christel. "But Sir Jacob will never be convicted. Saundra is dead, and twenty thousand pounds buys a lot of loyalty," she said. "It buys witnesses and tribunal verdicts. I am glad everyone knows the truth."

"He will not go free, Tia."

"I know."

Something in Tia's voice sent a chill down Christel's spine. She looked around her at the drawing room, then out the window. She stood and peered out the glass. The moon was bright tonight, but she could see the distant glow of firelight somewhere on the beach. She had expected Camden and Leighton to return by now. A cold chill went down her spine.

"Where are they, Tia?" She was not sorry for her anger.

"Leighton only said 'twould be finished for Westmont one way or the other tonight. Sir Jacob is dangerous to you as well, Christel."

Stars appeared only in patches in the sky. A fire burned on the beach. Camden's men from the *Anna* stood beyond the circle of light as a cloaked and hooded form was brought forward and dumped on the sand with little fanfare or regard to his rank. The ropes binding his hands behind him were cut and the black hood stripped away.

Jacob Westmont lifted his head. A hush descended on the firelit scene. Westmont's dark hair hung in his eyes, pulled out of a thong by the hood. His gaze first narrowed on Leighton, who stood behind and to the left of Camden.

"He is not the one you need to fear this night," Camden said.

"Carrick," he rasped.

Camden waited, gripping a sword in each hand, and for a moment he wondered if he was any less barbarous than Westmont. Camden wanted to kill him for the betrayal of their friendship, his trust, the harm he had done Anna, his threat to Christel.

Westmont struggled to stand, his boots digging in the wet sand.

"We are at sword's points, Westmont." Camden tossed down a dueling sword. "This fight is between you and me. No one else will interfere."

Westmont hesitated. "You wish to duel with *me*?"

"Would you pretend innocence? Pick up the sword."

Westmont grabbed the hilt, dragging the blade off the ground. The handle was smooth from wear, the balance perfect in his hand. He had held it enough during their practices. He raised his head. The shock of his capture had begun to wear away. "I will not fight to kill you, Carrick. We do not have to do this."

"What would you have me do instead? What would you do if you were in my boots?"

Westmont's eyes darted around the circle of men. His gaze returned to Camden. He raised the sword. "If 'tis any consolation, I would that it never happened between me and Saundra. But it did." He glared at Leighton. "Did your brother tell you about the gold?"

"He knows," Leighton said. "He knows you had six men killed in your search for it."

Camden and Westmont began to stalk each other in a circle. "You can never prove anything, Carrick. There is no one alive who can bear witness to any accusation you make against me. I will deny them all and see your brother condemned for the theft and hanged alongside Tianna Etherton."

"The gold will be restored to the king's coffers, Westmont."

"You are my business partner. If something happens to me, you lose your investments. If I go down, you crash."

"Did you burn Seastone Cottage?"

"My men have orders to burn out anyone suspected of aiding and abetting seditionists and criminals."

"What if she had been in bed that night, the same as the Fergusons had been in their cottage when your men set it to flame?"

Two steps, Camden met his attack. Naked blades flashed in the firelight. They battled around the clearing, the metallic click of blades sharing the night with the sound of waves breaking on the beach. Blood pumped through his veins, feeding life into his limbs. Westmont fought with strength and fury. Camden merely fought. Relentlessly. The battle carried the two men across the beach, the circle of men stretching outward to accommodate the duel.

"You are a fool, Carrick." Westmont's weapon glided against his. Standing nose to nose, their swords crossed over their heads, slid and met again. "For all the good this will do. You were my friend. I would have let you live. Now I will see you dead and every member of your family destroyed, including that little colonial bed warmer you have taken a fancy to."

Camden stepped behind the riposte and slashed his cutlass across the other man's blade. Westmont whirled at once, going for Camden's vulnerable side. "You are fighting like a Barbary pig, Westmont," he rasped in a cutting whisper. "Desperate."

"You are a traitor, Carrick. Like your brother. Ask him about the time he spent with your wife. Do you think I was the only one?"

"Aye, I do."

Camden swung his fist, hitting Westmont across the jaw and felling him. Westmont rolled and, barely evading Camden's fatal blow, came up slashing. The blade caught Camden's sleeve, tearing through the fabric. He managed to spin away before Westmont's blade sliced down across his arm. "You were my friend, Jacob."

Every blow smashed with relentless fury as he parried Jacob's moves. "You betrayed me. You betrayed Saundra. You betrayed the men who follow you and take your orders."

His breathing rough, his chest heaving, Westmont lunged. But for all the barbarity in his own heart, Camden fought with finesse and control. Blade met blade, glinting silver in the moonlight. He slammed backward against a rock and ducked, but his leg was less than agile and he stumbled. Westmont's blade struck stone. Sparks shattered the darkness. With a surge of force, Westmont pushed him backward.

At the last possible second, he deflected the sword with his remaining strength. And then, Camden sidestepped and his own sword sank into Westmont's side. Neither man moved. Their eyes held. "It could have been through the heart," Camden rasped. "But I will not let you off that easily."

Camden released Westmont and watched him drop to his knees in the sand. His chest heaving, his breath coming in gasps, he stood over Westmont, his hand clutched tightly to the hilt of his weapon, but something stopped him from the fatal blow. "What happened to you, Jacob? What happened to the man I knew? My mentor?"

Camden hurt deep inside him. His fury was gone, leaving something else. Regret. Grief.

"Where is your honor, Carrick? Have done with it."

Swaying on his feet, Camden tossed his sword to the sand beside Westmont's. "Honor is squandered on dishonorable men."

And women, he thought, thinking of the waste Saundra had made of her life. She certainly had not been worth killing for.

Camden staggered back, and something caused him to lift his head. He looked directly into Christel's eyes.

She stood just inside the circle of firelight, her hand clasped to the edges of her cloak, her hair a beacon of gold.

He reached his arm out as she ran into his embrace. She held him so hard that he didn't know if it was her heart he felt beating so hard or his own. And just that fast the world seemed to right itself back on its axis.

"You will leave Scotland, Westmont," he said. "My men will escort you to the *Anna*. I have a sudden want for fine rum in the West Indies, and you will be accompanying my crew. If you ever return, I will kill you."

"You cannot do this!"

"Get him in irons, Bentwell. Now." Camden stepped away. "I can. I am. 'Tis over."

Bentwell and three of his men from the *Anna* dragged Westmont to his feet. But with a roar, his hair wet from sweat, Westmont shoved away from the hands holding him. He ran toward Camden, reaching for the sword Camden had tossed to the ground, aiming for the final lethal thrust. Camden's leg would not allow him to drop and pick up the sword and stand again. His hands tightened on Christel to shove her aside as a flash of growling, mangy fury leaped across the sand and brought Westmont to the ground, landing him flat on his back in the sand. He screamed as Dog tore at his hand and arm.

For a moment, Camden didn't think Christel was going to call off Dog. She did, bringing the hound to their side as Westmont swore and shouted obscenities. "Good boy," he heard Christel say. "If he was a rabbit, you would have eaten him."

Camden knelt in the sand and touched Dog's head. "I think we can find a nice warm place at Blackthorn," he said.

"We can share the gold!" Westmont was shouting as Camden's crew dragged him away.

Camden leaned heavily into Christel as she settled her shoulder beneath his and helped him stand. "Do you want to share the king's gold with a murderer, *a leannen*?"

She looked up at Leighton as he came to stand next to the dog. "I want to take you both home. 'Tis time we all sit down as a family."

Chapter 20

There was no breeze as Camden strode from the stable, only an inland stillness that reeked of seaweed that came with the scent of low tide. When he finished his morning's business on the ship's manifest, he found Christel in her room. Folding his arms, he leaned against the door. She'd been spending a lot of her time in her room during these last few weeks. And that worried him. She was not eating. That worried him more.

Christel sat at her desk, bent over a drawing.

It had been almost a month since Sir Jacob had vanished with the *Anna*, a week since Tia's tribunal and her sentence—transport to Australia. Six days since the magistrate had allowed him to wed Christel so that Tia could be part of this moment. He had asked Christel to marry him before the tribunal had begun. She belonged with him at Blackthorn Castle. They would wed again in a larger ceremony at St. Abigal's later in the month when life became less chaotic. He'd been back and forth from Prestwick with a number of loose ends that needed tying, including his relationship with Leighton. They had made their peace, as fragile as it was.

"Leighton was given permission to go with Tianna," he said when Christel looked up to find him standing in the doorway. "As was Doctor White. We just received permission today. The English are building a new colony there."

Christel sat straight. "Doctor White? But he and Leighton were not convicted of anything."

"Nevertheless they will not allow Tianna to go alone, and the transports and colonies are in desperate need of doctors." Camden sat on the edge of the desk, where she was working on her drawings, and smoothed the hair from her face. "'Twas not too many years ago, prisoners were transported to the American colonies. Look where that got the empire."

Christel laid her cheek on his thigh. "But I only just began to know her, Camden."

"'Tis for seven years. If I know Leighton, they will not remain long where they are sent."

Christel visited Tianna one last time before Tia was loaded on the prison transport ship. They'd already said their good-byes. And as Christel and Grams and Camden watched the ship sail away that warm August day, she thought her heart would die. Christel brought Grams back to Blackthorn Castle, where she remained with the dowager and Anna for a week before she decided there were others who needed her: Reverend Nunn at St. Abigal's and the children at the orphanage.

One day in late September Christel finally sat down and wrote Daniel Claremont's sister Elizabeth and her husband, Lieutenant Ross. She told them about her new life and her husband and the child they had on the way and due next spring. She would love if they traveled to Blackthorn Castle.

Christel and Camden were married a second time in a formal ceremony at St. Abigal's that month. A poor man's ceremony, what some called it. Sir Jacob's prediction about Camden's financial fall had borne out, and they were now poor aristocracy but with big dreams. He still had the *Anna,* and humble beginnings did not mean he did not have plans. They faced each other and spoke the promise in their hearts, and as she met the conviction in Camden's gaze, she felt alive.

More than alive. She felt peace. She was not sure of anything except Camden's steadfast love and his promise that he would never forsake his family and a life they would begin together.

When Christel woke again, the next day, a silk dress made from spun gold and golden slippers lay on the chair. The note simply said, *"We never had our dance. C."*

She lifted the gown. Holding it against herself, she ran to the mirror. Gold was indeed the color of enchantment, as she'd once believed. The dress flowed around her as if she'd been seventeen again and a princess in her own fairy tale. The dress and shoes were the very same she had worn over ten years ago. The dress thankfully laced up the front, and, though loosened, the bodice was tight. Still, she had never felt more beautiful.

Christel saw him from the gilt-edged balcony overlooking the grand ballroom.

Camden stood at the bottom of the stairs, his elbow on the newel post. He no longer wore the dark royal blue uniform of a naval officer, but he was no less resplendent garbed in silver gray silk, white shirt and stock and dark breeches. It was just the two of them.

"Where did you find my dress and shoes?"

"Tia found the dress a few years ago in the attic at Rosecliffe. The shoes I have always had."

He led her onto the dance floor, and her pulse leapt, then raced as his body encompassed hers. He slid his fingers into the warmth of her hair and tilted her face. Their eyes met and loved in a timeless embrace before he lowered his mouth to her lips. "I love you," he whispered.

She loved him, too. Not the infatuation of a young girl's heart, but something deep and promising and enduring. Something she imagined her parents had once shared.

In her imagination music floated high above the spacious floor to resonate against the dome-shaped roof. "We could be the sun and the moon," she said in amusement, and he pulled her nearer.

His step was not perfect, but for her it mattered little. "You are the closest to heaven I will ever get, love," he said against her hair.

Heaven, where dreams were like the rolling waves of a summer sea, ever changing and infinite.

Where the magic they'd discovered one enchanted evening would endure to grow and nurture generations to come.

Where gold was the color of dreams that came not from the wealth in a man's pocket but from his heart.

She had found her treasure.

It was the end of the day, and the beginning of the rest of their lives. And with Christel wrapped in Camden's arms, the man once known as the Barracuda had finally brought her home.

5656

At Avon Books, we know your passion for romance — once you finish one of our novels, you find yourself wanting more.

May we tempt you with . . .

- **Excerpts** from our upcoming releases.
- Entertaining **extras**, including authors' personal photo albums and book lists.
- Behind-the-scenes **scoop** on your favorite characters and series.
- **Sweepstakes** for the chance to win free books, romantic getaways, and other fun prizes.
- Writing **tips** from our authors and editors.
- **Blog** with our authors and find out why they love to write romance.
- **Exclusive content** that's not contained within the pages of our novels.

Join us at
www.avonbooks.com

AVON   *An Imprint of* HarperCollins*Publishers*
www.avonromance.com